Seasonal Tribal Feasts

Novels
Meritocrats
The Gardens of the Casino
The Caves of Alienation

The Windmill Hill sequence
Centres of Ritual
Occupational Debris
Temporary Hearths
Houses on the Site

Poetry
The Function of the Fool

STUART EVANS

Seasonal Tribal Feasts

The final novel in the
Windmill Hill sequence

Hutchinson
London Melbourne Auckland Johannesburg

Copyright © Stuart Evans 1986

First published in 1987 by Hutchinson & Co. (Publishers) Ltd,
an imprint of Century Hutchinson Ltd,
Brookmount House, 62–65 Chandos Place, Covent Garden, London WC2N 4NW

Century Hutchinson Publishing Group (Australia) Pty Ltd
16–22 Church Street, Hawthorn, Melbourne, Victoria 3122

Century Hutchinson Group (NZ) Ltd
32–34 View Road, PO Box 40–086, Glenfield, Auckland 10

Century Hutchinson Group (SA) Pty Ltd
PO Box 337, Bergvlei 2012, South Africa

Set in Linotron Plantin by Input Typesetting Ltd
Printed and bound in Great Britain by
Anchor Brendon Limited, Tiptree, Essex

British Library Cataloguing in Publication Data

Evans, Stuart
    Seasonal tribal feasts.——(Windmill Hill
    series)
    I. Title   II. Series
    823′.914[F]   PR6055.V2

ISBN 0 09 168120 0

The author and publishers acknowledge the estate of
Sir John Betjeman and John Murray Ltd for permission to
quote from 'Indoor games near Newbury', and the
estate of Wallace Stevens and Faber and Faber for
lines from The Necessary Angel

Windmill Hill: campsite in what is now Wiltshire, Eng., believed to have been a centre of ritual and of seasonal tribal feasting in the Fourth Millennium BC.

Encyclopaedia Britannica

The occupational debris implies temporary hearths and there is no evidence of permanent houses on the site.

Stuart Piggott

1

'*U*nless I make a mistake, that is the scholarly head of Ben Oldfield bent over a learned book and a large whisky.'

'Unless *I* make a mistake, that is the lilting voice of Francesca Oricellari, presupposing the presence of her even more lilting figure. Francesca! What a marvellous treat! What will you have?'

'Gin and tonic, I think.'

'Ah, the gent behind the bar heard you. Thanks. Here you are. Let's sit down. It's lovely to see you.'

'But I shall interrupt your book.'

'Not a bit. I never take anything in on trains. It's just a prop. I find myself staring out of the window, or else going over the same page again and again.'

'Cheers. Where have you been?'

'London Library. Term ended last week: so I've begun my weekly summer treks. Either there or to the British Museum. Why don't we arrange lunch some time, if you're not too busy.'

'I'd like that very much. I am quiet at the moment, working up my autumn show. But it's all detail now. The excitement and temper and flashing scissors are over. How is your work?'

'At the boring stage. I don't know whether it happens to you, but I find that after I've planned something, fiddled with it and made reams of preliminary notes, I start with immense enthusiasm and then look at it all with growing weariness. I nourish all manner of wild ideas about what I'd rather be doing. And at the top of the list would be sipping a drink on

1

a train with you! What happy chance is bringing you to Oxford? I take it you *are* coming to Oxford?'

'Roger Ingestre has asked me to a ball at his college.'

'Lucky devil. I should think that will be a good do. How is he? I haven't seen him for months.'

'Much the same as ever. Very irritable about politics. He was disgusted by the results of the election.'

'Oh? I thought he'd be pleased. The Alliance did pretty well. I suppose it's the share of the vote in relation to the number of seats.'

'So I believe. Anyway, Roger is convinced that there is no hope for any of you until there is sweeping reform of the voting.'

'My dear, I've heard him say so!'

'What do you think?'

'I'm ashamed to say, Francesca, that I'm fairly indifferent. I try to be responsible and political. I go to the polls. But poetry in one form or another keeps getting in the way.'

'With me as well. I leave it to my brilliant diplomatic sister. You've met Clodia, haven't you?'

'Once. With Roger Ingestre, in fact. She's not someone one forgets.'

'So I am always told. They are very old friends.'

'As you are, surely?'

'Not quite in the same way. I'm not serious, you see.'

'Ah – yes! Well, I'm delighted to say, nor am I. I confess to the occasional pang of conscience when I look around and see the immediate local mess. Then I think there's damn all I can do about it. And then farther afield . . . Well! Helplessness takes over.'

'And with me. But I will not let it make me miserable any more. I ask Roger what good it is making such fuss on the edge of things. And Clodia in big rooms with important politicians. It's all just talking, talking.'

'I feel guilty all the same. They show proper concern. One of my colleagues just doesn't care. He describes himself as an apolitical scientist.'

'What is that?'

'According to him, someone who takes an informed, highly intelligent interest in politics without ever becoming involved in the blood and sand part of it.'

2

'Having his cake and eating it.'

'No doubt. He thinks this thumping Tory majority is going to split the country from . . . ah, right up the middle. Not immediately, but in a year or so. He predicts something really nasty. And there won't always be the gift of Falklands tennis balls.'

'He sounds depressing.'

'Not in the least. One of the least depressing people I know. He revels in the curse of living in interesting times. Come to think of it, you must know him. Very engaging, sardonic chap by the name of Peter Cameron.'

'Ha! I know his sister. Lady Dracula in person. Compared with Iris Cameron, Agrippina the Younger qualifies for *Paradiso*.'

'She's very – ah well, yes. I suppose you come into contact professionally.'

'As little as possible.'

'I know that she runs a model agency.'

'A front! You believe me. She is the top English *mafiosa*.'

'So you won't be having Sunday tea at Garsington.'

'Not bloody likely!'

'When's the dance? Not tomorrow? Friday's an unlikely day for a Commem.'

'Not until next week. I was invited to stay for the weekend by Eve Darrow. It's Isabel's birthday on Saturday.'

'Oh good! You'll be there. So shall I. Isabel and I are old chums.'

'Chums?'

'Yes . . . friends. You know . . .'

'You really are the most surprising man, Ben Oldfield. You have your eye on almost every pretty woman you meet and you have Isabel Darrow for a "chum"!'

'I know that she's very beautiful. Obviously. But somehow I've never thought of her in that way.'

'Of course not. She's a little young for you, after all. She must be almost your own age.'

'Several years younger, as a matter of fact. She's twenty-three . . . Francesca! You're laughing at me. In any case, Isabel rather favours older men herself, I think.'

'So who is the hopeless passion this year?'

'Henrietta Ball.'

'I don't know her.'

'She's a philosopher. Quite tall. Very elegant. Ice cool. Dark red hair and the most taunting and quizzical smile.'

'Oh dear!'

'Where are we? Ah. Skirting Didcot. Time for a quick one. The same . . .'

'No. My ah shout. Is that right? I'm richer than you are.'

'Well, thanks . . .'

'There you are. Is that too much soda?'

'It's just right. Thanks.'

'Cheers, Ben. What are you going to do in the vacation?'

'Work, I suppose. Quite a lot of the time. I'll probably take a week or so off in France or Italy. And I thought I might do a little writing on my own account.'

'That's wonderful. I told you that you should. Do you remember?'

'Of course.'

'What will you write? A novel?'

'I don't think so. I've been toying with the idea of a collection of aphorisms. Not necessarily for publication.'

'Aphorisms! Why the hell do you want to write aphorisms?'

'It'll be a complete change from literature and I've always rather regretted that I didn't become a philosopher. Not that I'd be much good at the technical stuff.'

'Is this the influence of your . . . who was it . . . Henrietta?'

'Good Lord, no! I doubt that she knows I exist. Just that my research made me take an interest in myth. The way we all seem to need myths – whether the grand-scale universal ones, or the small personal stories we invent and build for ourselves. To help us live our lives, as the poet put it in a different context. And then I became interested in the notion of a sort of spiritual or emotional parallax.'

'I don't understand.'

'Parallax? Look out of the window. Focus on that telegraph pole as the train moves. And now look beyond the pole to that single tree a couple of fields away. You see there's an apparent change of position. The pole which is nearer to you is falling away faster than the tree and what have you which is all farther off. You must have noticed the phenomenon dozens of times. Well, that's parallax. There's also a more technical astronomical definition. I just want to try to apply this to human relationships and to events in our own and other lives as they appear to different people. And then in some impartial, indifferent, for want of a better word, infinite perspective.'

'Are you suggesting that the nearer someone is to an event, the sooner it falls away? I don't think so. What about grief or love?'

'No, Francesca. But I might suggest that the closer one is to an event which involves grief or love the sooner it falls out of perspective. The farther away, the more it is seen in the context of the general landscape.'

'So: isn't the event the train? And the pole and the tree the observers. The whole thing's upside down. Am I making it clear?'

'Inverse parallax, by God! That's neat.'

'It's a metaphor, Ben. It's not a theory.'

'No reason why theories should not be expressed as metaphors.'

'And even more reason why theories expressed as metaphors should be written in poems. Not in aphorisms. Why do you want to be a philosopher? You'd be much more suitable as a poet.'

'First, I can't write poems. I've tried. And I'm no good. Second, I want to prove to myself I can think. I know so many philosophers and they make me feel thick. Stupid, you know?'

'This woman, Henrietta, is not good for you.'

'It's not just her. Have you met David Kelly? Or Marcus Ferdinand?'

'Yes. Kelly I know. He's a friend of the Darrows. Of Isabel, I think.'

'I don't know what you make of him. But Ferdinand . . .'

'A fat man who makes a lot of jokes.'

'Well . . . heavy. Ex-philosopher. Ex-cleric. Ex-existentialist. Very disillusioned and most formidable. Kelly's a close friend of Henrietta.'

'Aha!'

'Not a bit aha! He's very cool and clever and I suspect women find him sexy.'

'I don't. And I think I like Ben Oldfield the way he is. Just fun.'

'What an epitaph!'

'There are worse. Hey, here we are. We've arrived.'

'So we have. Well met by British Rail, sweet Francesca.'

'Isn't it lovely? I adore this place.'

'Oxford at the season of her high midsummer pomps, as Mr Eliot put it.'

'What is that?'

'The balls, the garden parties, the ceremonies. Public and private festivals. Like Isabel's birthday.'

'It's charming. Everything is so beautiful in the sunlight.'

'Perhaps. I have to go the Encaenia next week when they give out the honorary degrees and salute the prizewinners. One of the chaps I teach has won a poetry prize.'

'That is where everyone dresses up in gorgeous robes. I like it.'

'Hum. Shall we take a taxi?'

'No. It's a beautiful day. Let's walk.'

'Then let me carry your bag.'

'And I'll carry your briefcase. It's probably heavier.'

OLDFIELD'S APHORISTIC ODYSSEY

Introduction

I suppose this is the result of showing off to a pretty girl – as it happens a *very* pretty girl – on a train. The lady in question, although I meet her infrequently, will unquestionably taunt and tease me unmercifully if I fail to live up to my somewhat grandiose plan of justifying the ways of myth to man, or perhaps of man to Myth.

It is, however, only fair to myself to protest that my work on Eliot has made me think deeply, I hope, certainly extensively, about the necessity of myth in the lives of ordinary as well as extraordinary people. Eliot's vast erudition and powerful mind, as in the case of Joyce, mark him out from the rest of us: but we are all subject to cultural, religious, literary and quite banal personal influences out of which we gradually evolve a private symbolism which may in turn become an almost dominating myth of ourselves.

The rational man, the strictly rational man, asks questions about the nature of substance, being, change, appearance and reality, attempting to answer his questions intellectually, leading himself, quite willingly until recent years, into the labyrinths of metaphysics and moral philosophy. This is not to say that the rational man does not engage in what I propose to call 'myth-building' in the same way that the less rational or the frankly irrational among us look to myth, whether public or personal, to make sense of, support or endorse our motives and extempore actions.

In the broadest and simplest terms I am interested in the common need to identify at a 'cosmic' as well as at an intensely personal level with the experience of others through the fabrication of stories: the experience of wonder, awe, horror, terror, pity, compassion (quite separate from pity), affection and love. At no less intensity, we seek to justify our commonplace lust, envy, greed, petty resentments, jealousy and vanity by structuring them (I make deliberate use of that ugly locution) into a version of ourselves at a particular moment. This is to reinforce in us a perfectly respectable self-respect (sometimes construed as pride), or at worst an often ludicrous *amour propre*.

If I take as an example my own experience when I fall in love, or think I have fallen in love, I immediately build the beloved object (so to speak) into a story. Her concerns become my concerns, although viewed at a greater distance – probably from a different perspective. I am immediately more, or less, sympathetic to people in a similar predicament. (Being in love is always a predicament!) At the same time, I view their elation or tribulation quite differently from my own. And it follows that they, and dispassionate observers, look on me, the beloved object, and whatever is happening with sympathetic or irritated or impatient insouciance. Should there be a rival (especially one preferred by the beloved object in my eyes or imagination) the story becomes more complicated at once. The plot, indeed, thickens.

In my investigation of myths, conducted strictly from the point of view of someone whose training is literary and whose knowledge of anthropology, psychology, semiology and so forth is at most peripheral, I propose also to develop this notion of human parallax in which our relationships and our judgement of particular events in our own and other lives is governed by perspective, significance and our own position in space and time at the resolution of a particular sequence of events.

Myth-building seems to me to involve pure myth; the interpretation of history; the propagation of public or private, objective or subjective lies; fiction; the commonplace appetite for 'bad news' and its consequent supply; reportage – in the form of folktales, rumour, gossip, anecdote and press stories. And so back again to myth. My intention is to pursue a reasonably disciplined investigation using an aphoristic method: but I am all too aware that I am very susceptible to distractions.

. . . Looking around me, I have come to the conclusion that I do not qualify as a lecher. True I am usually infatuated by, in love with, or obsessed about some woman or another and I undoubtedly have a highly developed erotic bump: but it is tempered by some romantic infusion in my blood which commands tenderness and an approach at once gentle and I fear ingenuous. It is no doubt why I am so remarkably ineffective in such matters. My modest and delightful encounters which have come to a right true end have all been with girls whom I believed I loved at the time. This is almost reprobate in someone born as late as 1954.

Mendoza now! Only three years my senior, Mendoza possesses immense hircine impulses and energy which has him skipping from crag to crag with zeal and enthusiasm: so that even if he does occasionally miss his footing his natural instinct reasserts his balance and he is off to the next ledge, however precarious. Nevertheless, I do not like or admire Mendoza. Especially since his attentions have been focused upon Isabel Darrow. (No one will believe that we are and have always been very close friends and nothing more. In my less commendable moments I tend to bask in the reflection of such assumptions, because she *is* remarkably beautiful.) At the same time, it must be said for Mendoza that he is activated by straightforward and relatively honest lust. There are others . . . (Darkly brooding.) There are others who smile

8

and smile and are debonair, while nursing intentions, I suspect, of Middletonian depravity.

With my current craze (or mania!) for making categories and lists, I have isolated the following: the straightforwardly lustful like Mendoza, the romantic and erotic (me), the victims of wry desire tinctured with a certain *amertume* (Marcus Ferdinand), the coolly sophisticated (Henrietta alas!), the affectionate realists (Isabel Darrow), the honest and uncomplicated (Francesca Oricellari) and the plainly dishonest: the dissimulators. I think, Henrietta apart, that I have always distrusted David Kelly.

Lust is relatively uncomplicated: the opportunist grope between coincidentals, joyful copulation at the appropriate hour – a relief which it is to be hoped is mutually pleasurable as well as cathartic. Love is altogether more troublesome. Once committed to loving, one has given something of oneself away. Immediately, I (for example) become a prey to suspicion, mindless jealousy. Although I am capable of protracted affection, selflessness, generosity to her (whoever she may be), in my flashes of private spite towards her I glimpse the underlying dishonesties, deceits and self-deceptions which I nourish and which I suspect in her. Hardly so with Henrietta! I have not dared give voice and utterance. She, of course, is detached; she gives nothing away. And yet there is more than amusement or irony in the smile that rests on the sly, calm Kelly from time to time. Far too bloody often!

Dear Henrietta,
Please may I come to talk to you about F. H. Bradley. I am having great trouble defining the beloved object. I know that I shall present myself in the most vulnerable light and that you are probably scornful of Idealist philosophy. Nevertheless, it would be of inestimable value to be treated under the beam of your laser intellect.

Madonna of Norham Gardens, Regina of the Parks, should I presume? And if so, would you please tell me how. This pretence can not go on. The trouble is: you make me feel so thick: Your eager mind's so span and

9

spick. You make my own thoughts reel and spin – I'm such a lousy *in*-tellectual. To be serious, though, Henrietta: think how you could help me in the syntagma of my doctoral thesis. You wave a delicate and cruel hand: take away the Fool.

As I write, I see you sitting serenely across the room: your dark red hair sweeping back from a white, imperious brow, an eager and a nipping frost in your clear grey eyes, your highly defined breasts assured under a cream shirt with lapis lazuli cufflinks, your precise but deliciously modelled hips in a prim green skirt, your lovely legs crossed as my eyes find no rest in the long line of your thigh under the demure jersey.

The trouble is it is no joke. I am becoming socially incapacitated. If we are both in the same company, I find myself looking to see if you are laughing when I have said something mildly funny. I labour at conversational effects in order to attract your notice. And when I do . . . When I do, I detect in your eyes a benign, indulgent scorn. I know that you don't make a habit of touching people. Iris Cameron flirts with everyone; Francesca is temperamentally affectionate; Isabel is inclined to cuddle male friends (or perhaps, more accurately, they are inclined to cuddle her); even Eve, her mother, occasionally bestows on someone a lingering touch which has the effect of a very remote caress. All these women register a man's presence, confirm his identity, allow him to feel that he is *there*: but you, adored Henrietta, touch no one. Not even Kelly. And the kiss you give (always to others) on parting is cold.

Perhaps this is what excites me so much. I am told that macho men find pretty lesbians volcanically desirable. I am not macho, God knows. And I certainly do not think that you are lesbian. No: I dream only of softening that *froideur* as the early summer sun warms a grey college wall; I see you tender and lithe and trembling in underwear the colour of wistaria; I discover in you a gentle passion that no one else suspects, let alone has known. The frost melts in your eyes; your tense limbs become supple yet binding; your firm mouth is soft and sensual.

So: I have, at last made bold to declare myself. I make

this appeal, Eleusinian priestess, to be admitted into the Sunday complacencies of your peignoir, late coffee and oranges in a sunny swing on a patio with bougainvilleas. Let us, my darling, move away from our Henry James passivity, in which it is as though we are no more than 'convertible literary stuff'.

I am about to lock this letter away, addressed to you. It will be there for you to brood over when I am no more. I should add, however, that I have absolutely no intention of being no more if I can help it: but there are thundering buses, vespine malevolent motorbikes and fatal afflictions which give no warning. One never knows when the sun will go out on Venice.

Your adoring,
Ben Oldfield

THE NEED FOR MYTH

1 Oldfield's Telemachiad

As a small boy I was fascinated and frightened by mirrors. I used to look at myself with considerable interest until it inevitably occurred to me to wonder who I was. This is where the fright began. The first time it happened was a complete surprise: I said to myself: I am Benjie Oldfield, a little boy aged seven: I am . . . And I realized that I did not know what I was; what made me me. It felt, I still recall, like being swept into a vortex, like bathwater swirling away. I faced, as it were, for the first time the problem of my own identity. I was confused, made dizzy: frightened. Thereafter, cautiously, I would from time to time begin the same catechism without ever proceeding very much farther – trying to probe the mystery of my own existence as an individual, my uniqueness. It was not that I felt remotely special: I was a perfectly ordinary boy, moderately bright, quite imaginative, who preferred playing games to lessons and rather enjoyed being mischievous. Yet I was troubled by this urge to define myself and so, without knowing it, I began to subscribe to the myth of my soul, or at least of my spirit. As I grew older, learned

11

more, took this or that theory which might have been fashionable and tried to work them all into a coherent pattern to explain my own identity and that of others, I became less susceptible to this communion with my own image: though the same strangeness, in a much more phantasmal, paler way, gripped me now and then even in my early twenties. Becoming concerned in my work with the personal systems of symbols and imagery of certain poets, I began to examine my own minor capacity for myth-building and to guess that each of us, consciously or not, constructs a reasonably elaborate version of himself or herself based upon shared myth, fiction (from within or without), lies (once again subjective or supposed), a reading of a private past in the context of wider historical assumptions, an attempt to relate to the dread invoked by immediate events, and lastly a response to 'stories' in the journalistic or troubadour tradition as they may seem relevant. The more complex and contorted such personal myths may become may well depend on the intricacy of education or the variety of experience undergone by the individual concerned. At the same time, in an age of mass communication, the facility for myth is present all around: even if it extends only to the fruit-machine jackpot or the enormous win at some form of betting.

Let us start with Telemachus. Telemachus is alone. All the assumptions he is entitled to make about his future – his security and wellbeing – are under challenge. The suitors threaten not only his relationship with his mother (who is not much comfort, sitting up there spinning), but also his very inheritance. He is young and inexperienced. All the retainers faithful to him are ageing and incapable of much active resistance.

It is natural that Telemachus searches for moral support and help. (Surely it is not too far-fetched to find parallels in the predicament of Hamlet.) He idealizes his father; he seeks help from the old and wise (Nestor), from those chastened by experience (Menelaos and Helen), and (through them) achieves a Protean glimpse into the future which indicates his own destiny as well as that of Odysseus. Athene/Mentor is the resolution, the will, which impels the young and beleaguered man to act.

Telemachus illustrates a common (though by no means

12

universal) predicament experienced by young people made vulnerable by particular circumstances which make them question their past, feel uncertain about the present and look forward with anxiety if not fear. At school many of us were the children of broken marriages; more and more of the pupils I teach and my own contemporaries have known the same painful experience; and I understand that the proportion of schoolchildren who have lived through their parents' separation in inner cities and 'new' towns is surprisingly high. Some of these relicts of the failed marriage live with one or other of the parents; others have to accommodate to some new partner of one or both as well. (This is where Snow White steps up alongside Telemachus and Hamlet.)

In this situation it is immediately understandable that the troubled boy or girl looks for support; but other young people living in stable homes may find themselves obscurely threatened and go searching for other navigation points and bearings. (Many turn to cult groups of their own generation to merge identity in some uniform style or fashion; or else to assert individuality in an outlandish variation on an already rebellious pattern of behaviour. All of which is ably exploited to their profit by the manipulators of 'pop' culture. I do not see Telemachus or Hamlet – or even Snow White – as punks or skinheads, for all that.)

The search for an ideal father lost (or, as the case may be, mother lost) may become a quest for a father/mother figure. And this becomes complicated according to the sex of the questing child. 'Nestor' need not be very old or remarkably wise: but he must have common sense and must have been, at some time, 'a tamer of horses'. Menelaos and Helen represent the marriage which has survived, perhaps in the face of tribulation, let alone difficulty; the real or imagined paradigm of heterosexual partnership, betrayal and reconciliation. Menelaos's account of Proteus offers an insight into a painful and bewildering struggle with the forces of imagination necessary to the achievement of some kind of resolution to a particular problem.

I found myself at the age of sixteen, an only child, living in the wreckage of my parents' marriage. Although I had long been aware of weaknesses and faults in the structure, it was still a shock when the house came down. I lived with both of them when they set up separately. My father, a rather weak, gentle character, remained alone. My mother, who was more impatient and passionate, took, I think, several lovers, before settling with one. At which point I was, or at least felt, rejected. Subsequently, I found myself in search of both. Oxford became Ithaca; a tutor, his own teacher and various married (or unmarried) couples served as models for other figures in the original myth. My lasting attraction towards older women seems readily explainable. I was no Stephen Dedalus. I lacked the depth and penetration of mind, the arrogance and ambition and pride. I represented and to some extent still represent a much humbler, more typical Telemachus.

The Icarus/Daedalus story represents an entirely different, albeit powerful, perspective on relationships which are once again not uncommon. Here the generations are in alliance and conflict: first of all combining their exertions to escape from oppression and imprisonment; then at odds over the way in which to use their new freedom. If Icarus represents the heroic, impetuous, exulting fervour of youth, Daedalus stands for the wary, self-preserving calculation of experience. Or, as explored by Michael Ayrton, they illustrate the differences between the heroic and artistic temper. Daedalus also bears witness to the stamina and determination of the mature man in his exhausting flight to Cumae and his attempt to build something new. And so on.

I shall not concern myself at this point with other aspects of the Daedalus myth: that of the impartial craftsman who accepts an assignment whether it is to construct a golden honeycomb, a penitential labyrinth or a device to gratify the unnatural lust of Pasiphae. In passing, however, it is worth noting the frequency of shameful lust (as opposed to honest passion and desire) in myth: the fierce, merciless energy of Tereus; the semi-incestuous longing of Phaedra; the callous infidelities and betrayals of Jason and Theseus. All quite different from the situation of Oedipus who stumbles unknowingly upon his fate and who is appalled by what he has done. Freud's recognition of this myth as having had such powerful impact through the centuries because of its reflection of what he saw as shared forbidden desires may have generated rightly or not a certain confusion in some minds about the

14

intentions of the essentially good, just and damned Oedipus, who was himself a victim.

Enough illustration for the moment. It is time to attempt to isolate and examine the very many reasons which point towards the need for myth in individuals, societies, factions, nations, systems of government, cults and so on . . .

. . . That was a real nice clambake. I suppose I was mighty glad I came. In fact I was. I did have a real good time and always enjoy a party, even when it is not a particularly good one. And Isabel's birthday was splendid, because Isabel enjoys parties too. Naturally, there were her own friends – although quite a number of these are a few years older than she is. There was the lovely Francesca, the exquisite Henrietta, smiling damned Kelly and his pretty wife, always a little left out, Ferdinand and a few others. Mendoza had somehow wangled an invitation, glowing like a cathode ray if that's not out of date these days. For once it seemed that no one was specially concerned to prepare a face to meet the faces, except Mendoza for whom it was after all fitting to conceal his lust for Isabel; and Kelly, who seemed to spend more time with her than with Henrietta. Ah but Oldfield is not fooled! He would, of course: with his wife, Christina, present. Can't really understand why a public relations woman with an electronics firm should be so diffident – even nervous – at these semi-academic lustrations. I've noticed that any group of people who share some arcane language or levitical privilege – dons, musicians, actors, cricketers – do tend to edge people onto the periphery of any gathering, although I should have thought that Christina had been married long enough to Kelly to be used to it. Much of it is unintentional. Eve Darrow, serene and kind, perfectly adapted to being the Master's wife, will put her at her ease as soon as she notices. Charles himself, smiling and nodding, wishing he was somewhere else even at Isabel's birthday party, where for once, looking around, I noticed fewer perceptibly composed faces, compiled expressions of affability and goodwill than is usual at most of our rituals, whether public or private. There seems always to be a polite aura of obligation and social duty at most of our British functions: 'My goodness, this is a great day/splendid occasion/marvellous celebration/super party, I must be seen to appreciate it and therefore to be enjoying myself.' Even in the company of the delectable Francesca, to whom he seems affectionately indifferent, I don't imagine that Roger Ingestre *wants* to go to his college ball: but he feels he should support it and she is a highly decorative companion and he will rather enjoy it. I certainly don't want to go to the Encaenia to laugh dutifully at the Public Orator's Latin witticisms (well, titter undemonstratively): but I owe it to earnest Ernie Greaves and I'll enjoy the strawberries and champagne that Walter Harrington is laying on. There again: I don't suppose he wants to but it befits a head of college to acknowledge a small local triumph. And it gets our Walter out of the tiresome official tatharara, after all. All our ceremonies do light the way to an after-dinner sleep. Dining on Sunday evenings; sherry in one's rooms; this or that public lecture. I wonder if these rituals are a substitute for living our lives and that we mark out festivals and important seasonal rites to disguise and obscure the banal routine of daily observances, the canonical offices which we mutter smiling or yawning. I'm being less than fair to people with a zest for living: Isabel, Francesca, Iris Cameron (neither of *them* at the Darrows', I noticed), even me. I can't help noticing the way that the way of life has conditioned word and gesture in so many like Eve, who should be warm, has frozen Henrietta, devitalized Ingestre, soured Ferdinand and made a raging hypocrite of Kelly. (I still snarl in my Spanish cloister. Grrr!) Mendoza is something different: I suppose he's a public dissimulator to millions once or twice a week.

Fading light of a summer evening. The music rippling gently in the darkening, high-raftered room. The wistaria blossoms stirred quietly outside the heavy casement windows. The air was warm outside, for it was a summer occasion. I do not remember what the pianist was playing, calm and precise and delicate. Brahms or Schumann and I felt for a moment that I was part of the music, the kind of pleasure that will come seldom, if at all, again. And yet it was not like that. For all the time I was aware of her, translating her into music or transforming the music to be what I wanted to find in her. She was wearing a long white

16

dress, very pure of line. I could see the deep dark red glow of her hair still, but not her eyes, perhaps tranquil at last because of the music – those grey eyes still and tranquil. She was very still, yet I thought I could see across the dim hall the gentle rise and fall of her breasts responding to the notes as to the words or touch of a lover she herself desired, for whose words or touch she had waited. In the darkness gathering I could make out her white figure against all the absorbed silent gloom of others and the panelled walls aged into sombre solemnity. And the music, dying away into a romantic cadence of loss or despair or love remembered at the easeful moment of sleep, was suddenly tripping with joy . . .

The pianist's hand lifted in a gesture. There was a pause of indrawn breath, a little silence. Then applause. Lights went up. It was the interval. She was laughing at something said by her immaculate escort.

'Convertible literary stuff', by the good lord Henry! I feel somehow that I don't quite have the touch. The prose poem will not revive itself under the kiss of Oldfield's ballpoint Japanese pen. Henrietta is a hell of a name to scan (forgive me!). Four syllables all at a go. Still . . . Remembering it now, I can recall what I felt. Will I at forty or fifty still be painting lakes? I hope so. In a way. Much too early for my farewell to Florida.

Quite arbitrarily, I distinguish memory from experience. Memory is a flash of vivid recollection in which some usually pleasant, transcendentally happy event recurs in the imagination, bringing with it the rare and suffusing happiness of a delightful dream, from which it is disappointing to wake. Memory describes with unpredictable syncopation how it is to be unquestioningly in love, how some moments were elating beyond description, how forgotten friendships were warm and comic. Memory edits itself cleverly most of the time: but not *all* of the time. Experience will not leave anything out: the very awful must take its place alongside the very good. Where Memory offers the unattended flash of intense pleasure, sometimes almost ecstatic, Experience runs and reruns what happened before, then, and after like an unstoppable infinite videotape which cannot be destroyed or discarded. There is nothing mechanical, which is to say volitional, about either. You do not press certain buttons, or adjust various tuners, or get the man in to look at the aerial. Memory happens to you. Experience is always there. And Memory is the more debilitating. It is possible to spend too long and to waste too much time waiting for the visitations of past happiness.

Ah well: on with the bloody aphorisms. I think they have to be a bit more pithy. Shorter . . . That's it!

*　*　*　*　*

. . . I've heard that some people actually cultivate the lines and crevices of their faces to look interesting. Not yet. The bistred eyes of Giles Mendoza speak of infinite weariness already. Not actual bags beneath the eyes perhaps. Just the hint of bagginess. Marcello Mastroiani comes to Hollywell Road. Ah gloom. How long will Mendoza continue to charm the subelite of England. Good teeth. And all my own unlike so many I could name: but won't. Unprofessional. Tactful if not exactly charming. Would a moustache be telegenic? (That's a filthy word.) One of those walrussy, droopy efforts. Or a beard? Never tried and so I might not be able to manage the necessary hispid masculinity that sits so agreeably upon the features of so many of my . . . um . . . colleagues in the profession. Suppose I was wispy. How could *she* take in without gurgles of ready laughter a lover of tufts and floccules, a mere fimbriate, however ardent and woolly elsewhere. So much in the face I have learned in my craft or flickering art exercised when the moon rages for its violated magic. Come Mendoza. Pettishness before seven means a six o'clock drink with some sodding executive in shirtsleeves before you're thirty-three and the next day your contract desk and personal belongings outside your locked office in the corridor. What happened to Breakfast Television anyway? Urbanity, *mon brave*. Nose too long and eyes too sharp, anyhow. A beard or moustachios would overdo the whole face. Mendoza? 'You can tell he's one of them, can't you?' 'I don't know why they let these Australian Jews come on our programmes do you, Father?' 'Bloody dago! Not going to watch this, Jocasta.' 'Well, you know how it is, old boy, in the media: the Vatican and the Mafia hand in glove. God! What a perfect Renaissance

18

face.' As it were. Ah well. *Ach so. Eh bien.* Well, shit, baby.
I'll string along with you as you are Mendoza and these little
throwaway razors which get blunter by the package. No brand
names. Horror. If the BBC is Auntie, then the IBA is a not
very wicked Uncle. Or are they just the Ugly Sisters. Then
who is Cinderella. Not you, Mendoza. Boots Herbal suits me:
but I'd better wear Brut. Why should Buttons not get to first
base and farther before Prince Charming has noticed the
village green, as it were, as they so often say. *Ach!* The tang
of aftershave on the wily features 'composed in excruciated
compassion' (*The Times*); 'locked in knowing derision' (*The
Guardian*): 'showing elitist sneerocracy of the media as only
it can' (take your pick from the fringe press).

Enough of holding a mirror up to Mendoza superbly
shaved. Introspection done for a day. All the intimacies
complete. Not one to look at myself in the institutional lift
mirrors. The lighting is always so bad. And yet so many
executives do, mostly with satisfaction; though sometimes
with furry-tongued gloom. Orange juice; the humble
crispbread, lightly buttered, with Mrs Bridges Curried
Chutney; tea. What a neat kitchen! Compact and clean. Fit
for a princess. Talking of whom . . . The plot to seduce Isabel
Darrow: Phase II. Phase I, the direct approach, did not quite
work. And I'm still slightly miffed by the look of complete
surprise in those violet eyes. Unsubtle I may have been but
not coarse: she was simply startled. And very much amused.
I shall not forget that struggle not to laugh. She shall pay for
that! But no inflaming thoughts at this stage. Isolate the
competition. Any number of infatuated youth – one or two
of whom, it must be admitted, have certain physical advan-
tages if not charm: not significant. Oldfield: an innocent,
whom she regards as her private teddy bear and who sees her
as a sort of happy kitten; and yet their affection is evident.
(Odd how so many women show kindness to Oldfield, who
does so want to be an intellectual when the cuddling has to
stop.) Ferdinand: wistful middle age, too fat, an eye with too
much youth in it – so that he is increasingly acerbic; gone the
jolly jowls of yesteryear except in substance. David Kelly: the
most dangerous in that he is personable, quiet, very bright
(not that Isabel cares much for that!) and married to an
attractive woman; others might not notice, but I see small

exchanges of smiles and confidence between them, how often they seem to be together. Conquest rather than the man? Why not? Weigh against these and sundry visitors *ipse* Mendoza. Ah! The television presence who tickles your intellect with feather-duster wit in the living room and scours it ruthlessly in the loo; smooth radio voice starting stopping or just hitching up the week, sportive in quizzes, cannily quizzical on 'Kaleidoscope'; opera lover, first-nighter, *dégagé* clubman, who chooses to live away from it all at Oxford . . . (perhaps not tactful in view of Daddy etcetera) . . . who chooses to live away from false metropolitan glitter among his peers – after all was vivaed for a first and Aunt Dorothy left him a very pretty house. To all appearances, no contest! How can she fail to be impressed? But she manages pretty well. Likes me perhaps enough. I make her laugh. But then so does almost everyone with a gossamer of wit clinging to them. Phase II: I must concentrate on the youthful and urbane pitch. Obliquely erotic. What a mercy that I don't actually love her. That must be very miserable and inconvenient. So if I don't make it, I don't make it. There is the sad precedent of Francesca Oricellari with whom I have remained on the very best terms. (I think.) There seems to be a common assumption that she is the mistress of Roger Ingestre. Absurd it must be. Although she comes to Oxford often enough. Many friends, including the Darrows. At Isabel's birthday party and their guest, let me not forget. A joke? A discreet word? Oh Giles Mendoza! . . . I have heard of your winks and becks and oeillades, the lift of an elegant eyebrow, downward curlicue of a fulsome lip. Not the type. Fuck or not and never tell. Who needs to: arranged by Providence (so to speak) as she is? Not easy the laughter. Is that where Isabel learned to laugh? Very much: 'Well, if you do and I hear about it . . .' Enough. Paranoia is the Medusa wink to the wing-heeled amorist. Something down there shrivels or calcifies at the sound of merriment tinkling among the coffee cups. And yet what a wonderful body and what a lovely face and what poise. Isabel must have been about fifteen when I made my first pass at Francesca. Eight years. Is that all? And what of Iris Cameron? The truly liberated heterosexual woman. Unforgettable lust of one day and night becoming vague desire without the slightest urgency. We've had each other. So what? There was nothing else to do at the time. She was lavish and it was good, I'm sure. But don't count on me we said and still say with our eyes, laughing. I won't be there when you're desperate. What larks. Always the best of friends. The gossip about her and her brother? Does it matter? 'Shut your eyes and think of the Greek myths.' A nasty lot live here when you come to think of it. That, however, is all in the past. And I have barely savoured the piquancy of Mrs Bridges Curried Pickle. Back to Phase II. The sophisticated little darling (one of the tunes she likes) will not be impressed by the vast and trunkless image of my talking head. Thou shalt not covet thy neighbour's image etcetera. And she shows not the remotest interest in mine, nor my opera tickets, nor my privileged invitations, nor my introductions to the magnificent seven of broadcasting: (Fill in the appropriate coupon with your slogan: I like . . . because . . . no more than eleven four-letter words.) So what will impress her? *Who* impresses her? Not many people. It's not that she has any exaggerated sense of herself: simply that she takes others for what they are. She admires her father. As who should not? How to succeed in Academe without really trying. Eve Darrow, wonderful of coiffure and make-up, fragrantly and crisply laundered, yet suggesting a silken intimacy about her breasts and loins with every movement. Once an actress . . . And Darrow made it! From observation which befits one with his quivering paw on the national pulse, vibrating to every rhythm of the collective British minority audience, the thinking-person's dowser, I detect a certain wariness towards Henrietta Ball. Why should that be? Chestnut-haired Lorelei combing her tresses on the arid rock of modern British philosophy. Kelly must be the answer. But Kelly is so passive. Yet how many times have I caught them smiling across a room at some private joke, watched her laughing at some swift aside. Nonsense. And if so . . . well there is always his pretty Christina who might feel opportunely neglected. Worth bearing in mind. Time I was moving.

All quite difficult. Perhaps I should move away from Aunt Dorothy's comfortable and pretty house. Oxford isn't kind to personalities after the first intemperate gulp. I do much better everywhere else. Perhaps distance might lend a touch of enchantment even to Isabel. My new series. The BBC offer of an arts programme. Would not impress. Not very interested in the mind. Then why some pale white hunter like Kelly? It makes sense to take the BBC up. Not much more money: but prestige. Then in a few years perhaps my own show on my own terms. Abrasive charm, should it be? Or charming abrasion? I shall *not* turn into a telly bear – not even one with a sore head. That will work itself out. Not so Isabel. Who has become too much an obsession. I'd not have believed it a month or so ago. This obsession to hear from *her* those words and little cries and watch her face as . . . and see her vibrant and coaxing . . . and subservient to her before I leave no doubt about conquest. And domination.

Enough. Lights out. Taps all secure. Windows locked. Keys. Briefcase. Books. (Oh Christ!) All set. Mendoza squares his shoulders against another day and the drifting unalive of Paddington. Click. Clack. Stay secure until I'm back.

Mendoza steps out into the almost midsummer dapple of an Oxford morning blithely. And who is this that he encounters, on the corner of South Parks Road and Broad Street, high-heeled and elegant trim buttocks wafted by the light breeze which stirs the trembling leaves and scatters late blossom? It is Henrietta Ball also on her way to the station, also breathing deeply the overtemperate air. Bloody hot, already. Will she tell him that the sky is falling? Not the type. What will they talk about? Everyday banalities . . . As it happens not. Of course, I should have remembered that one of her pupils was shot a few weeks ago in Paris. Iris Cameron knew him, somehow, too. Sorry. Yes . . . I am. Sorry. A pity that such an attractive woman should be so forbidding. Perhaps only for me because I'm afraid that my intellect can't quite go the distance. Chat along George Street of television. Her philosophy series was scrapped, but now there is talk of something else on ideas that have rocked the world or something of the sort. Henrietta thinks it is all impossibly vague. Channel Four. Chiltern Television. Michael Dorf. Do I know him? We've met a couple of times. Large, self-congratulatory, acidly clever. But astute. Tell her about my BBC plans. Of course, says the elegant thinker to some purpose, *you* are the professional. Irony. She performs pretty well. Am I looking forward to it? Ah well: the world-weary face I was practising at the shaving mirror. There comes a time, faced with the

BBC's stand-up intellectuals in radio and television, when I feel like the second house on a Saturday at the Glasgow Empire or the front row of the old Windmill Theatre. My God, I've made her laugh. Inconsequential chatter. She buys *The Times:* I buy *The Times, The Guardian, Private Eye* and the *Listener.* Lurking already on the platform, lean and saturnine, Max Davenport. Shall we tell him the sky is falling or let it come as a pleasant surprise? Doesn't like me because I made it with Iris Cameron for whom he carries an enormous torch or some similar phallic substitute. She ignores him. Engages Henrietta in some intricacy of college politics which effectively excludes me. Hope the sky catches him the most awful crack on the head. She seems bored. The luxurious iridaceous memory runs again briefly through my private video. What a gloriously shameless creature she was! Was? Sadly, yes. Not again, I fear.

Train. Obliged to share a compartment. Not one of those long carriages with tables, so Davenport and I jockey for the best prospect of Henrietta's fine, long legs. I win. Henrietta, with ceremony, opens *The Times* and reads with that effortless concentration professional philosophers seem to have on tap. Davenport eyes me with undisguisable distaste, delving with a sneer into his briefcase for a tome as I leaf with merry humility through *Private Eye.* Henrietta glances at me as she turns over a page. Faint hint of a smile perhaps. What does she really think of debonair Giles Mendoza? Probably not much: but she is polite. I wouldn't dare. Suppose I do quite well all things considered. Except with Isabel. No: I haven't really tried. Women like me I think rather more than men: twerps like Oldfield are envious, filberts like Ingestre are indifferent. After all I am a household face. And unlike most of them, mine is a career that can't be touched: I am outside and well outside the narrow little dramas of *The Academic's Revenge.* Not that I suspect there's much adultery: lots of moping and pining, perhaps the wistful grapple in the cloisters but none of the Grade 1 laying that goes on in my world. Still Mendoza has never been one to man a moral strongpoint. And I've always seen ethics as a form of spiritual greed. What a shame Davenport's here. I could have tried that out on Henrietta. On second thoughts what a good thing Davenport is here. She'd have torn me into very thin fillets. Unconcernedly we read as the towers of Didcot simmer past in the morning air. Oh arseholes to you Davenport, now lifting his stupid little moustache in a snicker to descant upon a scholarly pitfall into which his Thomist has tumbled. Envious academic niggler: some happy bastard clearly beat him to whatever it was, *o felix bastardus*. Can't be, can it? Henrietta lifts cool eyes from the page, turns her nobly chestnut head with long-lashed indifference, suppressing a sigh which causes little silky ripples around her titties. She says indeed and crosses the delicious *jambes* the other way sparing me an admonitory look. Wouldn't dream of it, lovie. Wisest thing I ever did not to get a better class at Schools or but for the grace of Lucifer I might have been, how could it have been possible, another Davenport. Or with God's grace withdrawn another Ferdinand. Must be terrible to lose your faith like that. Careless at the very least. Henrietta not troubled by doubts, never having enjoyed anything else, I suspect. A flicker of white nylon for a moment in that elegant transposition encouraging thoughts of what lies under the crisp blouse and pencil skirt her hips were created to flatter. White slip with filmy lace around the bodice, one of those soft clinging brassieres rather severe in line with a dull sheen that make the most of a fine cleavage and then – ah what bliss – a scrap of lacy suspender belt, firm silky panties (none of your scrappy little bikini – good substantial items that ask for stroking hands) and long tan stockings with taut shiny tops. Definitely! Not tights! Much too cool a woman for such inventions of the sharp-faced wowsers on a hot day. Enough! Immoral stirrings have hardened into noticeable and purposeful will. Must conceal under the merciful *Guardian*. How suitable. *Private Eye* far too scant and (somehow) inappropriate.

And anyway it is Isabel, the beautiful Isabel, who should be the focus of my thrusting telekinetic imagination. I shall give a small, smart dinner party to celebrate my new series. One or two well-known public smiles, a couple of airy (no, forget it) wits. Amanda, who will flirt with me shamelessly. (God bless happily married actresses who *don't*!) Discretion. Good food and wine. Henrietta? Problematic. No absolutely *no* male academics. Top-drawer personalities – some of whom even have character. Isabel, my darling, how will you be able to resist?

*   *   *   *   *

Hotel Spap
Olympia
20 July 1983

My dear Rachel,
No doubt if he were not himself used to working hard in heat far in excess of this, Oliver would be thinking of referring me to one of his psychiatric colleagues. It is ferociously hot, but wonderfully peaceful. Perhaps even you, tolerant and understanding as I've always known you to be, will be asking yourself why the bloody woman with the entire summer in which to dispose of herself should choose the most blazing month for a trip around the Peloponnese. Answer: I had nothing to do until late August, will be busy in September, and was fed up with Oxford, tired of the banality of my thoughts and generally fractious with myself and others. So I booked ahead here and at a couple of other places, flew to filthy Athens, hired a car and set off chastely to commune with ancient wisdom and my less perturbed spirit.

It occurs to me that for such progressive twentieth-century people, Rachel Bailey and Henrietta Ball write an awful lot of letters. One reason, for my part, is that I hate the goddam telephone on which, as you know, I become incoherent. And this won't do for a professional philosopher, will it? What we are supposed to be is fluent. A better one, though, is that letter-writing seems to me to be the last civilized art left to those of us who are not consciously (or perhaps self-consciously) literary. I don't mean that one sets out to be a conscious stylist like Pliny, or even Cicero – who couldn't really help it – but it is pleasant, now and again, to write however inconsequentially about nothing in particular, rather than settle down to the drudgery of this or that learned dissertation or review, when phantom colleagues are always hovering over one's shoulder.

I hope you are having a marvellous time in San Diego. It was delightful to see you both at Oxford before you left and I'm glad that you enjoyed the little party. I found myself thinking a lot in subsequent days about our long and entirely accidental friendship and how very differently our lives have turned out.

25

It is always good to see you and Oliver together: you are so completely different temperamentally and so well suited. I know that things were not always easy while he was abroad and you were in Parliament: but you survived. And that, these days, is something in itself. *Circumspice!* What you said about sometimes wishing you'd had children rather than careers reminded me that I sometimes wish that I had a husband or at least (things being how they are) some man to share my life with. Don't think I'm being maudlin after too much Metaxa. Chaste though this journey is, you know perfectly well that I have sometimes used pleasure as a test of value. (Not me: Rebecca West.) And most of the time I don't regret celibacy much; it's just that the effort these days to be briefly unchaste and much more enduringly bored is increasingly wearing. I sometimes wonder whether I've ever enjoyed sex enough, but many of the people who tempt me are already married and I am not in that kind of 'change. Indeed, the confusion of people's lives, even from my corner of the cloister, is alarming. God knows (sorry, Zeus knows – I expect he would, wouldn't he) what it must be like in San Diego!

It was all so simple when you and I were young and it was possible to be gay without slur or footnote. There was no pill and young men had to be reasonably prescient if they expected to get anywhere. And it's quite surprising in retrospect how many of them didn't. Nowadays it is all quite different. And from what I see there are areas of human contact in which the generation gap is the merest hyphen, if that.

I was pleased that you liked David Kelly and Christina. Oddly enough, she is rather shy in spite of having a well-paid and responsible job with an electronics firm. David is quiet and clever and rather sardonic. He has lived all his life (after school) at Oxford and takes it for granted. She doesn't – which makes her nervous of people like me. You and Oliver, who doesn't give a damn anyway, were people she could like. You belonged to a real world she understands. Not that ours isn't real enough: it just seems not to be. I've known David for many years and I suppose that we are close friends.

But I'm aware that the easy charm conceals a certain ruthlessness. In private with me, he either talks very seriously or goes in for a line of sub-erotic banter which goes no further. This is, most of the time, something of a relief: though I'll confess to you occasional pangs of self-doubt in that I don't inspire him to more ardent efforts. I am, of course, being frivolous. He's an attractive man and knows it, which is what perhaps makes his wife nervous – although, in so far as I am aware, he is not promiscuous and is said even to have resisted Iris Cameron whom you *must* one day meet. I know we gossip most shamelessly about her.

At times, when I think about the instability of so many relationships, I suppose I am thankful that I am on my own and a free agent. One certainty is that I should not be easy to live with: I am often too fastidious and intellectually finicky for my own comfort let alone anyone else's. So far, to *my* knowledge, which is by no means a central intelligence unit in such matters, there have been in this academic year seven fairly serious affairs, three shipwrecked marriages and two long-standing arrangements which have sickened and died. It is depressing. Of course, the Darrows (whom I was surprised you did not already know) are a great comfort and reassurance. Charles is delightful, tolerant and wise and Eve is funny, eminently sensible and more glamorous with every passing year. She must be approaching fifty – the elder daughter, Isabel, is twenty-three – and I'm sure you'll agree looks fifteen years younger. Incidentally, the said Isabel is an unusually beautiful girl and works as a secretary at the faculty where she sees quite a lot of David Kelly who is librarian or something of the sort. They appear to be very chummy.

I suppose that you must be missing what involvement you still had in politics. However relieved you were to leave Parliament and however sensible I think your decision was, I've often seen the old light of fascination in your eye when chat has turned in that direction. What, I wonder, do you make of a political leader who takes a 'sabbatical' from active party work because he is 'depressed and tired'? Even Roger Ingestre admits a minor *chute de pierres* from the surface of the Alliance rock and others (SDP) are more scathing. I must say that it is a brand of Steel which seems to be lacking resilience.

You'll no doubt have read that hanging was once again an issue in Parliament about a week ago – just before I left England. It was an ingeniously framed argument by the rope lobby and I think many people feared – with the massive Conservative majority, many of whom seem righter than right – that it was going to succeed. There was a separate vote on several different categories of murder, including very emotive circumstances such as murder committed by terrorists, murder of police and prison officers and so on. They were all defeated and the overall majority against the principle was something like a hundred and fifty, which was a qualified indication that our legislators retain some respect for human existence. I can imagine how you would have reacted and felt rather sorry that you and a few others like you are no longer there to vote and speak on such matters.

Otherwise the political news is drab. The Defence Estimates are huge, as might have been expected. As you know quite well already, I am no raging left-winger: but it does seem absurd that a tiny nation such as ours is spending vast quantities on weapons of destruction we shall never be in a position to control let alone deliver, when the laborious structure of a humane and liberal society is flaking away where it is not visibly crumbling. With Gerontion at the White House I'm afraid that the Nuclear Cloud is a damn sight bigger than a man's hand. And I think I am genuinely afraid. How does it look over there? The Greenham Common women are making a pretty strident fuss, but they are so bigoted and so rabidly sexist in their antics that they must do more harm. And I'm not very keen on that highly equivocal priest who keeps appearing from behind the reredos.

All this, along with weariness of a selfish, libidinous, increasingly foul-mouthed ambience and the undoubted accumulative effect of the coenobitic life we live in the university, seems to have made me restive and disgruntled. But more than that, I think I am at last reacting to the wasteful murder a couple of months ago of one of my pupils. I talked to you about it briefly and would have wished to listen to your inevitably wise and gentle advice, but someone came up and it wasn't appropriate. The boy was barely twenty, very clever in a way but rather arrogant, slightly spoiled and unsettled. He was shot in Paris by a terrorist whom he bravely but foolishly tackled. The irony was that the murderer was in the wrong place going for the wrong victim. And perhaps worse, the boy had recently fallen in love with a beautiful girl, who seems (in so far as I have heard) to have loved him just as much. No one seems to know what has become of her. She was a fashion model who worked for Iris Cameron's agency; she, for all her failings, a generous and loyal woman, has done her best to trace the girl – to no avail. The young man was called Quentin Joyce. Although he frequently exasperated me and other people who taught him, he was dynamic and in a fashion attractive. His father, a successful architect, happens to be a friend of Charles Darrow. I met him only recently. Soon after, a very sane woman who is a close friend of someone we both know reasonably well, Evan Warrington. She was almost part of Quentin's family – his mother died while he was still a child. Then, coincidentally, the man with whom I'm discussing a television series, Michael Dorf, also appears to have known all of them extremely well. (They all live on a private housing estate in Kent.)

What I became aware of was that decent sorrow and a passing sense of futility and waste, a fleeting qualm of guilt that perhaps one has not done or did not do enough, cannot measure up to deep and real grief. I found myself trying to see this insignificant tragedy from other points of view, notably that of the woman involved, who was quietly, unostentatiously saddened. And in so doing I realized that an event I thought I had placed in perspective was not in any perspective at all. For me something which should have been of surpassing importance, the needless death of a young man for whom I had positive feelings, was merely an event that I had passed by, as though it were a road accident seen from a car or a sudden violent quarrel between a woman and a man in the street, or some recognizable but personally meaningless disaster in other people's lives reported on the early morning radio. Naturally, as Quentin Joyce's former tutor, we talked of him. His father was reticent: no doubt seeing the event still in frightening definition. The family friend, whose name is Maggie Eden, and Dorf were both anxious (I think) to explore their own memories and relationships. And I was struck that both were disposed to stress the way in which the passage of time altered their own view of the young man's death, but also the way in which the event had changed their own attitudes and affected their approach to longstanding and to new relationships. It made me think about myself not very kindly and to feel for the first time Wordsworth's 'unimaginable touch of time'. Fortunately not many of my pupils meet such violent ends: but there have been suicides and crashes and less drastic disasters which, in the past, I have always seemed to rationalize in a way that might have been insensitive if not callous. I begin to wonder what kind of woman I am and how others see me.

I can hear your sympathetic laugh. But it *does* matter, however silly and selfish it may sound. The people we know are always taking up – 'adopting' is a good word for it – moral positions. We all of us, even you and Oliver and Charles and Eve Darrow, are always talking about our moral preoccupations. And often these are only postures. Sorry: in impugning myself and one or two others, I seem to be obliquely attacking you. Too many of our acquaintances and some friends have made a religion out of the Apollonian 'Nothing in excess'. I wonder if some responses have not been frozen, if spontaneous feelings have not been harmfully held in check. I begin to think, sometimes, that the ultimate superstition is to place untoward faith in rationality and the scepticism we have cherished with untoward confidence. The paradox is, of course, that this supposedly moral severity is immediately relaxed for reasons of self-interest.

Sorry to be going on a bit. I'm passing through a

phase in which I wish I felt myself more a woman and less a philosopher. (Too soon, surely, for the change of life!) At my back I seem to hear Sir Philip Sidney: 'The philosopher teacheth but he teacheth obscurely, so as the learned only can understand him, that is to say he teacheth them that are already taught . . .'

It is wonderfully peaceful here. The site opens very early and I'm usually the first there – so that for about an hour I can wander around in complete serenity and the cool of the day before the group buses arrive with squawking gaggles of Americans with big bottoms in awful trousers. Olympia is, I think, the most beautiful site I know: less awesome and frightening than Mycenae, admittedly, but restful to the spirit which I have been known to disavow.

I shall move on in a day or so to Pylos or somewhere and then to the Mani, before making my way back to Athens. I should be back at Oxford in the first week of August. I'd very much like to hear how you and Oliver are getting on.

Love to you both, ever,
Henrietta

★　　★　　★　　★　　★

I suppose a fiftieth birthday, undiscussed and privately marked with a glass or two more of mourning brandy, is an emergent occasion. So I shall dignify this as a meditation when it is the sort of random jotting that I have made carelessly enough over the years and now resort to more frequently, which must be a certain sign of the process of ageing. 'Variable and therefore miserable condition of Man' indeed. This minute I was young, and I am rapidly, this minute, ageing. But Marcus Ferdinand is not John Donne – except that spiritually he was once well (at least, sanguine) and is now, this minute, ill (at best, melancholic).

Fifty is no great age after all. There is still time for *ayre* and *exercises*. At the same time, there is the oppressive consciousness that I have lived more years than I shall live. To little purpose. The sense of mortality that should have clouded my days some ten to fifteen years ago has come upon me like a dense patch of fog on a motorway that was not expected. I take very little comfort from Larkin's *Aubade*, though I am fortunately not a four o'clock insomniac and if I wake at that hour my thoughts are usually drowsily erotic. The poem simply reminds me of the blankness, the unbeing that is to come. It is not that my death is of any importance: so it seems feasible that it does not matter when it occurs, since my continued existence can also matter very little. But it does still to me. And yet I am not entirely sure: sentimental longing for a beautiful girl, good food and wine, pleasures of art, music and literature, friendship and conversation – are they enough? When I have lost all faith, all confidence in meaning, all courage to be good and identify what is right in an existence which seems increasingly meaningless.

It is much too easy to overdramatize oneself, especially when one is not John Donne: nevertheless I cannot help regretting all that lost young faith and hope and even a certain amount of *caritas*. In this mood of self-pity, it is all too easy to see myself as my own archenemy of promise, victim of a *sicknes* unprevented for all my diligence, unsuspected for all my *curiositie*. Rather, I suspect, caused by it. I stand accused in my own eyes of sophomania: I infatuated myself by hearkening after false knowledge.

And here I am, a little more than halfway through the wood, fretting still about right and wrong, good and evil, wishing I could have maintained my belief in the existence of sin which might have allowed me to cling to some kind of faith. In a minute a cannon batters all. Not quite a minute. It took some time, but once the conviction was certain, there was no alternative but to leave the Church. I wonder sometimes if my conscience would have triumphed as spectacularly if I had not been a comfortably placed rentier. Would I have been otherwise, like so many I know, a blind mouth still offering my lean and flashy song?

I think I did what was right. In so far as it goes, my action might be classified as good. I no longer know. Yet although I should not presume to describe the nature of truth and no longer dispute about these things, I think that what I did was truthful – in the sense that I was no longer carrying out a charade; or, in more commonly melodramatic terms, no longer living a lie. I was not a bad priest. My indolent goodnature and enjoyment of good things helped me identify with people and to listen most of the time with patience. The fact that my private interests were intellectual and some of my private desires were modestly sensual did not prevent me being a jolly old rector who enjoyed his glass and so on. I might have advanced in the Church; I might even have married: but I suppose I was always too lazy. And now when sad apprehensions and the artificial sickness of my own melancholy have made the irremediable natural human fever worse, it is too late. And I still brood about what is right, what is wrong, what is good, what is evil, half convinced that it no longer matters.

Right and Wrong. Right, according to the *NED*, is that which is consonant with equity or the light of nature; that which is morally due or just; accordingly Wrong is that which is morally unjust, unfair, amiss or improper; the negation of equity, goodness or rectitude. For definitions of Good and Evil I select from the same authority: Good (of personal qualities) commendable in the person, (of a state of things) right, sound, (generally) morally excellent; Evil the antithesis of good – bad in a positive sense, morally depraved, doing or intending to do harm, that which is the reverse of good, physically or morally, whatever is censurable, painful, disastrous or undesirable. My problem has been for many years that I have never been able to reconcile wrong and evil with the notion of sin, even in my earlier years as a priest. The idea that a particular act was a transgression against God rather than an offence against an individual or a collective group seemed to me to be absurd, except where some act of desecration or insult was directly performed against some religious institution. When I ceased to believe in God, then that issue might be assumed to have become irrelevant, but my aptitude for guilt wants to identify acts of evil or actions which are wrong with a form of transgression against man that amounts to a sense of sin.

Yesterday was the anniversary of Hiroshima. The arguments for and against the dropping of the bomb have been extensively rehearsed. For myself, I think it was wrong: but in the light of what evidence is a matter of public knowledge, I do not think it was evil. The subsequent bomb dropped on Nagasaki and the earlier saturation bombing of Dresden seem to me unquestionably evil, however plausible the motives argued by the perpetrators of both acts. The news is daily packed with reported violence on a much smaller scale. It is where this violence becomes atrocity that what is arguably wrong becomes unquestionably evil.

And I would so stigmatize the commonplace malice of our daily lives. Deliberate acts of sadistic cruelty, especially when the victims are defenceless, are naturally loathsome to all people of normal sensibility: but we excuse or affect not to notice other forms of more banal cruelty, treachery, betrayal or spite which, while they are not as grave as crimes of torture for whatever purpose, stem from the same roots of evil. This is especially so when our own interests are involved or where we ourselves are guilty of transgression. At the most trivial level, I have discovered in myself that what I thought was a sentimental attraction for Isabel Darrow is, in fact, positive lust: there is affection but certainly no love: it would be entirely wrong to seduce her (if it were remotely likely) and evil to rape her. I have no intention of attempting the one or the other. It would be just as evil to rape Iris Cameron: but not at all wrong to go to bed with her, in the least, since she is experienced and promiscuous. It is unlikely that I shall be offered the chance, but she just might out of sheer curiosity. Clerics who have unfrocked themselves, as it were, are not plentiful!

Commonplaces and trivialities are, however, nothing beside massive acts of hatred which involve indiscriminate murder. In our own time these are manifest in acts of terrorism in various places on whatever scale; they have always been with us in the slaughter and mutilation which has gone on in the name of religion. And, I contend, more than the bombing, we live under the collective guilt of the death camps. Even those of us who had no part in such persecution must cower in the knowledge that there is such a monster in a human frame, of whatever gender, of whatever intelligence. I devoutly wish that no intelligent, rational person could perform an act of cruelty or depravity: but I do not believe it to be the case. The excitement derived out of fantasies of evil and violence by so many are proof of some vicarious urge as is witnessed by the success of the allegedly vicious videofilms. But was it not there in the latent sadism, the degradation and humiliation of the films of Hitchcock which I and others of my generation admired and found amusing?

I hope that I shall see nothing again that will shock me as much as the pictures after Hiroshima and more – much more! – when the concentration camps were delivered. As a boy of ten or eleven, I first began to pray. I am not sure about my motives: they might have been: Dear God, don't let anything like this happen to me and those I love; or, Dear God, don't let anything like this happen. Or just: I am frightened – please help me not to be. I continued to pray through the beguiling indulgences of adolescence, of National Service (tedious but not without its pleasures) and of university. And then one day, in my own church, not long after becoming a priest, it stopped. The words and thoughts were no longer there. Reciting the liturgy became a substitute for communion.

Yet throughout these years I was never especially solemn: quite the opposite. People who knew me were very surprised when I said I wanted to enter the Church. Jolly, lazy Marcus Ferdinand a man of God – ridiculous! Underlying that cheerful exterior, though, there was, even then, a pervasive guilt and a pessimistic gloom not desirable in a priest. I had little enough to be guilty about. My sexual encounters, such as they were, were innocent and fumbling and, until I was conscripted into the army, consummated later in private. In Malaya and Cyprus in the early fifties chastity was at a very high premium. Whatever I did was not evil, even if at the time I was sure it was. I am not sure that it was even wrong: 'bad in a positive sense' – no. 'Morally unjust, unfair, amiss or improper' – possibly. And after leaving the army, there were one or two adventures. Pleasurable and meaningless. I did not find the celibate life difficult, and I did not stop desiring certain women in an agreeably, confessionably, casual way. Until I realized that I wanted Isabel Darrow whom I had known since she was an infant. Obviously I had watched her grow and been charmed by her complete carelessness, watched her grow into a beautiful young woman, whose beauty and youthfulness I admired as something clear and separate. And then one day I watched her coming down a staircase . . . The sentimental longing was transmogrified. And what I felt was wrong, though not evil. Unless the will to possess is also a wish to violate. Mendoza is more honest,

35

whom I detest: yet in his frank lust for the same girl which I brush as specks of dust off an ornament, I find a certain wrong but no evil. Then I ask how wrong does one have to be before becoming evil. Would I trust the girl with him? How easy is it to ascribe evil to someone out of jealousy – or even envy. I am not sure. There is the obsessional evil of Iago, bent upon destruction, as much motivated by sexual fury as occupational resentment: there is the implacable wrong of Cassius, fired by the small tinder of political frustration into a flare of impolitic rashness. And yet both wanted to destroy an individual.

In quite a different sense I cherish a mild envy of Peter Cameron (and not because he lives with his sister). Cameron, as perhaps befits a political scientist, does not care much about moral issues as they affect other lives than his own, whether private or public. At the same time he is good (within certain limits – in that he does not perpetrate harm), while not subscribing to what is emphatically right in ordinary quotidian conduct of the pragmatic affairs of domestic arrangement and national or international politics. Cameron is frivolous: he has evolved a theory of human categories based on the notions of Aristotle. His theories in fact have nothing to do with the categories and relate to Aristotle's four causes. Then Cameron has always been something of an intellectual fly-by-night: quick of movement and uncertain of sanctuary.

Cameron holds that the material, formal, efficient and final *causes* (which he calls categories) obtain as actively in people as in things. He blandly proposes himself and his sister as examples. They are what they are – produced by people already exercising the functions they themselves now perform. They have therefore each a separate formal nature and look towards (here he refuses to be specific) certain ends which are he says purposeful. As I understand it, the means whereby the formal entity reaches its quintessence is by some catalyst outside itself which nevertheless demands its cooperation. All very entertaining over too much port but surely this is teleologically unsound. What might one deduce (or indeed infer) about the purposes of nature from the behaviour of the Camerons? At the same time, as with so many of Cameron's theories, there is a kind of piquancy, and I have found myself applying such absurd principles to the lives of several

36

acquaintances and some friends, inconsequential as the whole thing undoubtedly is.

I digress. Is this preoccupation with right and wrong, good and evil merely a means to convince myself that there is some meaning in life where there is none? I see myself as a sort of Wallace Stevens snowman:

One must have a mind of winter
To regard the frost and the boughs
Of the pine-trees crusted with snow;

And have been cold a long time
To behold the junipers shagged with ice,
The spruces rough in the distant glitter

Of the January sun; and not to think
Of any misery in the sound of the wind,
In the sound of a few leaves,

Which is the sound of the land
Full of the same wind
That is blowing in the same bare place

For the listener, who listens in the snow,
And, nothing himself, beholds
Nothing that is not there and nothing that is.

I suppose I was only one of countless small children who wept when they looked out to find that their first snowman had melted and the grinning, black-eyed Mister had become a shapeless mound next to a forlorn battered hat. My father, on leave from the army, was sympathetic, saying that life was rather like that; my mother, who was intellectual and would like to have done something with her life, said it was silly to be sentimental and that it was important to learn early that all things were finite and that illusions melted without warning. I think I was five. And today I am fifty and this is *l'instant de boire* – the moment when everything turns sour and seems *wrong*. It occurs after a certain intake of drink, when the sober effort to be fair or at least neutral flags – and protest, anger, flares up. Sometimes it is righteous, sometimes not. The gloomy intimation of mortality: The *Sunne* who goes so many miles a minut, the *Starres* of the *Firmament*, which go so very many more, goe not so fast as my *body* to the *earth*.

So I fill in the little uncertain time left to me longing or desiring, or shake myself into some kind of mental respectability by brooding about right, wrong; good, evil. All right: (or, more accurately, so be it:) the idea of right and wrong is abstract and passive – one knows/does what is right; one knows/does what is wrong. Good and evil on the other hand are active, positive, sometimes impulsive, sometimes immediate, even involuntary – always the outcome of action which is conscious. One *does* good: one *commits* (always in full however swift cognizance of what one is doing) evil. Adultery where there is love is not evil: nevertheless it is wrong. Abstinence from adultery, in the same circumstances, is right and may even be good. And so to Bad.

Lou Andreas Salome thought that everything bad in the world amounted to a simple misunderstanding that it is always the subjective individual (poor *me*) who is the one injured. And badness is now almost an equivalent for naughtiness. Even wickedness has a grandmotherly gloss of affectionate scolding. Evil remains evil. Wilful harm in thought, word or deed towards another. Bad is something that happens to someone: evil is what someone chooses to effect.

We are at a disadvantage in that we have no comprehensive word in English to match the French *mal*, which implies pain, illness, disease, as well as a will towards evil. Wallace Stevens's *Esthetique de Mal* is effete figure-dancing on thin aesthetic ice compared to Baudelaire's gardening. The diagnosis of moral wrong in action is observed rather than suffered. And yet it was Stevens who wrote:

The field is frozen. The leaves are dry.
Bad is final in this light . . .

It is here, in this bad, that we reach
The last purity of the knowledge of good.

The crow looks rusty as he rises up.
Bright is the malice in his eye . . .

One joins him there for company,
But at a distance, in another tree.

Of course: any idea of what is good must rest upon an awareness and discrimination of what is evil. Enough: Stevens
again: 'We have made too much of life. A journal of life is
rarely a journal of happiness.'

★　　★　　★　　★　　★

29 August
Always a bad symptom when I resume keeping a diary. It
means I am either bored or guilty about something: usually
that I'm not working hard enough. It gives me an illusion of
doing something. Once thought I'd try to write a novel, but
after four false starts on four different plots decided I was no
bloody good and it would be a waste of time. No reason to
be bored, after all. La Baule is a thoroughly pleasant place,
the hotel is good, the weather marvellous. It's just that when
I'm on holiday all the things that I put off at Oxford, the
papers I intend to write, preparation of courses (although
such procrastination is of necessity limited), work on a new
book, become urgent and I become more aware of doing
nothing.

Still, Christina always enjoys our holidays immensely – even
more so since she has been busy at her new job. I'm pleased
about that. From the moment we stepped off the boat at
Cherbourg she seemed radiantly happy and the stops at Vitré
and Châteaubriant were a great success. C., knowing exactly
how to turn me on, was already dressed yesterday by the time
I'd had my shower, so I did not suspect the sexy new underwear and the sheer stockings until bedtime. And very
passionate it was. As we drive, she is (for her) remarkably
talkative. So far it has indeed been like a second honeymoon.
And if we go on like this we'll break all records set by the
first. Christina always prefers things when we are alone
together, best of all when we are away from Oxford. For some
reason which has always eluded me, she has never really
settled down. She feels out of place. God knows why: she
is not unusually clever like Henrietta but she is extremely
intelligent and she is very pretty without being beautiful.

39

Simply that she went to what used to be called a provincial university and came away without academic longings. Understandably a little wary of scholars and donnish conversation. And a mild sense of inferiority that she worked first in advertising and now as a PR. Then, Eve Darrow was an actress and it's never bothered her. And Isabel is almost aggressively unintellectual, if she were capable of aggression in any form.

I wonder if that is part of the problem. Several times recently when her name has come up, I've noticed C. looking very slightly tense. She becomes very still and silent. Admittedly Isabel and I see a lot of each other because of my work at the faculty and I take her for the odd drink or lunch every so often. We're obviously very fond of each other; but it's a sentimental friendship. Nothing more. And what is that? Well, it is closer and deeper than an ordinary friendship between a man and a woman and there is certainly an element of strong sexual attraction (which may or may not be mutual): no active sexual engagement – partly because the friendship itself might be impaired, partly because of other people who might be hurt. Yet Isabel Darrow is a beautiful, vivacious girl whom I am often seen with and in a community where everyone more or less knows everyone else there might have been gossip and perhaps a certain amount of malice. Henrietta has made certain comments – oblique and unmistakable. The word that something is going on between David Kelly and Isabel Darrow might well have been put about. And it is nonsense. Isabel is fourteen years younger than me, the daughter of old friends. I also happen to love Christina. Not very demonstratively, perhaps, except in bed: but I do love her.

Is this why I've started this diary? Am I a little guilty? Do I spend too much time thinking about Isabel? I have no creative talent: all that I have written has been more or less scholarly. Is this a way of sloughing off certain nagging worries while keeping Isabel firmly in mind? Rubbish! It's a way of filling in time in a café while Christina is shopping, because I loathe looking around shops.

Indeed a very enjoyable spot. La Baule itself has a huge bay on the Atlantic and what appear to be very pleasant beaches. Christina is dedicated to swimming whatever the temperature of the water, so while I sit sipping Ricard and reading, she has been profiting (as the French put it) herself. The rest of the town doesn't seem particularly interesting. Christina has bought some pretty trinkets and a becoming dress. Drives out of La Baule are charming. Best of all, around and partly through the salt marshes to Le Croisic, a pretty harbour full of colour, where we had the most terrific lunch at Les Filets Bleus. On the way Christina insisted that we bought natural salt and something called *salicorne* – I imagine a sort of pickled seaweed – from one of the several trestles on the roadside. Another pleasant outing to the walled town of Guérande where we met the weekly market. I like markets a lot more than stores and boutiques. I also met a local brandy called Seguin! Christina drove back.

After making the mistake of buying a newspaper a couple of days ago to find that Arthur Scargill in Moscow has branded Reagan and Thatcher as the principal enemies of peace, I resolved to absent myself from such fatuities and fill in idle moments by keeping up this diary which I shall undoubtedly lose or throw away. In fact, we have been active: driving around, walking; eating and drinking too much. And making love. Christina still astounds me. She is thirty-five – two years younger than me – and has the body of a girl of eighteen. After all the loveplay (perhaps more accurately sexplay), there is a fury of passion that should, but does not seem to, exhaust us. I begin to think that even after many years I do not know Christina, although I tell myself I understand her. Even so: such a quiet, demure woman full of inventive lust in bed; such a shy person a success in public relations of all things. I sometimes wonder if her insecurity (as I see it) is not a disguise: that she knows exactly what she is about, so that what I take to be her defences are, in effect, subtle strategies of conquest. Absurd. I speculate too whether Isabel's carelessness is a mask. Does she envy and perhaps worry about her supremely poised mother and her very bright sister (who also happens to be attractive in her own right)? Can it be that

Christina, whom I have always seen as insecure, is much less so than Isabel?

Why does Isabel come so readily to mind? I don't moon about imagining her undressed, much less undressing her . . . Well, that may not be *exactly* truthful. Then such passing thoughts are surely commonplace among heterosexual men who spend much time in the company of this or that pretty young woman. And of no consequence. Sex is certainly not the basis of our friendship. Henrietta Ball was undoubtedly caustic, intending to be so. I've had a long-running game with her which both of us have always known was a joke. Christina has never shown the slightest concern. Not indeed with Iris Cameron at her most Circean. Am I being more than usually dim? God, what a waste of time this all is . . .

4 September
Concarneau. What a delightful place. After walking three times round the ramparts, Christina has gone to lie down (as she puts it). I sit in the sunshine looking at the boats and the old town across the water with a half bottle of wine, full of contentment. Thoroughly good day. A time for constructive thought. A time in which I started seriously planning another book. I'd like a change. Something different along the lines of: *Wagner – an Evil Genius* . . . But I don't think OUP would buy it. More to the point: neither would the bloody public. I'd probably be much happier with Brahms, but I don't know enough about music. Schopenhauer, Fichte, William James all interest me in different ways and over the last year I've read a lot of Sartre. Perhaps something more general: *The Doctrine of the Will* – speculative essays on the ideas of Schopenhauer, Nietzsche, Bergson and William James. Or *Stuff and Dreams* – a reappraisal of metaphysics in the contemporary world. Great fun. Let it mulch in the compost heap I call a mind.

A very pretty girl goes by in tight jeans and high heels. At least I was not the only one who turned to look. And we were all middle-aged. There is something about young female beauty, the perfection of body, unblemished complexion, the features now finally moulded but not yet touched by sadness or disappointment or bitterness. Not always a matter of sexual desire, although obviously there is much of that: more a nostalgia for a sensual innocence that never was: Psyche, Chloe, Juliet. I suppose I'm as lecherous (in theory) as the next man: but I never intend doing anything about it. Henrietta said years ago that if she ever took me up I'd be out of Oxford by the next satellite. And when I consider Mendoza or indeed the merrily lascivious Camerons, I must declare myself harmless.

And yet. Isabel comes, alas with some inevitability, to mind. The idea of her in tight jeans and high heels is ridiculous: she would think it tarty and uncomfortable. As befits a daughter of Eve Darrow, she dresses with exquisite taste. Nothing expensive or ostentatious. I wonder if I think about her with this same slightly tainted nostalgia. Dangerous? I don't know. I remember Roger Ingestre's story about a girl he knew, one of his pupils and the daughter of friends. The girl had become infatuated with Ingestre who thoughtlessly put her in the way of a friend who was an experienced lecher. After a lurid affair in which the girl became less and less stable, her younger sister became somehow involved and there was an angry and bitter scandal. The girl herself was found dead in a quarry, though no one knew whether or not she had taken her own life. A sad little story and a salutary one.

The age difference must have been even greater than that between Isabel and me. I know young women are thought to be very wise these days, but it is still not difficult for an experienced man to exploit someone younger. And to my mind it is quite wrong, which no doubt is a very quaint attitude. I suppose what I do not like is lechery in action: the way that bastard Mendoza looks at Isabel for example. And at Christina, for that matter. Though Christina can look after herself as the years have proved. I suppose I wonder whether Isabel can. Oddly enough, of the two, for all her careless confidence and Christina's shyness, Isabel is or seems to be the more vulnerable. I don't think there is any relationship with Mendoza, but the very idea makes me shudder. In spite of his unusually undisciplined mind, Ben Oldfield is a nice, personable chap and he and Isabel behave like brother and sister. Not in the Cameron tradition! (Strange: the activities of those two, however shocking, don't bother me.) I think that I must have less to do with Isabel, all the same. There's been a certain coolness about Henrietta lately and I do not want people to get the wrong idea.

Oh dear, this is all very trite. I glanced at a paper this morning and saw that the frightful carnage in the Lebanon is still going on, as it is in Salvador and Belfast and Afghanistan. And all I do is blether sentimentally. Perhaps that's what diaries are for.

8 September

I think I love Christina more than ever. I don't know that we have rediscovered each other sexually, because I don't think we were ever particularly lost: but I think we give each other greater pleasure than ever. I hope it's as true for her . . .

Perros-Guirec is lovely. This morning we took a magnificent walk along the coast to a beautiful little port, Ploumanach, where we found an unexpectedly splendid restaurant and ate far too much. The walk back, past the most impressive rock formations and above a whole sequence of delightful bays, was leisurely. I was somnolent. Christina, energetic as ever, has gone swimming.

Brooding about the topic for a new book, I've decided I don't want to write one. Must be age: but the idea of all that reading and detailed note-taking fills me with a drowsy numbness. Think I'll do something frivolous like 'An Essay against too Much Reading'. That should be fun and thoroughly irritating to most colleagues.

There are times when I go along with Wackford Squeers upon my chosen discipline and career: if I remember:

' "Measles, rheumatics, hooping cough, fevers, agers and lumbagers," said Mr Squeers, "is all philosophy together; that's what it is. The heavenly bodies is philosophy, and the earthly bodies is philosophy; and if there's a screw loose in a heavenly body, that's philosophy; and if there's a screw loose in an earthly body, that's philosophy too; or it may be that sometimes there's a little metaphysics in it, but that's not often. Philosophy's the chap for me." '

Can't remember the rest. Look it up when I get back to Oxford. Something I've recited to myself in vacant or sleepless, hardly pensive I hope, mood. What's left is even more to the point. We're an odd lot when you come to think of it. And I thank God for Christina and Eve Darrow. Philosophers' wives can be very exacting. Understandably. But their own determined intelligence drives their husbands into deeper labyrinths of complexity where they can not be ferreted down or found out. Trim Marion Stallybrass with her no-nonsense face who has become a feminist over the last five years and as a consequence more humourless than ever, thus encouraging her husband's wry talent for academic irony. Anna Walton, who genuinely does have a first-class mind, has taken to wearing shorter skirts and crossing her legs a lot rather noisily. Understandable – because though shapely they are plump. Peter Walton doesn't seem to notice, always preoccupied. Fierce little Clare Arthur, resolutely analytical while Dennis becomes more and more vague. But there is also Samantha Wilkins, tall and cool with long blonde hair, who enjoys her children, likes running her home and Tom and giving dinner parties. I've never seen Tom out of humour. Is that unusual in a moral philosopher? I am the luckiest of the lot with Christina, even if she distrusts the others and is uneasy in the university ambience. And I believe that this holiday has proved that she is happy with me.

And what became of all the bright young Greats and PPE men of my time? Edwards: at the European Commission; Cassidy: working for American television – the most brilliant of all; Tomlinson, composer of elegant verses in Latin and Greek, now a highly paid executive at ICI; Stratford, the fervent admirer of Aneurin Bevan: headmaster at a public school. While I drifted into academic life because I couldn't think of anything else. I'm not grumbling: it suits me well enough. Can't help thinking though that I'm hardly one of the ones who 'made it'.

11 September
Dinard. A nice airy place with two good beaches, some interesting and untaxing walks and pleasant bars along the front, though those favoured by the young jangle the nerves and paralyse thought with their blaring music and bleeping of videogames. Not that my thought is ever up to much when I'm on holiday. And tomorrow we leave for home. In a way I'm sorry. I feel rather as I did when a small boy at the end of a holiday – a sort of nostalgia that it will soon be over. It's been good. Christina has been wonderful. And yet I rather

look forward to work. Something to concentrate on. I wish I had the kind of mind that was always occupied with worth-while ideas or indeed had some gift for abstract thought. (I don't mean solving problems or arguing some point of philosophy: real abstraction.) I wonder if I shall keep this diary up when we get back to Oxford. I doubt it.

Christina thinks it one of the best holidays we've ever had. She looks tanned and beautiful and very fit. My face and arms are brownish, but that's as far as it goes. It occurs to me that I only bother with things I'm good at. Swimming has never been one of them. And although I used to stumble shivering in after her when we were younger because she wanted to share her pleasure, she is now reconciled to my sitting peace-fully in a bar or a café.

I seem fated to associate with women who like cavorting in water. Isabel is another and must look pretty marvellous in a bathing suit. As does Christina. Surprising how often I've thought about Isabel at odd moments. I find myself looking forward very much to seeing her again. Which is all very silly . . .

*   *   *   *   *

Little Darling. No: Lil' Darlin', I think. And so you are, aren't you, he said, while we were dancing. Then gave me a pithy little lecture on Count Basie and big bands. Why should I be thinking of him? Straightforward association of the music. But I must have liked it. Yes, I did. It's nice to be admired. No complaints. Here, however, the dishy Swede obviously fancies Elaine, reading Malinowski or someone, in a bikini. Never understand my little sister. We've both managed to tan painlessly, but brown blondes look better. Ah well! Sigh. No complaints. And darling or not, I am certainly not *little*. In some respects . . . Vanity will get you nowhere, Isabel Darrow. Witness dishy Swedes. Elaine is the cool willowy type. So? I don't mind bouncing a bit. Did he mean anything? I hope *not*. It would upset everyone, including me. A bit. I like Christina though. And yet he is charming and funny. Not a Gloomsbury Bloop like Roger Ingestre. That's not entirely fair . . . except that I'm not sure I get on with liberals. Oh God! The gnashing American. Why haven't

I got Malinowski or Marcuse or something thoroughly off-putting handy? Elaine just turns off. Shut eyes, Isabel. Look ever so reposed and composed in blue one-piece outfit on pneumatic mattress. Help! What a train of thought! Gentle little snore might put him off. An anaphrodisiac pheeeeew. Freeze. How different we are. She so calm and serious. I suppose I'm frivolous. What a good thing that we like each other. Iris Cameron jokes about no sibling rivalry . . . I wonder if that can be true. Her and Peter. Surely not. Trouble is that Elaine's like Daddy and academic, Eve is a lot less hopelessly fizzy than I am most of the time. I try, but it's not much good. Not sex. Think I can handle that. So far at least. And Lil' Darlin' – I can deal with that too, if I have to. Mendoza is poison. Warrington is super, but happy with his headmistress. Always go for older men – except for the Swede. No. Elaine still reading. And he does so adore her. Poor boy.

Ikaros Village, I like you. Another thing: I *like* sitting around the pool. Think Elaine was a bit cross when I said that Knossos was a lot of Cretan bull. Why do I say these things? She forgave me. A family virtue, which is lucky. Just think of some of the people I was at school with and Quentin Joyce and . . . Warrington's headmistress knew him well. Said to be very upset. Funny boy. Older *women* possibly in his case? Not much to tempt me here, except Elaine's Swede. Twenty-four. I've had four men. Three men and a boy, that is. No urgency. I like wit, good company and laughter. Elaine and I never discuss it. I simply don't know . . . But she likes rock and discos and all of that which I don't. Also Stockhausen. Remember Mummy dancing once with a South American novelist and it was quite beautiful . . . No, of course she's never regretted it. They are happy and we all are. But has she ever been tempted, has she ever given in? Possible after all. And Daddy? No . . . No! But I don't think I know much about men. Must go into Mallia to buy presents. Then we can take a taxi to Agios Nikolaios, which is fun. Then tomorrow Elaine wants to go to the bloody cave of Zeus. Sorry Zeus. Can't imagine how Leda really felt? It's always been nice: but never ecstatic. Some day my Swede will come . . . What a very naughty thought.

I wonder about him and Henrietta sometimes. Poor Ben Oldfield – who is lovely. Well, she's elegant and has that dark red hair and the long legs. Cold though. Much good it does Ben speculating on whether she's wearing stockings or tights and the colour of her panties. Funny. Laughed for about five minutes when I asked him if he thought women wondered about male underwear. Isabel, love, how can men be sexy? Dear Ben, whom I trawl through Marks and Spencer to watch his eyes popping. Friends we are now: and friends we shall stay. Where did I hear that?

Eyes tight shut I hear the approach of the original Caledonian Bore for whom I'd commission my personal labyrinth. Ugh. I can *feel* his eyes on me. Still. Still! Wonder if disgust shows, rather than irritation. Don't mind admiration. No point in resenting it, built as I am and dressing as I do. But there are limits, if I knew where to define them . . . I should feel ashamed at not believing more things. Empty-headed Little Darling. Elaine is no virago but she is a feminist and she is for CND. Suppose I worry a bit about chemical weapons and MX missiles and whatever when I hear about them. Never for long. And if I'm a sex object for some, I know affection too and respect, I think. Learned from Mummy what it is to be a self-assured woman without being nervously aggressive. How does she see Elaine and me? Because she is *really* beautiful. Every movement even when it's just us. And I think they're still deeply in love. Cleverer than I am. And Elaine cleverer still. But then I'm cuddled more: because I don't mind and Elaine does. Still an uncomfortable feeling imagining them . . . Not until after my own first time. Such innocence! He tells me in passing that I'm beautiful. And others do. But I don't feel it. Pretty, yes. Good breasts, lithe hips, well-moulded legs. Black hair. Blue eyes. A little nose. Full lips. But I'm not beautiful the way my mother is. Or that Iris Cameron is. Or Francesca. Wonder what she can possibly see in Ingestre. Anyway it doesn't matter. Of course it would if I didn't. Wonder if Daddy minds that I'm not clever. Never showed it. I suppose if I were not pretty I'd care about Mummy and Elaine. Oh, little sister, give the poor Swedish idiot a chance! I'll look after myself . . . Does she know how much she and Malinowski are tormenting the boy who spends half his days in Nordic Twilight, stretching languourously in her yellow scraps of swimsuit? Don't have the figure for it. Still who's complaining. Walks well. Lilt.

Doesn't swing as much as I do. Little Darling be damned! That chaste September in Chersonesos . . . Hi, feel like a long cool drink?

★

'I don't think we've met. Ivan Whitehart.'

'Francesca Oricellari . . .'

'A very musical name.'

'A very unmusical character. You are obviously a friend of Roger.'

'An acquaintance and part-time colleague. I'm over here for a year on a visiting fellowship. I teach political science at Cornell.'

'Things must be looking up in Ithaca.'

'Excuse me?'

'I'm sorry: that must be a very exhausted joke.'

'Think nothing of it.'

'So: where are you teaching political science here?'

'Nuffield College. That's my base. I'm running some post-graduate tutorials and teaching a course of lectures. Are you connected with the university?'

'Only as a sort of camp follower. Roger Ingestre is a family friend. Which explains why I'm here.'

'Well, I'll certainly drink to that! Say, *you're* not the beautiful diplomat I've heard so much about.'

'That's my sister. I have a fashion business in London.'

'So you'd know Iris Cameron, Peter's sister?'

'It would be difficult not to. She runs an agency for models. It's not quite the same thing. But we are occasionally involved.'

'I've known Peter a long time. Obviously: we're in the same academic line. Can I freshen your drink?'

'Thank you. It's Scotch whisky. That's fine.'

'If it's not impertinent, I might say you'd make a great fashion model yourself.'

'I appreciate the courtesy.'

'This is a great party. You say you and Roger Ingestre are close friends.'

'We've known each other a long time. I think he's probably a closer friend of my sister. The beautiful diplomat. But she is in Buenos Aires. So I am . . . what's the word? . . . understudy.'

'You're obviously no stranger. Have you lived in England long?'

'Since 1975.'

'So you're properly acclimatized.'

'I'm not sure. In London maybe. Because you get lost there with so many others. Here I always feel, you know, different. Perhaps Oxford is a little like Venice. My father always used to say only Venetians felt natural in Venice. Is this your first visit?'

'My first protracted stay. I've been in England three, four times. I'm a dedicated Anglophile, but I've always felt a stranger.'

'Have you met David Kelly?'

'Over there with that very pretty girl?'

'That's right. He thinks the tribal instinct in the English is more or less concealed but very highly developed. Partly because the Welsh and Scots and Irish make such a belligerent fuss.'

'Is that so?'

'I don't think he's very serious about it. But he says the English don't really get on at all but pretend to be tolerant and subdivide into smaller and smaller tribal groups. Like here. He thinks Oxford is a great place for anthropologists.'

'There are certainly things . . . I don't know . . . taboos that still surprise me. What about this guy who's just had an affair with his secretary? The Cabinet Minister?'

'What is he called? Parkinson . . .'

'That's him. Well, would that have raised the smallest breeze where you come from? I know we have scandals in the United States, but they only matter if it's a question of money or dirty tricks.'

'Or dirty language.'

'Point taken. But all this fuss about a little off-duty . . . excuse me . . .'

'Fucking? Is that the word you want?'

'As you say.'

'Incidentally, it was not an invitation. I'm not Miss Cameron.'

'No . . . well to get back to what we were discussing. I

50

don't think back home it would have been more than tittle-tattle. Jesus, we've lived through generations of Kennedys after all. What's scandalous about sex?'

'I don't know. With the Germans it's security; with the French it's . . . when I think of it the French don't seem to worry much; with us it's the Mafia or the Vatican or both; with the Scandinavians it's gloomy drinking. Thanks. You can freshen my glass, as you say with elegance.'

'Talking of elegance . . . And don't get me wrong. I am truly *not* making a pass . . .'

'Sir! I don't even know whether you're married!'

'All right. *Kamarad* . . .'

'You were talking about elegance . . .'

'Well, I just thought you might think it was a kind of preliminary gambit . . .'

'You're safe. What were you going to say?'

'Doesn't it surprise you that so many academic wives and sweethearts are so . . . well, sophisticated?'

'Not any more. These aren't typical. Well, that is to say some are. Lady Blakemore is . . .'

'Excuse me? Lady . . .'

'The tall woman in grey. That's what the party is all about. Her husband has been made a lord. And he's a very old friend of Roger Ingestre.'

'But why?'

'I think for being there. And if you're thinking of Eve Darrow or indeed your friend Iris Cameron, they are exceptions. In very different ways.'

'Who is the tall woman with red hair?'

'Red . . . Ah that is neither a wife nor a sweetheart, that is Henrietta Ball. She is a philosopher.'

'She is a *what*!'

'And I understand a very precise philosopher.'

'Has anyone ever told you that you talk very good English? Or is that insulting?'

'You don't do so badly yourself.'

'All right. Let's get neutral. Have there been many changes in the time you've lived here?'

'A great many. A new political party. Four million unemployed. Violence. Right-wing dogmatism. How has it been in America?'

'I was being quite serious, Francesca. I think things are deteriorating. What I liked so much about England was the sense of tolerance.'

'Not when it came to being European.'

'Well, when I first came here, there was some enthusiasm.'

'When was that?'

'I suppose the early seventies.'

'I don't know enough about it. Ask Roger Ingestre or any of these people. They're all European and so bloody English.'

'No reservations in Italy?'

'No. We don't have native Indians.'

'I don't think you like me.'

'Tell me about life under the cowboy president.'

'If you'll listen. Stop scoring points. All right? It's hard being a liberal in the face of so much redneck bigotry. How old are you?'

'Thirty-eight.'

'I'm forty-three. I grew up, almost, when you *had* to be radical. Everyone who thought at all that you wanted to know was angry. And now the kids I teach are either wild revolutionaries or staid suburbanites wearing the generation uniform.'

'So Reagan will be re-elected next year.'

'Without a doubt. I don't like the way things are going. At home. Here. In Germany. It's all so solid, sticky right.'

'I understand how you are a friend of Roger.'

'I'm not. We just met at Charles Darrow's. And we both happen to be liberals. Us liberals have to stick together.'

'And draw the wagons round in a circle?'

'You're very smart, aren't you, signorina?'

'I get by. And I think I don't dislike you . . . Ah Ben! So you've come out of the wood . . .'

'Woodwork, love.'

'Of course. Ben, this is a charming American professor . . . I'm sorry. I've picked up English manners. I don't recall your name . . .'

2

*P*hase II progressing. Not going badly I think. Mendoza
in effortless command of elegant dinner party. She
does look lovely, but then she can't help it . . . the
violet eyes, the dark tumbling hair, the full lips . . . oh stop.
Laughter. Good sound at a dinner table. She's laughing.
Oldfield neighing away. But she wouldn't have come without
security. She can't possibly . . . not with such a nurk. But
she likes him. What is he? Safe. No threat to her . . . No,
she is surely not a virgin. Doesn't look or behave like one.
And I think I know. Just no trouble and a good cover. It
would have to be David Kelly . . . Loathes my guts, but it's
worth the effort. Good turnout. Zara and Miranda Hogg top
catering: *Classique* Zara austere in black with little Miranda
frilly white with a pink apron – such efficiency . . . Sisters
be as it were buggered. *Bisque de crevettes, côtes de veau grati-
nées au fromage, fromages* in their own right, *vacherin Chantilly
aux fraises.* I can hear it on cue, darling Amanda with Giles!
Where did you get such delicious strawberries in October?
My secret darling and secret smile from tight-bosomed Zara,
high-necked, discreetly bending, elegantly arsed. But thank
you conspiratorial Amanda. Pouring the good wine: Meur-
sault, Chambolle-Musigny, and in due course with the bloody
fraises Château la Tour Blanche. Must slightly impress Llewellyn Gray but not over the top. Retired executives have their
pride. Don't like to be patronized. Especially not the erstwhile
Welsh. Very good Zara – a nice squirm of the hips. I suspect
the good Llewellyn prefers fluffy little Miranda flouncing . . .
oh come here bach against the kitchen sink, oh lovie what
you wearing tights for? Nevertheless . . . nevertheless . . .

And is *she* impressed? Ought to be. Amanda is wonderful and enjoying herself, flirting always with me and Gray and leaving Humphrey Mattingley alone for Alexandra cool flowing-haired and tight-thighed he'll be lucky. Amanda Tait I wish you were not so faithful to Roderick Gough-Thomas M bloody P. And yet those merry, laughing eyes entice so . . . I thought . . . well she wouldn't and there's an end. Now famous herself: Tenant of Wildfell Hall and Henry James Galatea and Thea Coloris in a new thriller in which she almost bares rather little tits . . . Zara I wish you wouldn't do that brushing past. Lovely Amanda shoulder-long silky wafting hair the dancing eyes the unequivocal hands off. I like you Giles, I want us to be friends but No. So I've cut my losses: she's good to be seen with and R. Gough-Thomas is sure of her and himself and his career. Unless that is . . . Oh forget that! She couldn't keep up an elaborate deceit. Does she suspect . . . yes, of course, that Isabel is the object of this whole . . . wit about Cecil Parkinson and his secretary. Support of Thatcher. Mattingley in the know glitters: she is being loyal less to him than to her own unshakable vanity which tells her that she cannot make wrong choices. It's the magic-mirror-on-the-wall syndrome. Gray, more solemn, recalls the public flaying of Profumo. Mattingley eyeing Alexandra Fleming, always cool, across the table. Once married to Charley Hampden sweet girl I used to know when she was still a flowery and determined virgin. An impeccable shit, Mattingley: but impressive for all that with his centre-page column, punditry on morning radio and late-night television. In the know. Knows everyone. Alexandra meets his eyes frostily I think. Flounce of Miranda with *beignets de courgettes*. Proud Zara breathes deeply at the sideboard. Her breasts seethe against the satiny black. What a waste. Even Oldfield notices.

Is she impressed? Should have guessed that she'd know Llewellyn Gray and Jocelyn. The endless Darrow connections. But surprised that *I* know them so well. And they are quite a catch. Who was Albion Television and God knows what in the City and she is a little lined but still glamorous. Michael Dorf might have served the purpose more immediately depending on his mood, but I needed a married couple obviously affectionate to enhance respectability. Time for television chat which will cut out Oldfield and his arse-faced reflections of all that is irrelevant. Thanks Amanda. I'll do the same for you one day except that it will hardly be necessary.

. . . My new series. Yes. I've decided to give it a go. Of course, the Beeb don't pay as well as you used to, Llewellyn. But it's quite a challenge. An arts programme presented by a leading philistine. No, it's true, Jocelyn. That's part of the whole idea.

Mattingley snidely in with my well-known sceptical razor. Just what we need. Isabel? Not bloody listening. Laughing at some witty remark of Alexandra Fleming which must be something of a record. Oh God she is lovely! Imagine her lifting her arms to tie up that tumble of dark hair and the tilt of her breasts or in a black silk one-piece camisole being deliberately tarty the violet eyes misted with real lust. Oh Isabel! No. Must listen and concentrate. Get her attention.

. . . up to a point. I mean there is a place for unpopular culture which is not the property of an esoteric minority, although I don't suppose Ben Oldfield would agree.

Shouldn't let him in but it succeeded. She's listening. Out it all comes T. S. Eliot, Joyce, Ezra Pound. Does it mean she really does care about this twitterer? Can't be. Kelly I can imagine except that his wife is herself pretty special. Or Peter Cameron. Not interested. Told me as much. Said he'd like to fuck her mother. Well so would we all. I wonder about him. Used to think he'd had more women than me. Iris said they both did it more or less at random in the right social grouping. Just the once she was terrific and I must have been pretty good. True that they do it together? Perhaps it's all fantasy based on her. Two or three years older than her brother. So it might have been one bored afternoon when she was feeling randy (and doesn't she!) and they never looked back. Would have been quite easy for her. What about that sniping bastard, Warrington? Oldfield's tutor at that. No: Senior Tutor at Daddy's college wouldn't risk it, would he? And he has that headmistress in the tight charcoal or navy suits. She must be a handful in the right mood . . . Oldfield's drone subsided. Question . . .

. . . it seems it was between me and an Irish poet, Brendan Mullally. What Humphrey calls my sceptical razor or his acidly ingenuous charm. Anyway, they settled on me and the minstrel boy to the wall has gone.

Actually made her laugh. Or was it something Gray said in an aside. Change of tack. Can't really yet veer it back to my programme. Nobel prize to Golding. Where do we all stand on that? Walesa's Peace Prize. Mattingley scathing. Always thought he was a very left sapper masquerading as a rifleman. Suppose I'm right, not that anyone cares.

Politics however will shut up Oldfield. Isabel never talks much: the odd shaft of unexpected humour, the smile, shake of the head, swirl of dark hair, flash of violet wicked eyes, ripple of tits. Zara has a brooding menace and Alexandra Fleming the ultimate cool assurance and Amanda the hint of delicious mischief and Miranda the prettiest flounce in the Common Market, but Isabel is perfect . . . Now what? Election of Kinnock to Labour leadership. Gift of the gab but not much proven substance says Alexandra. Charm says Amanda. Gray with the venom of a radical turned commercial quotes a dedicated class hoplite. Mattingley glimmers amusement. Gray is also Welsh. I don't trust them. So is Warrington. But she couldn't. And he would surely not. Not Charles Darrow's Senior Tutor. Jocelyn Gray says that the trouble with meritocrats is they can't stand the upper and upper-middle classes. Llewellyn laughs untowardly and tugs his left ear. Why is he not a knight after all? Christ they've made Robert Blakemore a lord. Must be bloody short of lords. Political chatter back to poor Parkinson. *I* can understand it. Lots of men spend more time with a secretary rather than a wife. Imagine Isabel . . . Kelly does with her. Oh shares her but . . . not what I want to think about. Pull yourself together Mendoza. I *don't* love her. The fuck's the thing. A few rehearsals and then that great as it were First Night . . . Pay attention. Mattingley being clever: Have you noticed in any gathering Tory politicians always go for the most senior woman present, while Labour surges towards the prettiest. Isabel asks wide-eyed: Where does that leave the SDP? Whinny from Oldfield but Gray and all the women laugh. Leaving Mattingley on the edge of sulking if Etonians know how to sulk. Amanda gives me one of her most basking smiles which Isabel notices and then unsolicited Alexandra Fleming what's in it for her says Giles tell us more about this interesting new series. So I do. Why the favours? She knows and I know that we've been through the sparring and she wasn't interested. No hard feelings. Part of my charm. I don't dare push it with Isabel. That's what the groundwork is about. Is chummy Oldfield a front for Kelly? What was that joke her sister made? Very oblique. The three-legged Riley. But Isabel understood and was angry. Rare. Wonder if she is an *allumeuse*? Polite word for a prick-teaser. No. Consider Amanda . . . Well yes, consider Amanda. She knows perfectly well the effect of the dancing eyes and mischief and is absolutely sure she will choose her distance. Possible but Isabel's eyes sometimes flash but don't dance and there is that deep blue gaze sometimes slightly misty. Much more dangerous. Cleverly disguised intelligence. Wit rather than fun . . . Shouldn't be so limp at my own dinner party. Zara waltzes past with brandy and Calvados. That unimpeachable arse. Imagine her with little fluffy pink Miranda. Oh don't! Not so limp all at once . . . The televising of Parliament. Oh Jesus! Not again. Radio broadcasting a bad thing. Load of yobboes. And so they are on both sides. Have to admit the Alliance lot behave quite well. Does it mean that I am some sort of repressed Whig? Terrifying! The resurgence of Mattingley: Kierkegaard (note the impeccable Danish noise on the last syllable – Isabel almost giggles. Not impressed. So why did I invite him? I don't like the bastard and I did like his wife who was a friend of Sandy Fleming. Of course! So that would set up some tension. Why did she accept? Didn't know of course. But why did he? Convenience and I have a certain influence after all). What about Kierkegorrrr then? Categorized people into officers, serving maids and chimneysweeps. So who is what in modern politics? Gets his laugh at last and chatter. Very frivolous. Gray tugging his ear. Always a jovial sign. I almost patted Jocelyn's thigh in my abandon. *Not* a good idea. Amanda has as it were withdrawn. Not that it would much bother her. Doesn't mind the fleeting caress if it's fun for you and nothing at all to her. Gray turning to Isabel. Is it ever avuncular when a woman looks like that whatever the comfortable familial background? Can't tell. She has the misted violet look. What I need is someone to take me very seriously. Why in addition to my television couldn't I be one of a think tank? That's what does it. Look at them. Mattingley

– left-wing intellectual bloody pundit. Gray ex-left-wing intellectual bloody pundissimo. Oldfield even passes for an intellectual . . . How the fuck did we get on to Proust? Somehow by way of Kierkegooorrrr and Sartre I imagine. Can't stand the bastard.

. . . sometimes in the right company, I feel that I might actually *read* Proust . . .

Amanda's encouraging chuckle tells me it didn't work. The put-down put out. Icy-eyebrowed flicker from Alexandra F. Fixed Gray grin. Indifference of Jocelyn. Oldfield–Isabel transference of some wry footnote of amusement. Mattingley yawn hardly stifled. Balls-up. Not that I don't appreciate loyal and mischievous Amanda. How can she be married to that out-and-out bloody rottweiler? How to retrieve? Back to my new series . . .

. . . Include real live political stuff. After all Third World writers are deeply involved in day-to-day politics. Think of it: Latin America, the Caribbean, Africa. So as I see it any valid arts programme should have its vigorous political component without following a line that's in any sense doctrinaire. It will mean I get about a bit to some interesting places as well.

Rather sly grin in Isabel's direction. No reason why you shouldn't see the world with me. Gray wants to know what shape the programme would take. Isabel full-lipped pretty mouth tilted in politeness that I fear is deeply bored. Nonsense. Have faith in Mendoza, Mendoza.

. . . As I see it and you know, Llewellyn, as Sandy and Humphrey know too, it won't be entirely up to me, although I have some significant muscle, broadly in fifty minutes, three main items and a couple of ironic quickies. Unless of course there's something really special that week like a major exhibition or somebody's death or defection one way or another. So let's say a fairly iconoclastic interview, never anything sycophantic; a sharp feature with a political or social slant; two brief bits of piss-taking, if you'll forgive me, I mean the arts are crawling with pseuds; and something immediately topical on film.

Very original Oldfield says. Sarcastic little toad. Isabel coughs. This should have worked and it's bloody not.

. . . Of course I shall have a direct say in the editing. Some of my best friends even now are on the cutting-room floor . . .

Touch not very sure tonight. Though the professionals laughed. Mattingley, sucking up like mad, asks Gray about his time in television. Long story about Guy Walker who killed himself. Cut his wrists. Remember hearing about it. Alexandra F. interested in the sad story. Beautiful wife. Tortured relationship. So what. Holding the attention though. Mellifluous Gray effortlessly tugging on his erstwhile left charm, flashing his compassion. Miranda with the coffee. Discreet exit of both she and Zara to her taffeta or Z.'s pinewood room depending on which is in charge. Guess that it's often the little fluffy one. Not the point. Phase II not working out so I have to put my mind to other enticements. Blackmail wouldn't work even if I had the wherewithal. Teasing thought though – Angelo and Isabella. Come to think of it I could use someone languishing in a moated grange. He will not come. Don't bet on it, darling. Just hope he won't come too quickly. If she is having it off with Kelly, I'll make sure there's trouble. Supercilious philosophic arsehole . . .

General flirtatious conversation I can make use of at last. Gray paying court to Isabel, his wife confident and amused, Isabel playing up. Amanda and Alexandra Fleming on their mettle. Mattingley glittering. One day Isabel will travel a lot, see everything. Step in quickly . . .

. . . Anyone as beautiful as you are would need a reliable travelling companion. I'm sure I can think of several who'd volunteer.

Warm violet-eyed smile, little upward tilt of mouth. Can you? the bitch says. There are some precautions it would be almost vulgar to take. Laughter all round.

Phut.

*   *   *   *   *

Lady Margaret Hall
Oxford
15 October 1983

Dear Rachel,
Thank you for your letter and your trans-oceanic view of American life and politics. I don't think the man is

mad so much as dim. Accordingly just as dangerous, for the belligerent bustle he affects is frightening. It's a mercy perhaps that the Kremlin leadership seems to be in a state of collective coma. But one can never be sure. Someone came back from Moscow the other day with rumours that Andropov is very ill. Anyway if the California Kid is re-elected we might hope for a more measured drawl off the teleprompt. I must say the extreme right still make me tremble. When I remember how you and I fretted as gels about Goldwater! My God, compared to the existing resurgent right and the hideous reborn, Goldwater seems to have been a raging liberal. At the same time I suppose one should weigh the martial carnival of Grenada against the altogether more prudent, even precipitate, withdrawal from the Lebanon. All that bellicose maundering can only encourage the different Peace movements to more exhibitionist antics as we are seeing throughout Europe, exploited by the crazy left. Even I, no Greenham Common woman, begin to hop up and down as I detect the carving of a slaughter benchmark of history.

Meanwhile back at the palace mews. Horsies and doggies all fine and falcons unjessed for the good of the image. Not that it matters. If the lunatic left give me the cold waking horrors, it's nothing to the rabid (literally) right who are disturbingly noticeable here and in France. The idea of 'consensus', as it is now called – I think we would have said something drab and old-fashioned like 'common good', has become a victim of the Boojum. It is exasperating that there are men like Jenkins and Heath around so remote from real influence let alone power when we have these two mediocre choirs howling each other down. Nevertheless, there seems to be growing support for Labour since the glib though not very substantial Kinnock has been wished upon us. I don't suppose this will please you or Oliver. It certainly has Roger Ingestre invoking his ginger paws and whiskers. I'm not sure. The implacable lacquered madam *wants* confrontation and the little Welsh pepper-head is going to enjoy the garrulous challenge. The trouble is it encourages extremism. Here perhaps there is some hope.

I still believe that the British are essentially sane. Sapped by television, exhausted by the greed and lust engendered in advertising. But still sane. So it may just be possible that sane politics and humane policies will prevail. Oh what a mess.

Enough. As you will have detected I'm in a sour frame of mind. I'm a victim to a persisting restlessness which I still can't properly account for. But I shall try. It's what I'm trained for, after all. It seems that at forty-three my sexual juices are flowing too quickly again. You will remember Tim all those years ago. And Helmut more recently. Both married – though Helmut, as far as I know, is still alive. These were passionate affairs. Apart from them I've only had two fleeting encounters where there was no question of love. Now I find myself wanting that ridiculous abandon where I am desired by someone whom I myself want desperately. I'd like to have a whole sequence of empty days set aside for fucking and little else except empty hedonistic pleasures shared with someone also recuperating for the next glorious fuck. You alone know me too well to be shocked by any of this and I dare imagine that you too, even inside the security of your most enviable marriage, may sometimes have been stirred by immoral longings. I wrote abandon and I mean it. No strings. No one hurt. Is it possible to become suddenly (at my age) a nymphomaniac?

Of course not. I think I've been jolted a little by David Kelly. I'm sure you remember him. Balliol philosopher: sort of tawny, bright brown eyes, quiet, smiling. We've known each other well for years. His wife, Christina, is very pretty, rather nervous. I think you've met. David and I have always behaved in a light flirtatious way which I suppose, over the years, has become intimate. He's made various elaborate figurative passes but no actual physical advances. I've responded in much the same way. All good fun. I've always assumed that he and Christina were erotically totally compatible, if less so in other respects. Now I may be wrong and I certainly have no right to meddle or make mischief, but I think he has become deeply involved with Charles and Eve Darrow's daughter, Isabel, who is (part of the time) his secretary.

She is a beautiful, utterly feckless girl, more intelligent than she lets on, and (I suspect) irresponsible. What bothers me is not that they are having a brief mad fling, although I would not like to see someone as vulnerable as Christina hurt, but that *I* should be jealous. And I must be. Have I, all these years, wanted to curl up with Kelly and renounced the pleasure because of his wife, only to find that some well-laid-out little number, without a thought in her curly head, has slipped into the sleeping bag? All right, *cojones*! I shall prepare a monograph: 'Bourgeois Love and the Theory of Identity'. Thanks for listening. I'll start taking cold baths again.

Term is a week or so old and for the first time that I remember I'm bored by the whole prospect. I've always liked teaching and I used to enjoy all the rituals – even when I knew they were interrupting my own work. Not any more: everything has become a chore. I'm having some comic relief in preparing a lightheaded series for Chiltern Television, which will be broadcast so late that it will be watched only by desperate insomniacs or alcoholics who take life seriously, which I suppose is something of a relief. I shall, naturally, be teased about it by colleagues: so I shall wear a specially short skirt and fishnets. I sometimes think I have the mentality of a rather conceited stripper. I don't know whether I've ever confessed that when I was at school and chivvied about being an intellectual or a swot, I sometimes undressed slowly in front of my mirror. And I'd say to myself: so what Julie, so what Sue, so what Liz. Then when I got down to the knickers, I'd think: *and* I have a mind as well.

Is this the mid-life crisis? It has to happen sooner or later. A man called Marcus Ferdinand who was once a C. of E. priest until he applied for voluntary unfrocking (a moral stripper) told me a long story (which I suspect he made up) about a Jesuit and a female moral philosopher who were made joint guardians of the same adolescent. According to one version the Jesuit seduced the moral philosopher by the intensity of his gaze and the softness of his voice; according to the other she seduced him by a calculated disorder of the dress. At all events no one was in any doubt about what happened. Perhaps I should meet a nice Jesuit.

Serenity is something I long for. You have it. Eve Darrow has it. But I don't think that happy marriage is a precondition. I met a very calm lady the other evening whom you used to know called Marie White. She claims to have been a camp follower of the group you and Roger Ingestre once belonged to. Ingestre says she was and probably still is quite a girl. Perhaps that's why she is so cool and detached.

I'm due for a sabbatical in the next year and I've had an attractive offer from Cornell. I think, though, that I'd rather stay in Europe if I can arrange something suitable. Ingestre and the Darrows send love. Look forward to your next letter. Love to you both.

Ever,
Henrietta

★

Es schadet nichts, gottloss zu sein, wenn man Gott nur wirklich los ist. There is no harm in being godless if you are really rid of God. The wise Lou again, who reached the conclusion at a surprisingly early age. I wonder if she was really successful. After all Nietzsche, God's undertaker, and the devoted blasphemer, Baudelaire, were never really rid of God. And I think I know myself that I can deny a faith which ceased to have meaning or passion for me, but that in denying God I am implicitly admitting the possibility of such a being. My own minor excursions into existentialist wildernesses came to nothing when I realized there is no *Néant*, no nihilistic Eden, because that Voice is still there muttering if not exactly thundering any more.

The mind of winter once more beholding 'nothing that is not there and the nothing that is'? I think not. Rather *Man* who is the noblest part of *Earth* melts so away, as if he were a *statue*, not of *Earth*, but of *Snowe*. In which regard, we are all Snow Men. But it oppresses some of us a great deal more than others. What prompts this emergent occasion is a happy evening with Isabel Darrow and others in which I realized that I did not even pose the threat of nuisance. It has not crossed her mind that I am anything but a harmless, intermittently amusing, lazily clever and ageing labrador. Mortality beckons in the careless sparkle of her eyes.

I doubt that many people of my acquaintance suspect me of melancholy: they see a corpulent, mildly bibulous, easy and directionless *bon vivant* (within the limits of comfortable but not lavish financial resources). What they do not detect is the underlying ennui. Boredom is not an adequate translation. Perhaps I write this because I am reminded of Baudelaire. Victim of acedia as Eliot noted. I should go further and diagnose more than spiritual apathy: a definite disorientation, the kind of spiritual alienation which we now call anomie. I do not believe that I present an extreme case, but there are what I take to be symptoms. Hardly psychopathological: just a feeling of emptiness, vacancy, of simply not belonging. Perhaps it is all an affectation I put on for myself. After all, the persona I present to the rest of the world is affable, almost jolly. I wonder if my parents had lived longer whether I should have been quite as ready to cut loose from things that once mattered to me, that made some sense of life. They were always kind and I was fond of them – especially, I suppose, of my mother. Without benefit of brothers and sisters, I had nothing to deflect their attention from me. Had it not been for my father's insistence that I be sent to a boarding school, I might very easily have been spoiled. Whenever I returned home, in those years, I looked on my mother with adoration and I suppose I have always tended to idealize women whom I think I love. Isabel is the latest and presumably because I am an elderly fool it is more painful than it once was.

Here, however, any fanciful parallel with Baudelaire ends. The critics, as far as I know, agree that to be a Satanist one has to believe in sin as something positive, which means one has to believe in God. I have never considered being a Satanist, which always seemed to me while I kept faith silly, and now that I have lost it seems even sillier. Also however idealistic my wistful amours may have been, I have no voluptuary talent at all. Apart from one or two essays in fantasy featuring my more opulently respectable parishioners in whom I thought I detected a certain eclectic sensuality – usually full-bodied, comfortably married and over thirty, my incursions into professional luxury before my ordination and after my fall have been characterized by embarrassment rather than orgiastic triumph on the one hand or orgiastic disgust on the other. At the same time I have derived pleasure from my modest erotic demands and I am not able to see the sexual act between men and women, let alone the genuine act of love, as having anything remotely to do with evil. I am personally repelled by the idea of homosexual relationships, but I should not describe the more orthodox of these either as being evil, though I may consider them to be wrong.

Here I am at odds with Baudelaire's grim resolve to suffer, to nurture the sickness of a soul he believed to be damned through the disgust of sexual excess. And reading Eliot's essay on the man again, I am at odds with the critic who is all too ready to understand how such a course of self-hatred and abasement is achieved, seeking thereby to justify the poet's latent sense of Christian values and his ultimate fixation upon a God capable of dealing out salvation or damnation. There is in Eliot's own early work a revulsion from, sometimes a horror of, heterosexual encounters with the implication that they are certainly sinful if not evil. Eliot does not share Baudelaire's almost Jansenist attitude in which evil and its retribution are predestined by the aptitude of a particular individual, but the freedom of choice which he seems to have accepted does not veer from the Puritan conviction that sex and physical love are essentially bad. I am not sure that I understand Eliot's distinction between 'moral Good and Evil' which he says 'are not natural Good and Bad or Puritan Right and Wrong'. But I am in no doubt when he writes, 'So far as we are human, what we must do must be either evil or good; so far as we do evil or good, we are human; and it is better, in a paradoxical way, to do evil than to do nothing: at least we exist' that he is relating this statement to one which implies that an understanding of the sexual act as evil rather than one of 'cheery automatism' is 'more dignified and less boring'. Quite apart from my own view that the sexual act is in no sense evil (although betrayals which accompany it may be wrong), I am unable to see that it is better to do evil than to do nothing. Would the crimes of some sadistic murderer or torturer, the molestation or battering of children be even faintly vindicable, because they confirmed the existence of their perpetrator?

Baudelaire who saw in children 'des Satans en herbe'. Anyone who has spent any time in some institution such as a boarding school or doing military service will have met some malignant, even devilish, personalities: but I am not a misanthropist, I refuse to be That perverse man that barell'd himself in a Tubb. While I have no great confidence in the aesthetic taste or intellectual energy of the majority of people, I do not believe that many are malignant or cruel – unless they have fallen victim to religious or political fanaticism. And it must be considered that while the psychopath is readily drawn to opportunities of extreme violence, it is the fanatic who exploits him or, indeed, her. In the Middle East, in Latin America, in Northern Ireland, the evidence is most apparent. I would contend, however, that a similar exploitation of the relatively few totally malignant people in different societies occurs at a more subtle level, less obviously, in the East and the West at the hands of men and women who are *not* demonstrably fanatics. Yet I believe firmly that most of us – at least those not afflicted with too much thinking, which brings about *atonie*, the loss of force which perhaps may be mistaken by some in themselves for anomie – are decent and on the whole well intentioned. Whether the functioning of the social and cultural ambience in which they are obliged to live is conducive to these higher qualities is questionable. Triviality has always been with us, but violence as a means of entertainment is something we are now experiencing on a smaller scale and in (at the moment) simulated form but which calls to mind the most savage days of Rome. We hear of small children watching horror films on video machines and playing back the more bloody bits. *Satans en herbe*? If so, it is we who have prepared the fertile ground. And it is people like me and like my friends who have perhaps failed. At least have not shown courage in not protesting against the landslip which is becoming an avalanche.

Is this merely 'the demon of noontide' or the reaction to an evening when it became clear to me that the beloved object saw me with radiant benevolent indifference. Then what did I expect? It may be true that love is simply the urge to make oneself loved: but I think it is also a means of justifying oneself, of insisting that there is one other being, at least, who is, at a given moment, more important, more complete, more alive. So that the act of devotion becomes one of immolation. An abnegation of the self in an act of worship. My experience of sex, indeed of love, has been such that I have never known this physically, but I have heard that some men and women have lived this ecstasy. Does one emerge from the flame like a phoenix (there is no Phenix; nothing singular . . .)? It is absurd to think, even in passing, of the possibility of physically possessing (or being possessed by) Isabel. Of course I have imagined her undressed or at various stages of undress, of being gently and skilfully seduced by her. I see the nearly perfect figure, the high, beautifully moulded breasts, full but not heavy, the long silken limbs, tumble of dark hair, the merry blue eyes, the . . . And what would she see? A bulky clumsy man running to fat, with heavy jowls and a barrel of a body, and apparently complacent face. I would like to think that she would find something kind and sympathetic in the eyes. No: it is ridiculous and enervating. I should be content just to adore. She probably thinks of me, if she thinks of me at all, as old, past it. And there is somewhere a lurking fear in me that I might fail, that the defilement of that lovely body would be beyond me. I fear this! Who have held that there is nothing evil in the sexual act and who would conceive of such love as something sacred! I am making Isabel into Mme Sabatier. The twists and turns of the protean self-obsessed fancy.

It was Baudelaire though who compared love to torture or a surgical operation. 'Even when the two lovers are very much in love and full of reciprocal desires, one of the two will always be calmer or less possessed than the other. He, or she, is the operator; the other is the patient, the victim.' At least he has, eventually, the satisfaction, however much it tortured him, of knowing that Mme Sabatier desired him and consummation. With Isabel there is no question of dominance or submission. It is what people are pleased to call a non-event.

I suppose I should attempt some sort of Aristotelian progress from physical need to intellectual resolution. *Mañana*. I suppose it would be wiser to avoid Isabel's company, because I feel more lonely afterwards. Practical but not really feasible. I suppose I could become an eremite and revel in my noonday accidie. Not yet.

Solitude is a torment which is not threatened in hell it selfe. Even when you do not believe in hell.

*　　*　　*　　*　　*

10 November
The diary seems to have become an intermittent habit, indicating that I've found nothing better to do with any spare time on my own when I don't feel like reading. I'm still no nearer deciding on the book I'd like to write, although the publishers have been making encouraging noises. As I understand from colleagues and acquaintances, this is fairly rare these days, which is no solace to my guilty idleness. I've thought again about the idea I had on holiday – essays about Schopenhauer, Nietzsche, Bergson and William James under some kind of umbrella title. (Not sure that *The Doctrine of the Will* is right.) But I've turned up a couple of other ideas: one to do with Idealist philosophy; the other, which interests me rather more – the putative influence of Dostoevski as well as Nietzsche on later existentialist thinkers. It would in fact be a sequence of separate essays linked by a general theory, which I have yet to work out in detail. And it would afford the luxury of involving myself in literature as well as philosophy.

Until then these scribbles. That isn't entirely the truth. Since term started I seem to have become more involved with Isabel. Not by design – hers or mine. The fact is, all the same, that we are spending more time together and (I rather fear) seeking to spend more time together. That's as far as it goes and as far as it will go. There is certainly no question of infatuation on Isabel's part – much too sane and self-mocking, but she obviously likes me very much. Briefly after that one kiss at the Camerons' party, I was confused and foolish, but I too am not infatuated. Intense as it is, the friendship will remain sentimental. I suppose it accentuates the difference in age between us. In early middle age I am the one more likely to become moonstruck. Quite apart from not wishing to hurt Christina, I do not intend to be unfaithful. And remote as the possibility is I would not want some feckless affair in which Isabel might also be hurt. And so might I be. Self-restraint is often self-protection. Fourteen years is quite a gap even today. I should not like to lose or damage my friendship with Eve and Charles. Little sister, Elaine, has already made one or two witty remarks: 'What a pity it's not the nineteenth century when you could write her beautiful letters.' For a paranoid moment I wondered if I was for both and perhaps for others a figure of fun. Little sister is very bright, but she doesn't have Isabel's easy, happy disposition. Just as some people want to talk about whoever it is preoccupying their attention, losing no opportunity of bringing up the cherished name in conversation, I am finding some oddly vicarious satisfaction in writing this stuff.

Another excuse for keeping the diary is that it enables me to record, as irreverently as I please, college and university rituals – and events such as the Camerons' Hallowe'en party. I'd heard about their notorious parties: the more scandalous allegedly at their house in Garsington, but fairly riotous evenings in Peter's college rooms. All this was long before Christina and I were invited to one. Iris and Peter both seem to attract prurient and highly imaginative rumour. Both are thought to be promiscuous. Perhaps Iris is. If it is true of Peter he is admirably clever about it. Mendoza has it that they are incestuous. His account (very likely all his own work) is that Iris (aged seventeen) seduced her younger brother (aged fifteen) one wet Thursday and that the relationship has matured over the years. How Mendoza could possibly know may be questioned, but he claims to have slept with Iris (if that is the right way of putting it) and implies that he is in her confidence. Reckless of her; if it is true, which I doubt. At her most prim, Henrietta disapproves of both. One of her pupils, called Quentin Joyce, whom she liked, met a beautiful girl at a Cameron party – one of Iris Cameron's fashion models. This girl was with Joyce in Paris when he was shot by a terrorist (ironically it appears in the wrong place) whom he stupidly tried to tackle. He was killed. Peter was the young man's tutor in politics and he seems to have been a favourite with Iris. I am sorry about what happened to Joyce, of course, but he always seemed to me to be something of an arrogant show-off and his foolhardy gesture was in character. Henrietta, departing from her customary icy logic, seems to blame Iris for this concatenation of events. Christina, on the other hand, likes Iris and is much easier in her company than she is with a lot of other people. She finds Iris warm, natural and envies her talent for not giving a damn. Ever malicious, Mendoza hints that Iris's warmth extends to the pick of any crop of her brother's pupils, offering in return the most likely model on her books. I am sure this is not so.

The Hallowe'en party was certainly no orgy. The Camerons have a big house, inherited from a rich family, so I daresay compatible people slipped away, from time to time, from the main action. Iris was wearing a glittering black mask, a scarlet tabard and the sheerest of black body stockings which generously displayed her beautiful legs. There were a number of extremely pretty girls whom I took to be fashion models. Mendoza was flouting his image – not without success – and gyrating in an ultracrepidarian way to the very loud music which these days seems to be inescapable outside the more dignified gatherings. Christina was twirling gracefully with Peter Cameron, using her supple hips to full advantage, watched by a glassy-eyed Ben Oldfield, beaming genially from the sidelines in close touch with a bottle of whisky. Isabel was dancing enthusiastically, but without Christina's seductive rhythm, with a chap who teaches history at Corpus, a friend of Peter Cameron of like reputation. It was colourful, brash, alcoholic and very noisy. Skirts swirled with more abandon where they were not already too short to matter, to the delight of certain leaden-footed lechers who caught the odd enticing and old-fashioned glimpse of stocking. The girls in the very short clothes uniformally wore different coloured tights, so that their appeal, if aesthetic, was less arousing. After a while the cachinnation and the insistent beat of the music got the better of me, so I wandered out of the room, intending to get a breath of fresh air. Most doors were open but one or two shut and I thought it unwise to enter. Peter Cameron's library, however, which is well stocked, was empty; some untouched bottles on the long table with his glossy word processor. I poured myself a drink and was looking idly at the books, when Isabel appeared. 'I saw you go out,' she said. 'You haven't talked to me all evening. Come back and dance. I know you say you can't, but I'll teach you. Christina is marvellous.' 'That's why I'm reluctant about it. I'm astoundingly clumsy.' 'I'm sure you're not. Anyway, they've stopped playing rock and they're switching to smoochy music, so you won't have to thrash about.' She had come up to me and put her arms lightly on my shoulders. I put mine on her hips. And so we kissed. Nothing torrid. The merest brush of lips. The violet eyes were bright, laughing, and yet tender. Neither of us was aware of Iris Cameron at the door. 'I'm sorry to interrupt,' she said. 'I came for some more gin.' She put her finger to her lips and whispered 'Sh.' I was confused. Isabel laughed. 'We're going to dance,' she said. Iris said we'd make a lovely couple, with an ironic gleam. Christina was dancing very close to Cameron, both moving beautifully. Isabel and I did not. We stood together sipping our drinks until someone else claimed her.

14 November
With Christina away for several days in Birmingham at some kind of conference, I was quite pleased, for once, to accept an invitation to dine at another college this evening. Usually the obligations at my own are quite enough and there are certain unavoidable social chores. Christina never complains, but it's a good week when she is not left on her own for a mere two evenings. She says she doesn't mind: she reads, watches television, catches up with her own work and does odd jobs. I suppose academic wives become used to periods of comparative solitude (as indeed do academic husbands) when the spouse is working at something; which is why, no doubt, Christina enjoys holidays so much. Of late, though, I have tried to make sure we do more things together.

Henrietta is a good hostess and it was a lively evening. There was a certain amount of glinting curiosity about the Camerons' party from several of those dining. Evidently rumours have begun to spread and I suppose I experienced a mild *Schadenfreude* in dissipating them. True, things gathered pace again as the evening wore on, but it was far from a Fellini rampage and apart from some harmless exhibitionism (such as Iris discarding her tabard and one or two of the younger girls of firm build their blouses) such liaisons as occurred were discreet and clandestine. Or so I imagine.

Fortunately gossip soon becomes tiresome when there is no focus for malice or innuendo and the conversation over dinner was amusing and enlightening. Henrietta complains of feeling jaded. I thought her wits were sharp enough reviewing the recent outpourings of colleagues in various allegedly learned proceedings. On my other side sat a pleasant English specialist called Paula Bradshaw who is working on a book about Trollope. She was self-effacing but most entertaining. It was all very agreeable.

After dinner in the commonroom, things became more intense. Innocently enough an expert on the Eastern Bloc from Nuffield, called Korolev, set a spark to the kindling by observing that Andropov had been missing from the Red Square parade. He was politely asked what he interpreted from this conspicuous absence. It is virtually fatal to ask experts on the Eastern Bloc to interpret anything, especially when they have uninterrupted thick hair which rolls back from a plump face redolent of uninterruptible smugness. I have heard such people discourse on everything from the Boyars Plot to the death of Mozart to 'faction' in contemporary literature at one time and another. Korolev met his match in Bridget Ross, a formidable Marxist, who belongs (I think) to the same SCR as Roger Ingestre. His analysis of the political stalemate between East and West was credible enough: the Soviet enervation while they wait to decide whether a gerontocrat or an aparatchik will succeed; the American stasis, albeit apparently bellicose, while Reagan bids for a second term and Congress sits nervously upon its sweating hands. It all led, not surprisingly, to nuclear gloom and a bold argument for the Greenham Common women positively protesting against Cruise missiles based upon British land, put forward by a rather dowdy woman called Enid Wellbeck. I was surprised that her main opponent was not the preened Korolev but Bridget Ross. Leninist (rather than Marxist) logic at its most formidable. Mrs Wellbeck's point was that the women might well be shot by American guards if they infiltrated the site. Heseltine, intellectually debonair as ever, had said as much. Ms Ross pointed out that such action was inevitable and justifiable in that such intrusion constituted an anarchic threat in itself. Of course, she disapproved of the bases and favoured British disarmament: but while they existed they must be defended by responsible professionals. Until dismantled by political agreement, they must be secure. Furthermore, Bridget Ross claimed, the real disarmament assault was being occluded by what she described as buffoonery which had little to do with feminism. That really set things going. Henrietta crossed her long legs and sipped her Madeira, looking unperturbed. The unlooked-for mercy in a Senior Common Room is that no one is going to turn and say, 'You're a philosopher, tell us what it's all about.' Philosophers are just things they have to live with.

When it was all over, Henrietta saw me out and kissed me on the cheek. What had I done to deserve that?

17 November
Christina has returned from her conference with the news that she has to go to Stockholm for the company in a week's time. She is untypically distant and most unusually snappy and impatient. I have known her to be in the past edgy sometimes, nervous: but she is a gentle, tolerant woman. I have worked at equanimity. Nothing in excess, as Henrietta would no doubt have it. So our marriage has been even and peaceful – very few spats, let alone quarrels. Now there is some minor tension, especially, I notice, if Isabel comes up in casual conversation. There is a minute but perceptible flicker in Christina's eyes, or a slight furrow of her brow or around her mouth, sometimes a deliberately sardonic smile. I wonder if somehow she has been told in exaggerated form of that insignificant moment at the party when Isabel and I kissed. Iris Cameron is the last person I should suspect of malice – except for her hatred of Francesca Oricellari, which is professional. At the same time, Iris's own careless sexuality must devalue the importance which others, even today, attach to erotic peccadillos. She might have joked about it to someone, perhaps her brother or (heaven forbid!) Mendoza. And Christina might have heard some casual gossip.

It would be a pity. Our summer holiday was marvellous. We've made love since: but not often and somehow without passion. I think that there has been mutual pretence, which worries me a little. She may well go to New York in December. I said that I could travel with her, since term would be over. She was evasive. Her schedule would be very full; there would be business lunches and dinners; anyway what about the book I am allegedly planning. Without putting it into so many words, she did not want me on the trip.

The people she works with are pleasant, fairly intelligent, extremely well dressed. One or two are good-looking. None of them, outwardly, have shown anything other than friendly interest in Christina and she is not, apparently, attracted to any of them. In fact, since we have been married, I have very seldom heard or seen her take much notice of another man. It's possible that she is having an affair, but I'm inclined to think that she is worried about Isabel and me. How on earth can I reassure her without lending credence to whatever rumours she may have heard?

24 November
It is strange how easily one tends to forget people who were once very important. Then the same name crops up within a day or two in quite separate conversations. With Christina away in London overnight, I had dinner at New College as the guest of Tom Wilkins. Among others present was Robert (now Lord) Blakemore, austerely pleasant, and a sort of wandering scholar, called Harold Hassett, who has been a diplomatist, academic, civil servant and *chef d'équipe* at the European Commission. He is currently writing something thoughtful at All Souls. One of these men who effortlessly and deservedly seem to fall very lightly on their feet. This was the first time that Guy Walker was referred to.

I did not know the man well. When I was a young man, he gave me an early opportunity on BBC Radio. We met here, at Oxford, and I must have impressed him in some way, because I was invited to do something about intellectuals in the French Resistance. As far as I know, it was moderately successful: but soon after Walker left the Corporation and any hopes I might have nurtured about a supplementary career in broadcasting departed with him. Now and then I am dredged up from the bilges of their filing arrangement, hardly to any purpose or account. Such is vanity that I seldom turn them down. Guy Walker became distinguished as a publisher, a newspaper editor and finally a television executive. Henrietta and various others worked with him. And then one summer's night or day he went home and slashed his wrists in the shower. It was not very long after the death of his wife. Blakemore and Hassett, both of whom knew him intimately, were talking about his energy in encouraging others to new

74

and rigorous efforts. Hassett said something about waste and despair. Then both became guarded and circumlocutory, which is not unusual among men of their type.

Within a day or so I ran across Evan Warrington in the Lamb and Flag. Isabel had some appointment or other, so we didn't have our usual evening drink. Warrington (who is Senior Tutor at Charles Darrow's college) courteously invited me to join him and a couple of friends: a grizzly, gruff but entertaining writer called Jack Maddox and the woman (attractive and much younger) who evidently lives with him. Her name is Jean Morgan and she is softly Welsh, where Maddox himself preserves a flinty acrimony which is only emphasized by acquired English vowel sounds. Warrington, also Welsh by origin, although he has lived all his life in Oxford, was once taught at school by Maddox. They are good friends.

Maddox, as I gathered from conversation, is a freelance lecturer who does a little reviewing and various other odd literary jobs. I seldom read fiction, but I have come across one or two of his books. The girlfriend (what a trivializing little phrase!) has a responsible job in insurance or banking, which is hard to credit in someone with gently curling auburn hair falling to her shoulders, pretty green eyes and a demurely enticing smile. Then who can tell about these things: Warrington has (I should guess) a splendidly curved mistress of unmistakable allegra who turns out to be the head of a London comprehensive school.

I can't remember how Guy Walker's name entered the conversation. Perhaps it was on my account. Maddox was a great deal more forthcoming than Blakemore and Hassett had been. Apparently he knew Walker well and spoke with the respect the others had shown for his energy, diverse talents and his driving enthusiasm for encouraging others. Maddox ascribed his own publication and continued efforts in fiction to the interest of Walker. 'After he died,' he said, 'I didn't do very much. I played around with ideas and wrote one thing that was too private for publication. But things have changed now.' As he said this, he looked across at Jean who smiled at him. It was a curiously tender moment. Warrington asked why Walker had killed himself. 'Several people wondered about that including that ichorous icicle Blakemore whom you know. A friend of mine called Morgan Rice was asked to get up some memorial and a few of us tried our hands at remembering without success. In the end Rice had to do it all himself in a short biography. He was a tormented man, Walker. He and I used to drink heavily together. I'd had two marriages which ended in a shambles and I was I suppose, at that time, coldly promiscuous. Walker was different: he was married to a beautiful – a really beautiful woman, called Imogen, who was loved by a lot of men. As far as I know she was entirely faithful, but Walker was insanely jealous – not only of attractive acquaintances and friends, some of them close. He accused her of picking up the rough trade and gave her a hell of a time, while he himself had violent affairs and one serious girl, eventually, who was almost as lovely as Imogen. Oddly enough he never seemed jealous of the other women and went on worshipping the woman whom he said he believed was always betraying him. The truth was very different. I guessed and Morgan Rice discovered where Imogen Walker's most compelling sexual urges lay.' We all looked surprised. Maddox nodded. He went on to say that Imogen had become terminally ill over quite a long period, during which her husband showed every devotion. When she died he threw himself furiously into work and became a chief executive in television. 'Rice,' said Maddox, 'ascribed that savage suicide to grief and Walker's growing obsession about the cheapening of what we are pleased to call our civilization. But I don't think it was that. I think some of the things he knew about his wife and mistress finally deranged a brilliant but unstable mind, afflicted by an almost paranoid jealousy.'

There were a few more desultory, rather chastened, exchanges, before the conversation turned to other topics. Of course, what I have written here is a paraphrase of what I remember; but it made my thoughts wander from what the others were saying. Despite all appearances now of detachment and confidence, I was once capable of wild, irrational jealousy. 'I have drunk and seen the spider . . .' I ruined several relationships and can't honestly explain how Christina put up with me at first. Through her I gained confidence over the years. Apart from flashes of sudden doubt, I was able to conquer such a susceptibility. To my dismay, I realized after what Maddox had been saying that, while I was perhaps worrying Christina by seeing so much of Isabel, I could detect symptoms of jealousy in my attitude to both women. Christina's business absences and late evenings. She looked disappointed once if I had to go out on some college or university business. No longer. Perhaps the recent strain I thought existed between us was nothing to do with Isabel and me. And Isabel herself – pursued and flattered by many men more attractive than I am. Oldfield is hardly to be taken seriously, but he is lively and implacably good-natured. Mendoza . . . That hardly bears thinking about. And although she is mildly disparaging (for Isabel) about him, might this not be a way of disguising a sort of Jacobean fascination? Ridiculous! I am now mature. I have made a profession of rationality. I have no intention of living again through the flatness of that misery. Nevertheless it was with some effort that I dragged my attention back to a thoroughly agreeable conversation, remembering it was my turn to buy a round of drinks.

27 November
The fictogenic properties of Iris Cameron are indeed remarkable. Since their Hallowe'en party I have heard five scurrilous, varied and utterly inaccurate accounts of her stripping, dancing naked, seducing five different young men, doing a go-go dance dressed only in a body stocking and being discovered in lesbian embraces with two of her models. It is true that at one stage of the evening she *was* wearing only a body stocking which concealed very little of her quite admirable body and that she did caress one or two people to whom she was offering a drink at some given moment. I daresay that she danced intimately with relatively selected partners. But at no time were her admittedly uninhibited cavortings very depraved or especially shocking. All that within a month! A little month! And yet I, too, have speculated idly (with nothing better to do) on aspects of Iris's private life. Christina was quite angry about the gossip and blamed it on the lubric, semi-monastic tradition of Oxford, a mere microcosm of upper English behaviour in which women are playthings or potential bedmates or out-and-out whores. A bit strong even from Christina these days. I did not argue the fallacies of her supposition. (It was hardly an argument.)

Marcus Ferdinand tells me that my mind is sodden in trivia and will remain so until I set myself a worthwhile project outside teaching, lecturing and the occasional learned exercise. Quite mildly I remonstrated with him that he was nothing if not intellectually lepidopterous. To my surprise, although he made light of it, I must have upset him. The large, bland, pallid face showed a spasm of something like pain and his eyes were momentarily hurt. In spite of his easy manner and bonhomie, I know from very infrequent conversations alone with him that his is a very perturbed spirit which will not rest or be still. I'm not sure whether he conceals a procrustean conviction that all is for the worst and that what we fondly call 'democratic freedoms' must give way to arbitrary government which might readily become totalitarian. (Warrington believes this is happening under Thatcher and that every single breach of social discipline injects some poisonous muscle-building steroid into the system which will surely destroy imagination, identity and ultimately will.) Ferdinand, however, has a cheerful resilience. The morning after, if one chances to meet him, he will present the usual placid, benign face. I suppose it is after years of pastoral accommodation. For all that, I hope I did not touch a sensitive nerve. He is a kind man who does not deserve to be hurt by some facile aside.

Isabel is fond of Ferdinand, because he is gentle and amusing. I told her about my mild misgivings. She looked untypically wise for a moment or so, then started chattering about some semi-farcical incident which she and Ferdinand had shared when punting on the Cherwell. It was a funny, affectionate story. I have always thought of Ferdinand as a celibate cleric still, without giving much thought to his sexuality. Our conversations have veered nowhere near any such confidences. Now it occurs to me that he too perhaps is attracted to her. I chuckled at the absurdly wayward thought. Isabel looked questioning, when Iris Cameron herself rippled in. Iris needs no invitation to join people she likes. She was buoyant as ever, floating like some exquisite, shameless dryad on the billows of gossip. Except for one cloud: the abominated Venetian harpy (Francesca Oricellari) had mounted a highly successful autumn fashion show in London a week or two before. The newspaper columns had been rapturous. Furthermore the inveigling harlot had managed to appear on *television* as well as radio. Understandably, I knew nothing about it. Isabel was tactful – though she later confessed to me that Francesca's collection was stunning. (Her word.) I asked why she never wore such clothes. She answered that she could not afford them and, anyway, that wasn't the point. Francesca herself didn't wear her own designs. I didn't quite follow. Iris is indifferent to snubs and sometimes insults which come her way from people who are envious or jealous: but she cannot stand Francesca. Is it because she is very attractive and highly promiscuous, while Francesca, even more attractive, is evidently not? After one drink Iris left to meet her brother who had just heard that he was going to a lucrative American symposium in December, so was taking her out for an expensive dinner.

Leaving the pub, we ran into Henrietta in Broad Street. Pleasantries. Then Isabel had to dash. We watched her tripping away, lithe even in a winter coat. 'There, no doubt,' said Henrietta, 'is the most recent princess in the dynasty of Venus.' It took me some time to track down the allusion. It referred to 'indiscriminate love and misguided affection'.

$$*\quad*\quad*\quad*\quad*$$

It seemed to Isabel that it was always now much busier than it used to be and she rather liked it. Her father, a lovely but sometimes cautious man, had always taken much longer to adjust to changes than Eve whose efficient serenity she envied. At first, she thought that, while pleased to be the Master of his own college, he was not enjoying it much. Now that he had acclimatized, his fit of caution was over and he was energetic and enthusiastic, which meant a flow of guests and visitors (some important), undergraduates, graduates and dons to Sunday lunch, what Ben Oldfield called (not disparagingly) 'food rituals' – dinner parties and cocktail parties and what have you. Isabel and Elaine played their parts – although Elaine, much the more reluctant, was able to plead some academic chore or other when she really couldn't face another bout of social chat. Eve had always liked entertaining and was effortlessly good at it. She'd encouraged both daughters to bring friends home, when they had lived at Bardwell Road, before Daddy's elevation. Elaine's invitations had been sparing, but Isabel had taken full advantage of her mother's friendly, relaxed attitude. Since the friends were reasonably intelligent, personable and not specially noisy, there had never been any problems. And now that she had grown up, many of her friends were older people whom she was lucky to share with her parents.

Now with term about to end there had been three Sunday lunches on the trot. Around the table on 4 December, the day after full term, were an agreeably disparate collection. Next to the Master on his right was a formidably corseted life peeress in a handsome grey suit with hair moulded to look soft and unblinking dark eyes, who in spite of her severe mien seemed to laugh a great deal and rather musically. Otherwise on Isabel's stretch of table, next to her, were Francis something, an undergraduate who was shy and surprisingly an extremely good actor; and, on the other side, Peregrine Prideaux, tutor in comparative theology at the college, whose name suited him – he was wearing his toupee dropping brahminical seedlets of wisdom for all who would listen. Isabel thought of him as the guru with the fringe on top. Beyond the portly little don was a lively girl from Hull called Doris, allegedly an excellent mathematician, and a toothy youth, whose name she hadn't caught, who was explaining to Eve the theory of the transit of Venus. While Eve was listening, wide-eyed, thrilled by the intricacies of planetary parallax, Alexander Fitzallan, graduate of the college and now something important at *The Times*, trapped in the conversation, had assumed a glassy expression. Elaine, sitting next to him, was unable to rescue this massive, likable wag because she was receiving courtly attention from a double blue, called Adams, almost as massive as Fitzallan, who had given up Isabel after one night at the theatre, three dinners and two unsuccessful forays because she had giggled at an inopportune moment. Being the well-brought-up athlete that he was, he was now politely cheerful or cheerfully polite as the occasion demanded. Next along the table was the elegant Henrietta Ball, whose dark red hair Isabel admired. She was a friend of her mother's, although they had remarkably little in common. If Eve represented poise which was warm and outgoing, Dr Ball's composure was cool if not chilling; furthermore she was an intellectual and Eve (like Isabel) was most certainly not. On her right Evan Warrington, once Ben Oldfield's revered tutor, wore his habitual ironic smile, listening to Henrietta with his eyes absent-mindedly on Isabel's breasts. There was more appreciation than lust in the abstracted stare, but Isabel was aware that her favourite dark blue dress fitted to snug advantage and was quite pleased about it because Warrington was attractive and was known to have a mistress. Finally, a mousy little student who had begun timidly was now talking in voluble bursts to kind, lovely Daddy who was twinkling and prompting her, sometimes mischievously. It was all quite fun. Isabel noted the skilful arrangement of her mother, not least in the disposition of Elaine and herself. And it worked.

The double blue was making Elaine blush. Isabel knew quite enough about him to be certain that it was not from any impropriety or louche reference. The distinguished *Times* alumnus (how he would have hated the description!) was animated again in the full glow of Eve. While the Venutian transitourist had found in mathematical Doris someone who really understood him. She heard Peregrine Prideaux mumbling something, somewhat peevishly, about a female theologian (the very idea made him choke over his baked potato) at Cambridge who had developed an absurd theory based on an impeccable source. Isabel heard herself saying that it needn't matter: what was source for the goose was source for the gander. Peregrine was plumply unamused, but Evan Warrington across the table caught the remark and laughed, which surprised Dr Ball and the little girl who were talking across him, assuming his attention. He nodded at Isabel, appreciatively. A nice man.

It reminded her that while it was all very pleasant, she hoped that it would not go on too long. Christina Kelly was away (again) somewhere and Isabel had said she would have tea with David, if the weather was good, at a little place at Iffley. They would walk along the towpath and she was looking forward to it. What was so good about David's company was that there was never any need for effort. In all fairness, there wasn't much effort at any time in being nice to people: but with him conversation and laughter and gossip just happened. Isabel did not see why some people (Daddy) thought him solemn, others (Eve) too cerebral, others still

81

(Elaine) dull. At this point, she noticed Dr Ball looking at her in an impassively unfriendly way. She listened more attentively to Peregrine Prideaux, smiling, nodding her head at intervals, not taking in a word. That first kiss, a little tipsy – certainly not drunk. She had opened her already moist lips just a little, so that it was not just a peck. No reaction from him, which was probably as well since Iris Cameron appeared. And so they sometimes kissed quickly now on parting of an evening, never on meeting. Isabel wondered if she loved him a little, in a way, knowing that she thought about him too much. Ideally she would like the kind of brotherly-sisterly relationship that the Gloop Ingestre had with Francesca. Not that she had ever quite believed it. Still, the Gloop was odd. Reddish hair now greying, but still quite handsome. Indifferent to women and yet patently not poofy. Isabel thought that she wouldn't want to be, at her age, any man's sister. She remembered her mother's calm eyes upon her months . . . quite a long time . . . ago when she had been laughing with David. Had Eve recognized something Isabel hadn't even imagined then?

She looked up and down the table, animated, scuffing the port over the instant shine, to catch the brief smile between her parents. Contentment, confidence. Love, indeed. The ingrowing – no, the ingrown marriage. She was not ready to settle for that as Eve had been when more or less her age. Isabel listened to the blur of good-natured chat and passing humour with almost sleepy pleasure into which she deliberately intruded a goad of discontent. She should leave Oxford, cut herself off from academic life, learn to know herself in a much, much rougher world. Eve had given up what must surely have been a good career as an actress for her husband. She had never shown a moment of disillusion or disenchantment that Isabel knew of. When Isabel and Elaine were not too little, she had appeared again in plays, in rep. Some happy girl or other always pleased to look after them. Then she had given it all up. And if becoming Master of a college was success, then they were successful.

Isabel, still bubbling as required, was beginning a review of academic life, comparing her father and Ben and David with people like the nice Ferdinand and the odious Mendoza who had renounced it, but found it hard to keep away. Then there was Warrington and Roger Gloop and Peregrine Prideaux. There was Professor G. S. Walton! There was Henrietta Ball opposite her. And all the people at the faculty. It was surely only women like Eve and Samantha Wilkins, an ex-Wren officer, who tended to turn assumptions upside down, who contributed to comparative reality. Such profundities were interrupted by a general upheaval. The immediate 'food ritual' was over. She would ring David and arrange to meet for tea. Not that she was hungry.

They met on Folly Bridge. It was a bright winter afternoon. They greeted each other happily without touching. David was wearing a smart sort of duffel coat, quite unlike Isabel's father's threadbare and shapeless old thing, from which he would not be parted. Across the river was the sadness of the elms in Christ Church meadows and David remembered the days when the opposite bank was a succession of brightly painted bar barges from Talboys, the boat builders, to the brick boathouses of the more recent colleges. Not so long ago. She listened to his memories and images of the time when he was younger as she had listened to her father and to others. They were all a part of Oxford as it lived and changed: but it had become the thoroughly agreeable factory in which they worked (where the company in Japanese style looked after loyalty), sometimes complaining about conditions mildly, sometimes angered by a change too suddenly imposed. But it was not *their* Oxford. That belonged to twenty-one-year-old Charles Darrow just after the war and National Service, from Balham; to eighteen-year-old David Kelly straight from one of the last grammar schools in the Northwest. Isabel remembered that Warrington had lived in the town all his life, as indeed had she. It was pleasant. But neither of them was remotely sentimental about the place. Nor was Elaine: but then Elaine was seldom sentimental about anything. She watched him as they walked, remembering her mother's wary, quizzical look, Henrietta Ball's masked hostility, Elaine's sharp jokes, Iris Cameron's blue and sideways flicker. 'You'll make a lovely couple.' What the hell! It was sometimes claustrophobic. Suppose she confided in Eve or Elaine that she was having a wild affair with David Kelly. No: it would not be fair to Christina, who might indirectly be hurt by some childish whim to cause shock waves. And her father would be upset.

It would be silly, let alone dishonest, to pretend that she had not imagined making love with David. Not to be too coy about it, heartily fucking. But it was all illusion and best left as illusion. Isabel knew exactly that she had a good figure, long, well-shaped legs and that she was pretty. She had first had serious sex when she was seventeen and a few times since. It had always been enjoyable but hardly ecstatic. She was quick to react but . . . But . . . And quite often, as with the double blue Adams, she had suddenly thought how funny it all was. Not when it was the final fuck. But all the preliminaries. And Double Blue had no chance of getting much further. Male vanity was amazing. Isabel thought it was a pity that she had never been in love. And she wasn't in love with David. Only in a sort of way. Wistful and out of the question. She liked sex, enjoyed caresses, was pleased to give pleasure. That was all and enough. A long way from that look she had in a second seen pass between Daddy and Eve. Could either of them *ever* have been unfaithful? Did it matter that much?

The teashoppe was pretty. Chintzy and matronly. David had buttered crumpets, Isabel had cucumber sandwiches (very thin). Both had Black Forest gateau. And talked about nothing much. Compared to the conversation at lunch, it was all so trite. And happy. Was this nonsense – just being with the bloody man – what people thought of as being in love? That sudden look again between Charles and Eve. Not sudden: it was slow in a moment, it was always there. Not being *in love*. Just loving. Isabel wondered if the quiet, blushing Elaine knew something that she didn't, after all.

David said that he'd promised to look in for a drink in Roger Ingestre's rooms. Gloop. They took the bus into Oxford. David said he wouldn't stay very long because Christina was expected back from London some time during the evening, so he thought it would be civil to prepare a cold supper. 'Civil' – an odd word in the context. Isabel said that Christina was evidently doing well. David said, 'I think she must be. She's certainly dedicated.' It was best left at that. In a way she was glad that they were not to spend the evening together.

Roger Ingestre was as usual pleasantly furrowed, kind and

physically relaxed. He was already entertaining a former pupil, Stephen Kent, and his wife Charley (short for Carlotta, a name she couldn't stand). They were a good-looking couple. Steve was tall, blue-eyed and rosy faced, probably about thirty but looked younger. Charley was small, neat, fair, also blue-eyed and enviably slender, about the same age. Isabel liked her immediately and felt that, in turn, she was liked herself. She didn't talk a lot but when she said anything it was either funny or remarkably to the point. Furthermore, she listened and laughed when other people were running the chat. Stephen Kent had evidently been a favourite of Ingestre, so there was a tolerable amount of standard Oxford flattery all round. All the same Isabel thought that there was a certain constraint between the two men, a wry turn of phrase, a flicker in the eyes, a sentence allowed to trail away. She thought that Charley was aware of it too. David, once catching her eye, hinted something by a movement of his mouth and interlinked fingers.

Then conversation, as was inevitable in Roger Ingestre's company, turned to politics. Elaine fretted much more about such things as Cruise missiles and disarmament than Isabel did. It was not that she was indifferent or unconcerned: she simply recognized that there was absolutely nothing that she could do about it. Her sister, on the other hand, believed that protest was positive and that eventually even politicians of the stamp of Reagan and Thatcher must take notice. Isabel had asked, 'What about the Russians?' Elaine had accused her of being disingenuous, a line of thought which she had been unable to follow. Ingestre and Stephen Kent (who was to be the Social Democrat candidate for an unpromising constituency in the next election) favoured multilateral disarmament, pursuing what Isabel thought was a very woolly argument. David and Charley were not for nuclear disarmament but against the disposition of new weapons. Isabel listened, thinking if it has to be done, when 'tis done, let's hope it's all over quickly. The talk moved from the earth-shattering to the earth-yawning: Roger Ingestre glooped about the resignation of Eric Varley from his constituency at Chesterfield which would open the way back into the Commons for Wedgwood Benn if he put himself forward and was selected. David, teasing perhaps, said that surely this could only be good for the SDP. The more Marxists or crypto-Marxists there were in public view to frighten the electorate, the better for them. Neither Charley nor Isabel was in the mood for political hubble-bubbling, so they chatted together. Her first impressions had been sound: they got on very well. Charley was a year or two older than her husband and had been married once before to someone whom Isabel might have heard of called Humphrey Mattingley, described by Charley as a national windbag. Recognizing, uneasily, how easily it was for a relatively small and supposedly elite bunch to meet and make contact, Isabel said that she had met him at Mendoza's. Charley laughed. Mendoza indeed! More or less a contemporary of hers. They swapped Mendoza stories. The approach seemed to have found little variety over the years. But Charley was surprised that Alexandra Fleming had been there, an old friend whom she'd seen less of since she married Steve. She had always loathed Humphrey and couldn't have known they'd be at the same table. It was typical Mendoza. Even so, Isabel was not entirely sure that either Alexandra Fleming or Mattingley had shown many symptoms of mutual loathing. In response to Charley's questions, she talked a little about herself. There was, refreshingly, no inquisition about her relationship with David. They must meet again. Yes: Isabel would let Charley know when she would next be in London, which was not very often. Everyone joined in general, fairly funny chatter.

When they left, Stephen Kent took Isabel's hand warmly in both of his and said they must all meet again. Ingestre cautiously kissed her cheek, which was unexpected. As they walked towards Carfax, David said that they had been witnesses at a reconciliation. Isabel's instinct that there had been some miasmal strain between Roger Ingestre and Stephen Kent had not been merely fanciful. What David knew was second-hand: oblique comments from Henrietta Ball and asides from Ingestre. Years ago one of his pupils, a pretty but rather silly girl (according to Henrietta), had been steered in the direction of a fairly ruthless lecher by Ingestre himself, who was bored by the girl's attentions. Kent had, at the time, been infatuated by the same girl, who was killed in an accident which might have been suicide. Not surprisingly the slurry of blame had hit the fan. David could not remember the name of the girl (as she must have been), whom he had never met. He had written one or two books for the publishing house run by the dead girl's father, a quietly intense man, Jeremy Taylor, much saddened by what had happened. There had also been peripheral scandal which David did not know or care about. Suddenly Isabel thought about Elaine – for no reason whatsoever. Suppose Elaine, serious and by no means alert to such things, should fall into the clutch of an unscrupulous older man! The melodrama of her protective spasm made her laugh aloud: Elaine *was* serious, eminently level-headed. The laugh startled and perhaps rather shocked David. 'Sorry,' Isabel said. 'I wasn't laughing about what you were saying. It's very sad. I was just thinking of myself as the prey of Giles Mendoza.' Not strictly the truth, but the proper explanation would have been too complicated. David looked at her rather coldly. She managed, this time, not to laugh. The now usual perfunctory kiss under the Martyrs' Memorial. David went briskly along St Giles. Isabel turned back towards Broad Street.

Eve was watching 'Mastermind' on television – a programme scorned by Elaine and even mildly derided by Daddy. 'Would you like a drink?' she said.

'No thanks. I've had several at Roger Ingestre's.'

Her mother's elegant eyebrows reacted. 'I didn't know that you and Roger were such good friends.'

'We're not. Not particularly. David was invited round and so I tagged along.'

'Ah,' said Eve, looking serene.

They watched the rest of the programme together and a comedy which followed. Isabel's attention wandered. David's sparse account of the unfortunate young lady troubled her obscurely in some way. She was in no doubt about her own ability to cope with erotic or emotional squalls. But she was uneasy and, without warning, restless in a very specific way. It was a long time – well, two or three months – since she'd had any active sexual contact and then it had amounted to deep kisses and some fairly passionate caresses. All at once she felt like the real thing, a long vigorous carnal night of it. It wasn't like her. And she didn't know what had brought it on. People, she knew, thought it odd that she had no regular 'boyfriend'. And she wondered if this was, after all, because of David Kelly. She had registered her mother's studied calm, she remembered one or two sharp asides from Henrietta Ball. Was she hiding something from herself pretending that their relationship was genuinely platonic?

'Would you like something to eat?' Eve said. 'Daddy's out and Elaine's at her film club watching something depressingly Central European.'

'I'll make it,' Isabel said. 'What do you want?'

'Well, there's some cold beef and some chicken.'

'Sandwiches?'

'Thank you, darling. I'll open some wine.'

Soon Isabel had snapped out of her woozy mood and was briskly carving meat and buttering bread.

*　　*　　*　　*　　*

'*Ciao*,' said Francesca Oricellari. 'What a pleasure to see you.'

'Very nice of you to ask me to lunch,' said Henrietta Ball. 'Odin's indeed. This is very grand. Well, first of all, warm congratulations. Your autumn show seems to have been a triumph.'

'Thank you. Everyone was very kind.'

'You deserve it. It was a beautiful collection. You'll be pleased perhaps to know that Iris Cameron was said to be furious.'

'Why? I didn't use any of her girls.'

'Exactly. And it was a success. And those wide innocent eyes do not fool me, Francesca.'

'Well, she is impossible to do business with. She wants to run everything. I think she should have been a pirate or a highwayman. Anyway, it's all history. Back in October. What have you been doing?'

'Nothing much. In fact I've been vaguely depressed. No. That's not accurate. Down. Out of sorts. I don't suppose it ever happens to you.'

'Don't believe it! Shall we have a drink while we order?'

'Thank you. Gin and tonic, I think.'

'*Ciao*, Liam. A large gin and tonic and a Campari soda. So: why are you depressed?'

'I don't know. I certainly have no earthly excuse. I've got a fair crop of students – one or two quite bright, I'm just about to record a television series which is very well paid, though I doubt that it will have an audience, and I'm due for a sabbatical. So why should I complain?'

'What about love?'

'Oh heavens, I never think about that! Sex, perhaps, as don't we all from time to time. And I don't imagine it keeps you awake often. Sorry, I didn't mean that to sound . . .'

'Of course not. It's funny. As a matter of fact, I find it quite simple to be pure. In a manner of speaking. Chaste. That's more exact.'

'Delighted to hear it. Thank you. I drink to chastity and all that.'

'Cheers. But you mustn't laugh. I only go to bed if I am in love. And it is so much more difficult all the time to be in love. I think I will be a feminist.'

'Very drastic, don't you think?'

'Sorry. It's the way I speak English after all this time. I meant I think I am becoming a feminist.'

'Because you don't . . . how shall I put it? . . . "fall in love" as often?'

'I like that. But I've never had it out of focus, you know? I don't know how you feel. It's more difficult being a woman than it used to be. Do you agree?'

'I'm not sure. In my job, I've always had to inure myself to male arrogance and (worse) condescension. Things are much better at the university than they once were, but it's still riddled with prejudice. Slyer and more subtle: still there. And now, what courtesies there were, however demeaning in implication, are in rout before the forces of belligerent and quite mindless feminism. And I'm sure *you're* not in that particular cohort.'

'No. Most certainly. People in the rag trade aren't exactly popular with the militant women.'

'I'd hardly call your end of it the "rag" trade . . .'

'All right. The sort of pretty frothy rags that a lot of us still want to wear. It makes the lesbians wild. And they are crazy enough to start. I mean God! I am Italian. I was brought up as a Catholic. Of course I believe furiously in women's rights. But I also believe in being a woman.'

'If that's being a feminist, it puts a new slant on it. No.

Sorry, Francesca. I was making a rather poor joke. I know what you mean.'

'It's funny, really. But I have been brainwashed. There was a time I didn't mind being a sex object.'

'And now you do?'

'I'm much more prepared to resent stares and suggestive remarks and the assumptions some men have. You must know about it.'

'I doubt that I've experienced as much . . . what's the phrase . . . harassment, as you have. Academics tend to be circumspect. I suppose I've come across more intellectual discrimination, which I must say makes me livid. I'm sure it's possible to be a responsible feminist and still be a normal woman. Have you noticed the word "feminine" has become a pejorative?'

'I've never liked it. I think of a fluffy little girl in calico. Very pretty: but no chic. Not what you have and what my sister has.'

'I'm flattered. Not what you have either, if I may say so.'

'Oh, I am too fat! I had a good figure once. Perhaps we'd better order. What the hell!'

'I think I'll have the set menu. It looks good.'

'Why don't we eat *à la carte?* What are you doing for Christmas?'

'Getting out of Oxford! That must sound very uncharitable. But it does honestly get a bit oppressive.'

'Yes. They're all lovely people, but I can imagine.'

'And I rather like being on my own. I'm going to Nice. What about you?'

'I will go to Venice. Clodia will be there. And even now that Pappa is dead, there are still old ladies and old men who like to have us there together when it's possible. Venice is lovely in the winter. Anyway, I like it – perhaps it reminds me when I was a child.'

'How is Clodia?'

'All right! Great. Except she is trying to get out of a Women's International Conference in Nairobi in 1985. For the moment, she is enjoying her work. She'll be over later – well, next year I suppose. Nineteen eighty-four.'

'Don't! Can you imagine what the first few days will be like?'

'At least you'll be in Nice and I'll be in Venice . . .'

'Your wine, signora.'

'Thank you . . . That's good.'

'*Bon appetit*, ladies.'

'Thank you . . .'

'You don't have a family, Henrietta?'

'No. Parents dead. No brothers or sisters. There are various relations. But we're not in touch.'

'Still you have a lot of friends. What I think I like about Oxford is the welcome I'm given. There are so many interesting people. Where exactly did we meet? It couldn't have been long ago.'

'At a party, I think. Isabel Darrow's birthday?'

'That's right. And then again at Roger Ingestre's thing in honour of Robert Blakemore. Ben Oldfield rescued me from an American called Whitehead . . .'

'Whitehart. Didn't you like him? I think he's rather pleasant.'

'I just got completely wrong with him, you know? I thought he was brash and conceited. He thought I was a bitch scoring points. Anyway, I think that Ben was only pretending to rescue me. He really wanted an excuse to join you . . .'

'Oh? Ben Oldfield?'

'Yes!'

'But surely . . .'

'I am most indiscreet. But Ben Oldfield is in love with you. He confessed to me on a train where all the best confessions are made. But I should tell you: I have known him be passionately in love before. Several times. He is a great romantic. Not with me, by the way.'

'But that's absurd. I hardly know him. I mean, we see each other around and say polite things. And I'm years older.'

'Why should that matter? He's quite attractive and very amusing.'

'I suppose he is in a puppyish, enthusiastic way. Well, you surprise me. I shouldn't have thought I was his type at all.'

'He would like to be a philosopher. He is working on a book of aphorisms.'

'He's *what*! Good Lord, I hope I don't have that effect on people. I thought he was writing something about Eliot or Stevens or someone of that sort . . .'

'No. This is in his spare time. I told him he should write poems. He says he can't.'

'You seem to know him very well.'

'I do. I don't see him all that often. But we are both extrovert and we liked each other straightaway.'

'Then why on earth hasn't he fallen in love with you?'

'I don't know. But he hasn't. Oh I think he appreciates whatever I have going for me. But I'm not spiritual enough for Ben.'

'I was going to suggest that you steered him tactfully in the direction of Isabel Darrow. But if you're not spiritual enough, I'm sure she's not.'

'They are "chums". That is Ben's word. She's a lovely girl and very beautiful.'

'She's beautiful. I think I'd like her more if she spent more time with men of her own age who weren't married . . . You look surprised and it was somewhat bitchy but . . . I shouldn't gossip.'

'You mean she's having an affair?'

'I wouldn't go so far as to say that. But she and David Kelly see a great deal of each other. I know she works for him, but people have started noticing . . .'

'He's such a quiet man. Shy.'

'He's reticent. But he's not in the least shy when you get to know him. He's flirted with me for years, all in fun of course, which is why I'm worried about Isabel. I'm not being prudish, but I like Christina, his wife, very much. Have you met her?'

'A few times. Rather nervous.'

'Vulnerable. In spite of the job she does and I understand does well, she's not at all sure of herself. Least of all, I think, where David is concerned. I think I won her confidence a long time ago. And I'd hate to see their marriage run into trouble because of someone as basically frivolous as Isabel.'

'She has a lot of fun, but I don't think she's malicious or predatory.'

'I'm not suggesting she's malicious. I think she is simply irresponsible and utterly careless of other people. Except for her family. I wonder that Eve hasn't had a tactful word with her. Perhaps she has. I don't know.'

'Have some more wine.'

'Thank you. This is delicious.'

'Great! Henrietta, do you think I should say something about this to Eve? I know her very well, but they are such a close family.'

'I don't think so. Perhaps things had better be left to sort themselves out. I'm probably exaggerating.'

'People do when it's a pretty girl. I'm not saying *you* are. But if others are talking gossip. It must have happened to you?'

'No. As you say, they are close. I doubt it would do any good. I don't know Eve well enough. And Charles keeps his distance from more or less everyone. In any case, I've no experience of that kind of intricately knit family concern.'

'I do a little. Pappa was against the Fascists and suffered for it. Then after Mussolini, the Communists and others said how could a Venetian aristocrat not have been for him. So things were still tough. I don't remember much. Clodia could tell you a lot more. But it made us close then. Mamma died: but we were always encouraged to look at the world. Clodia went to school in Switzerland, which is why she speaks English better, without an accent. I wouldn't go away then.'

'You and Clodia are still close. And, incidentally, the accent is delightful.'

'True. And thank you.'

'My mother and father were very restrained. He taught classics at the boys' grammar school in the town where I went to the girls' high school. My mother grew flowers. I read books and played on my own when I was little. When I was older, I read books and had friends who read books. Girls for the most part . . . God . . . it must be unheard of these days! . . . I remember the terrifying excitement when a boy first fondled my breast. And I think I went absolutely rigid. At the same time I knew I had a fairly attractive body and wasn't bad-looking: but that was a secret I kept with myself. One day . . . It took years before I was able to take sex easily. I don't think I've ever been in love.'

'I have. Three times. I'm not so shocked as you are if Isabel is having an affair . . .'

'I understand. I think I'm being stupid. You live in the real world after all. My father and mother kept the world at a distance and when I left them, I went up to Oxford, eventually read philosophy. Academic discipline imposes its own perspective on life, but it doesn't provide any prophylactic against feelings and longings and nostalgias that were bypassed when they were possible. So the distance shifts. The perspective changes. Sometimes I am involved and then it's different from the times when I am disinterested or even mildly bored. Once, recently – fairly recently – I did feel involved in someone's death, someone I had taught. But . . .'

'I don't think I live in a real world at all. Who does? Except people actually suffering. Still, here we are. Are you going to have the sorbet or the mousse?'

★   ★   ★   ★   ★

OLDFIELD'S APHORISTIC ODYSSEY

Why do we need myths? Personal, public, collective, universal.

To probe the mystery of being here at all, of being me: to explain little man (me) against the notion of man (*man*) being important in an immense cosmos which defies understanding.

To investigate the possibility of gods or a God.

In this way to try to justify disaster in whatever form it happens. (The Reason for Bad News – see below). In this way to explain away or justify war, tyranny, atrocity; or at a lower level any kind of political shift of emphasis in circumstances which preconceive domination.

To enable an individual to explain to himself his own actions in terms of universals: that they are commonplace and nothing to worry about; that they are of a superior nature and something to be proud of; that they contribute to a private narrative which makes that individual unique and important.

To alleviate the ecstasy (in which there is usually fear) or the pain (in which there is sometimes hope) of loving someone else.

To justify family conflict: envy, rivalry, jealousy; to explain hatred among kindred where it is thought to be unnatural (among blood relatives – parents, children, brothers, sisters) or anti-social (among warring family factions).

To allow the discussion of aspects of sexual lust, whether

permissible or forbidden, natural or unnatural; to persuade oneself that others are just as guilty or much more depraved.

To identify with great or heroic figures, whether historical, contemporary or genuinely mythical – paradigms exalted in story.

To create (where they do not exist) such heroic fictions in a world of irreducible evil. (The ruthless detective, the western hero obsessed with pursuit or vengeance or his own code, the battling slum priest.)

To establish, for whatever reasons, a patriotic illusion or a folk identity or a national fervour. Usually for political ends: that is to gain power.

To suggest to humble people that they might become rich, beautiful, famous.

Allied to this, to sell products or ideas or personalities.

To project the future at its worst in order to stimulate or pacify existing fear. (Nuclear catastrophe, various forms of science fiction and fantasy, social anarchy.)

To investigate notions of magic and occult theory.

That'll do to be going on with. I shall expand a little and then get on with discussing the nature of myths – ancient and modern; tragedy and farce as against comedy, which is in essence hostile to myth; myth, fiction and lies; myth, history and lies; parallax and myth. There will no doubt be digressions of one sort and another of a personal nature.

I have heard it argued that fiction is a holiday from reality for the writer as much as for the reader. This implies that in its highest form, which is literary, it is as escapist as it is in its lowest form, which is television or radio soap operas. The difference is in the attitude of the author. Is he churning something out as a mere distraction; or is he entering into a conspiracy in which the reader is actively a part to cheat reality?

The fictions (sometimes described as fantasies) of our daily lives become, if we take them seriously enough, personal myths: that is, they underwrite our assumptions and so modify our behaviour. What distinguishes a fantasy (Ben Oldfield is gracefully seduced by Eve Darrow; Ben Oldfield scores a hundred against the West Indians; Ben Oldfield becomes Professor of Poetry) from a personal fiction is that the latter is a state of mind, a recognition of oneself in a certain guise, fulfilling a certain role, which may be for the most part false. Most of us are capable of considerable self-deceit.

At the same time, Eliot wrote of Joyce's method in *Ulysses*: 'It (the use of myth) is simply a way of controlling, or ordering, of giving a shape and a significance to the immense panorama of futility and anarchy which is contemporary history . . .' So, I contend, in attempting 'a parallel between contemporaneity and antiquity', we try to make sense of the futility and anarchy of our personal lives having despaired of making sense of an apparently futile, anarchic cosmos.

There is very little point in my trying to identify with someone I admire greatly – author, philosopher, cricketer, actor. I don't know any saints. The very fact of admiration recognizes in someone else superior prowess, charm, personal magnetism, intellectual or spiritual power. Contemporary fictional heroes can (at best) involve me in a conspiracy which ends when I close the book, (at worst) stimulate in a desultory way my lazy imagination. But in order to reassure myself about myself, I need the friendly participation of a Doppel-gänger who has survived the mountain mists of the ages. I choose Telemachus. In so doing I am immediately creating a role for myself and wilfully, knowingly, cultivating a form of self-deceit.

This allows me to impose roles upon others whether or not they might agree or approve. Warrington (not yet fifty) becomes my Nestor, as Jack Maddox, his former English teacher, appears to be his own. More fancifully Charles and Eve Darrow, Isabel's parents, become my Menelaos and Helen. The university itself (personified, perhaps, in Marcus Ferdinand) becomes Proteus.

Oxford, the city itself, home of marmalade and motorcars, represents the reality of Ithaca – a reality which has little to do with the metamorphoses, metempsychoses, transmogrifi-cations and transformation scenes of the perennial academic pantomime.

. . . Eve Darrow. I don't understand how, as a friend of Isabel's, I could have known her so long without appreciating what an astonishing woman she is. She has a trick which I have noticed more than once of unexpectedly (I don't mean abruptly) taking off her earrings in the middle of casual conversation. Why this should be so seductive I do not know, but it was certainly this casual, graceful, unaffected movement which focused my attention, making me realize how beautiful and how complete she is. For a while, admittedly, I was besotted by Henrietta Ball and her frostily elegant allure. I think I recognize in Eve a much more real woman.

Hardly Menelaos and Helen. She and Charles seem to have an effortlessly serene marriage. And yet she is a very controlled actress. The blue eyes (not as dark a blue as Isabel's), the dark hair swept upward, the exquisite bone structure and complexion, the hint of humour and gentle mockery, her slender and tall and fully rounded body.

I have no ambition to play at being Paris. (Always thought Paris was a bit of a shit, anyway.) Oldfield's conscience strikes again. I like a certain man very much. Suppose that I fall in love with his wife. Am I already immoral? Assuming his indifference, if I seduce the woman or we agree to make love, because she has some interest in me, is this immoral? Has the husband been betrayed by her and insulted by me? Now then: suppose that the woman and I admit love for one another, but abstain from sexual commitment. Is this not dishonest as well as immoral? Are we not guilty of some sin of omission in denying one another transient physical expression of a love that is real enough (in a loveless world)? *Pourquoi faut-il aimer rarement pour aimer bien?* Camus. Was it? Yes. Here! More aphorisms! I must not allow myself to be put off by Lady Henrietta Disdain. 'Surely all this parallax idea of yours is implicit in James Joyce. Read the essay on "Proteus" in Hart and Hayman.' So I bloody did. And all it does is to validate my theory which is quite different from the intricate interweaving of the great man.

J. Mitchell Morse in op. cit.: 'Berkeley says distance is a relationship among objects; that therefore we do not see it, but learn from experience – experience of "the connection between the proper objects of sight and the things signified by them" – to estimate it and adjust our ideas accordingly: e.g. that a castle on a hill far away, which seems to our eyes to be two inches tall, doesn't change its size with our distance from it, but that God makes an apparent change by way of informing us of our distance from it; and that the system of such apparent changes constitutes an "optic language", whose rules, though as arbitrary as those of human language, are as regular.' He notes too Stephen Dedalus's phrase 'coloured on the flat'. And adds: ' . . . we see flat, "then think distance". We see the signs then think the things; and our unrestricted or unreflective naiveté thinks we see the things . . .'

It is the same with individuals, if we substitute that word for 'objects'. We learn from experience. The difference is that our estimation and the according adjustment of our ideas is not a matter of static or relatively immobile 'things', whose existence has nothing to do with our perception of them, but of people with a free range of physical, emotional, intellectual and spiritual movement. So that we may be utterly wrong in our estimations. We 'colour on the flat' or indeed flatten out the colour. We see flat and 'think distance': that is, we allow our imagination to interpret situations in an involved or a detached way that is coherent with our experience or consistent with our interests.

If I dislike someone intensely, I will read into events which have nothing whatsoever to do with me, spiteful, ignoble, petty or even depraved motives. If I love a woman, I will view her other relationships with suspicion, jealousy, anxiety, and an uncritical sentimentality: I will persuade myself that she is unhappily married, unfulfilled, repressed or ragingly lustful according to my mood or design.

Where self-interest is not in question, I am able to look with more dispassion at the circumstances of others. But I am still capable of grave misinterpretation and false (even though irrelevant) judgements, because of latent prejudices or predilections in me. This is at a personal level of observation or anecdotal evidence (gossip).

I am also inclined to think that *physical* distance has some bearing on our reactions to 'public' disasters. A bomb outrage in Oxford or London would startle me more than one in Belfast or Paris or Tel Aviv, although my moral indignation would be similar in all cases. If I have recently travelled on an aeroplane and hear a day or so later of a violent hi-jack, I am more sensitive to the suffering and fear of the passengers than I would otherwise be if I had sat in a library for months. The unremitting savagery of sectional battle in the Middle East, the famines of Africa, natural disasters when they occur become commonplaces of television. First of all deeply shocking, then something we learn to live with. It is only when disaster is immediate that we do not judge from a distance.

It is then not surprising that we often set greater store upon trivialities than upon world-shaking events. Except in extreme circumstances, one of the 'reasons for bad news' is that it helps us live with minor tribulations in the knowledge that far, far worse accidents of fate or history or human evil might befall us.

If my identity is an enigma and independent of the existence of others, my awareness of personal well-being or wretchedness depends on an intelligence of relative suffering.

Fuchs writes of Stevens's supreme fiction (a private myth based on the determined imaginative reconstruction of reality where there is no God and no transcendental impedimenta) that it occurs in the face of 'his awareness of the personal disorder of our time'. It is in 'bad news' that we register this awareness and construct our own fictions. By projecting ourselves into the disasters of others, we escape the mediocrity which threatens our individuality.

In our happier, lighter moments we share individual pleasures with others. True comedy (as opposed to farce or wilfully destructive satire) is a matter of sharing. Tragedy is an exercise in isolation, where we identify with a necessarily lonely figure at odds with universal forces. Someone wrote: 'We participate in a tragedy, at a comedy we only look.' This may be true as far as it goes. My contention is that tragic participation is ultimately selfish, assistance (in the French sense) at a comedy is not. Alfred Hitchcock told a German female star that 'the whole point of comedy is to reduce dignity'. She answered, 'Not in Germany.' (And I hope the obese egomaniac was for once put down.) Anyway, it is not true. It is the purpose of farce to reduce dignity. Farce is the reverse side of the tragic coin. Tragedy asserts dignity as the tragic hero is humbled. Farce humbles ordinary, unremarkable people. Comedy enhances the commonplace normalities by making us share in laughter at our daily weaknesses.

. . . Not sure I'm very good at this. Perhaps Francesca is right. I'd be better trying to write poems as a lovely hobby. The trouble is I desperately want to be serious and I am not a serious man, which is why I get on so well with Isabel who is also not serious. Her luck is that she doesn't want to be. Elaine is very different. And the delectable Eve? Hard to tell. After all, she was once a professional actress (according to Ferdinand and Ingestre, of considerable subtlety) and no doubt in perfect command of whatever velleities and carefully caught regrets she has in mind.

After the cinema (a happy nonsense *Victor/Victoria* which had Isabel bubbling and me rolling about) I went back with her for tea, which turned into gins and tonic for her and Elaine and whisky for me. Elaine was glooming about Christmas impending. Typically, Isabel was looking forward to it. She enjoys any celebration and wondered why people were so joyless. She'd heard some priest or other on a radio programme identifying the idea of Father Christmas with unspiritual acquisitiveness. It had annoyed her. Even more when the same remote and ineffectual cleric had been rebuked by the irate mother of an upset five-year-old, only to respond that he and Father Christmas were on the best of terms. When Isabel is angry (not very often) she looks quite stunning. Elaine, always a realist, thought about all the children who would *not* be getting presents of any kind.

Then Eve came in, looking marvellous. She was wearing a white blouse and a straight bright red skirt. Blue stud earrings. Cool and slender. Isabel gave her a drink. Lapis lazuli. Conversation is always easy with Eve and Isabel, but my own contribution was none too bright. I was trying not to gaze helplessly at her, imagining what an affair with such an inaccessible woman might be like. Once I noticed Elaine, who is always perceptive, quietly smiling: so I said something inane which made them all laugh. I had been imagining some languid afternoon with lilacs, entirely civilized, no ungainly hurry for consummation, towards the end of the affair. Eve twirling the flower in her long white hand – both of us perhaps recalling things that other people have desired. If I am to epitomize youth that is cruel and has no remorse, then she must surely be the eternal humorist, the eternal enemy of the absolute, twisting my vagrant mood as she does the flower. The mild December evening comes down (not many smells of steak from passageways these days) and we move into the exquisite nocturne as I gently remove her lavender silks, she

100

having already dispensed with her earrings. Oh Ben, she murmurs wistfully . . .

When it was time for me to leave, Isabel was merry and kissed me lightly on the cheek. 'Don't worry, Ben,' she said. 'Sooner or later everyone falls for Mummy. She's used to it.' Then am I not merely inane but bloody transparent?

The best reason I know for growing a beard is that it obviates daily communion with one's own increasingly banal face. I no longer play the identity game, but after conversation with a most unusually unjovial Ferdinand I found myself tracing the skull beneath the skin. Mortality, it seems, has been whispering to him. Ferdinand assumes that he has already lived more years than are left to him. He is fifty: I shall be thirty next April. (The cruellest month.)

How soon hath Time, the subtle thief of youth,
Stolen on his wing my ninth-and-twentieth year!
My hasting days fly on with full career,
But my late spring no bud or blossom shew'th.

Now that we talk of dying, indeed! Back to the aphorisms. It is difficult, when young, not so much to think of oneself dead or moribund, but to imagine beautiful women dead: the graceful Eve, the lovely bubbling Isabel, the effervescent Francesca. Dust hath closed Helen's eye. Lord have mercy on us.

At best death must represent the unbeing before birth. Nothing. A blissful nothing without fear of oneself or threat from outside. No dreams. Yet now that I am aware of my certain end, the crisis of identity is shuffled aside and I am afraid. I do not want not to be.

When I was little I prayed for fine weather because we were to have a picnic or to go to a cricket match and I prayed in a more routine way for my parents and friends. Eventually I prayed that my mother and father would like or love one another. I prayed that I would win my scholarship here. I did. And I fell away from the habit of prayer.

I no longer expect God to help companionable weather, of course. I no longer expect divine mercy. Look around! I understand the need to explain thunder and the urgent desire to find in all the mysteries of quantum physics and the most

101

advanced mathematics an explanation, an idea of order, a God who is utterly beyond imagination or explanation or configuration. A state of Godness that passeth all understanding and has nothing to do with religion.

And yet, when I contemplate my own death (as Ferdinand who is godless and was once a priest has been studying his own), I begin to wish for some respite from oblivion. When oily politicians invoke God and adumbrate what they call Heaven I feel sick. The idea of judgement is repellent. But I do not want to stop being. How do I dare question in the face of Eliot or Dante? Why can I not find solace in the exotic defiance of Stevens or in Joyce's exiled cosmic urbanity?

Winter morning on Port Meadow. Icy lacustrine pallor of sheeted water. Low flight of solitary birds. Stillness of the cold. Silence because the birds do not call or cry. Unbroken high cloud denying the pale sun. Even now I am a fiction: a stark, black figure against the flat white and faded green looking out at limbo, wishing for monsters and torment rather than a limitless nothing, apprehending the mood of winter in which there is no conception of spring, no possibility of hyacinths. A sad tale's best for Winter.

I am usually quite buoyant even in December, so all this brooding is unusual. Still, it is the darkest time of the year and I do not enjoy the short days. I am certainly not melancholy because of frustrated infatuation for Eve. It is all far too comic – even if she did notice me gawping. No doubt Isabel is right and she is entirely used to admiration. I suppose that even retired actresses thrive on it. Perhaps I should go away for Christmas as Henrietta Ball is doing. My God! A month ago and I would have given my doctoral thesis to go with her. A little month. Frailty thy name is Oldfield. Oddly enough she has seemed to notice me more of late, in spite of what she thinks about my theory of parallax. But what would be the point? I'd be on my own whereas here I'll be entertained. I think I'll give a small party myself on Boxing Night.

On my way back from my lugubrious walk I made a detour to the Lamb and Flag. There to find David Kelly and Isabel sitting quite close to each other and laughing into each other's eyes. I do not like or trust that man, so I hope that Isabel, who is a smashing girl, is not . . . No that's ridiculous. They welcomed me immediately, as they must, but there was for a moment, before they saw me, a distinct aura of intimacy about them. Not just someone having a drink with his pretty secretary. Sheer and rather mean fantasy. Isabel was as lively as ever and Kelly was in his quietly sardonic philosopher's hat. I sometimes think that philosophers largely discount the accident of their private lives, in which they have much in common with slaves.

Ah well. Enough of this. Time for an invigorating aphorism or two.

3

*D*ear Rachel,
It's a bit late to wish you a happy Christmas, but I
hope this will reach you in time to send best wishes
to you and Oliver for the New Year. As you will see from the
address, I have decided to be festive all on my own in the
sun (in which I have not been disappointed) and to get away
from Oxford or indeed English rituals and the feeling of being
the woman who came to dinner when the family really want
to put on paper hats and pull crackers. The hotel is in a
delightful place on the little promontory between the Baie des
Anges and the road that dips down to the old harbour. It is
run by efficient and uneffusive young women (it seems),
which suits me. From my window I look out at the sea, the
bay, the sweep of the celebrated English promenade and over
the roofs of the old town where I eat and drink splendidly
and safely. So far at least the *clochards* are still in tenure and
one is more in danger of being shat upon by pigeons than
mugged. What I so like about France is that a woman can be
alone without fuss. The occasional optimistic approach, yes:
but no arrogance of waiters, no simmering stares across the
chrome and velveteen imagination of solitary males.

Ironically enough, shortly before leaving, I had a reasonably
tempting proposition from an American visitor called Whitehart. He would be alone over Christmas in London and
thought it might be fun if we spent a little time together,
caught the odd show or choral event, maybe. (Of course, you

will know about this: but the Mass in B Minor and Mozart's Requiem are choral events.) I'm not being fair to Whitehart. He is charming and attractive, unflabby and fairly bright. He simply has these appalling turns of phrase. Having already booked a holiday here, there was not much difficulty. Furthermore, Whitehart had the grace not to suggest that he join me. It wouldn't have been difficult. But I was not in the giving vein. Silly of me, perhaps. We shall see.

I don't think that on orthodox lines he is in any way outstanding. He doesn't compare with David Kelly or your Oliver or you or me for intelligence, let alone the top luminaries whom we both admire, but he had an ingenuous and impetuous enthusiasm for curious ideas. In the terms of *1066 and All That*, Hitler (according to Ivan Whitehart) was a 'good thing'. I can hear you exploding. This is how he argues: if a more enlightened policy had emerged from the deliberations of Versailles, Hitler would have been relegated to the mediocrity which he deserved. Weimar would have had a chance. Without his rise, devolution of empire would have been slower, more reluctant, more careful. The superpotency of the USSR would have been detained. Japan would admittedly have become more significant in the Pacific; but this would have meant that the USA could not afford isolationist policies and would have had to forge alliances with the UK and other imperialist nations with Asian interests. Separatist national forces would, however, have flourished as stupidly as ever in Europe. There would have been (what Whitehart calls) 'a retardation in class sublimation', and a spinning-out of the imperial dream. Social and liberal progress, as we know it, would not have made such advances. Hitler (says Whitehart) accelerated the course that history was to take. Nonsense, of course: but entertaining nonsense for a cocktail party. I asked him if he was a Marxist or a determinist, which shocked him to the very balls. He then recovered promptly enough to make a pass at me. Why can't I have *ordinary* conversations? So, while waking alone at three in the morning, I might wish for the firm hand of a Whitehart on my indolently palpitating thigh, it is probably all for the best.

I have hired a car which I park in a hotel reservation under the flower market. That is what is so beautiful: to walk in December among such a profusion of colour in the Cours

Saleya – roses, those vast bundles of carnations, violets and the absurd Christmas cabbages luridly decorated. Then to sip a drink in really hot sun watching the children and the dogs. I daresay the sun is hotter and the pavements are most certainly cleaner in California, but I'm not envious. Tomorrow I shall drive to Cannes and eat a huge Christmas lunch in one of the restaurants near the port: then if this glorious weather lasts, I shall laze in the gardens at the end of La Croisette until I feel light enough to drive.

It is good to be away and to see my own life and those of others in perspective. I brought Dante and Shakespeare's late comedies. Not a good choice. Heretical as it no doubt is, I find the *Paradiso* hard going and always have. There is something about the whole Beatrice business which obscurely annoys me, probably because I am theologically thick. And while *The Winter's Tale* is marvellous, I have always been exasperated by Prospero and find *Cymbeline* and *Pericles* ludicrous. What was the old examination question: 'A tired man with one eye on the box office: Discuss.' I have accordingly devoted far too much time to a French version on television of the romance of Albert and Victoria. You can have no idea of what really went on in cross-Channel ferries and the like.

I was delighted by your account of the conference in Florida. I can imagine the impact that Oliver must have made. It all sounded rather glamorous and perhaps I should think again about the American offer. I shall have to make up my mind in January. The problem is that you and Oliver enviably do things together, you have someone to share the joke or the tribulation or simply the new experience. I know it wasn't always so when you were in Parliament and he was with the WHO, when even your marriage knew a little strain, yet you have always had reliable reserves of trust, shared experience and (in your case) laughter to draw upon. And indeed love. What I've always admired in you, from the days when we were both at the university, is your capacity for affection. I know that I am capable of considerable loyalty but I lack the gift of natural warmth. Apart from the passing illusory transports of some erotic encounter, I doubt that I have ever loved anyone – certainly not any man whom I might have married. I can hardly complain because I have done pretty much as I please, but now well past forty I sometimes long for companionship and I get rather sour about friends like David Kelly recapturing adolescence. He is still much taken, it appears, with Isabel Darrow. Now and then I have an uneasy feeling that I may be jealous.

I think I'm also becoming slightly maudlin. I had a fascinating chat with a waiter in an empty bar about '*la politique anglaise*'. He was a warm admirer of Madame Thatcher ('*quel courage et en même temps quelle élégance*') and was surprised that I wasn't. He had very little time for Mitterand whom I've always rather liked because he seems able to read and think. Then he told me I was '*très charmante*' and asked me to have dinner with him on his evening off, in spite of our political differences. So all is not lost. I wonder how often he is successful. I might add that, as charmingly as I knew how, I excused myself from this little adventure. I surely don't look like an easy lay. Perhaps this enterprising chap varies his approach: the fact that I was reading the political pages of *L'Express* with evident interest might have suggested to him a clue to my conquest.

It is excellent news that you will both be back in England in the spring. I shall welcome you with an appropriate feast. Oliver will make a terrific professor and it will be lovely to have you in London.

It is time for a half bottle of champagne and Albert and Victoria. The luxury of it! So my warmest love to you both and again my best wishes for the New Year, if you can face all the blether there is likely to be about it being nineteen eighty-four.

Yours ever,
Henrietta

*   *   *   *   *

Well, Christmas is a traditionally lonely time, though I seldom remember noticing it before. And since my parents died within a couple of years of each other more than twenty-five years ago, I have spent many, indeed most, Christmases alone. Solitude is a torment which is not threatened in *hell* it selfe. Then, Donne was very ill when he thought that. I am in my usual sanguine health, at least physically. When I had the care of a parish, there were the services on Christmas Morning and then the visits to one or two lonely or recently bereaved people and to the local hospital: but I ususally spent the evenings alone, cooking and eating a solitary but very good dinner, drinking well, listening to music. Sometimes, because I was thought to be a fairly jolly parson, I was invited out. I suppose I miss the contact, though pastoral work for me was always a duty rather than a pleasure. If I am gregarious, it is in seeking the company of like-minded people, given to lively talk and urbane laughter. It means, I suppose that I am something of an intellectual snob. When I am alone and become aware of it, I do not enjoy it. Left to myself, I am too conscious of a certain morbidity. Even so, just as I did in holy orders, I conscientiously observed the seasonal feast again this year in solemn isolation: avocado vinaigrette, two plump poussins with my own redcurrant sauce, a baked potato and mushrooms, a salad, Stilton. A half bottle of Pinot-Chardonnay and a good bottle of Savigny-les-Beaune, 1974. A little brandy. All that for one already overfed man. Self-pitying. For the first time frightened at being alone. But why doe I exercise my Meditation so long upon this, of having plentifull helpe in time of need? Is not my Meditation rather to be enclined another way, to condole, and commiserate their distress who have *none*? How many are sicker (perchance) than I, and laid on their wofull straw at home (if that corner be a home) and have no more of helpe, though they die, than of preferment, though they live? Still true enough of Conservative Britain in 1983, as we celebrate the mass of Christ. . . . Who hast given us thine only-begotten Son to take our nature upon him, and at this time to be born of a pure Virgin: Grant that we being regenerate, and made thy children by adoption and grace, may daily be renewed by the Holy Spirit . . .

So my recitation each Christmas Morning for all those years. And in short I was afraid. *Death* is in an olde man's dore, he appeares, and tels him so, and *death* is at a young man's *backe*, and saies nothing; *Age* is a *sicknesse*, and *Youth* is an *ambush* . . . Always the fear then was of dying. I have lost that and lost too the fear which prompted defiance of the apparent order of the meaningless firmament and lost too the fear of oblivion . . . and they shall all wax old as doth a garment; and as a vesture shalt thou fold them up, and they shall be changed: but thou art the same and thy years shall not fail . . . What comfort indeed! I will not, I must not, I *cannot* die. Can I?

It was easy to be happy as a child in rural wartime. A quiet household with my father's books and my mother's embroidery and flowers. There was a pretty maid who cuddled me whenever I wanted. It was one Christmas I remember being bored with the droning afternoon wireless when I went to look for her. Her name was Rosemary and my mother, through her customary haze of solemn sweetness, had told me that she 'had no one'. I'm sure that this was never the case after she left the service of my parents, whatever may have obtained before. My father was sleeping unobtrusively over a book, probably Sir Walter Scott who was festival reading; my mother was endlessly drawing thread through tautened gauze. The King was giving everyone his message. I wandered away and knocked (as I had been taught to do) at the half-open door of Rosemary's room. She was lying on her bed reading *Girl's Crystal*. She was seventeen perhaps or eighteen. She had taken her afternoon dress off and was wearing a pretty silk petticoat. At the time I thought it was silk. Rosemary was a proper girl. She immediately pulled it down over her thighs. Without permission I climbed onto her bed and snuggled up to her. She put her arm around me and I nestled against her bare shoulder, loving the sweet-sour scent of her body so different from the cologne of my mother. She told me I shouldn't be there, called me 'poor little chap', and went on reading, while I tried to get even closer, touching, without reproach, her soft, thinly clad body. Such was my first voluptuary experience and I was very happy. Occasionally, when she was turning a page, Rosemary ruffled my hair. Eventually she had to get up to serve tea. She explained that I must not make a habit of coming into her room: but that it didn't matter on that day because it was Christmas. Before she dressed, she kneeled down and put her arms around me. Then I was sent away. I remember with tears, even now, that thin, gentle child's kindness to a small boy with a heap of Christmas gifts and no one to cuddle. It was the first time, although of course I did not recognize it, that I experienced sexual excitement, however passive: I went to sleep imagining I was lying next to Rosemary for several nights. I went away to school and the maid left. I don't remember why, but there was no acrimony: I imagine that she found someone who wanted to marry her. I hope she is and has always been contented. After the war we could no longer afford a maid, which may have been as my senses awakened just as well. I recall seeing *La Ronde* when I was about sixteen, when I was untowardly aroused by lost possibilities. What I now recognize as quite ordinary guilt began to oppress me. As I read more, while experiencing little, I was at once sensualist and worshipper, urgent for physical satisfaction and for adoration. National Service allowed me opportunities to gratify experimental lusts, after which I decided to be chaste. Becoming a priest helped – though there were holiday lapses. What an absurd waste of natural vitality! So now here I am pathetically languishing for Isabel Darrow.

> Tes yeux, où rien ne se révèle
> De doux ni d'amer,
> Sont deux bijoux froids ou se mêle
> L'or avec le fer.

What arrant knavish tomfoolery. She is no Jeanne Duval and her eyes are unusually merry and expressive; dark violet eyes. *L'instant de boire* . . .

It's not often that I have the chance of speaking to her alone even in a room full of other people, so Ben Oldfield's small Boxing Night party was a particularly felicitous occasion. Perhaps it was simply that she was escaping from Mendoza and she thinks me, alas, safe. As always, she was the perfect Euphrosyne, buxom, blithe and debonair to a fault – unless buxom is too gross a word. As always we talked in amusing generalities and I trust I disguised my farcical longing under an unfrocked urbanity. Catching sight of myself in Ben Oldfield's mantel mirror, I saw my great beaming ingratiating face, my fifteen-stone bulk reflected and her own tumbling black hair, the straight back, the beautifully moulded *derrière*. As always, she was friendly and funny. I think I, too, made her laugh, although I do not remember what I said. She showed no more favour to anyone else, except perhaps David Kelly, who was there with Christina. This rather surprised me as I had the impression that Oldfield didn't like him.

110

When Kelly's voice was distinguishable, I noticed that Isabel's attention drifted. Not only when talking to me, but to others – for, of course, I was watching her throughout the evening.

Oldfield, who is amiable in spite of the fact that he would like to be cleverer than his natural endowments will allow, seems to know any number of pretty girls, three or four of whom were present – quite apart from Isabel and her sister, whose quietness is almost sinister. There were one or two young men, very civil and convivial of similar Oldfield status, Evan Warrington, and (as always late) Peter and Iris Cameron. Iris arrived in a high-necked black winter coat, trimmed with fur around the collar and hem, looking ravishing, her face flushed and her yellow hair gleaming and silky. Peter looked more like an apprentice demon than ever. When Iris removed the close-fitting coat, she revealed an even closer-fitting dress (light blue – a colour which she must know becomes her because she often wears it). In spite of the season she did not seem to have favoured a brassière. There is much silly, sometimes malicious, gossip about the brother and sister. She is openly concupiscent without being predatory. He is rather more restrained in manner but is said to enjoy a sexually eventful recreation from his academic labours. They live together and show public, tactile affection for each other. As far as I am concerned it would not matter, but I doubt that it is the stuff of gutter headlines. Iris's impact on a room is always interesting. Men's eyes narrow or frown appreciatively while an unmistakable gleam flickers and is hurriedly put out. Women (most of them) tend to straighten their shoulders, touch their hair or make some slight adjustment of posture or dress. Isabel could not care less. She waved and called some greeting across the room. Iris, equally confident, said something mildly ribald. It was interesting to see Christina Kelly also smiling unselfconsciously – until I realized she was looking at Peter Cameron. Of course, I may have been guilty of misinterpretation, but I thought the look that passed between them was strangely intimate and I was surprised.

My conversation, such as it was, with Isabel lasted not much longer. The truth, I fear, is that we have little to say to one another: she has wit and a keen intelligence which she chooses not to use, but it would never counterbalance the leaden cast of my own thought at its most jocose. I must desire her in affable futility. I don't suppose she gives me a second thought. It was a good party. Looking round, I saw that we were all (the ones whom I knew) lonely people. Even Isabel? Perhaps even Isabel, laughing at the side of David Kelly, as Christina put her hand briefly on Peter Cameron's arm . . .

One of Ben Oldfield's friends turned up the old chestnut about the loved old dog, the unknown baby and the fine work of art in a burning building. What to save? He presented it in a way which bypassed traditional argument: the precaution of saving oneself; get the bloody dog out and then work the rest out from there; human life is sacred – it might be the infant Mozart; it is the last unproved cartoon of a Renaissance master. Oldfield's friend reduced the situation to your lovely wife, your adorable old mother and your Rembrandt. Someone asked about the old and faithful black servant. She was told not to be digressive. (I think it was Elaine Darrow.) There was the usual mindless if harmless chatter which attends such foolish games, until Isabel said, 'I'm sure you're all absolutely right, but I'd say: Hey you lot, don't just stand there. Give me a hand with the bloody Rembrandt.' It broke the illusion. Perhaps that is her talent: one of weaving and breaking illusions.

As I walked home I found myself for once not so much drooling about Isabel as relating the facile game to an old existentialist argument. 'It does not matter: the choice of a gratuitous task (or object) or of an absurd object (or task) is better than no choice at all.' That and a last late brandy put me to sleep. I suppose I must have read it somewhere.

And so I woke today with the familiar sense of emptiness. Is it simply a function of understanding that one is alone? In the eyes of Nietzsche I might qualify as modern man: 'stupid, short-sighted, selfish . . . since he no longer holds metaphysical views, he looks upon his short life obsessionally and no longer needs to build lasting institutions over hundreds of years. He wants to take all the fruit from the trees without replanting trees which will need the care of generations but which will offer them shade and shelter.' And it is a just accusation. I am alone. I understand that I am alone and I have ceased to care (in only the broad and meaningful term) about the well-being of others. Occasionally I feel remorse when I listen to the epideictic flights of Roger Ingestre, or the comforting sardonyx of Warrington or even the acid all-round but concerned scepticisms of Peter Cameron; but current events bore me and talk of the future is meaningless. Outside the factor of people suffering, it does not seem to me to matter that an essentially distorted or existentially desperate world should achieve destruction.

I am thought by many to be an unabashed hedonist. Isabel herself, teasing, said it must have been a relief for me to leave the Church so that I could pursue the career of a *bon vivant* without worrying palpitations of conscience. Yet I think it was Aldous Huxley discussing the Greeks who suggested that hedonism is the natural companion of pessimism. I think it is rather a sort of Saint Sulpicerie which recognizes and reacts against the Jansenist who lurks inside me. I cannot find the courage to admit instinctive evil rather than natural goodness, which is perhaps why I pursue futility where nothing matters.

No man is well that understands not, that values not his being well; that hath not a cheerfulnesse, and joy of it; and whosoever hath this *Joy*, hath a desire to communicate, to propagate that, which occasions his happinesse, and his *Joy* to others; for every man loves witnesses of his happinesse . . .

I see her vividly laughing (with Kelly) across the room and I wonder if I were bold enough and she were kind enough whether declared love for her, even at a distance, would purge these pestiducts of accidie. I am a fat bland man of fifty who sets his traps in the midst of dreams.

⋆   ⋆   ⋆   ⋆   ⋆

29 December 1983
I find myself in my usual seasonal fog. I suppose I must have enjoyed Christmas when I was a child, but from early adolescence it has been a considerable bore. Often I have chafed at the social obligations which have prevented me getting down to work. This year the waste of time has been emphasized by the fact that I am not doing any worthwhile work and the gloom of the New Year is given a hideous miasmal light around its edges by endless references to *Nineteen Eighty-Four*. Powerful though I found the novel when I first read it, I have never been inclined to see Orwell as a

visionary any more than as a sick, embittered man damning a future in which he was not to share. On the surface, life in Western Europe, at least, bears little resemblance to existence on Airstrip One. Scratching a little deeper, however, there are disturbing symptoms of a totalitarian death wish all around. In France and England as much as in America. The power of television is terrifying – whether it is the ray that such vapid trash as 'Dallas' seems to beam into so many lives, or the obsessive news coverage of violent events which can only breed violence and enhance its impact. 'New technology' is equally alarming: the instant data available, the speed of informational transactions. We are millimetres away from the telltale telescreen. Only, so far, thank the Lord, the political will to use such tools seems to be lacking. Where Orwell was most certainly right was in his fears about the degeneration of language and the way in which imprecise and muddled speech and writing brought about and are bringing about slovenly habits of thought which will allow in turn for social and political deceit upon a monstrous scale. It has happened before and we are no wiser. I must ask one of my classical friends about the slide of a language from gold to silver, whether it is connected with general decadence in a society as it would seem to be. The English language, as used in public communication, seems to me to be going through an age of lead or some other very base metal.

Unseasonable moping. I suppose in a way that the inevitable dinners and parties shake people like me out of untoward and unconscionable dejection. Not that I would have thought myself at other times of the year to be markedly gloomy. I managed (I hope) to be cheerful at Christina's dinner party last night. No university people. The Wilkins couldn't come and Christina did not talk of inviting the Camerons (either/or). So it was three couples (one the statutory unmarried) from her electronics firm. All very agreeable, suave, festive. I suppose that in the company of businessmen and their wives, splendid in ruffs and plumage, I feel as out of place as Christina does among the people I take for granted. If that. It was very jovial: although I do not fully understand the apparent hostility these people have for academic life. The ivory or Cotswold-stone towers are surely of their imagination. And it is less blood and sand down there than machine oil and silicone grit. I wish them lungs. They are a highly scented lot one can imagine in pink energetic shirtsleeves about the office and popping out for a noggin, half-pints only, at midday. One has a friend who owns a private aeroplane at Weybridge. What they talk of as perks seems to me to be cheating. Christina understands them.

Very different in form and content from Ben Oldfield's little gathering on Boxing Night. A donnish collection – except for Isabel and Iris Cameron. And, of course, Christina who seemed to enjoy it. I know that she likes Iris, however outrageous she chooses to be, but she has become noticeably more distant to Isabel. There is, possibly, gossip about us. Iris may have reported that trivial incident at their party some months ago in a light if unmalicious way to someone disposed to make mischief. It probably looked more erotic than it was. I spent very little time with Isabel, who talked at length with Marcus Ferdinand and flirted generally. During the few minutes we were together, I thought I detected distinct signs of unease in Christina.

If she is really upset by idle talk, it is worrying. Iris, who is a professional in such matters, has on occasions teased me, but I'm sure would not dream of hurting Isabel or me or most of all Christina. Mendoza, who is jealous and malign, flagrantly desiring Isabel for himself, has made several snide shafts. I am more concerned, however, with a passing remark of Roger Ingestre who seldom shows interest in the putative meanderings of senior members of the university with secretaries, undergraduates or casual acquaintances of either sex. After predicting (somewhat gleefully since it would benefit his SDP–Liberal Alliance) a year of bitter industrial dispute, general disruption, an increase in public violence, anarchic protest and dire economic prospects in the face of intractable Thatcher dogmatism, he turned happily to lighter topics. Friendships and seasonable rites. Isabel's name came up somehow. Beautiful girl, said Ingestre, *but* rather high-spirited. You see rather a lot of her, David, don't you? Ingestre's mild frown. He still frets, I think, about what he sees as his part in the untoward death of one of his women pupils, which accounts for his deliberate show of unconcern about whatever is going on around him. The implication of his casual remark was therefore of some small impact. I made no comment. Perhaps I should explain to Christina how innocent the friendship is, though that would not necessarily dispel her doubts or fears, such as they might be.

It would be foolish and dishonest to pretend that I am not attracted by Isabel – and not just physically. I am also intensely possessive of Christina whom I love in a way that I could not love laughing Isabel. When have we ever had a serious conversation?

I watched Christina with Peter Cameron in animated conversation, detecting in myself the first ratsfoot scrabbling of jealousy: her frequent trips away from home; they were coincidentally in America at the same time. Now smiling at each other. His hand briefly on her shoulder. The turn of her head as they parted company, wistfully assured. Their eyes meeting. I was once bitterly jealous soon after we were married, but she reassured me about the man I suspected, a very clever politician sometime fellow of All Souls. And then there was no doubt on either side, except for one lapse when I noticed a mark on her neck which might have been a love bite and a bruise upon her thigh which I had not made. It was at the time when someone had recently told me about the disastrous holiday of a man who, suspecting his wife of infidelity, had noticed two heavy fingerprint bruises in the mesial cleft where she was presumably unaware of them. He did not challenge her and she could not understand his callous indifference. I did not ask any questions of Christina at that time and was soon convinced that it was a bout of madness. It might have been better if I had profited more from the opportunities of my coming (allegedly) to maturity in the sixties. I did not and I have not been unfaithful to Christina. Would it matter if she had been having or was in the process of having an affair? I recall Bloom reflecting on the supposed adulteries of Molly, considering reactions of 'envy, jealousy, abnegation, equanimity'. And excusing his own complaisance on the grounds of 'the futility of triumph, of protest, of vindication; the inanity of extolled virtue; the lethargy of nescient matter; the apathy of the stars.'

Of course I have desired women other than Christina, as I desire Isabel. For a year or so I was tempted by Henrietta Ball in silk summer dresses to the extent of imagining her at various stages of erotic fervour, but (at that time) her cool indifference was the best conceivable deterrent. Nothing in excess. Know thyself. Remember that you are a very fallible human and not a god answerable only to the vindictive energies of other gods. All thinking must be safe thinking. Hubris is protean and knows a host of insidious forms.

I wonder at the harm and misery we volitionally inflict and whether this is part of Sartre's notion of man aspiring to be God: an instant conviction of power felt in deciding whether to cause or spare pain. Very few animals kill or maim for pleasure. And Nietzsche, whom Freud is said to have admired for the extent of his self-knowledge, wrote: ' "I have done that," says my memory. "I could not have done that," says my pride, and remains inexorable. My memory gives in.'

I opted for philosophy because I thought I must become rational. Kindly, altruistic: but rational. Good at maths, I was never troubled by the technical analytical problems. Not unduly. So I made the mistake of turning to moral philosophy and dabbling in old-fashioned metaphysics. The Squeers interpretation I partly remembered on that very happy holiday with Christina runs: ' "Measles, rheumatics, hooping cough, fevers, agers and lumbagers," said Mr Squeers, "is all philosophy together; that's what it is. The heavenly bodies is philosophy, and the earthly bodies is philosophy; and if there's a screw loose in a heavenly body, that's philosophy; and if there's a screw loose in a earthly body, that's philosophy too; or it may be that sometimes there's a little metaphysics in it, but that's not often. Philosophy's the chap for me. If a parent asks a question in the classical, commercial, or mathematical line, says I gravely, 'Why, sir, are you in the first place a philosopher?' 'No, Mr Squeers,' he say, 'I an't.' 'Then sir,' says I, 'I am sorry for you for I shan't be able to explain it.' Naturally the parent goes away and wishes he was a philosopher, and equally naturally thinks I'm one." '

In my bleaker moments, it is how I see myself and my kind. At the same time I take some comfort from the wise and good Miss Murdoch: 'The role of philosophy might be said to extend and deepen the self-awareness of mankind. Such a definition will cover both analysis and metaphysics. What the psychoanalyst does for the particular consciousness of the individual, the metaphysician does for the intellectual consciousness of the group he is addressing, and through

117

them perhaps for the consciousness of the epoch. He presents a conceptual framework which is an aid to understanding. The answer to those who wish to eliminate metaphysics is the "moral" answer: that it is proper for intellectual groups to make this particular sort of effort at self-comprehension. That the influence of such attempts, for good or evil, is not limited to the groups concerned is evident from the history of philosophy.'

So let that, at least, be a cheering thought for 1984.

★   ★   ★   ★   ★

In the opinion of her father and sister Isabel and her mother were quite evidently mad to plan a shopping trip to London on New Year's Eve, particularly as it fell upon a Saturday. They were, nevertheless, enjoying themselves. Temperamentally similar, although Eve was much cooler in manner than Isabel, they liked bustle and lights and lots of people, just as Charles Darrow and Elaine hated crowds and glare and the implied rapacity engendered by sales. They had bought some very pretty things and were now having a leisurely lunch at a favourite Italian restaurant in Romilly Street.

'I don't think,' Eve said, 'that I should have connived in those saucy scarlet knickers you bought for Elaine. She might be very cross.'

'Not a bit,' said Isabel. 'One of these days Elaine is going to melt spectacularly and the scarlet panties will be a terrific visual aid.'

'Possibly. Sometimes I'm not sure whether I wish Elaine was more like you. Or that you were more like Elaine.'

'Well, you bought all sort of frou-frous yourself, I noticed.'

'It's not polite to take an interest in the sex life of your parents.'

'I agree. One good turn deserves another.'

'You might have found a more elegant way of putting it. At the same time I've never had to tax you with being too serious.'

'You don't fuss Elaine either. Nor does Daddy. That's why we're such good girls. Anyway, she's the mysterious, quiet type that men find irresistible.'

118

'You don't do so badly. When I was your age everything seems to have been much more complicated.'

'Ah well – I've been careful not to fall in love.'

'That's what I mean. When I was twenty-four I'd been desperately in love five times. On two occasions with men far older who fortunately thought me an idiot. Then I met your lovely father.'

'And the consequence is you're still buying frothy undies. I hope I'm as lucky.'

'You're going to be at lunch tomorrow, aren't you? I've asked Ben Oldfield.'

'Mamma! Ben and I are the emotional equivalent of Noddy and Big Ears or John and Janet or Cinderella and Buttons. I wish people wouldn't keep making up stories. Who else is coming?'

'Francesca Oricellari, which is nice. She's on her way to New York and had to cut short her holiday in Venice. She sounded quite relieved. Marcus Ferdinand, because I think he is lonely and won't admit it. Sir Everard Carnaby and his wife . . .'

'Who!'

'Sit still and eat your gruel, child. He's someone very important in the world of grants who was once at the college.'

'Ah!'

'Walter and Lucia Harrington.'

'Ugh!'

'Would you like a bi-sodol, or would you prefer to go on grunting like a disenchanted warthog at the jungle ball?'

'Go on.'

'You'll like the others: Tom and Samantha Wilkins and Evan Warrington.'

'Is Elaine coming?'

'No. Elaine is going to Greenham Common with some friends of hers on some entirely arcane mission. Did you know that Elaine is working on the theory that all governments should have a proportion (thirty-three per cent at the last count) of young mothers in government? No heads of state should be under forty or over fifty. And she has alarmed your father by citing a passage from Molly Bloom's soliloquy to support her argument.'

'Well, Elaine *is* terribly well read.'

'I should have hung you up on the drying rack when you were two.'

'We don't have a drying rack.'

'We did when you were two.'

'Who's the odd woman?'

'What odd woman?'

'God knows we know enough odd women. I mean to balance Warrington. I thought that would be Elaine.'

'Oh dear. I forgot about that. Are you suggesting that Warrington fancies Elaine?'

'Mamma! I'd put strychnine in *her* gruel. No, of course not. He has that headmistress with the hips.'

'Yes. I've heard your father annotate.'

'In a scholarly way, naturally.'

'How else? So I'm one woman short. We'll use the round table and some lucky male shall sit between us. I had thought of asking the Kellys, but Christina wouldn't much like Sir Everard Carnaby or Walter Harrington, would she?'

'I've no idea. She seems to run her own professional life without much trouble. According to David.'

'Oh? Indeed?'

'And she was getting on tremendously with Peter Cameron the other evening . . .'

'At Ben Oldfield's, of course. I wish I could like that man. Cameron, I mean. I know damn well that I should never like his sister.'

'She's honest . . .'

'Yes. 'Tis pity. And so on. You must see quite a lot of David Kelly.'

'Only in the run of our professional lives. You must have worked with a lot of leading men.'

'I wish I could describe them all. Are you going to have cheese before pudding? We've still got quite a lot of wine.'

And as she had cued her, Eve spun delightful fantasies about Jerome and Crispin and the old provincial editor (53) Caspar, and the gentle theatrical buff (only 47) Patrick. Isabel liked her mother but she resented the intrusion into her own life, however discreet. She despised the account of infatuations that had never taken place. What did it matter to her how many times her mother had been fucked? What did matter was that she and David Kelly were thought to be fucking, distressfully, disdainfully, harmfully, meaninglessly: *when they were not.*

Her mother talked expertly. Intelligence, natural aptitude and professional training had equipped her well for situations even with an alert daughter. In a way, Isabel thought, Elaine (much cleverer) would be easier to handle. Daddy could help. Isabel was neither actress nor academic: she did not care. She was herself. But she wasn't going to spoil the day out.

At the same time, as her mother talked with ease and confidence, while Isabel smiled and nodded, she felt angry. Since that first insignificant little kiss with David Kelly at the Cameron party, when she had been a little drunk, the sentimental weight of their close relationship had been like an allergic headache. Not there most of the time and then nagging behind the eyes in moments of repose. Elaine's sharp asides, Mendoza's innuendoes, the *froideur* of Henrietta Ball (who was probably jealous), the anxiety of dear old Ben Oldfield expressed with typically clumsy affection. And now, in a characteristically unconcerned charade, Eve herself. Isabel did not worry about Christina who, she was sure, would make her own arrangements. Christina was pretty, calculatingly sexy and very shrewd. Isabel had grown up among clever people and understood how easily they could be fooled into believing how uneasy or vulnerable someone apparently less bright could be. She was vaguely disappointed that her mother, who had always personified a cool reason (or rationality) that so many others claimed to control and did not, should lapse. Isabel loved her father, liked her sister and admired her mother. She had never cared whether she was intelligent or not. It did not matter. Any more than the fact that people said she was 'beautiful'. She was Isabel. She had fucked, she had even 'made love', but she had never loved properly. Least of all with David Kelly. What nonsense people made of their own lives. But what pernicious nonsense they made of the lives of others. It was almost tempting to play up to their suspicions. Isabel doubted that David Kelly had a sufficiently developed sense of humour.

' . . . a very attractive man,' Eve said.

'I suppose so,' said Isabel, having no idea who was in question.

'You don't think so?'

'Well, yes. I think the Senior Tutor's all right.'

'Evan Warrington?'

'Yes. He talks to you as if he assumes you are there. And if you can't pick him up, too bad.'

'You know the headmistress you were talking about?'

'With the hips.'

'And what we called, in my day, pretty good tits . . .'

'Mamma!'

'All right, little lady. Did you know that she was a close friend of Mathieson Joyce?'

'Quentin's father.'

'Yes. I talked to her for a while after he was killed. We both did. Charles and I. She was very deeply . . . I don't know the word . . . I suppose the one that fits is an old cliché people no longer use: she was cut up. Torn apart.'

'Are you saying that . . .'

'It happens. Young men fall in love with quite elderly ladies. It isn't necessarily reciprocal. But if things happen to go wrong – things entirely beyond control – it can upset your life.'

'Has it happened to you?'

'Yes. Fortunately, the boy concerned was not shot by accident in a street in Paris, so there was no grief, only the understanding that passes for peace in a woman who knows that a good marriage is a sacrament. And you know that Charles and I are neither of us religious.'

'Can we have brandy with our coffee?'

'Of course.'

'What are you telling me?'

'Simply that people invent romances for themselves and others. And one person's romance is another one's scandal and someone else's misery.'

'What David Kelly calls "nothing in excess".'

'I'm pleased to hear it. Two black coffees with cognac, please. That was delicious. What are we going to do this afternoon?'

Isabel looked at her delightful mother, marvellously composed, and thought that (apart from the saltimbocca) she had taken in enough ham to fill a prayerbook.

*   *   *   *   *

'Francesca! How delightful,' said Ben Oldfield. 'I thought you were in Venice. You've met Marcus Ferdinand, haven't you?'

'A comparatively recent pleasure on my part,' said Marcus Ferdinand. 'But one which has much enhanced my declining years.'

'I'm not supposed to be here,' said Francesca Oricellari. 'At all. But something came up in New York with a millionaire's widow which I could not afford to turn down. So I am stopping over. All the people I know in London are somewhere else, so I called Eve and she invited me for 1984.'

'I shall raise my glass willingly to that. Won't you, Ben?'

'I shall. Long may your London friends be somewhere else in this portentous year or any other.'

'Thank you. This is nice. What is it?'

'Berry and Rudd Number Three. Charles is not bigoted about most things, but sherry is one of them.'

'As opposed to Marcus, Francesca, who is bigoted about everything that happened after Laker took nineteen wickets and Fred Astaire stopped dancing.'

'Who is Laker? Stop. I know. Roger Ingestre talks about him. He was a very cunning bowler. A Machiavelli of cricket.'

'Oh, I wouldn't go *that* far, would you, Ben?'

'I've always had my doubts about Ingestre. I think he mixes up cricket and history to the detriment of both. Viewed dispassionately, that is.'

'Are you still writing aphorisms, Ben?'

'Aphorisms? What is this?'

'Didn't you know, Marcus? Ben is making a book of aphorisms. About myths.'

'Much as I have always admired him, Ben is irrepressibly solemn. Why don't you write poems, Ben?'

'That is what I say too.'

'And why don't you both stop taking the piss out of someone essentially harmless. Happy New Year. Long may you both avoid Room One-O-One.'

'Who is the fat man with the wig?'

'Hush. Or you will be spirited there in a trice. Tell her, Ben.'

'That is Sir Everard Carnaby, a senior civil servant in the Department of Education and Science who was once a member of Charles's college. We are expected to be nice to him.'

'I'm always nice.'

'Well, without being, I hope, untowardly sexist, it's not difficult for you. Ben has much more trouble. And I am notoriously fat and ponderous. Although slimmer than Sir Everard. The lady in the perruque is Lady Everard, as you might put it. Equally important and senior: rather less civil, if that were possible.'

'Who is the man with Isabel?'

'That's Walter Harrington who is about to be Vice-Chancellor of the university and brings Ben's old tutor, Evan Warrington, out in a severe allergic rash.'

'Why so?'

'People mix them up. Walter Harrington is a Thatcher Conservative, if not a Powellist. Evan is a Social Democrat of some animus. Furthermore, he is better looking.'

'I was about to say. I don't think I would be confused.'

'And some people, Marcus, think they were both invented by Meredith.'

'Who is Meredith?'

'Ben is merely being confusing. Charming Victorian man, like Clough and so many others, born out of his time. Very good and drastically underrated. I think you should know, Francesca, that Ben although solemn to a degree is not very serious. He has an elfin streak. Imagine Benedict in *A Midsummer Night's Dream*.'

'All right. If you want. Imagine Titania in a garden of Messina.'

'You're a lucky man, Ben.'

'What? Sorry . . . I wasn't listening.'

'Isn't it always the way. Titania wafts through the wild thyme and nodding violets and Bully Oldfield wasn't listening.'

'What are you going on about, Marcus?'

' "Going on about!" This from someone preparing a thesis on Wallace Stevens.'

'I was looking at Samantha Wilkins.'

'The best cook in Oxford. You are excused.'

'She is also worth looking at. I'd like to have long blonde hair.'

124

'You too are excused, Francesca. In my young day, Ben, spirited young men went in search of more sherry.'

'Yes. Of course. I suppose I have a more suitable figure for the press.'

'Oldfield on page three, at last . . . He's what you call "nice", isn't he?'

'He's what I call innocent. Naturally.'

'Is Isabel?'

'In a way. But more childish. Is Ben good?'

'Not very. Not many people are. He's kind, though, which matters quite as much.'

'And you are fond of Isabel?'

'Why should you think that?'

'You asked. I answered. You looked as if I had thrown my drink at you.'

'Spreading ageing wings, perhaps. Ben's found a decanter.'

'I'd like to know you better. Do you love her?'

'I'm much too old for such indulgences. And too fat. If I cherish fantasies, they would be for Iris Cameron.'

'I will pray for you in that case. Next time I get around to it.'

'Ah Ben, you found some sherry. Do you have fantasies about Iris Cameron?'

'I suppose I do, now that you mention it.'

'There you are, Francesca. Incapable of deception. That is innocence.'

'Any fantasies I have about Iris are not remotely innocent . . . What's so funny?'

'Quite honestly, I don't know. Nor perhaps does Francesca. Time for all of us to talk to Samantha Wilkins.'

'Because she is a good cook?'

'Not entirely, my dear. She was once a psychologist in the Wrens and gave it all up to marry Tom.'

'He looks happy.'

'Precisely.'

'Odd when you think about it: Oxford wives. Samantha and Eve and Christina Kelly. Quite remarkable the difference.'

'Very profound, Ben.'

'What about mistresses? Not, of course, that I qualify.'

'The supposition would be less than gallant.'

'The trouble with Marcus is that he always interrupts a fluent train of thought.'

'Nonsense, dear fellow. *You* interrupt. *I* interpolate.'

'You understand that he was in his Heraclean infancy a philosopher before he learned to strangle serpents. I think it's high time they were all nationalized. Like most service industries, they operate at a loss . . .'

'Nice work if you can get it. I'd much rather have been Bradman or Fred Astaire. What about you, Francesca?'

'I've never thought about it. I think I'd like to have been someone sexy and wicked. Always excluding Iris Cameron.'

'Poor misjudged woman. I'm sure Ben agrees.'

'I think she's fun.'

'There you have it. What horrors can there be in a woman whom Ben thinks is fun.'

'Has Ben told you about his theory of parallax in literature?'

'I'm sure that Ben has long been concerned with the transit of Venus, one way or another.'

'It's all nonsense, in fact, Marcus. Henrietta Ball pointed out that Joyce had worked it all out ages ago.'

'Burke had a word for people like Henrietta: if I remember accurately, "Nothing can be more hard than the heart of a thoroughbred metaphysician." '

'You're only persuading him to write his bloody aphorisms. I think he should write stories. He's always making things up.'

'Pour us more sherry, Ben. I detect from Eve's eyebrows that she is about to collect us. Time for a quick swallow as T. S. Eliot must have eclectically had it before the days of floppy discs. Ah . . . Eve, you've been missing us. Samantha! I want to talk to you about banana and onions with a light cheese sauce and good gammon . . .'

'Ben . . . is that a rather unhappy man?'

'Marcus? I shouldn't think so. He fancies Isabel a bit. But it's all under control. He was a priest, you know. And he chucked all that in without much distress. So . . . No!'

'And do you "fancy" Isabel?'

'Isabel? Well, she's very pretty and so on. But, quite honestly, Francesca, lovely as she is, she's a little bit thick.'

*   *   *   *   *

OLDFIELD SETS OUT FOR ITHACA

The syllogism of Adam. According to Father Arnall in Joyce's *A Portrait of the Artist*, Adam did not have the moral courage to resist Eve. According to Milton in *Paradise Lost*, Adam ate the apple out of love for Eve so that she should not alone be doomed although he knew that he was damning himself and mankind. The syllogism: self-sacrifice demands a lack of moral courage.

Marcus Ferdinand says this is less a syllogism than an enthymeme where the premises are likely rather than demonstrable.

Ferdinand can be a right pain in the arse.

I admitted that the logic of my proposition was nonsense. Ferdinand agreed. 'Of course, it is nonsense: but how much utterly flawed logic offers us, if we are lucky, a glimmer of truth.' If I am in a position to be conducted into the realm of the shades, I shall choose Ferdinand as my psychopomp. Psychopompous is a good word to describe Ferdinand. His gloom, when it shows, is transcendental. So he would have instinctual sympathy with the natural gloom of the domain of Hades and would be able to find his way about. Useful. I'd much rather chat to Odysseus or Machiavelli than have to watch Sisyphus or Ixion.

Ferdinand would not discuss Catholic and Protestant attitudes to the Fall. He insists that Milton, for all his faults, was a humanist of much more practical use than visionaries like Dante. Furthermore he believes that 'Original Good' preceded original sin – as suggested by the generosity of Adam. And yet, Francesca is right: under the plump affability the mind is bleak.

Awareness of Evil is necessary to us.

> The death of Satan was a tragedy
> For the imagination . . .

The Reason for Bad News is partly to compensate for this great imaginative lapse, partly to remind man that he is a poor forked animal who is more or less entirely defenceless.

The Reason for Bad News is that it reminds us of the possibility of a God who is retributive, indifferent or even hostile. In one light it is a validation of mortality implied in the Incarnation. In another it is the random justice of Zeus.

Bad News means we must acknowledge the quotidian hostility of nature as manifest in floods, tornadoes, volcanic eruptions, tidal waves and drought. Also wicked or perverted tendencies in people (whether on the scale of some massive atrocity or some act of private depravity). Also sudden disasters which befall innocent individuals. Bad News is the fanaticism that destroys lives in an act of terrorism and which might, conceivably, destroy civilization itself in nuclear suicide.

Bad News is testimony to provable (as opposed to supernatural) fear, whether actual or potential. Myth has always been the last system of defence against fear whether specific or undefinable.

Myth is the only defence against death – that is: no longer being. I should dearly like to believe in Elysium, but the sad shades of the kingdom of Hades and the tormented spirits of the Inferno seem to me at the age of thirty to be preferred to an everlasting sleep in which the body of Ben Oldfield, such as it is, will surely rot.

Even now I am making or borrowing insignificant private myths for myself, imagining myself conducted into a dream kingdom out of this lotus-eating land of dreaming. (It still seems to me that the manufactories of dreams are the only ones we staff adequately. Perhaps the apt word is overman.)

. . . But however unimportant the stories we make up to placate or justify ourselves, if they cause pain and do harm, we should try to break ourselves of the habit. Is it possible for any of us not to (in one way or another) make up stories, any more than it is possible not to dream? What concerns me immediately is my concern that Isabel is having an affair with Kelly whom I have suspected in the past of bouts of reasonably remorseless lechery on the quietly shady side of the street. Get your gown and get your cap/Leave your morals on the doorstep/But still keep discreet/etcetera. Now what bothers me is not that Isabel should be having an affair. It would be very odd if such a pretty girl did not. But I am fond of her and I wish it was not Kelly who, I am certain, will eventually discard her. Affairs do not interest me: but I am sensitive to the breaking of lasting relationships – perhaps from early experience. Other people are inventing rumours which I should normally ignore. What troubles me is I find myself anxious to believe them, or at least to acquiesce in belief, because I have suddenly discovered Christina. I've known Isabel long and well enough to ask mildly what exactly is going on. She would laugh. No harm done. I have not asked.

Simply because a little while ago, on a Saturday morning, I saw Christina at the launderette where I take my stuff that doesn't need ironing. I didn't expect to see her – wife of a well-set don and successful in her own right – looking relaxed and singing to herself as she loaded the machine. For the first time I saw how very attractive she is. Quite different from the rather tense woman one meets at parties or college functions or whatever. She looked happy, light-hearted and touchingly innocent. She did not see me and it seemed an inappropriate moment (carrying my off-licence bag crammed with underpants and socks and thermal vests) to descend upon her like a mountain lion. I thought, though, that I was seeing someone I didn't know and had never seen for what she really was. I wanted to know her. So I invited them both for Boxing Night. They accepted: to my surprise. Presumably they had nothing better to do – but if they had turned it down, I should have thought of something: though of a peaceful turn of mind, we Oldfields of Laramie are a resentless lot. Now I find myself almost wishing that this delightful and carefree woman is being betrayed. I am no Mendoza. I am not looking for suave opportunity. None of your slick sonatas for me, ephebe. (Come to think of it that evokes a vexing memory. Henrietta across Jesus hall with Schumann and the steeped atmosphere of mediocre cooking. How could I?) And yet I am concocting a little tale where violet-eyed Isabel is being borne across the brown-ale Cherwell by the foxy and cunning Kelly so that rosy-fingered Christina will, whitely diaphanous, play ball in my court. Enough: I shall become inflamed.

She is lovely, in fact. On Boxing Night she was relaxed and as I, unobserved, saw her happy: at the launderette. Christina gives little away, but there are glancing lights in her eyes. She was affectionate to me. Otherwise she talked to Peter Cameron and Mendoza mainly, without, I think, the same immediate softness and warmth. I watched for Isabel and Kelly, who said very little to one another. She spent much of the time with Ferdinand, who is hardly the Errol Flynn of Bardwell Road, even in his top boots. I wonder what they found to talk about. Iris was, as she often is, the centrepiece of attention. She would never be as obvious as to wear a see-through garment, but her clinging light blue dress and black, seamed stockings worked on the imagination: the colour and pattern of her knickers and suspenderbelt – if she was wearing the former at all, for example. Isabel said something once about the male obsession (in fiction and elsewhere) with female underclothes. I must admit I share it. Why not (she asked with wide violet eyes) descriptions of the male undressing or undressed. I see in my inward eye the contents of my carrier-bag – thermal vest, Marks and Spencer's Y-fronts, tired socks. Not quite the same. But I wonder how many of us – the men, of course – in that room had not, at one time or another, stripped Iris Cameron layer by layer; the more layers the merrier the eventual lay.

Ah well! The Camerons themselves are a rich vein of local myth, by comparison with which my own fabrication of Isabel and Kelly, Christina and me, is a mere folktale. Why are so many different people (including me) titilated by the idea of brother-sister incest? So he is satyrnine and she is – what would be the word – aphrodine? Neither is right . . .

In this way trivialities of gossip, the observation of others, the moral evaluation of conduct affects our conception of ourself – or in the jargon of the day 'our image'. Sartre's examples in the essay include the peeping tom who realizes he is being watched or the man walking in the park whose demeanour is affected by the appearance of someone else, who until then was also alone.

It is a commonplace. If I am behaving in a lackadaisical or stupid way, I am naturally chastened. I behave as Ben Oldfield only to myself. To others I respond to their image of me, as I apprehend it. And I adjust that image variously. If Christina had been aware of me at the launderette, she would not have been singing to herself in such a carefree manner. Of course, there were lots of other observers, but they didn't matter. It is those who recognize us individually who do; or else those strangers who catch us in some guilty or innocently foolish act.

So Iris may act and display herself in the way she does partly because it is expected of her and partly because she wishes to show defiance and contempt for such expectations. Iris is determined to assert herself as an individual (in more or less the Sartrean mould – although she would dismiss such an intellectual assault with a bump of the hip). As, in a rather different way, is Isabel.

Observation is determined by moral certitude or prejudice or else by unabashed (though often unconfessed) self-interest. Most of the time I am unconcerned about the activities of those around me: sometimes I am tangentially involved. My attitude influences my judgement.

The few novelists I know tell me that they are endlessly interested in the activities of strangers at café tables, in railway compartments, across the piazza or along the avenue who do not realize that they are being observed. With very few exceptions I believe this to be so. Unlike poets, novelists are not very interested in themselves. Warrington's teacher, Jack Maddox, once said to us: 'A poem is just an erection, while a novel is almost a fuck.'

. . . So be it. Ferdinand stayed late on Boxing Night. Pretty drunk, rather sad, but never maudlin. He was interested in dissimulation rather than distorted judgement: although evidently both circumstances are related. I wasn't exactly sober. Discoursing on the protean nature of the life we all seem to accept, Ferdinand suggested that we were all too clever – too clever at dissimulating. There is a difference he suggested between being protean: changing shape and form to protect arcane knowledge, almost (he said) an epistemological duty, and being deliberately devious in the intention of protecting oneself or one's interests. Athene commended Odysseus for being such a sly bastard. Best liar she'd ever met. Addicted to deceit and lying words. Ferdinand recalled his reply to her rebuke for not having recognized her: 'What mortal, goddess, can recognize you when you take on so many forms, assume so many personae?' And Athene is the patron goddess of wisdom (said Ferdinand) and wisdom is the commodity that our kind and this university claim to trade in. In my cups, I suggested Henrietta Ball as Athene and Kelly as Odysseus. Ferdinand, further in his, proposed Isabel and Kelly as Pyramus and Thisbe (which is when traced back quite a tragic little story). Ferdinand was to be Moon, Mendoza the Lion and myself Wall. It all seemed very funny at the time . . .

Back to Bad News.

1984. Hardly surprising that Orwell is everywhere, before and after the midnight doom-strike of Big Ben. Pundits predict and critics carp. Optimists observe that it's turned out nice again; pessimists probe the latest consignment of smoking entrails. And they are always available. Surely the grim myth makes one final and desperate point: that an individual may be so degraded as to wish alternative harm and suffering upon someone cherished. I hope it is not so. I believe it is not so. I have yet to prove it and hope that it will not fall to me to do so.

On the first of the month of January Cruise missiles (operational) were in position at the Greenham Common base. In El Salvador guerrillas mounted a new offensive. Christians and Druse and Shi'ites and Palestinians shot at each other. The Middle East smouldered out of its sullen crater of mindless hate. Religious fanatics simmered just off the boil. The Pope informed the world that nuclear tension and hunger were its two major problems.

It is true that the nuclear cloud is always billowing somewhere to the north and east of the playing arena, but the myth is not one we wish to take on individually. Let the doom programmes on television (fact or fiction) frighten us. We can always switch off and fiddle with our immediate fantasies or find something personal to worry about.

And yet the very notion of tragedy (a word much misused) is out of date. Whether it is in Spengler's 'illogical blind accident of the moment' or the life which 'matures inwardly towards a catastrophe', that arrogance which defies the gods – or persists against religious, perhaps specifically Christian, submission – no longer obtains. It is no longer possible to go against the gods or God: there is only the State or the Party or the System. Certainly there are heroes, very brave and enduring people. But they are not *tragic* heroes. For my own part, I doubt that Antigone was a tragic heroine, while Phaedra and Pasiphae and perhaps even Lady Macbeth were.

We are stuck with disaster. Particular or general it does not ennoble us. We may share or sympathize with the suffering

132

of another (fact or fiction) but we may no longer spiritually profit from its defiance of uncontrollable forces; we may no longer be encouraged by such examples. Tragedy is as dead as God. There is only catastrophe on whatever scale: the cot death, the crashing car; the flooded valley; the terrorist assault; the big and complete bang.

Eliot no doubt held the prayerbook at the beheading of the poor beast. Joyce and Stevens were away and somewhere else making up rigmaroles to enchant the elusive beauty whom they would, in their different ways, call reality.

Reality is not tragic. It is a matter of grief, compassion, fear. At best, it is material for comedy.

One of those bloody European sages (I forget whom, but I'll look him up) said the essential problem for European writers was how to come to terms with Marxism. That too is out of date. Marxism is as impotent as Christianity. The forces that hold sway, secular or religious, are fanatic and anarchic. Unpredictable and beyond control. Trotsky could write: 'It is not enough to create a programme, it is necessary that the working class accept it.' The US marine formula was and probably still is: 'You can't win over their hearts and minds until you have them by the balls.' And the terrorists (or partisans) learned the lesson.

But secular or religious martyrdom is calculated, however much inspired, and works to a purpose. The victim may be great or good, may or may not have some vicious mole of nature wherein he is not guilty: but he is not a tragic hero in that he is not daring the universe to destroy him. Nevertheless, we need public myths and public heroes: so we are insatiable in our desire to find martyrs. Those who are against the system.

Kierkegaard's knight of faith, he said, looked like a tax collector. Yes: and he votes for the SDP-Liberal Alliance. Today's knight of faith is trying to escape myth and martyrs in the name of decent common sense. And there I am making a myth out of the most commonplace man as he steals into the polling booth on his way to catch his morning bus or train.

Ah well . . . 'Still I think out of the dreary sameness of existence, a measure of dramatic life may be drawn. Even the most commonplace, the deadest among the living, may play a part in the great drama . . . Life we must accept as we see it before our eyes, men and women as we meet them in the real world, not as we apprehend them in the world of faery. The great human comedy in which each has a share, gives limitless scope to the true artist, today as yesterday and as in years gone.' James Joyce. Who else?

There are cadences in the looks or gestures of some pretty women, not necessarily young, not evidently sensual, which remain in the head like a snatch of some tune, perhaps trivial. A delightful melody remains for a while as might a few bars from some pleasing but inconsequential song played on the barber's transistor radio or heard through someone's open window on a summer morning. The music pleases as the woman's smile, or blush, or unexpected movement, might. For a day or so the pleasant memory remains. But then: that same woman seen again – a second and third time, perhaps more often, and the characteristic look or movement is no longer a trite, delightful phrase of music. It becomes a beautiful theme which stays with you in moments of repose. And it is no longer a trivial catch. And very soon it may cease to be pleasing.

. . . I should desist from passing fancies:

The doll was called Christina
Her under-wear was lace
She smiled when you dressed her
And when you then undressed her
She kept a smiling face.

Until the day she tumbled
And broke herself in two
And her legs and arms were hollow
And her yellow head was hollow
Behind her eyes of blue.

. . . .

He went to bed with a lady
Somewhere seen before,
He heard the name Christina
And suddenly saw Christina
Dead on the nursery floor.

I frighten myself. When I think of the mischievous havoc I can invent out of other people's lives (and I do not believe myself to be malevolent), it occurs to me that professional fiction is a sort of blood sport. It is, after all, a matter of playing games with the misery or uncertainty of others. Seldom with their happiness. The unobserved observer, the maker of fictions, complacent in his corner toying with events which cannot touch *him*. Out of innate reserves of conceit, the poet may deal in his own lamentable state; but the novelist deals very calmly in despair and delight which are not immediately his own – even when his private despair is comprehended in his material. I am inclined still to challenge Wayne Booth's assertion that 'though the author can to some extent choose his disguises, he can never choose to disappear.' But I am not as sure as I once was. If the author is not revealed as he really is, readers will make fictions of him. That is, of course, if they are that bothered.

Perhaps I should do better to emulate Mendoza's erotic fabling rather than to try to make sense (which is to say fables) out of what I observe.

Let the old Muse loosen her stays
Or give me a new Muse with stockings and suspenders.

Ah Christina . . . I've lost my thread again. O Lord, will I ever make an aphorist. Perhaps I should chuck all this into the bin and concentrate on my proper work. And my bloody teaching. Term starts on the 15th.

the MA gown
Alphas and Betas, central heating, floor polish . . .

Forsooth! I think I'm a bit pissed. Aaah, Christina!

*　　*　　*　　*　　*

Hello. The show, as you will already know, is 'Somewhere Under the Rainbow' and my name is Giles Mendoza. Good to be back with you. '*Under* the Rainbow' you ask, as we fully intended you should. Why? Well, we're a programme about the arts, which we spell with a small 'a'. And some of us feel – no doubt many of you who haven't already turned at this hour to 'Rape in Reno' or 'Litter in Lambeth' may feel the same – that the arts (with a small 'a') have been *over* the rainbow for too long. Now: this doesn't mean we intend to belittle or demean the fine work and very hard work done by all the artists who will talk to us and appear on your screens. But we intend to ask questions. Why another programme on the arts? Who the hell cares? Why not have snooker or darts? So, if you want to, turn over now. All I promise is that we are taking nothing for granted: we'll bring you something respectfully disrespectful; we'll try to relate what artists are thinking and doing to the political and social scene: we'll get about the world and see how other artists manage in regimes more hostile than our own. And they *do* exist! And there will be the occasional squib under the administrative, pompous and pretentious backside. I shan't carry on like this at the beginning of every programme. Unless there's a good reason. And there are something like eleven people who will make sure I don't find one . . .

Keep it going. Four out of the eleven want the show to succeed and me to flop. Two want the whole thing to collapse like the temple of Dagon. And the other five are neutral, but hope we'll make it. The girl I want is up in the gallery. Having brought her bloody sister. Ah well.

. . . So here we are. Nineteen eighty-four, in case you hadn't been made aware of it. Eight days into an apocalyptic time. And here we all are. Pritchard Lofthouse is not . . .

Film of one of the tormented paintings with everything coming apart. Black and white. Speed up. Montage of colour. Decaying surfaces breaking up from jagged fragments to glutinous splotches of blood and flesh and torn sinew out of which emerges the image of Lofthouse in his environment, looking like a transfixed toad in a cloth cap.

. . . He lives on the island of Eriskay where, alone, he pursues a ferocious, terrified vision . . .

Lugubrious twit now wandering in convenient mist. Couldn't

stand him. Thank God for helicopters. Ah the profile glooming at the gannets on the spiked headland. Vision in voiceover. Cutting to painting of dead and half-devoured creature on cold beach shimmering into fragments. Technically very adroit, of course. Now he speaketh. *I choose to live here because there is at least a sort of peace.* You can hardly credit it. A gannet diving. Dead carrion on a broken road with ugly black birds tearing at it. Some kind of hawk falling on a bloodied rodent. Good television. Must have taken a lot of time and patience. Here he goes again. *It's a raw rough peace that sometimes passes understanding: but it is true. It is natural.* Recapitulate to hawk and bloodied rodent and mix to one of his paintings. *Unlike the destruction we will upon ourselves in the city.* Close up of that monotonous gloom in distort. Rapid sequence of his *Infernal Limits* group: swollen faces, clawing hands, distorted lips, limbs awry and diseased, eyes tearing out of their sockets in some tile and concrete ambience, walls streaked with unreadable shit graffiti as they fall and flounder. And (ah well) the predictable explosive oeuvre. Before we come back to the charoniferous jib muttering: *God's not man's destruction.*

And in dulcet Mendoza the story is taken up. Pritchard Lofthouse lived, taught and struggled in so many mean cities before he found this freedom. Manchester, East London and all the rest of it round about 1948. Camera as the eye of bloody Lofthouse. I don't need to listen to this. Remember the scene in the Wagner film. 'Listen to this, Nietzsche. Listen to this.' 'I don't have to, Wagner. I wrote it.' And what is *she* thinking, up there in the gallery, waving of her delicate knickers, with little sister, the minder, Orfamay Darrow. No: Bébé. The Adèle of silence and sudden corrosive mirth. Not impressed I'm sure. But what have we here. *Ipse* Mendoza in his anorak having done the dulcet bit effortlessly climbing a scree or whatever the hell the bastard things are called to join the massively mournful gumboil up among the haar and sheepshit with a brisk hey nonny Lofthouse. What the fuck is this all about? And a ha cha cha!

Ipse: . . . You abandoned the grim vision of *Infernal Limits* – thirty-one pictures, some large-scale, other almost miniatures of despair – for the even longer sequence *Fragmentations* which

137

many people found even more alarming – perhaps because you showed us disintegration in harsh jagged colour. And then you abandoned the city itself. And since you came to live here, alone, your imaginative daemon seems to have taken you in another (for me) terrifying direction . . .

Camera moves in the course of windswept hollering from the searching but sensitive gleam of Mendoza to the ravaged gumboil, whose face is trenched rather than lined. Eyes utterly without laughter. Deep growling croak. Ah well. Here he goes. The bacteria must need pitons to get over those cheekbones . . . Images of the degradation of the inner city: derelicts on waste lots sprawled among all kinds of filth, rotting animals. Good stills. So to the Lofthouse vision. I have to concede it is horrible. More horrible than the real thing. Black and white. Ochres, slate-greys, umbers. On drones Zarathustra. The death camps. Relates the corpses to the living dead. Single eroded face of an old diseased vagrant. *A society capable of allowing that* . . . Cut to massive canvass of piled-up bodies, some dead and decaying, others alive still and mad . . . *will not for long keep this in memory*. Back to death camp film. *Or even this*. Hiroshima sequence. The agonies of Lofthouse. First *Fragmentation*: garishly adapted versions of the most famous stills. Car smashes, air crashes, rail disasters. You name it. The gumboil was in there fragmenting everything capable of shatter. Always returning to the nuclear blast. Don't imagine Isabel thinks much of all this. Not much in the way of happy, girlish laughter. Isabel! I can't see her, but she can see me from the deep purple up there. What a test, Mendoza! An air of professional calm, suitable concern for what is being shown, slight hint of amusement at earnestness of Lofthouse and all the time indifferent awareness of Simeon Langley-Gross, lined up on camera 4 for impending interview. How does the man keep so many balls in the air and yet he can't manoeuvre the two that matter into the right adjacency?

Ah the rugged and oil-skinned braver of deranged gumboils out there on a bleak ridge gazing out at the grey and swollen sea sullen with the menace of Nature biding her time.

Ipse Mendoza: . . . Some people might say that in coming

138

here you had escaped. Run away from the horrors of city life, the fear of crowded annihilation and its aftermath . . .

Such gaunt anger. Glad they caught that. *Escape!* he croaks. Longish film of Lofthouse brooding over craggy mountains and grey-grassed glens bespattered by black stones, glowering at the stirring sea, materializing out of the mists as he contemplates some ghastly aftermath of nature while explaining that when annihilation comes, as it must, he will face it alone as part of the destructive course of things. Some quite fierce shots (I know they were on location for weeks but these must be stock . . . Thank God I wasn't needed in the pissing cold rain), interspersed with his obsessive pictures of things luridly coming apart in every cell and fibre. *There is nothing but cruelty.* No sequence of pictures now. Each one is itself. Still he sells them. And at a good price. And he agrees to let us put him on television. Grabby gumboil, wanting it all ways.

Abrasive Mendoza: And you don't miss any of it?
Gumboil: What?
Mendoza: The world in which you once belonged, the critical acclaim that has been yours for some fifteen years, the stimulus.

Bitter flexing of the creused jowls. I suppose that was a grim smile. *Miss it? We managed to survive the death of God: we are now witnesses at the tearing apart of Prometheus – the vultures tearing each day at the vitals of the living arts. There can be no heroic rescue. Prometheus will die of sheer exhaustion. It is carnage more deliberate and mindless than the natural atrocities of my pictures.*
Suitable Lofthouse carnage exhibited. Back to him fading on a dire glare into a filthy-looking fog out of which some massive bird of prey beats upward. Ah well. Alive, alive o . . .

. . . Simeon Langley-Gross, now a back-bench MP, still the most tenacious public watchdog over the arts in Britain. Here we are. Nineteen eighty-four. Are things falling apart?

Langley-Gross has perfected the knowing smirk public. 'After what we've just seen, it would perhaps be more apt to describe me as a Cerberus. But let that pass . . .' Clever sod, isn't he. Unfortunately he bloody well is. Tread softly, Mendoza. Isabel is watching you and so is acute little sister.

. . . Of course I know that as company director, journalist and Member of Parliament you're used to wearing three hats, so I should have thought about the three heads. Seriously though . . .

Seriously repeats Simeon. The genial whimsy has in a twinkling frozen into solemn disapproval of my frivolity. Most politicians are vain, so one has to remember that they have, as of right, a monopoly of any wit or rhetoric that happens to be on the market. We'll see. Seriously (he says) it must be evident, must it not, even to professional philistines that the arts are in pretty good shape. Return of twinkle, smirk dribbling down from the sinuses. Finest theatre in the world, opera, ballet, orchestras to compare with if not excel the very best in Europe and America. Hardly tactful to talk about television in present company: but responsible journalism, intelligent drama, probing documentary, truly wonderful features. I am affably cool. The film industry? Serious publishing? Lists he gives me. Titles. Names of greybeards, winds, dragons, all the bright young kongs and pungs. Wonderful clutch of poets, he says. (Bloody good word for them.) Always a chronic shortage of money, of course. And everything that much more expensive.

. . . That's admittedly a comprehensive survey of the elitist arts and I know that you'll also pay tribute to our vivid contribution to international pop culture, but in the context of the season should we not perhaps be talking about repression, censorship, the dangers of the deliberate dissemination of lies, the distortion of history?

When he thinks he's going to win a point the twinkle runnels downward into a nose-girding smirk. 'Well, surely Giles, if we're getting back to Orwell, the main source of trash and trauma was television. And as I've already suggested, you know a lot more about that than I do.' Bastard's contradicted himself hasn't he. *Habilissimus* Mendoza. I shan't point it out.

. . . In a purely technical sense, possibly. But as a politician you know infinitely more about manipulation, I imagine. What I'm really asking (hope they got the smirk) is that given the purely commercial let alone the propaganda potential of this medium, must we not fear that the arts themselves, the serious arts, will be so degraded – not in Soviet Russia, where they are not as savagely put down as they were in Nazi Germany – but here, in Britain, so as to be meaningless? In Orwell's *Nineteen Eighty-Four* there were no discernible arts. In Chiang Ching's China, they were what she said they should be, while she watched American movies. Don't you think that there are signs that artistic functions are increasingly used for political ends?

Simeon Langley-Gross knows it is my function to fly hares and start kites, but am I seriously suggesting that (twinkle, smirk, droop) GLC festivals and pop protest concerts and things of that sort could turn into Nuremberg rallies?

. . . Used in the right way, Yes. Devalue the coinage and it becomes meaningless – so you can pass off valueless trash. Promote anarchy and people welcome the ensuing discipline, as long as it satisfies their appetite for junk food and circuses, however repressive and vengeful. Cruelty would be part of the circus.

Frowning anxiety corrugates the bland political forehead. Pervasive monochrome gloom of Marxist states, yes; brutality, injustice and inequality of right-wing dictatorships, yes. Simeon has never seen, much travelled as he is, anything to approach the omnipresent misery depicted by Orwell. Ah but that irrepressible twinkle prefigures the humorous face curdling into whimsical condescension. 'I must say, Giles, this is a very bleak not to say melodramatic scenario that you create. Rather surprising in a programme designed to extol the arts.'

. . . We extol, as you put it, what is admirable or, at least, worthwhile. We're equally anxious to see it flourishing in a free society. (Signal to gallery. Mah Jong! I think, already swivelling.) Simeon Langley-Gross, thank you.

Full swivel to camera 3. Red-hot wires of hatred up my arse. Pity the public can't see geniality transformed into sullen fury.

. . . A good many novelists have hired costumes from the Apocalyptic Wardrobe Company. Timothy Waddell tailors his own, so that it's not surprising they sit more easily and even elegantly on his long, lean frame. *Breakdown, The Pyrrhic Sword Dance, The Oracle of Sandal Street, When the Satyrs Dance, Dead-End Gate* and (soon to be published) *A Kinda Kulchur* – the titles perhaps speak for themselves. Waddell's view of the human character and of the future is uncompromising and grim. So it was something of a surprise, when we travelled to his home in Biarritz, to find a jovial, epicurean man albeit with a wickedly ironic gleam. Let Timothy Waddell take it up from there . . .

Canny old sod wouldn't be interviewed. 'Tell me what you want and I'll serve it up. I shan't need prompting.' Didn't even make a note. There he is, lank in an ancient cardigan, strolling above the Plage des Basques. Lovely day. Atlantic obligingly crashing in. Eleven novels before *Breakdown* – about three psychologists, contemporaries at university, two men and a woman who agree on a programme of clandestine behaviourist experiments carried out on schoolboys, prisoners and servicemen. Nothing obvious: no mental or emotional torture, no physical devices to induce reactions. The aim to discover who will crack and how under subtle pressure. At the end of the novel they have set up a consultancy and look forward to contracts with a multinational firm and the Ministry of Defence. Close up of Waddell, eyes probing and sinister. Cut to him flapping along past the chateau on the headland. Voiceover. *The Pyrrhic Sword Dance* was really just an extension of the previous novel – the refinement of environmental pollution into a means of warfare. Inevitable scenic shots. How banal! But they wouldn't listen. Strictly a Northwest European/North Atlantic game. (But of course.) Controlled defilement of the habitat of others without resort

142

to chemical or biological weapons in a *military* sense. A means of economic asphyxiation. And of course the twist when the wind blows the other way. Atlantic breakers roll in. Now with the Rocher de la Vierge in the background in a roll-necked sweater, hands in pockets of an old tweed jacket: *The Oracle of Sandal Street*. Serious book. The other two being a bagatelle of laughs! Cult religion. Charlatan sets himself up. Acquires local following. Wider reputation. Engineers sensations. Television interviews. America. Television spot. Huge following. World conflagration of devotees. The piercing, unblinking eyes again with that same gleam: 'Religion has always been more of a threat to man's survival, let alone his dignity, than any ideology. And it all started in Sandal Street.' Wonder if he gets all his titles out of Suetonius. Never thought of it before. Cunning bastard! Now the Oracle of the Place Sainte Eugénie is sipping something at a café table eyeing two succulent whores in tight clothes of flamboyant colour. Very good they are and so they should be for the fee we paid the model agency. (Christ! I wonder if Iris lets out her girls on such missions. No. On the whole she tends to be mother-hennish. Though not always. There was that boy whatwashisname who was shot and the particularly lovely girl. And Iris set that up, so they say. Perhaps it's just me. I wonder if it was any good. I thought it was. Did she? Apart from all the delightful writhing and flattering gasps?) Meanwhile Waddell's piercing glance traverses the 'whores' one of whom loosens her shirt as the other crosses her thighs. Oh God! Why don't they listen to me. The master of the revels is nothing if not obvious. Still we have winsome twitches of irony on the face of Waddell, a narrowing of eyes, slight elongation of the mouth on one side as he takes a long puff at his frog fag. Meditative exhalation. His novel *When the Satyrs Dance*. Exploration of sexual licence as a social disease in itself. Significant theme of a society in which drug taking, if not drug addiction, is a matter of course. Governments who can't beat it join it: exploit it. The satyrs dance more wildly. The predicted plague of the sages of the Group of Rome is at hand. Back to our models displaying. Picked up. The master of the revels is nothing if not trite. AIDS I suppose is what he implies. Well, who knows? Waddell stubs out his *mégot*. Frightening bloody book, all the same. Tomorrow *was* another day. The author on his sunlit patio. Brief description of *Dead-End Gate* – a landmark in Pompeii, he explains. Hadn't known that. Reconstruction in fiction of several sites and moments of vast destruction in which the central characters through thematic imagery, echoed phrases, parallels of feeling suggest (God save us!) 'a metempsychosis of human suffering which must end in annihilation from which nothing will rise – the Dead-End Gate.'

Newly lit up within easy reach of the gin basking in the Biarritz autumn, he settles with amused intelligence to discuss his oeuvre. He won't say what *A Kinda Kulchur* is about. Perhaps we can guess? His wicked smile. Half-smile. Pleasant grimace. Many main characters. Focal innocence. His puritanism, in spite of his complete scorn of religion . . . Oh yawn. I've heard it all. Seen this bloody film about nine times while the master of the revels was losing his. I daresay he might too. Hope he was watching the bit about AIDS, if that's what it was. Four minutes twenty to run. Waddell on loving and Love: Eros, Agape and Charis . . . Phoo! Wonder what she's making of it. Can't help being impressed. Look at the crinkled old bloater gassing away. At Mendoza *off* camera! Shouldn't do it to a dog. Little sister will certainly get in the way in the piss-up. Launching champagne might have just done it. The SS *Isabel* and all who sail into her. Now they'll be skimming back to Oxford in that filthy yellow car the bloody blonde pipstrel drives. Gels of that age didn't have cars of their own when I was a boy!

What next from the kippered brahmin of Biarritz? Ah yes. He thinks that as slatternly use of language has contributed to the general degeneration of the modern mind, so has sexual promiscuity undermined the modern spirit. When did it not, for God's sake? Nothing very new about promiscuity or pornography. More about love and loving. No Mendoza to beguile the screen and I've heard all this until I'm up to there. Wonder what she thinks of it? Not much hope with bloody Elaine around. Party and overnight in London might just have worked. Old enough to be out on her own after all. Wonder why I'm so nervous. Never used to be. And I've had my successes after all. Twenty-three. Twenty-three doesn't break any records but it's not bad. Iris was the only one with whom it was understood as once off unless . . . But she didn't ever come calling for more. Was it any good? Was *I* any good? Another minute forty-five of this apocalysm. Oh what the hell it doesn't matter. I might try Sandy Fleming one day. No Iris but not passionately discriminative for all that. If Benedict Passoa could make it why shouldn't Mendoza? Wonder if Mattingley did. Now there is one of my lasting sorrows: thought I couldn't fail with little Charley Hampden when up through the trapdoor from the cellarage popped suavely Humphrey bloody Etonian Mattingley. And that ended in tears. Not quite I suppose. Seems happy enough with her political bantam, fuckit. Trouble is no one takes me seriously enough. Patronizing academics and even though Isabel makes fun of intellectuals some of it must rub off. Daddy and festering Kelly and even disorganized and woolly Oldfield. Likes him. Must have premature degeneration of the balls or they haven't dropped. Portrait of a preorchic puppydog. And I *am* serious. Too right wing to be fashionable, but three books to my name. One documentary, one 'genuinely funny' novel, one anthology. Featured articles. 'Abrasive wit'. And Kelly's not much more than an academic poolroom loafer. Still, come to think of it and not for the first time, there is always Christina . . . Christ! Wake up, gentle Giles. They're wheeling in the panel: Llewellyn Gray creasingly affable oozing cultivate Welshness, ex-TV tycoon; Honoria Bannerman, the most decorously accessible tits in *Debrett* it is said, TV playwright; Lancelot Coote, short-arsed poet all glare and hair, TV critic. And guess what we're going to talk about . . . End at last of the Pyrenean smokie.

. . . And so we look nearer home. Television – a sinister force in Orwell and always under censure from the hierophants of apocalysm. (Like that word.) So we've brought together three people well acquainted in different ways with the monstrous creature. Is the menace a myth? In 1984.

Introductions and off we go. Bet I can predict every word of it. What good luck to have been born under an irreverent star. I don't think I can possibly be ambitious. They'll never believe me. Wonder if she'd like me if I were more Mr Niceguy. They wouldn't believe that either. Come Mendoza, concentrate. It is time to be acute.

4

*I*s Brutus guilty of a considerable deception in Act IV Scene iii of *Julius Caesar* and consequently of moral turpitude? If, in pretending to his officers that he knows nothing of Portia's death having already talked of it to Cassius, he is more or less lying, what are his motives? To bolster morale by showing how bravely he can bear sudden shock, or (more ignobly) to puff up his own reputation for courage. Warrington puts it all down to a mistake in the preparation of the text, holding that an expunged and rewritten scene was mistakenly left in. Oldfield insists that Brutus is deliberately acting a part consistent with Shakespeare's portrayal of an intolerably conceited prig, interested only in what others will think of him. Why else should he peremptorily shut up Cassius ('Portia, art thou gone'), if not later to dissemble? The implied contempt for Cassius (according to Oldfield) contributes to his failure of spirit from this moment on.

An amusing, thoroughly good-tempered pub argument: no more. But it set me wondering about the real nature of stoicism, a way of looking at the world which has always rather repelled me. Of course, it would have been improper for a Christian priest to countenance such a belief for all its emphasis on virtue and oblique obeisance to the will of God. Such detachment from suffering would never do. And for the caring existentialist, however defiantly he faces the meaningless chaos of the sun in which he happens to occur, it will not do either. Surely, though, it would fit someone entirely without faith or belief, bereft of intellectual conviction, even if nagged at by one dilemma or another of the mind while the

146

body lives and it is still of account. In the extreme it seems to me that the stoic, in his detachment or indifference, approaches the psychopath. Not, of course, in the sense that he is capable of doing indiscriminate harm without feeling: but in the sense that he is capable of indiscriminate indifference. To protect his own equilibrium, the detachment of stability, the stoic will ignore hurt or suffering in others, even if he is the agent of such distress, even if it involves showing no response to love or affection. If the stoic must suffer he will, to keep up appearances, do so without complaint. This does not require him to make every effort to avoid the likelihood of any form of pain.

Yet there is the example of Epictetus, living in the reign of Domitian, teaching that endurance and abstinence are the secrets of the good, peaceable life, which is not far from the Epicurean doctrine that pleasure (the avoidance of pain) is the only good that we are able to apprehend; Epicurus, too, advises a virtuous, gentle way of life free of excess. We should not be afraid of God; in death we shall feel nothing; it is possible to achieve goodness and to endure evil.

I have been studying how I might compare the prison of my being with the world of more effectual men and women, not afflicted with fits of surpassing melancholy, recognizing a waning in any courage I once possessed. If I have avoided serious hurt and suffering, it is more from indolence than theoretical effort. Stoicism is a gospel of endurance rather than hope: but does it teach its adherents how to endure their own thoughts, the banality of their very existence? My attention in recent months has never been very far from the prose of Donne, which moves me more than his verse, and I am grateful to Ben Oldfield for acquainting me with Wallace Stevens. In very different ways, both men show undaunted courage: the one firm in faith, the other prescribing different aspects of hope while fully aware that 'The death of one god is the death of all.' Marcus Ferdinand is resolute in an entropy of despair. The man on the dump, sifting through the garbage of the ages and finding nothing.

Donne can write: O who, if before hee had a beeing, he could have sense of this miserie, would buy a being here upon these conditions? But it is no impotent wail of complaint. Donne's courage is vested firmly in understanding and acknowledgement of weakness: '*Fevers* upon wilful distempers of drinke, and surfets, *Consumptions* upon intemperances and licentiousness, *Madnes* upon misplacing, or overbending our naturall faculties, proceed from our selves, and so, as that our selves are in the plot, and wee are not onely *passive*, but *active* too, to our owne destruction; But what have I done, either to *breed*, or to *breath* these *vapors*? They tell me it is my *Melancholy;* Did I infuse, did I drinke in *Melancholy* into my selfe? It is my *thoughtfulnesse*; was I not made to *thinke?* It is my *study*; doth not my *Calling* call for that? I have don nothing, wilfully, perversly toward it, yet must suffer in it, die by it; There are too many *Examples* of men, that have bin their own *executioners*, and that have made hard shift to bee so; some have alwayes had *poyson* about them, in a *hollow ring* upon the finger, and some in the *Pen* that they used to write with: some have beat out their *braines* at the wal of their prison, and some have eate the *fire* out of their chimneys: and one is said to have come neerer our case than so, to have strangled himself, though his hands were bound by crushing his throat between his knees: But I doe nothing upon my self, and yet am mine own *Executioner*.'

Surely my own failing of courage, failure to endure, is not simply that I am pining after a pretty woman half my age, that I lack the vigour or endeavour to pursue some romantic or erotic liaison which would 'take me out of myself'. For whatever reasons, I was not, as a rather overweight young man, quick enough of mind but lamentably unathletic, attractive to women. A quiescent libido might have awakened, I suppose, had I not found my way out of embarrassment through the Anglo-Catholic bolthole of celibacy. And for many years I was not sorry, apart from brief fits of passion which I suspect were for the most part self-induced, when the glimpse of an amply filled brassière leaning over the Christmas treat jellies or of a shiny stocking in careless genuflection, convinced me that I was master of some demon of marvellous potential. Marriages I made some study of seemed usually to be (while they lasted) tolerant accommodations, necessarily irritant pacts of humours mutually indulged or occasionally reviled: not just among my unpresuming flock, the more so here among the acute minds and delicately tinctured sensibilities. Of course there are happy couples whom

I envy such as Wilkins and his Samantha, but most seem to struggle on doggedly or cynically: secret disobediences, secret repugnances – and murmuring, murmuring about Iris Cameron, or, of late, Isabel. The most amiable and affectionate relationships I know are those between Ingestre and Francesca Oricellari which is languidly decorous and between Warrington and his headmistress which is neither but underscored with laughter that they can hear when others cannot. I don't know what to make of Charles and Eve Darrow.

Is it then some menopausal spasm which makes me aware of all the sexual pleasure, companionship, love that I have missed, largely from my own choosing, which brings on these protracted fits of enervating gloom? Out of which emanates despair. No possum, no sop, no taters to look forward to. Ever. And this frustration focused, quite artificially, on a beautiful, light-hearted girl now the subject of much murmuring and some malice.

No. It is more than that. We do not live in a tragic time, but in one of mindless fanatical atrocity. And I have come perhaps to realize that, alone, without the solace of someone more important, it is increasingly difficult to bear the random horror which is part of the daily news. The very (justifiably) restrained presentation of such items as five hundred unidentified bodies discovered in a mass grave in Buenos Aires, with signs of torture and mutilation, takes several seconds to work upon the inattentive mind – simply because such information has become commonplace in some land still far enough away for it to be unreal.

In the Senior Common Room of Charles Darrow's college, in the most civilized company, Warrington was putting forward the theory that it was impossible for a hero to be both Christian and tragic. Ingestre and Darrow were disposed to argue in the name of factual martyrs, having conceded several Shakesperean and Jacobean characters. It did not occur to them to argue that while the ancient tragic heroes defied the gods, the notion of universal order, any such worthy of the name, these days, defies religious fanaticism or ideological dogma equally certain in the knowledge of destruction. This, of course, would not have exploded Warrington's technical literary point, but it might have broadened the discussion. Perhaps I am too susceptible to an intense fear of religion in whatever form. Islam is an older enemy of Christianity than Marxism, perhaps: but Christianity has itself been the enemy of civilization in its various chimerical forms. No religion is free of the guilt of personal sadism or mass cruelty in the name of some holy purpose. And the highest idea of 'the Good' was Greek, against the background of a repressive, slave-based economy.

Once again *l'instant de boire*: the moment of twilight over stagnant pools at batflight. Well, Eliot found a Rock to cling to. I have slipped on a patch of treacherous weed while reaching for a handhold and now lie crumpled in this brackish pool, my mind wandering in and out of trivialities: Professor Eucalyptus and Mr Apollinax, the dry commonplace, a bitten macaroon. Mendoza's snickering innuendoes about Isabel and Kelly. A struggle all too readily given up against the image of that tumbling dark hair, changing light of the deep blue eyes, high breasts, narrow waist, strong but slender hips. Her laughter in which I pretend to join but no longer understand. What if I had met her when we were *both* young? The laughter would probably, however gently, been at my expense. 'The priest desires, the philosopher desires. And not to have is the beginning of desire.'

Oldfield, untroubled by Isabel, derides Mendoza's thwarted murmurings. But as the days pass with less certainty. For Mendoza she is *la vivandière des faunes*. Clever malice. And I am only annoyed with her for being too charming, for having become the intolerable obsession.

Ben Oldfield appears to have lost his passion for Henrietta Ball (with whom I am to dine terrifyingly on Sunday) while hacking his way through the tangle of his latest impenetrable theory, rooted in some fertile swamp of literary confusion which he calls parallax. When he gets to a clearing, Ben (and by his example the rest of us) will be better able to understand the motives and behaviour of others, so pondering more significantly our erstwhile failures of perception. Whatever Oldfield chooses to call it, it seems to me that he has discovered synaesthesia: the correspondence of feeling between different people as they develop sympathy for each other, or the transference of impressions from associations and images derived from quite different sources. Fanciful as it may be, this is perhaps an aspect of parallax. Oldfield insists on dispassion on the part of the observer and some degree of passion on the part of those directly involved in the action, whatever it may be. All very well: but would it work. I am dispassionate about Iris and Peter Cameron, whatever the murmurings: yet I suppose that I desire her in a speculative way, I like them both, and I enjoy their company, worldly and sardonic as they both are. I watch Ingestre and Francesca Oricellari with curiosity that is hardly prurient, but more than disinterested. And, undoubtedly, my love for Isabel distorts my attitude to Mendoza, David Kelly and his wife, and even her family. In each case I am an observer and what I observe changes perspective according to my own emotional tilt. Synaesthesia is not parallax.

In our relationships we are not snowmen with a mind of winter: more often Proteus slopping ashore at midday to doze broodingly among the rank seal herd of our prejudices and lusts, for ever changing form until pinned down . . . So all these officious and mutual assistances are but *complements* towards others and our true end is *ourselves*.

And that is a matter for courage:

It is in this solitude, a syllable,
Out of these gawky flitterings,

Intones its single emptiness,
The savagest hollow of winter-sound.

It is here, in this bad, that we reach
The last purity of the knowledge of good.

The crow looks rusty as he rises up.
Bright is the malice in his eye . . .

One joins him there for company,
But at a distance, in another tree.

★　★　★　★　★

24 January 1984
If there has hitherto been gossip about Isabel and me – and there has been I've no doubt from Henrietta's frosty asides,

Elaine's witticisms, Ingestre's cautious probing and Iris Cameron's wry amusement – now they all have something to gossip about. And we are both as chaste and innocent of scandal as ever, except perhaps in thought.

I was mildly surprised when Isabel showed interest in a paper I was to contribute (on Nietzsche – who else!) to a symposium on existentialist thought at Bristol. With Christina away in Amsterdam for several days, I jokingly suggested she might come with me to hear it delivered. She said she would. It was a Saturday engagement just for the day, so there was no question of an illicit weekend and our arrangements were so open as to place them completely above suspicion, even though Eve Darrow glittered with irony at her elder daughter's abruptly awakened interest in moral philosophy. Then my car broke down outside Marlborough on the Saturday evening. Since I am an idiot about machines of any kind, I was indeed lucky to find a sympathetic garage man. I'd noticed a sort of sparrowy twittering for a week or so, but my car is not very old and I had failed to guess that my 'clutch release bearing had buggered itself'. There was a grinding noise a juddery halt and a walk into Marlborough at this most inappropriate time.

Isabel thought it funny. I hope that others see and understand the joke with the same untainted gusto. The logistics were straightforward: it would take the amiable mechanic several days to put my car right, but if I turned up on the following day he would arrange for a hire car, which I could return when I collected mine. The alternative was a complicated rail journey involving infrequent buses and several changes of train. Or so I understood it. We decided to put up in separate rooms (not that this was discussed) in a fairly comfortable hotel.

The psychological implications were more complex. Suddenly there was considerable constraint between us. The opportunities were evident. It was up to me to make the first move and it would be ridiculous to pretend that I was not tempted. At the same time, fate and all such dramaturgical machinery apart, it did not seem right. Isabel herself was noticeably cautious: as delightful and funny as usual, but waiting to see if I should try to force the moment to a crisis.

Uncertain, she told me on the following day, whether she wanted me to or how she would have reacted.

We took time over a relatively palatable dinner with a sufficiency but not an excess of wine. Isabel telephoned her mother and returned to the bar looking flushed and perhaps a little angry. She went to her room. I had another drink. We were assiduously careful not to touch. No good-night kiss!

On the following morning, the friendly garage owner provided the promised car which did not twitter, chirrup or complain. It was a lovely winter day. I suggested to Isabel that since we were probably compromised in the eyes of anyone who was likely to find out about the adventure, we might as well enjoy a leisurely return to Oxford through Avebury and the Vale of the White Horse with perhaps a good lunch. I had by no means lain awake tormented by images of Isabel without a nightdress or covered softly in some undergarment only a few yards along the corridor, but they did cross my mind. Now she was immaculate and I was as little dishevelled as possible in the circumstances.

'Well, we made it,' she said. 'Congratulations.' I wondered if there was a certain ironic edge. I began to fumble for words. 'Of course, I did,' she said. 'But I'm glad it didn't happen – if it's ever going to – in quite such a farcical way.'

I thought it best left at that, vaguely encouraged that I hadn't been entirely dismissed from her premorphetic thoughts. Such is the vanity of male middle age as it approaches. We walked around the Great Circle at Avebury and climbed a little way up Windmill Hill. Isabel knew a lot more about it all than I did. She said her sister had once been keen on archaeology and that she'd always tried to take an uninformed interest in the family obsessions, having few of her own. The thought of Elaine bothered me momentarily. If Eve chose to be tactful, as Charles would certainly be, no one need know about this absurd interlude. But Elaine . . . Ben Oldfield . . . Ferdinand and so on . . .

Some kind of mutual enchantment possessed us. I don't know what Isabel was thinking. For my part I was trying to call up in imagination the culture to which this place had given its name: the dangerous emanation of a civilization trying to express itself in simple domestic artefacts as it determined to survive. And to what purpose? The structures of contemporary life, quite apart from the underlying destructiveness, seemed to me suddenly to be very fragile. Fantastical, perhaps, such reflections looking at great standing stones. Perhaps.

This hardly idyllic train of thought was rudely jolted when we turned a corner to find a huge BBC pantechnicon trailing wires in all directions with all its lights and screens and booms and batteries, a great number of people standing about doing nothing, and bloody Mendoza in a sheepskin overcoat.

Now Isabel and I will surely have to live with the euhemeristic fantasies which will proliferate.

27 January 1984
One brief glimpse of Isabel since the malefic encounter with Mendoza among the megaliths (where, of course, he was filming for his wretched programme). She favoured me with a lingering deep blue look of undisguised promise, which was not lost on Professor G. S. Walton who was with me. Walton is seldom aware of other people's concerns, least of all their conversation, since his own offer him the utmost fascination. Except where sex may be involved: then his narrow features expand and light up, his ginger whiskers bristle, in the hope of vicarious lubricity. Fortunately he did not comment or I'm certain I should have lost my temper. (Why so touchy, indeed?) It is extremely unlikely that Walton would have heard chatter about the events of last weekend, since he does not move in Mendoza territory, which makes Isabel's irrepressible mischief the more inconvenient. He is a great dispenser of scandal in his own right. If she has been provoked by someone, Isabel may well have decided, as she once hinted she might, to give the blabbermouths something to ruminate. This might seem all very well to someone of her mercurial sense of humour, but it might also cause trouble that neither of us would ultimately enjoy.

My forebodings are not dispersed by the aloof poise of Eve Darrow, whom I met outside Blackwell's. With much calculated concern she asked after the wellbeing of my car and the whereabouts of Christina. It seemed to me that mawkish explanations were out of place, so I answered factually. I doubt that Eve frets deeply about the virginity of her daughters, but her own marriage is apparently blameless and I imagine she would have forceful views about one of them breaking up another which seems to be (and indeed is!) perfectly happy.

Fortunately most of the week has been taken up with teaching and sorting out the problems of one of my pupils who has had enough and wants to drop out. This would be a pity since she is quite clever and not in the least eccentric. It is simply a bad attack of nerves brought on by Wittgenstein. (My God! The number of times I've wished that the bloody man *had* become an aeronaut!) We are also experiencing one of the sporadic outbreaks of militant students demanding an alternative philosophy syllabus: a mere nuisance, but occasionally disruptive. Nothing like the hysterics of 1968–69 when I was still an undergraduate myself just about: but though fewer in number and less rowdy, this new crop of *soi-disant* radicals seem a lot more vicious.

Now I have to reclaim my car and return the one I hired from the excellent Les Downs at Marlborough. He referred to Isabel as 'your good lady', without any hint of a leer, wink or nudge. Why should there have been, after all? Fourteen years isn't very much and she might have been what Les would have called my 'missus'.

As it is, the incumbent returns on Sunday. It occurs to me that one of the meanings of the word is that which falls upon someone as a duty or obligation.

31 January
I thought it premature to explain to Christina on her immediate return about the farcical events at Marlborough, which may have been a mistake. We made love but it was less than ecstatic – as though I were indeed fulfilling a duty politely and she responding with a certain resignation. Since, sooner or later, she must hear some distorted account from someone or other, I made a great inconsequential joke of what happened over supper on Monday. That, too, might have been a mistake. Christina has moments of stillness during which she suggests that the effort is hardly worthwhile because she has heard it all before. I elaborated. Christina asked if it had been a good dinner.

I suggested that there might have been rumours about Isabel and me. Christina shrugged. This was disconcerting.

Assuring her that there was absolutely nothing between Isabel and myself except affection, I admitted that we had perhaps sometimes played up a little when sharp-faced by the proliferate Mrs Grundys of either gender. Christina said nothing, smiled vaguely and asked if I would like some ice cream.

Her unconcern was becoming maddening, though I was determined not to show pique. In fact I find myself rather worried that she is herself having an affair, or perhaps several, which her protracted absences on company business would make entirely feasible. She is very attractive, sexually alert and sometimes passionate. Away from academic circles, she is lively and assured. At the various conferences and on the many business trips she must meet men who interest her, perhaps more than fleetingly. Or else she may have an arrangement with a particular lover who joins her when possible at some suitable assignation.

I declined the ice cream and said that I had work to do. She started clearing away the dishes. In my room I glared at the *Breviary of Aesthetics*. When I was grumbling to Oldfield that I could not find a theme to interest me enough to attempt another book, he suggested Croce. Unsystematic as he is, Oldfield's enthusiasm is boundless, so that he keeps 'discovering' people others have lost sight of. Although I have become very interested in the subject and may well pursue it in Collingwood, Santayana and perhaps Cassirer, I did not read a line. Instead, I found myself cursing the fact that I had not gone to bed with Isabel at Marlborough. Or at least tried to. Then I remembered how she had been decidedly guarded and began to brood about her sex life. Is her flirting with me a playful disguise to divert attention from some other more dangerous liaison. I found myself running through a list of contenders. The obvious selection is Warrington, whom I know she likes and whose company she enjoys. Surely that is absurd. Warrington is an astute, mature man (far more, so I discover, than I am) with a comely mistress: but then Isabel's physical attractions might bend the sanest, most sceptical mind.

I at last saw how adolescent all this maudlin speculation was: first worries about Christina's fidelity which I suppose I have some right to expect, then about Isabel's upon which I have no claim whatsoever. The rodent of jealousy at work again. In theory I have no objection to modest sexual licence and have often said so. Now I discover that I uphold this as long as it does not apply to *me*. Exculpation came in form of reflection on 'moral' positions generally. For the most part they are *attitudes* which are struck, rather than opinions which are believed in and consequently held. I drank too much whisky and fell asleep.

3 February

Mendoza has been at work. I met Peter Cameron in Turl Street the other morning. If less extrovert than his sister, he is nevertheless usually high-spirited: on this occasion his manner was quizzical. (I can't think of a more appropriate word.) There was about him an air of slightly patronizing amusement, which is not typical. The customary polite inquiries were in no sense charged with insinuation, but they were more personal and less professional than they are wont to be. Or so it seemed to me. He asked after the wellbeing of Christina. Nothing particularly sinister in that, I suppose, except for the sensitive circumstances. He then talked about the various chores we had to undertake in addition to teaching: his own as tutor for admissions and mine at the faculty library. Yet he supposed there were certain compensations.

Perhaps more to the point, I was taking a glass of sherry with Roger Ingestre when a visiting American called White-hart appeared, as it seemed unexpectedly. This chap has been around for several months. He is genial and generally well liked. Christina and Isabel have both commented favourably about him and find him handsome. I've barely exchanged a dozen sentences with him. Ingestre said, 'You know David Kelly, of course,' in the usual way. And Whitehart perhaps ingenuously said, 'Who else? The luckiest man in town, with a lovely and delightful wife and the glorious Isabel Darrow as secretary.' Whitehart is deceptively American primitive. Cameron and Ingestre assure me that he is erudite (in political theory) and intelligent. I have yet to notice the evidence and would have dismissed the effusion as just that, if Ingestre had not flapped, interrupted, knocked over a table and changed the subject. It amused the American, justifiably no doubt, as he responded to Ingestre's queries about Reagan's State of the Union message and his announcement that he was preparing to stand again for the presidency. A confirmed Democrat and liberal, Whitehart's appetite for scandal (such as it might have been) was overtaken by political gloom. He could see no way (*sic*) in which the ghost rider from the sky could be defeated. Ingestre was more hopeful (without much tangible evidence) of the demise of Madam Thatcher. But the SDP and their chums seem to live on such optimism. We stumbled around in a maze of political topiary for a while before I had my surfeit of hedges and left.

In an attempt to subdue my righteous irritation, I plunged into the *Philosophy of the Spirit* in a sort of bellyflop reminiscent of my intellectually inelegant youth. Leaving Radcliffe Square I almost met Ben Oldfield in Catte Street, but he saw me first. For a moment he halted like a stricken rabbit then darted back into the High. Ominous. Ben is imaginative, industrious, inoffensively ambitious, disorganized and most of all decent. Perhaps, after all, Isabel is more than a chum. I hope not. For his sake.

Christina was home before me, which is rare these days. She had cooked savoury pancakes which were *à point* when I came in. It was an auspicious start to a placid evening. In which we did not talk to one another.

*　*　*　*　*

In retrospect, though it had not occurred to her at the time, Isabel was surprised at how easy it had been to resist the temptation of fucking with David Kelly – and the surprise was not especially unpleasant. It meant that she was well in control of herself and their relationship. She had thought, first, about Christina – faced at last with the reality of betraying a friendship; then, she had thought of the artificiality of circumstance – it was not as though passion had stranded them in Marlborough, just a faulty clutch; finally, it would have been cheap: opportune and cheap.

At the same time, she wondered, if she found herself in the same situation with Evan Warrington or Peter Cameron, whether she would have been quite as contentedly passive. Both were bachelors, after all: though neither had shown more than speculative male interest in her and always behaved with the tense courtesy of sexually vibrant men in the presence of an attractive and aware woman. So be it.

What would have happened if David had been more ardent? Isabel would certainly not have repulsed him, although she knew now quite certainly that she did not love him. That had all been fantasy of which she was a little ashamed. There had been *no* ardour. He had looked wary and nervous throughout dinner. Next morning, he was himself again, if self-conscious. Had he been (in Isabel's eyes) timorous? Would she be a little insulted that the expected pass had not been made? On the following day, to preserve a friendship that she valued, she had tried to find suitably reassuring phrases. So that is how an infatuation ends. No harm done.

For this reason alone the knowing looks and passingly vague disapprobation irritated her immensely. Elaine had abandoned pert sniping for tactful disappearance. Eve was fastidiously unconcerned. Daddy was smilingly furrowed and solicitous. For God's sake! It wasn't a question of having it away. As long as she was not raped or hurt no one had shown the least concern about *that* since she was of the age of consent. Mendoza, Ben, the Double Blue . . . Warrington. Not an eye would have batted. There would have been no deathless hush in the cloister. It was the suspicion that she might have contrived (how could they be so bloody naive) a dirty night with a married family friend. Elaine continued to evade her. To confront her father would be embarrassing to both of them. That left Eve.

'Look,' Isabel said, 'I've no doubt that Mendoza makes a habit of spreading a little calumny as he goes by, but nothing happened between David Kelly and me. And would it matter that much anyway?'

'I'm not the slightest bit interested in Mendoza,' Eve said. 'What's it got to do with him? I've never known you to be a liar: but I know, *from experience*, that there are times when one is not entirely truthful. We've known David and Christina reasonably well for some time and I wouldn't want any of you hurt.'

'Which presumably includes me?'

'Of course it includes you. But you are the least likely to be lastingly hurt.'

'My God . . . '

'Isabel . . . I've tried to put it to you discreetly. There's been a great deal of talk about you and David Kelly for some time. Even Francesca asked me if you were having an affair . . . '

'Francesca!'

'Yes . . . she'd been talking to Henrietta Ball . . . '

'Who is probably lime-green jealous . . . '

'Quite possibly. At the same time . . . '

'At the same time, nothing! Forget it, *Mummy*!'

'You're going out?'

'Yes. I'll cycle to Garsington to find out if Iris Cameron likes pretty girls as well as her brother. That should give you all something to smitter about.'

'Isabel . . . '

In the street, tearful with anger, Isabel immediately was sorry about the whole wasteful scene: but her sense of personal vexation was still strong. It was raining and cold. She hunched her shoulders and walked in the direction of Holywell Street, thinking that perhaps she might look for Ben Oldfield. Then, he, too, had been behaving untowardly. At moments like this, Isabel wished she did not think in the language natural to her father. Ben had been behaving like a fucking wimp. In any case Mendoza had a house in Holywell and she might run into him. Instead, she bumped into, of all people, Iris Cameron.

'You look as if you need a stiff drink,' Iris said. 'White Horse or King's Arms?'

They went to the White Horse. Isabel looked with something like envy at the confident, eloquently trim figure of Iris in her close-fitting black coat as she ordered drinks at the bar. Iris couldn't care less. Whatever her reputation and the scandal she invited, there was no disputing her generosity. Eve disliked her intensely and had little time for her brother. Her father had reservations about both which he did little to disguise. Isabel had always liked the brother and sister and had found them lively, funny and undemanding. If Iris had enemies, she was a formidable adversary in her own right: but once on your side there was no more loyal or unquestioning a friend. She came over to the table with two large gins and tonic.

'They've been getting at you, I suppose,' Iris said. 'About

David Kelly. Don't talk about it if you don't want to, but remember it's all so much yaffle. And I *know*.'

'The point is nothing happened.'

'I can well believe it. Saving your own preference in the matter, the man must be certifiable.'

Isabel laughed. Iris unbuttoned her topcoat, crossed her legs and lit a cigarette.

'Cheers,' Iris said.

'Thanks. How did you know what was bothering me?'

'It's been in the tea leaves for some time. And the word gets around. You know that Giles Mendoza fancies you rotten?'

'I guessed.'

'Well, you can't blame the poor sod. You are pretty special, you know. As it happens, he's not at all bad. But I daresay you don't feel inclined. Why are you so upset? I always thought that you were one of us who didn't give a . . . the word that comes to mind is hardly appropriate in the circumstances.'

Isabel explained the circumstances, the meeting with Mendoza. Iris Cameron laughed. For the first time in many years, Isabel felt like a little girl in the presence of someone vastly sophisticated, though not much older. And yet Iris must be over forty. Two bluff young men swathed in scarves were eyeing them. Iris winked, crossed her legs the other way, flamboyantly and shook her head.

'Never on Tuesday,' she said. 'Cold shower. Long row. Another cold shower.'

The young men were discomfited.

'People have dished the dirt, as the original said in the song, about me since I was fifteen,' Iris said. 'I suppose it's hurt once or twice. But not much. The advantage of being thought a tart without exactly looking like one is that you can be thoroughly outrageous. And I have been. But nothing like as often as people imagine. I've never been in love and I enjoy fucking. Sometimes it's the little bistro round the corner and sometimes it's the Tour d'Argent. It wouldn't be the same for you. And it shouldn't be. But don't get upset.'

'It must seem very silly. I feel like an idiot.'

'Don't.'

'It's just that my mother . . . and Francesca . . . '

'Oricellari?'

'Yes . . . '

'The creature from the black lagoon. Oh forget it! I can't stand her. For that matter, your mother and I are not exactly buttercups and daisies.'

'I don't think she was being malicious. It was something Henrietta Ball said.'

'Ah well . . . Are you thinking what I'm thinking?'

'About David?'

'Yes. It's an exemplary case. Curious the way the ritual works. Lust keeping its distance. I'd better not go on. Do you love him?'

'David?'

'Prince Andrew, McEnroe, Lester Piggott: take your pick.'

'No.'

'Good.'

'I thought I did for a while. But there's Christina. And I am very fond of her. I couldn't . . . I am very mixed up.'

Iris Cameron's blue eyes flickered. She shook her long fair hair almost impatiently. For a moment Isabel thought she saw the formidable harpy of local legend. The negligent kindness was gone: there was anger, resentment, hurt.

'I wouldn't worry about Christina,' Iris said. 'Her kind has an instinct for self-preservation. Think about yourself, love. Do what suits you. None of it is *that* worth worrying about and not much is serious. I know quite well what people say about me and about Peter and I don't care. I encourage scandal. So does he. But he's a man and belongs to Oxford. So it's done differently. I belong nowhere. If they want to twitter about me, I'll give them something to twitter about. And I think that as often as not my bed is as unsullied as your mother's or Francesca Oricellari's. I shouldn't bet on Henrietta Ball's. Why don't you get us another drink?'

★　　★　　★　　★　　★

'That was an absolutely delicious dinner,' said Francesca Oricellari. 'I heard you were the best cook in Oxford and it is true.'

'Thanks,' said Samantha Wilkins. 'I heard you were the

162

most beautiful visitor to the dreaming causes. And that is also true. You like this place, don't you?'

'Yes. Very much. Don't *you*?'

'I'm not over the top. I like Tom, though. He's happy here. The kids go to reasonable schools. And I have a smashing garden. Pity it's dark and wintry. You must come in the summer.'

'I'd like to very much.'

'Be warned in advance that Tom takes it into his head to have barbecues sometimes, whatever the weather. He's out there huffing and puffing in an anorak and we're all expected to be little Oateses and Evanses. Though we, too, stop short of eating the dogs. The labrador is Barnaby and that woolly fellow is Cornelius. Whop him on the nose if he gets too familiar.'

'I hope you don't think this is rude: but how does someone like you become the wife of a professor of philosophy?'

'Accident. Good luck. Sex. The Navy used to be very keen on drama. For all I know still is. So they sent people on courses at the British Drama League. I was in the Wrens. Tom was doing National Service in the Royal Marines. They put us together in a scene from *Desire under the Elms*. And the elms had it. I hadn't the faintest idea that he was a philosopher at the time. Not that I suppose it would have made very much difference.'

'It sounds idyllic.'

'It certainly wasn't. I had to wait a year and a half until my commission ended during which time Tom had come back here on a pittance and I was pregnant. It was a laugh a minute. But it's been fun. Sometimes a bit claustrophobic. Then so was the Women's Royal Naval Service.'

'It's a lovely house.'

'Well, Tom turned out to be quite clever after all. It's hardly the sort of place that suggests we're exciting people to know: but with four children and two dogs who would be? Tell me about you. I've met your sister lots of times.'

'There isn't much to tell. She's the one with the brains.'

'But, my God, running a fashion house can't be a game of hopscotch. I love your clothes – when Tom can afford them.'

'I was admiring your dress.'

'This is Diana von Furstenburg. I didn't want to be obvious. Do you know Iris Cameron?'

'Is she a friend of yours?'

'I think I take the point. Not exactly. But I quite like her. She's outrageous and this town, or certain sectors of it, can use a little outrage.'

'My only contacts, thank God, are professional. Why do you need the outrage?'

'Everything is too complacent. They all take themselves so seriously and don't bother enough about the *real* world. I sometimes think that if there was a riot in Cowley, they'd manage to have Magdalen Bridge barricaded and make suitable arrangements at Folly Bridge and the Woodstock and Banbury roundabouts. Then they could all analyse the causes of discontent. Look at your Roger Ingestre . . . '

'He's not *my* Roger Ingestre!'

'Sorry. I wasn't being nosey and I was simply making a point. But he and Tom and David Kelly over there and a dozen others will wag their heads about what's to be done and flick their tails like sagacious horses and look for the most shady tree. Don't mistake me. I am not discontented. I have no reason to be. But I have four children growing up in an increasingly nasty world. And I am sometimes exasperated when clever people theorize endlessly and do nothing.'

'What could they do?'

'Good point. Ineffectuality is built into the system. Not always, though. Think of the Second World War. And, all things considered, Tom wasn't a bad Royal Marine subaltern. It's just the lazy assumptions. How long have you lived here?'

'What is it? Nineteen eighty-four . . . Ten or eleven years. I travel quite a lot in Europe and America. It's still more civilized. Not as happy as Italy; not as comfortable as France. But not as dangerous. Under the surface.'

'I wonder how long that will last?'

'What do you mean?'

'Trouble on the streets. It must come. Look around here: can you imagine a more compassionate, caring bunch. Tom, Roger, David and Christina, Henrietta Ball, Ivan Whitehart – well, he is admittedly American which makes a difference, Charles and Eve Darrow. They all *care* like buggeration, but

164

they are all steeped in assumptions of privilege and class which they can't even recognize.'

'I admire English . . . I should say British, shouldn't I? . . . tolerance?'

'Fine. As long as it's at a distance. I'll tolerate you grandiloquently as long as I am not offended in any way by your existence. As long as I can retreat into the coterie which understands *me* and shares my reservations about *you*. It's all too comfortable. Sorry. I'm preaching and that was my pinger. Time for coffee. Slaves to the galley as the call went when I was a sailor.'

★

OLDFIELD IS VARIOUSLY BUFFETED

Comedy seems to me to be inimical to myth, where tragedy and farce are not. The heroic myths were as often as not tragic, allowing for the occasional idiosyncracies of Heracles. Quite often the myths relating to the sexual aerobics of the gods are farcical, although the line between farce and tragedy is thinly balanced. Ares and Aphrodite enmeshed was rich farcical fare for the rest of the pantheon: but not surely for Hephaestos. True comedy, however, is rooted firmly in reality. Comic narrative relies upon the observation and recording of things as they are, the natural ironies of life and vagaries of character which are part of our everyday awareness. It does not exaggerate, embellish or embroider to create an effect.

I see that earlier in these deliberations I have announced (in a grandiose way) the death of Tragedy. I must add a footnote: that her little sister Farce is alive and kicking.

Why is it that what should be high, light comedy turns into trouser-slipping, knicker-dropping, stage-wetting tomfoolery at the slightest nudge. *You should use stronger elastic*. And, after all, you can't blame the great impresario in the sky: he merely created the circumstance in which elastic was possible.

Example: Kelly and Isabel are stranded in Marlborough. (Surely that is farce enough on its own.) Off on a scholarly jaunt and his car breaks down, crumph, just outside Marlbor-

165

ough. (I don't think this qualifies as an aphorism.) Never mind. Isabel tells me that nothing happened and I believe her. No one else does. Although I have the most devout doubts about Kelly, I think Isabel tells the truth. And then what happened . . .

. . . Forget the aphorisms. A St Valentine's Party at the house of Peter and Iris Cameron! I can hear the pantheon falling over in hysterics. I was dancing with Iris Cameron under protest. It was what used to be called a slow foxtrot. Iris was so near that my own readiness was all too evident. She said nothing. She gave me a long sigh and wriggled closer so that I was durably aware of the fork of her thighs as we danced. She said nothing except as the music ended, 'We must do that again some time.'

Well we have. For the rest of that evening and early morning I cooled my passions with very long iced drinks. Many of the other guests were people (especially women) whom I didn't know, so I was able to be more or less interesting. Iris danced, without conspicuous effect, with several other men, while I was unable to dismiss that inflammatory moment: a simple, probably rather drunken, wonderfully sensual rapture.

Some ten days later, she telephoned and asked me to lunch at Garsington. It was Saturday. When I arrived there was no one else. Peter was away for the weekend. Lunch was designed to be leisurely. At no time did Iris make a single provocative movement. It was relaxed and mildly scandalous. Iris thought the Kelly-Isabel incident was merely funny, except that it was bothering Isabel. She has reservations about Kelly. 'Nice enough, but self-interested,' she said. 'He talks one of the best fucks in the trade. That's all.' I said I should have guessed that accolade might go to Mendoza. 'Oh no,' Iris said. 'Mendoza means it. He's the louche that goosed a thousand hips and screwed the topless tarts on valium. Quite indiscriminate, but he does live up to it.' And so we went through the cold beef (Scottish forequarter spit-roasted) and chocolate mousse with a good Morgon and curaçao. Slanders came thick and fast. Clodia Oricellari was the incarnation of the diplomatic bag; Henrietta Ball – 'When she thrusts out her chin you see a jaw that could be used for smiting Philistines.' Remembering my erstwhile admiration for Henrietta's elegant

166

delicacy, I felt guilty at being so amused. Happily Iris said nothing about Isabel that was not kind. She didn't mention Francesca, whom I know she does not like.

She left the table and walked through the alcove to switch on the record player. 'Dancing time,' she said, holding out her arms. I suppose I must have noticed that she was wearing a black dress that buttoned all the way down the front. I had not expected her, as I approached somewhat stiffly, to start opening it up. Underneath she had on a glossy light blue bra, a scrap of matching blue lace between her legs, a suspender belt of the same blue, and stockings. 'I'll give you a toothbrush,' she said. 'You can use Peter's electric razor. As far as I can tell, you have everything else you'll need. Let's dance. This is going to be one hell of a Saturday night.'

So it proved. Iris's erotic vocabulary was vast and quite abandoned. Quite apart from everything else and incidental to the intense pleasure, it was a considerable education in racy terminology. As we lay side by side on the carpet of what (presumably) is the Cameron sitting room, myself breathing heavily and Iris's bosom gratifyingly heaving, still more or less in the glossy light blue bra, she turned her head and said, 'Good. Now that we're over the convulsive bang, let's go up to my bedroom and have a long delicious honey-fuck.' So we undressed each other. (Shoes and socks on such occasions are a surprising embarrassment.) It was certainly delicious but not notably long. Then Iris rolled over from the missionary position and said I could now give her the ride of her life. This was ecstatic: Iris knelt across me and writhed like a maenad first soughing and eventually almost shrieking.

We lay still for a while, for which I was grateful because I doubted how long I could keep up this pace. She got up, put on high-heeled slippers and swayed slenderly out of the room, astoundingly graceful, to return with a bottle of champagne which we sipped. With about half of it gone, she swung off the bed again and held out her hand. She was in complete control so I obeyed. I was led into a gleaming luxurious bathroom, where Iris stepped into the light blue tub. 'Wash me,' she said. 'All over, except my hair. Thoroughly.' It was an amazing sensation. I was required to pat her dry. Then she left.

By this time I understandably needed a shower myself. Iris

called, 'I'm going downstairs with the champagne. We have to keep up our strength. Don't bother to dress. I've left a dressing gown on my bed.' It was one of her own. At least not a flimsy negligee, but a silky very feminine kimono. I nevertheless felt absurd. Heracles at his most whimsical. Fortunately Iris was not dressed mannishly, because I don't think I could have dealt with that. Indeed she was wearing a sort of extended light blue camisole with suspenders which held up black stockings. She was cooking toasted cheese. Her luxuriant pussy was not as fair as her hair, but it was very pretty for all that. We ate and drank a little more, during which time she sat as decorously as was possible in the circumstances and I remained excitedly concealed under my all too sensuous kimono.

And so Saturday evening progressed. Once, passing a *bouquiniste* on the left bank of the Seine, I saw with curiosity a book entitled *Les 12 Postures d'Amour*. At the time I was too shy to buy it. Such *pudeur* has sloughed off after Iris. I calculate that I had learned seven of them and no doubt might have improved further if the farcical Muse had not intervened. After an active night we took separate baths. Looking unbelievably fresh, she was brewing coffee in the kitchen wearing only her high-heeled slippers. 'Well,' she said, 'I imagined that it was going to be one hell of a night and you did *not* disappoint me.'

Suddenly she thought that we had not done it straddled on an upright chair. She explained that it was quite something, with bilateral thrust (not entirely satisfactory in a knee-trembler) with the added advantage that I could fondle and kiss her tits. I've no doubt that it would have been marvellous, but such was the increased sensitivity in my genital area that I realized at once that a sudden tension on her part was not a venerean contraction. 'You're back early,' she said. Behind me I heard her brother's voice. 'So I see,' he said. 'I should have knocked. My God! *Ben!*' 'What happened?' Iris said, swinging off me with absolute composure. 'She had an attack of guilt,' he said. Clutching the kimono about my subsiding but still erect person, I backed out of the room.

It may be as well that I have not heard from her since. Such a complete in-service sexual training might become an obsession like jogging or weight training. In the succeeding days various lascivious images have formed in my mind, so that I have had to concentrate extra hard on my work. The hardest of all to chase away is the memory of Iris's black silk thighs around my head, her own wild pleasure, my grunting – subjugated and ecstatic. Rovola on Rhodope . . . Donne's eighteenth elegy . . . Oh dear! What's going to happen next? Be firm, Oldfield! That's the entire bloody problem.

Thus I too have become a victim of the volatile spirit of Farce. Kelly and Isabel stranded together: how delightfully embarrassing! Professor G. S. Walton walking into the Isis, still talking: how justly hilarious! And now Ben Oldfield bestraddled in a Garsington kitchen by a colleague's sister, having to hide his excitement behind her very kimono.

Farce thrives on bad news. Folktale, rumour, gossip, anecdote, stories in the gutter and roof-sluicing press. Admittedly many are full of fear and horror and pity: but just as many are founded upon malicious glee in the discomfiture or humiliation of this or that man or woman, preferably famous, rich and (if possible) good-looking. If unavailable the postman and the vicar's wife will do very well, or the headmaster and the head girl. Makes you scream, doesn't it.

Iris and I are safe enough: but suppose (instead of walking into the river) Professor G. S. Walton had been stranded in Marlborough with his secretary, Mrs Higgs. (Quite a thought, when you get round to it: thirteen stone if she's an ounce, but personable still.) And however lubricious his mind, Walton is supposedly respectable. No one cares much about what youngish single men such as Mendoza and I get up to, but suppose Charles Darrow was compromised with Henrietta or Iris or Samantha Wilkins. Samantha! *Sensation forte!*

My own ludicrous moment was private. Peter was taken aback but hardly discomposed: and Iris seemed entirely unmoved. It will remain so as far as he's concerned, but in one of her wilder moods Iris might tell it as a funny story. Yet what of all the whisperings and winkings there have been about Isabel and Kelly.

In our immediate ambit we need people to tattle about to make us feel snug in our own cocoons of self-esteem; beyond that we need stories of the folly, greed or malice of people in the wider world to make us feel superior or virtuous. If the sufferings of the heroic breed in us the hope that just possibly we might endure as courageously, the cavortings of the Olympians remind us that the great gods themselves can be reckless, silly and found out.

Most of us are egocentric, always centre stage. At worst characters in a strip cartoon with bubbles of glowing delusion over our heads. The salvation, such as it is, is the moral doubt we experience when made suddenly aware of others and realize that we may be distorting what is really happening by our interpretation. At one level or another this fictive bloodlust seems to me to operate from time to time in most people.

There is, however the reality of bad news. When it is on an enormous scale – a famine or a serious natural disaster – the listener (even more so, these days, the viewer), however appalled, probably feels powerless beyond contributing to some fund or other. Few of us are men and women of action.

What is more serious is the increasing malaise which many people I meet have experienced and describe about the underlying moral disintegration in our own society. Surely there *is* something to be done, some effort to be made. Unless it is too late.

. . . The winds of argument and contention were blowing furiously from all directions an evening or so ago in the SCR on this very subject. It was a Sunday guest night so there was an even wider spectrum of opinion than usual with infra-reds like Bridget Ross (or so she would have us believe) and ultra-violets like Christopher Makepiece, who is one of the young bright thinkers of the new Conservatism. When not dressed formally, as on this occasion, Makepiece wears large-brimmed hats and extravagant foulards. Also present were Lord Blakemore (high Tory), Henrietta (left of centre), Ivan Whitehart (fairly left Democrat), Max Davenport (acid), Henry Farnaby (crossbench), me (not very political) and Professor G. S. Walton (talkative). Diagnostic to begin with, in a thoroughly Oxford pattern, it became more heated. Bridget Ross makes a profession of being fiery: equally, Makepiece has high qualifications in supercilious irony. Henrietta's incisiveness, Davenport's sarcasm and Walton's irrelevant reminiscences about how various events from strikes in Australia, to riots in American cities, to uprisings in the Middle East had affected *him* added to the general excitement. I dismissed anodyne thoughts of the blue sheets of Iris

Cameron's bed because they were not especially soothing, thus surrendering myself to the argument.

There was consensus that there was soon likely to be trouble on the streets. The threatened miners' strike falls due in about a week, there is huge unemployment and there has already been sporadic rioting since the early eighties as proof of discontent fomented by racial antagonisms. There consensus stopped. As far as I recall (in no particular order) our state of cultural unrest was the result of the decline initiated in the sixties by the obsequious acceptance of 'pop', opening the way for permissiveness, general laxity and imminently pervasive narcosis; arrogant politicians especially on the Conservative side; the subversion of the militant left aided by prominent figures such as Benn (newly elected at Chesterfield) and Scargill (about to become very noisy); rampant commercialism exploiting particularly the discontent of the young and the rapacity of their elders with only an eye for profit; the encouragement of such an attitude by a cynical monetarist government interested in entrepreneurs rather than working people of whatever class; the idiocies of egalitarian fanatics over the years encouraging indiscipline, with the consequent decline in the quality and motivation of teachers; the intransigence of Thatcher and her sycophants creating vast unemployment, the source of much social unrest; the cheap standards of the popular press, television and a good deal of radio aiming at the lowest popular taste; universal greed.

Although never exactly degenerating into insult, feelings ran high. Lord Blakemore, cyclopeian at the best of times, looked even more awesome as he was suffering from some cyc-complaint and wearing an impressive patch. He contributed little to the sound and fury except to add barbed footnotes to the more sweeping generalizations using his encyclopedic knowledge of history which called upon various stages of Roman civil strife, sundry mediaeval rebellions, the decadence of nineteenth-century France and the blind folly of the tsars – among much else, to challenge, undermine or simply flatten this or that point. Impressive as he can be, Blakemore, in this company, did not have everything his own way: some of the others may not have known as much, but all (except perhaps me) are quick-witted and I suspect the two expressing the most extreme views are paradoxically the most clever.

171

Henry Farnaby, a mild enough man, diverted the main lines of conversation in an idle moment by quoting Luther: 'A ruler who is a bad man and prudent is preferable to a ruler who is a good man and imprudent.' He went on, however, to say that he thought that this might well have applied to Richard Nixon. In Henry's opinion, Nixon was not such a villain as had been made out. This incensed Whitehart, normally the most pleasant of men, who pronounced a vehement diatribe in which Henry himself might have been thought to be one of the discredited politician's closest intimates.

With the departure of Makepiece, followed soon by Bridget Ross, who no doubt was disappointed by the withdrawal of her most combative adversary, the evening became more relaxed. Henry did not take Whitehart's tirade personally and we were joined by two or three more convivial fellows and guests. Upon leaving, I found myself in the company of Robert Blakemore, which would not have been entirely of my choosing. For some reason, the noble lord, without the mitigation of other company, freezes my very soul. I know him to be an exemplary husband and father, devoted to his dog, of fair if severe mind, liked by a good many people whom I like, and admired by several more: yet there it is. As we walked he reviewed the evening's conversation quite kindly. We fell to discussing welfare organizations and charities, prompted initially (I suppose) by our passing the Oxfam shop. 'Ah well,' I said, as we came to the parting of our ways, 'I think it was H. L. Mencken who said: "If I am convinced of anything, it is Doing Good is in bad taste." ' *Infelix* Oldfield. Blakemore fixed me with his functioning eye. 'We spent a great deal of time this evening, Mr Oldfield, in analysing the causes and symptoms of social turbulence the world over. We did not discuss intellectual triviality: the quick mind which makes some glib observation, retort or jibe in order to shock, titillate, or else to elicit some immediate response – usually idle laughter. Personally, I have never felt much regard for Mencken, but I am mildly disturbed when such *jeux d'esprit* become the stock-in-trade of those who might be thought to be scholars. I bid you good night.'

He strode away, straight-shouldered, arrogant as ever in the confidence of his own inflexible integrity, limping very slightly. (An old war wound, no doubt.) I turned, waiting almost for the clatter of a biscuit-tin . . .

If I remember rightly it was Juvenal who suggested that, in his own time, the preference for myth and mythical themes indicated a flight from squalid and dangerous reality. How true is this of 1984? I think Juvenal was castigating other writers for their laziness or pusillanimity, while I am thinking of the reaction of audiences, especially television audiences.

There is, I understand, a proven appetite for costume drama. If I follow my adaptation of Juvenal's thesis, this is understandable. The machinations and violence of other ages is comfortable because it is all over: the Tudors, the Civil War, or, however luridly misrepresented, the life of Claudius. Even safer the long excursions through Galsworthy and Trollope; the distancing of the world of Waugh or Paul Scott's India. And yet there is an appetite for contemporary violence seen to be avenged as shown in the relatively amiable Kojak (as opposed to the loutish Starsky and Hutch), who is in the tradition of the countless good men obliged to be violent for altruistic ends. Exceptionally ferocious, bloody, violent or pornographic video films are watched not only by lolling, jaded, largely mindless adults (for I cannot believe that they are *all* depraved), but by giggling children who know no better and who might well expect *never* to know anything better, who rerun the especially nasty bits. So violence becomes acceptable and violent sex in all its forms is a matter for apathy, opportunism or the gratification of some instant savage impulse.

The adult audience cannot be accused of escaping from real contemporary horrors. The same television screens show, daily and nightly, slaughter, murder, outrage, brutality as it actually happens. There is the occasional bland caveat that 'some of the following sequences may upset more sensitive viewers.' It is small wonder that the audience escapes from news and current affairs into fantasy, absurd games based on greed, situation farces which are often cruel, the inane chat of topical swanks or endless serials which supposedly lend dramatic glamour to the kind of monotonous lives that most people lead. (My God! Grumble as I often do, seldom a day goes by when I do not bless my own good luck!)

None of us can escape all of the news all of the time. It is

173

dinned into us, remorselessly flashed before our eyes: the hostage body dumped onto the living-room carpet, the screaming child with its clothes on fire running desperately towards us. People dragged out of bombed buildings, victims of natural disaster and starvation – part of the daily, increasingly uncomfortable world in which most people know they are helpless.

How comfortable, then, to know that accessible, fictional villainies will be dealt with in a way which will come out right in the end, whatever the interim suspense. Human kind cannot take too much reality. Not exact: but it will do for the moment.

I have watched more television recently than I've been accustomed to in the interests of pursuing ideas of 'mythologies' as defined by Barthes. (To my mind not an exact phrase for myths or mythic simulations. Mythology is surely the *study* of myths?) I doubt that I am much the wiser.

At the same time, I am much more aware of my own susceptibility to what is presented, especially when I am tired. Such vulnerability is limited when it is a matter of advertising: I am relatively impervious to soap powders and detergents and to the nugatory claims of various household products. Not so to drinks. I have often found myself drowsily reminded of a Guinness or a brand of lager which I have not drunk for a while. I am beguiled by style even when I have no desire or need for the thing advertised. And while I am quietly appreciative of technique in films that I have already seen, in films or plays which have caught my brief attention I find myself avidly partisan – even when the retribution handed out to some sadistic and unspeakable monster is itself untowardly savage.

In someone trained for more than ten years in scholarly literary criticism, this is surely reprehensible.

Am I, which is to say are we all, thus becoming conditioned to the imagery of television: whether the obviously unreal picture of the world as portrayed in advertising, the contrived and carefully plotted scenarios of film and drama, the glamorous personae of living people made up and produced by public relations consultants, agents, and fatuous puppetmasters who believe in what Mendoza calls 'good television'?

If so, I am surely in a state where I will respond to slanted

174

documentaries or news stories. The direct party political broadcast is unlikely to deflect me: other less obvious methods of presenting events might very well influence my moral (as I see it) attitude and hence my political commitment. I am accordingly easily exploitable.

Television defines the object in such a way that perception is no longer a matter for the individual.

What is shown on television may not tell the viewer what to think, but it selects what he is to observe and thus conditions thought, often interpreting what would otherwise be seen subjectively in some cases, objectively in others, on the viewer's behalf.

I must read Barthes again. But not yet, O Lord, not yet.

The face of Garbo/Striptease. I suppose these represent the ambiguity of desire in a lot more men than me. On the one hand, the unreachable, icy princess who will never be possessed; on the other, the shameless but safely untouchable female whose job is to stimulate a form of lust which she will not be called upon to satisfy. Not personally. The facility with which I am attracted to women is quite nonsensical and I have more or less learned to live with it. I am disconcerted all the same to find myself, slightly tipsy, bored, fairly tired, drooling in fantasy over some woman on a television screen.

Not so much of late. Oh Iris, where the hell are you . . .

. . . I don't see how it can end there. In spite of the farcical denouement, too much happened in those twenty odd hours to be shrugged away. I don't love Iris and I'm damn sure she doesn't love me. Should I try to get in contact? Is she away? I have to admit I'm afraid that the telephone will be answered by her brother in his inimitably mocking vein. Why hasn't she tried to get in touch (unfortunate phrase!) with me? The gentleman's privilege. Or duty? I doubt that either would be of much importance to Iris, even if I pass for what used to be a gentleman.

It is not possible (at least for me) to think of women in the same way as I think of men. If I listed the twenty or thirty people I like most, the difference of attitude would be soon apparent to me. It is not simply a matter of sex, although sexual attraction would be a strong element in my interest in most (though not all) of the women concerned. But liking is more important than lust. And liking itself is not enough, not

175

quite enough. There must be at least a hint of love. Now: is it possible that there could be real love without desire? Things become much more complicated. When is desire not raw lust? To me perhaps the relationship between Isabel and Kelly is as sentimental as that between Leda and the Swan. To the people I teach, and God knows to others less sheltered, our mannered tea dance of lechery is Anna Neagle and Michael Wilding in *The Barretts of Berkeley Square* – a guilty eye over each shoulder and ears alert for a nightingale. There are horrors we know nothing of. I should like to *talk* to Iris. I have an uncomfortable feeling that she is wiser than most of us – certainly wiser than I am.

I cannot forget the excruciating pleasures I had with her, but I can no more rid myself of a sense of shame which is daily more oppressive. She could exorcise this – even though I knelt literally at Circe's altar.

The images crowd in again. *Opulent curves fill out her scarlet trousers and jacket slashed with gold.* Such fantasies cannot compare with the reality of possessing her or being possessed by her. And yet the memory of her encourages them. *Her ankles are linked by a slender fetterchain.* Not bloody likely. Not Iris.

It is all nonsense – almost sentimental. One carnal night – well, afternoon, evening, night and forenoon – with a highly sexed woman leaves me blaubering to myself, still wanting her and almost frightened of her. Love's old sweet song, be damned. You're hot! You're scalding!

Oh I had heard the rumours often enough and I had imagined her naked and half-dressed: but never such splendour. Now, as I wait for her and find myself in some trance of indecision, mildly besotted, I wonder how easy it is for her. How many others have spent such a night or such a weekend: to find themselves weakened by her, irresolute. In a way mocked, symbollically castrated. (That's rubbish: I'm mixing up me with theory.) She will never tell me and I should never ask, passing still for a gentleman. Perhaps it is all true and she had to face the fury of an incestuous brother. Then where the hell had *he* been? With whom? The one who was suddenly guilty? I wonder, innocent that I once was, how many of them are game: do it in the shake of a lamb's tail.

If I have plunged into infatuations and will no doubt do so

again with fatuous abandon, I have usually thought myself to be in love. Not with Iris, which perhaps makes her and what happened important. Her confidence and self-knowledge do not allow me to deceive myself. I think that we gave ourselves to one another physically for a few hours, expending a little spirit without any waste of shame. Not much else. Laughing witch: 'Come into the music-room and I'll peel off.'

Such music too. Variations that I shall never understand although we play them together, having forgotten the theme: not caring any more about the theme. Improvising. I see you now, entirely without care, ever without shame, disdaining modesty, swagger towards me. A dancer in complete control of her palpitating audience. You ask for submission, then demand a form of conquest, if only in the eyes that meet yours, until you wish to reassert your power. You relent and surrender something but never all your pride, keep briefly dormant some fury that is in you. And you laugh inside. You bewitch – not in the finery you choose to wear to tease, not even in the texture of your thighs and breasts unclothed. You promise no mystery for there is none. As you give, as you demand, those eyes, innocently blue, promise nothing. There can be no betrayal, for there was never any pledge of faith. This is how it is, this is how and who we are. Why ask for anything more?

She is difficult to idealize. And probably wouldn't want to be Aphrodite on anyone's page. No man's goddess and yet an enchantress, allmoist seductress, ready to enthral, to make mad, even if only for a night, in order to practise her art. I sit here, the two-headed Oxford don – Philip Sober and Philip Drunk without my lawnmower, computing a list of her likely lovers over more than twenty years, jealous and laughable in my own eyes, rueful about my one moment ever of terpsichorean ability . . .

At last she telephoned. She came around without my knowing what exactly to expect. She was cool, gently amused and never more attractive in a black leather jacket, which she threw aside, a white blouse and light blue narrow skirt, black shoes with very high heels, her eyes merry and her fair hair shining. She took a gin and tonic, lit a cigarette and crossed the faultless legs which I remembered all too vividly disposed in other ways. 'I'm sorry,' she said. 'I should have been in contact before, but I had to go away.' She explained that it had nothing to do with the unexpected appearance of her brother. 'Just business,' she said. For a while she watched me wondering what to do, wondering what she wanted me to do. Then she said, 'It was good, you know. Very, very good. Much more than I'd imagined. But you know that was *it*, don't you? Not because of Peter arriving. Because I'm the woman I am and you are the very dear man you are. It would be mad to pretend otherwise. As far as I'm concerned, it's happened before and will happen again. You couldn't take that.' I asked if we were never to make love again. 'Was that what it was?' she said, smiling and shaking her head. 'I don't know, Oldfield. We shall have to find out. But it will have to be sheer chance. I shan't risk hurting you. You don't love me, do you?' I said that I did not think so. 'Good. I hope we'll go on seeing each other. Can I have another drink?' And that was that. Typically she had come to my rooms not to shirk such intimacy by suggesting that we meet in a pub or a restaurant; typically she had come immediately to the point without for a moment playing down her intense physical attraction, without underestimating the emotional tie which she recognized was mutual. Of course I desired her and still do. I have tried to think of her many lovers: dominated as I was, controlled as I was, by a harlot sorceress. But I find that I admire her.

Past was is today. What then is will then tomorrow as now was be past yester. Parallax, indeed! Come home to roost. Ah well, time for Barthes.

*　　*　　*　　*　　*

The bitch shuddered. Little bitch actually almost squirmed when I touched her. And it wasn't as if I'd reached for her tits or tried to put my hand up her skirt, the merest touch on her upper arms and she tensed and trembled, her shoulders hunched and she was very still. Perhaps she was surprised because I came up behind her. Unmistakable revulsion all the same. And yet the whorelet can sit in fucking public with her hand on Kelly's twilled thigh. Hastily withdrawn, of course,

as I approached. Fluttery simper and his bland smile . . .
Well, hel*lo* Giles! Hello be fucked! When I just touched her
that shiver of complete distaste which ran through me too
like an electric shock. Involuntary? I'm not sure. Perhaps it
was designed to hurt and so repulse. Oh she apologized. Took
her by surprise. But if you are startled you don't recoil in
quite that way. You jump. And *you* don't apologize. You say
what the fuck d'you mean creeping up like that, stupid
bastard. Frightened me.

All right, little lovebird, it's over. I thought it would be
hard work but that I'd make you in the end. If you're someone
else's *tartine* I'll choose the *crêpe surprise*. And I'm not staying
awake another moment with such hatred and pain as I did
last night. *Why?* Why let it get to me? It doesn't matter. God,
I have the proof of years that I'm attractive enough to women.
Not to anyone until now in some way loathsome . . . No,
Marion, I don't want to be bothered about that now, I'm
collecting my thoughts for the Cherubim and Seraphim who
continually do cry for something different. Let it go. Never
one for the sharp allusion, Marion. No glimmer of a smile.
Only woman I know whose eyes can flash sullenly. Says she'll
leave the papers, folds her arms across her fine tits in a black
wool dress and goes out wafting her shapely arse from side to
side with hauteur. What about *her* for example? Doesn't like
me but I'd soon get over that and she'd enjoy being the
dominant one from time to time. Dark, tall, good-looking,
great figure. Why not? No. Wouldn't do. Not bright enough.
Besides there are something like thirty other possibles just as
attractive. My trouble is I go for the classy broads, Henrietta,
Eve Darrow which is dreaming the impossible dream,
Samantha ditto, Isabel even if she is a little tramp, Christina
. . . Now there's a thought. Yes. Stir up a little mischief and
profit from a bit of insider trading. Ghastly man Cecil Hanover
I interviewed fixed his son-in-law by some frame-up when
Passoa was having it off with Sandy Fleming. Old bloody
goat with his scraggy face trying to look aquiline. Literary
politics in the thirties. I took him apart. Christ! I *must* collect
my thoughts for the glorious company. What time is it?
Quarter to. Fatal flaw, I suppose: classy women and the need
to be thought a heavyweight. Part of the same thing. Now
then: marshall the arguments . . .

Fucking telephone! Yes. All right, Marion, put him on . . .
Rupert! You cunning old bear! *Was gibt's sonst?* How are
things at Hentzau? . . . Good . . . Yes. Series finished at the
weekend. Usual thirteen-week run . . . I'm glad you liked it
. . . Great. (What's this about? He wants something.) . . .
Well, that was the general idea. Rub a little salt in. Arts
programmes are too bland most of the time . . . I agree . . .
Next autumn, keeping the same format, I hope . . . By no
means, old friend! You should know what the Beeb is like.
There are one or two in the midwifery who wanted it stillborn
and now they want to take it off life-support. I'm just about
to have a meeting with them . . . Contracted for two series
. . . Well, they'll have to pay me off or find something else.
I wouldn't mind *that* much. Don't exactly want to be slotted
as an 'arts' presenter. (When is he going to get to the point?)
. . . Lunch? Sure. Let's see. I'm free on the 18th. Next
Wednesday. Two days before Good Friday. Suit you? . . .
Great . . . The Rue St Jacques, Charlotte Street? Hey,
Rupert, this must be something special . . . What . . . You'll
explain then . . . That's fine. I'll look forward to it . . .
Wiedersehn.

Wonder what's up his sleeve. Sounds promising. Independent company. Perhaps he really *did* like the series. Can't be
anything this year, so I'll be in a strong position. Either take
him up if the offer's good or put up the ante with this lot.
Should be moving. God, wish I could get that little cow out
of my head. Shudder. Should move in fact right away. Sell
Aunt Dorothy's house. There are those who'd swear that I'd
have sold Aunt Dorothy. And they'd be wrong. But I'll never
be anything there. A curiosity simply because I'm *on* television
and radio and write for magazines they pretend never to read
and occasionally the odd piece for papers they do. Not for
myself, though, or any qualities of mind I might possess.
Oxford abhors a heteroclite. Academic Oxford. Too independent for them. And what does she matter or any other of the
supercilious bitches. Iris is the only one worth anything and
she *won't* fucking conform. Neat way of putting it. Never
fool myself that I love whoever it is but have to admire the
woman I'm screwing. Otherwise sex is nothing. Might as well
feel up one of the dollies around here or zip through a whole
chorus who'd like to be laid by a personality. Or go to an

expert expensive tart. I can afford it. Just won't do for Mendoza. I hate that little *salope*.

Get on your fucking bike, Mendoza. I'll have to think on my feet. Wonder who'll be there . . . OK Marion. I'm just going. In no shape for a tricky meeting. Right. No question about Austin in the chair which no one has had the foresight to electrify, Wolfe who left his fabulous Central European charm back in Austria or Hungary or Liechtenstein or wherever else he took refuge from but has forgotten that it's still there in some scuffed railway *consigne*, Mabel Senior who glittered as a presenter but who has acquired executive furrows between her eyes and has to high-heel her way through daily dross like Marie-Antoinette through the cowshit. All certainties. Ah no – Peregrine Hyde will be there, although it's nothing to do with him, because he never misses a meeting – any bloody meeting. It is after all the function of anyone of his seniority in the Corporation. With luck that'll be the lot but I doubt it. Wolfe wants to kill the programme to make room for some scheme of his own with Naomi Baron and her teeth . . . Ah shit! Already in position with Hyde beaming isometrically (always some thin balding bastard everywhere with a name like Peregrine or Egremont or Fenelon in all the committee rituals). Plain, bluff and pompous, yesterday's Mr Cinders, Wally Bacon, and tapping a menacing pencil Gilbert Slack of the pale-lashed sideswept eyes. This Mendoza is a hiding to nothing. Not my week.

Entrance (stately) of Mabel Senior, long of handbag and slim of briefcase. Gone the days when she chatted in a moderately low-cut blouse to Jim the Jumbo or flirted (glitteringly materteral) with The Passing Clouds, The Rockalls and other pop groups on their way (but not fast enough) to oblivion. Now trim in a check suit which reveals how well she has kept her figure and in high heels which express the curved tension of her excellent calves, she pleases us with a glimmer of the smile that entranced Jim the Jumbo and countless children and pensioners in the early sixties. Still as executive producer of the series she will be an ally. My producer, Shem Jenkins, shambles in with what he hopes is cool arrogance sitting as far away from everyone as possible wearing an old unpressed shirt ungreeted.

'Mabel, what did you do at the weekend? We've been

181

comparing notes.' Treading upon eggs we wait for her to say that she was laid by her husband Cecil, Bert the local bobby and Frieda her neighbour's au pair. Well, she says, I didn't watch the programme. We had people in for dinner so I spent most of Sunday cooking. Wally Bacon had a really good afternoon in the garden. Josef Wolfe read the latest Milan Kundera and a little George Eliot for relaxation after tea. Hyde watched, ha ha ha, television. He thinks that Maggie Thatcher must have seen Flora Robson as Queen Elizabeth in *The Sea Hawk* and believed it. Peregrine was left wing up to a point during the satirical sixties and likes to keep up delusions. Bacon amiably joins in his laughter, Wolfe smiles in a way that suggests he is trying not to vomit (such charm!) and elevates his fine Transylvanian profile, Slack sniggers weakly, Mabel flickers a little, I chuckle obligingly, Shem Jenkins yawns. Shem will have to go. Hyde travels ceaselessly through committees.

At last bustling and explosive appearance of Danby Austin, pursued by his capacious arse, waddling urgently into the room his spectacles shining with indiscriminate malice. Usual sychophantic rhubarb as Danby manoeuvres his posterior into the specially reinforced unelectrified chair. Plonk. Not one to stand on ceremony Danby comes straight to the point: 'Right then what about this f — sodding series?' A recognitive glance at Mabel since it is well known that Danby was brought up in a tough school and respects no one when it comes to effing and blinding. Good sign. The f — sodding series was Danby's idea with abrasive little me up front taking the f — sodding flak. Mabel crosses suave tights (I imagine) and works up her skirt a little to ease the tension as it were. I'm the only one in a position to admire which of course she does not know. Not a chance! Or at least I'd be very surprised . . . Shudder! That humiliating slut! Not a time to feel downtrodden. It's all coming. But not in *that* way.

Warts and all. Iron out the corrugations. TCP on the pimples and Germoloids where it matters (Ha, ha, ha: Hyde) Danby thinks it was a fairly successful venture which could be f . . . pretty fucking good. Ah well. Mabel uncrosses her legs and *is* wearing tights with an appealing gusset. I wonder why? Gusset I mean. Recrossed slitheringly all is mystery again.

Josef Wolfe spreads his hands and uplifts again that curiously noble nose, his vestiges of accent and experience, of worming his way into the establishment significant in every gesture as he presents not only the tablets but the glory of his own intellectual acumen to all present. 'I'm sorry, Danby: but I don't think it came off. Forgive me, Giles. This is no reflection on you, or indeed on Mabel.' Snort from Shem Jenkins who is doing himself no favours. Wolfe pauses to lean his lupine face upon his hand. Broods for a second. Then the hand opens in a controlled, reasonable gesture: 'We have to ask ourselves if we were right conceptually. We were rightly, in my own opinion, aiming for a programme about the arts which was different. The challenging style of Giles helped. *Some* of the political items worked well. A few of the squibs went off, but others were decidedly damp and one or two backfired.' Amusement from Hyde and Wally Bacon. Strictly token BBC amusement. Mabel sits with her rather nice mouth compressed, eyes stony, still (happily) unaware that I have a four-star view of her thighs worth a detour but not a special visit. Danby Austin never laughs at any jokes but his own. Slack taps his baleful pencil. Wants us chopped as badly as Wolfe but hates him more than he does the rest of us, even Mabel Senior a rival executive producer. 'All right, Josef. Anything constructive to say?' After all it was Danby's own bright idea. 'Yes. The problem as I see it with the concept was (perhaps I should still say is) that, like all the other arts series, it treated the arts as something apart from daily life. I think and I will come straight to the point that it should be replaced by another series which relates the arts – and I do mean the fine arts – not to concepts of society but to the real society that we live in. And it should not be too serious. There should be laughs.' Coming from a man who has to exercise his facial muscles for five minutes every morning practising smiling, this observation is received impassively by all except Shem Jenkins who snickers. I catch Mabel's eye and allow myself a small ironic grin. She remains stony but shifts position and in so doing reveals an inch or so more thigh. Not at all bad when seen in longer perspective. A lecherous eye still at such a moment in my career. As Wolfe contracts his shoulders and extends his arms in a shrug which signifies: And there you have the not entirely unestimable wisdom of Josef Wolfe which you may take or leave but you would be fools to ignore.

Mabel uncrosses her legs and leans forward, about to speak, which makes the prospect the more enchanting even if the thighs are still decorously compressed. All the more exciting to etcetera. Ah but Gilbert Slack is in first. Hair, eyebrows and eyelashes the colour of authentic powdered ginger, features arranged in what he took to be scrupulous concern in his days as an interviewer, inescapably shifty, his soothing voice anxious but not quite wheedling he cautiously bites his thumb at Wolfe before presenting it to Austin. 'But Danby, we are after all discussing a series about the arts. And not at all bad. As you've said yourself, there are hiccups to be cured. But we should remember that we haven't congratulated Mabel and Giles and – ah – Shem Jenkins for what they actually *did* achieve.' (General murmurs of BBC assent.) 'What troubles me is that if we broaden our approach to the arts, which need every scrap of support that a public corporation can offer, we will detract from the impact of a programme like "Rainbow." After all we have enough programmes of general concern from the news magazines to our own output.' Of course. That is the point. Not Slack magnanimity, simply the fear that Wolfe is going to make a territorial claim in his *liebensraum*: Who could believe it of the archetypal freedom-seeker? But still. Slack is safe enough with 'Citizen Jane' a woman's view of the world we live in and 'Down the Market' the thick person's guide to social economics, but he is evidently worried about his pet projects 'Grasshopper' our culture like what she really is and 'What's News?' stories that really matter for ordinary people who couldn't give a toss for Ronald Reagan and Maggie Thatcher and God and that. He is also planning 'Dispute It' – a series that will really dig into issues others want to cover up, however prescient their motives. Slack, his wan face a study in anxiety, clips any altruistic impulses with his fingernails at least twice a week.

Before Mabel can try again Danby Austin flabs a paw at her and in my general direction. 'Perhaps we should go around the table and then let Mabel and Giles have the floor to make our – which is to say their – case. Peregrine?' Mabel leans back her hemline long forgotten. And Hyde begins. Danby drums his fingers on the table and thinks about his CBE,

Wolfe closes his eyes and thinks about his profile and lunch with an attractive ballet dancer from Vienna or Budapest or Croydon, Slack thinks about ways to do down people likely to get in the way of Slack and keep them there, Wally Bacon conducts a plain man's tour around Wally Bacon just as Peregrine will hang-glide over the wisdom of his own words when it is Bacon's turn to speak, Mabel is seething, Shem Jenkins points to his watch and leaves without being noticed. I fix my eyes on Mabel's legs and think about Christina. Nothing like keeping the mind clear. I know what I'm going to say and how, jokily, I'm going to say it. Feel better. Stopped bothering about that horrible shudder. Thanks Mabel. Thank you in advance, Christina. Anyway it doesn't matter: we're all right. Danby Austin will cover himself by saying it's ultimately up to the Controller but . . . Oh Lord, she's noticed: a rapier glare as she tugs at her skirt. Who knows though? First tentative gambit. Peregrine meanders on seraphically.

★　★　★　★　★

Hotel Concordia
Venice
Easter Sunday, 1984

Dear David,
This letter will probably be a surprise that you may not entirely welcome. I decided to come to Venice for a few days after one or two conversations with Francesca Oricellari had aroused in me a nostalgia for a place where I was once very happy. I was quite young and probably much less defensive than I later became. Something I am now inclined to regret.

I suppose it is that nostalgia and the memory of being in love which has nerved me to write to you in quite this way.

It's a strange feeling when you have imagined yourself as someone fairly central to the action to find yourself in the wings, waiting to make an occasional, unimportant entrance. That probably sounds like, and perhaps is, nonsense. But I have that feeling of being an onlooker when I might have been something other – an amusing secretary or maid in a Coward comedy without the funny lines, when I might have been the other tempting woman.

Perhaps I never did tempt you and all the dashing chat was just a joke after all to which I kept up a studied (and now you will know how carefully studied!) indifference. In the last few months, especially when I've watched you with Isabel Darrow, I think I might have been a fool. I think I was always a little in love with you without daring to admit it. I'm not even sure that I admit it now. And I'd be lying.

Relationships are *always* difficult. My trouble has always been that I have never been able to judge distance. I suppose we were an affectionate undemonstrative family without ever being close to one another. As I grew older, I became aware that what interested me was either dismissed by my parents or else it puzzled them. Naturally enough they were pleased when I did well at exams and won prizes. They said they were proud of me but I somehow felt that they wished, in their separate ways, that I had turned out differently. I was much more undemonstrative than they could have wanted. I was physically attractive as well as bright, but I didn't have boyfriends whom they could like or else warn me off. Of course I did: but here too I was restrained. Not inhibited, simply restrained. I felt sexy enough. My fantasies were quite passionate, though, not surprisingly, innocent: but I could never reproduce the passion when someone to whom I was genuinely attracted touched me. As ever, I was damned by reason. Even as I was failing to respond with the fire that I (and no doubt the disappointed boy) wanted, I could think: Ah well, at least Gavin X or Johnny Y knows what my breasts feel like and will have the memory of his hand *so* far between my legs. And then it was all over. All perfectly friendly when Gavin or Johnny fancied someone else, because I didn't care that much. I wanted sex but did not seem able to give in to it. It was much the same when I went up to Oxford, except that the petting, as we used to call it, was rather more inventive.

Since then I have had lovers whom I've never talked

about except to a very close woman friend. I learned to give myself, never entirely convinced that I was only looking for carnal satisfaction which was rather getting in the way. When I fell in love, at last, I began to understand myself and another person. He turned out to be married. Thereafter, perhaps a little more competent at the technique, on the rare occasions when I had an affair I kept my head. *En cas d'incendie gardez votre sang-froid.* More than anything I was determined never again to become a threat to any practicable working marriage, even one in difficulties. Once again it was a matter of judging distances.

Most of the time I am entirely contented. Of course I dress carefully and (I think) prettily in order to play up the reactions of those who expect a female philosopher to look quite different, but I seldom intend to be provocative. Except with you. Not always, but fairly often, I behaved wilfully in a way designed to remind you that I was first a woman, then a friend, then another philosopher. You responded. It never went beyond banter and persiflage as we are both well aware and that was enough. You were aware of me and I was not doing any harm to Christina with whom I was sure you were happy. Although I don't think she enjoys the circles in which we usually move, I think she and I have always been perfectly at ease and have become reasonably good friends. I shall now confess that sometimes, when I was in an unusually randy mood or when you said something untowardly arousing, I was tempted to seduce you. I've no way of knowing whether I should have succeeded. I genuinely believe, however, in the 'nothing in excess' axiom: so I settled for your company, friendship, the occasional flurry of sexy chat. If I admitted that I was a little in love with you then, I became more and more certain as I watched you becoming increasingly involved with Isabel. Hardly improbable. You see each other frequently: Isabel is young, very beautiful and lively, obviously attractive to many men of all ages and fully aware of it. However she has greeted the advances which have no doubt been made to her, Isabel, unlike Iris Cameron for whom I have a grudging (*very* grudging)

187

admiration, behaves with perfect discretion. I haven't thought about it much until the last six months or so, but I have in the past wondered why such a remarkable girl has no steady relationship with someone more or less her own age. It's apparent that she prefers the company of older men, but it can hardly be an intellectual preference and I wonder if it is not mildly destructive.

Now I see her from time to time with you, when both have abandoned any discretion. I shan't pretend that my concern is for Christina, although I would not wish her any more hurt than I might once possibly have caused. I am simply jealous for the lost elegance of a love affair we might have shared, if I had been a little less astringent and perhaps a little more tart.

For a while I tried to deceive myself that it was all some quirk of pique. Whitehart suggested we spend this or that weekend together and I almost did. Francesca told me, merrily, that Ben Oldfield had taken a fancy to me. And for a moment I felt like taking up the option. It wouldn't have worked. Still a question of distance. I know enough now to go through the motions effectively, but that's not appropriate. Ridiculous and demeaning for a sexual desire to matter as much, which is, perhaps, why I am exaggerating what I feel for you.

Venice is beautiful. Why can't there be some congress of European philosophers here which we might both attend and be taken in some Jamesian trance? I woke at five this morning, the hour and the day when Dante ended the *Inferno*: it is now beginning to be light and it will be a lovely day. I doubt very much that I shall send this letter, while I'm not sorry to have written it.

No reproach, just regret and love,
Henrietta

5

29 April 1984

*I*t is strange that, apart from keeping a tedious, somehow jumpy, holiday, we do not make more of a fuss about Easter. I suppose, in all fairness, proper Christians do, so it behoves the rest of us to treat their observations with respect. At the same time, it is unusual for the essentially secular throng not to take advantage of a Christian festival to set up some essentially secular ritual. At Easter it doesn't happen. The commercialism is there: bunnies, eggs, fluffy chicken toys and the rest – but there is (perhaps mercifully) little of the jolly goodwill which writes off Christmas and the New Year for about two weeks of unnecessary entertainment, making it a time of evergreen boredom. Then Easter should be, for part of the time, a season of dutiful dolour: yet for believers the moment of resurrection and rebirth should signify great rejoicing. As a humanist, it is none of my business, but even as a child I was conscious of too much solemnity. In those days Good Friday was (as I recall) always sunny and after going to church I was free to play football – not a proper match, just a few of us fooling around on any odd patch of grass. Now in my thirty-eighth year I find myself longing for an inconsequential kickabout. According to Evan Warrington's friend, Jack Maddox, Easter was always a great occasion in Nonconformist Wales in his own childhood when entire villages, except for drunks and members of the Church of England, turned out for massive ceremonies of singing which even the apostate radicals held in tacit respect, while withholding their support.

This comes to mind because, for once, I should have

189

welcomed companionship when nothing at all is happening. Easter falls in a vacation, so everyone is away or catching up on neglected work or even springcleaning. No one seems to have the urge to entertain, or indeed be entertained.

Christina claims to be tired and says she will enjoy a few days' rest. She did not want to drive to a pleasant hotel in the country (of which there are a dozen within thirty miles of Oxford) to spend a lot of money and tramp through muddy footpaths. She did not want to telephone a few friends, perhaps enfogged in similar torpor, to arrange an impromptu rave-up. She made some acidulous asides on the reliability of my car (her own, when she chooses to use it, is provided by the company) and we left it at that. I have worked at my notes on Croce, Christina has watched television. We meet when it is time to eat.

1 May

Another term which I greeted with rather less lethargy than usual. It's pleasant to see Isabel regularly, looking very lovely, but perhaps overplaying her mischievous charade. I'm quite sure it means nothing to her; for me, however, the most casual intimacies remind me how desirable she is and I have to admit that I want her.

It was odd to receive a letter from Henrietta, posted on Easter Day at Venice and then to bump into her outside Marks and Spencer. She is a prolific writer of letters, usually addressed to Christina and myself. This was for me alone and was obliquely admonitory. Could it be that she took the game we have played over the years more seriously than I did? If so, it is not a very agreeable irony. She and Christina have always been friends, but there is in the letter a hint of something else. Nothing explicit. No direct reference to Isabel. She asks me to be careful. It is so easy to hurt and be hurt. *Qui aime bien châtie bien*. A busy morning in Cornmarket Street is hardly the time for sensitive colloquy. Besides, Henrietta was in a hurry.

It is becoming evident that Isabel and I should either call off the game or else play it seriously. Sometimes I wonder if there is a latent instinct for destruction in her. Fantastical it may be, doubtless evoked by Henrietta's description of a spring day in Venice, but I find myself thinking of the story

I read somewhere of Merlin the Enchanter building the most beautiful city in the world for a peasant girl with whom he fell in love. The girl of great beauty would not be satisfied until he had given her his magic ring. Laughing she threw it into the sea, whereupon Venice and the girl vanished, with Merlin left alone and weeping on a deserted marshland. Well, that is far too much. At the same time Isabel's laughter, most of the time merry, sometimes seems to me to be derisive. Quite as intelligent as her sister and her mother, she makes a deliberate point of setting aside all the things the rest of us presume to care about – perhaps because she sees through the presumptions. And yet she wanted to come to the symposium in Bristol and Ben Oldfield tells me she has been reading Baudelaire because of something Ferdinand said to her.

Unlike her sister, who cares fiercely about any number of current predicaments, Isabel doesn't seem to give a damn about anything. Before we became close I remember wondering why she dawdled around at Oxford when there were glamorous jobs she could walk into with her looks and family connections – in politics or broadcasting or publishing. She is more beautiful than Francesca Oricellari and just as alluring as Iris Cameron. Even this she laughs away. Is it the arrogance of slender, youthful, self-evident perfection? It is difficult to believe that she is cynical, nihilistic. Destructive. I shall have to talk seriously to her. I am too old to be a plaything.

6 May
I think I shall know when I am finally old and thoroughly jaded when I stop fretting about my Schools candidates. The nice little girl who was almost shot down in flames by Wittgenstein is still airborne. She won't get a first, but she will perform well enough. As always there are a couple of walk-overs; one noisy, the other quiet. Much will depend on last-minute nerves. They should be all right. I am more worried about George Boniface who has taken to walking up and down the room during tutorials. He is sharp, witty and (I suspect) desperate to do well. He wants to prove himself so badly to someone: possibly himself. The rest of them will do as well as they can. May be one or two surprises either way. At least most of them will find some kind of work. That, as Ingestre

and Warrington are for ever pointing out, is the cruelty of Thatcher-Lawson Britain. These kids work very hard. For what? And how much thought do pious buggers like Ingestre, Warrington and me give to the 'low achievers'? I was never worried. None of us were: Henrietta, Ingestre, Warrington, Peter Cameron. We *enjoyed* examinations. It was a polite way of showing off. And *here* we all are! There are the consolatory presences of Ferdinand and Ben Oldfield to remind us that thinking can be pretty rugged and tiresome, if one doesn't take it up professionally: but it is the women among whom we manage to survive who represent what it is worth living for. In their different ways: Eve Darrow, Samantha Wilkins, Francesca Oricellari, Iris Cameron (indeed!), Christina who turned away from it all, and Isabel . . . No. I am not going to think about her.

10 May
Christina in Brussels again. Lunch with Roger Ingestre and Peter Cameron, during which the conversation, as might have been predicted, was about politics. Interesting all the same: while Cameron teaches politics, taking a 'critical' view which may be impartial but does not err on the side of the imputation of noble or generous motives towards politicians, Ingestre, the historian, is still the dedicated idealist. Ingestre was gloomy about the implications of the Libyan Embassy siege and international terrorism. So indeed were we all. And once more, as Cameron pointed out, it took the shooting of a policewoman in a London square to make us properly aware of daily atrocities in Beirut or Belfast. None of us could even sketch a scheme to combat fanaticism: Cameron, disturbingly clear-headed, pointed out that it was hardly possible in a liberal (or relatively liberal) democracy. 'Once you say let's bomb the bastards, you've given up. They're justified. They're winning.' Ingestre wondered what would happen if the Soviet Union were involved in some major terrorist outrage upon its citizens or dependants. Cameron thought they would manage things behind the scenes in a way which the Americans in particular and the West in general could not because of the insistence of the press and competing television channels looking for sensation. 'We seem to be saying,' said Ingestre, mournfully, 'that democracy and freedom of

192

expression work against a decent, civilized way of life.' Cameron nodded. I didn't commit myself.

Looking back on it, our conversation was pretty depressing all round. With the miners' strike approaching its ninth week, there seems to be a fair amount of violence and intimidation. Ingestre foresees more and more trouble on the streets, fomented by the extreme right but much more significantly by the extreme left, leading to the organization of a paramilitary police force on the lines of the CRS or the *carabinieri*. After all, such a force already exists in Northern Ireland. Compared to both Cameron and Ingestre I am an innocent about politics, so I was alarmed to hear both quite calmly discussing the possibilities of repression and revolution. Ingestre, naturally, sees a solution in the adoption of centre politics with the existing Alliance reinforced by defections of reputable men and women from the Conservative left and the Labour right. Cameron is not as hopeful. He considers the Alliance to be well meaning and ineffectual, which is the central nervous disease of liberal politics from time immemorial. In an entirely uncommitted way, he thinks much will depend on the schismatic impulses of the unions, a growing prosperity among those in work, the strength of the black economy as against the anger of the unprivileged or (curious word) dispossessed.

We left Ingestre, after a very good lunch with a delightful Moulin à Vent, whistling not very convincingly in the twilight. Cameron and I walked part of the way to our respective colleges together, chatting inconsequentially. Oxford is always at her best in May sunlight, so our mood lightened. Not, I suspect, that Cameron allows his political reflections to weigh heavily upon him. I daresay he must hold some convictions, but he is in the true sense a student of politics as I am a student of philosophy and Warrington (for example) is a student of literature. He inquired about Christina and suggested that we come out to Garsington one summer afternoon. 'I wondered,' he said, 'about inviting Isabel and Ben Oldfield, but perhaps that wouldn't be the right mix.' That might mean a dozen things.

12 May

Some good work on Croce. I have become particularly interested in his view of the passivity of nature until it is under the artist's focus, which, if I remember rightly, was part of Baudelaire's aesthetic theory. I shall have to look it up. It is too early to work out a theme and I have to read a great deal more, but I can see a pattern emerging in an examination of reality and ideality which would involve extensive research in Santayana and Collingwood. At least it keeps me busy. Teaching is going well and there are no alarums from my examination lot.

I found myself wondering as I wandered around the Parks today and around the early blossom trees of the roads leading away from the town how much Oxford had changed in twenty years. I arrived here in 1964 in the autumn, when it was not particularly turbulent, even if no longer respectful of authority. Then there were a few years of threatened disturbance. In retrospect nothing that the majority of undergraduates could not and would not have put down, but distressing, at least for some of the dons. Hence we have evolved again into something quite different. My undergraduates are so solemn and worried. Ingestre and Ferdinand remember Suez and Hungary and the earlier CND demonstrations. Robert Blakemore recalls Hogg winning an election against Lindsay in the 'Munich' by-election of 1938. Blakemore is a very unconvincing Tory, but I should never dare suggest it: he believes in academic impregnability, a kind of courage in warfare, decency towards everyone. Right or wrong, Disraeli represents Conservative thinking for Blakemore in a way in which Mrs Thatcher, Macmillan and even Heath could not. *Noblesse* has to bloody *oblige*. At heart Blakemore is a Whig. I should be the last to wish to tell him so. And I have heard Peter Cameron's political morality compared to that of Metternich. It is very confusing. Parliamentary democracy will see the lot of us in a mass grave, into which we wandered by mistake. Then, moral philosophers are no judges of expediency.

Summer. Summer approaching. I wonder about the old men and old women remembering times I never knew. The little lost love affairs which must have mattered so much at the time, passing glances of affection, moments of recognition, all the clichés of half-heard songs which were in an instant real enough. Not all that difficult to realize. *Réaliser* in the French sense. Reality and ideality. *Un film de David Kelly.*

Here I am then, aged thirty-eight. Settled. Not much farther to go, unless I leave Oxford. Adequate, respected, considerate to the students. No ambition, other than to write some decent books. Slightly lost. I was sharp but never original. For a philosopher that is not quite enough.

Christina came home a few hours ago. Very tired. She met Mendoza on the train from London. I cooked supper during which she told me that he had hinted that Isabel and I were having an affair. I said it wasn't true. She shrugged. 'He thought it was a good time to make a pass at me,' she said. 'Was it?' She laughed.

*   *   *   *   *

It was a lovely warm evening in late May and Isabel was on her own. Her parents were in London and Elaine was at her college working. She had not seen David Kelly for over a week and was not quite in the mood for the irrepressible good humour of Ben Oldfield. As it happened Isabel did not mind these occasional moments of privacy. Most of the time she was expected to be the happy, laughing one. She knew that she could be funny without being malicious, while realizing that she, in common with most people, occasionally did something or said some casual word that was hurtful. When Giles Mendoza had suddenly gripped her shoulders, her reaction had been involuntary. When she had turned, though, there had been a deeply hurt look in his eyes which she still remembered after several weeks. Isabel did not want to wound anyone, however unintentionally. Mendoza actually did put her off and there was fair evidence that he had directed a certain amount of malice towards her and David Kelly. Their own fault, perhaps. Since the initial, thoroughly misunderstood accident of the car breakdown, they had perhaps courted scandal in an irresponsible way. It was ironic that David was much more concerned, as far as she could tell when they were alone together, about Christina's indifference and his suspicions that she was having her own affair with a person or persons unknown. Isabel was not enjoying her line

195

of thought, so she decided to take advantage of the weather and go out.

As she crossed the quad, various people smiled at her in a tentative way. The days seemed to be over when they would have engaged her in light chat before suggesting a quiet drink or a decent curry or (rarely) something grander out of the *Good Food Guide*. Why she had become unapproachable mystified her, because Elaine was evidently still thought to be biddable. Pity, she thought: an evening out would have been quite fun. Things improved when she turned into Broad Street where she met Evan Warrington. They told each other it was a beautiful evening. He was off to the Turf beer garden for a pint or so of Old Hookey.

'That sounds lovely,' Isabel said.

'Why don't you come too, if you've nothing better to do.'

'I can't think of anything better to do. Thank you.'

'My pleasure.'

'But you've got a book. Won't I be a nuisance?'

'The nice thing about books is they keep.'

And so they went along to the Turf Tavern and sat in the waning early summer light, talking peacefully. Warrington was reading a novel by a writer whom Isabel did not know of called Vargas Llosa. It was called *Aunt Julia and the Script-writer* and sounded interesting.

Warrington did not condescend. He talked about Latin American writers as though she might have read them all. She had heard of Borges and Neruda; she knew that Garcia Marquez had won the Nobel Prize, but the other names he reeled off meant very little. At the same time he was sharing something, rather than talking to himself. It was the way you talked to someone over a glass of beer. You assumed intelligence. Given that your companion was a woman, you did not push it. Not at all.

'I've been talking too much,' he said. 'I'll ask you something impertinent? Why don't you get the hell out of this place?'

'Easy riposte. Why don't you?'

'Good. I did for a while. I had to be in the army, which was not at all unpleasant. I went to teach in Canada. Then they took me back. It's comfortable. But I'm in my late forties and you're *not*.'

196

'I think I'm quite happy.'

'I rest my case.'

'Can I ask *you* something impertinent? You like women. Why aren't you married?'

'Frank but not exactly cheeky. I've seen too much married misery and it frightens me. I don't want to bring unhappiness into anyone's life which is directly attributable to me. Cowardly it may be: but moral cowards, on the whole, do not inflict pain. Now there are obviously all the examples you could cite . . . '

'All right, I know. My parents, Tom and Samantha . . . '

'As you wish. You've met Maggie Eden. I have a long and happy love affair with her. There are times when I think it would be a good idea to make it sacramental. Perhaps she does. But she's a headmistress in London and I work here. We don't love each other the less, but I doubt that we could bear each other's daily company. And there are other things.'

'I knew Quentin Joyce. His father and mine were friends.'

'Observant of you. It's complex. If he hadn't been shot in the street with one of Iris Cameron's models looking on, Chernenko and Reagan would *still* be slack-mouthed over a leaden chessboard with immovable pieces. It doesn't matter. I didn't like the boy. I don't suppose you did much. He fancied Maggie, which is understandable: but he should have fancied you.'

'And you don't.'

'Objectively, I'd be less than a man if I didn't. But you're not an object. And I like to think I'm not a chancer.'

'I'm not sure I understand.'

'I think you do. Very well. Proust said (as far as I remember) that it is a mistake to speak of a bad choice in love: as soon as there is a choice, it can only be bad. Mind, I'm not sure that you and I and Proust would have been on the same wavelength.'

'Are you teaching?'

Warrington laughed.

'I believe I am,' he said. 'It becomes a habit.'

If there had been a suitable intimate spell, it was now broken. Isabel was powerfully attracted to a man who was not going to commit himself for a moment to a potentially destructive and unhappy effervescence with a young, rather bored woman. They both laughed. He went to fetch another drink.

When he returned, he asked her again why she stayed in Oxford when there was not much reason to. Isabel told him, entirely truthfully, that she did not know. She had always been happy at home. As far as she could tell she had no ambitions.

'You just let it flow over you?' Warrington said.

'More or less. A lot of women do, I think. And here most of the men do. My sister wants to change the world. I don't.'

She watched him frowning in a tutorial way.

'Sorry,' she said. 'You are political. You, too, want to change the world.'

'I'm a member of the SDP,' Warrington said. 'I'm not sure it's the same thing. I just want to try to keep what's left of the world liberal and decent.'

'Two Lost Souls,' Isabel said.

'I'm sorry?'

'It's a record my mother plays sometimes called *Damn Yankees*. A Faustian baseball player and his temptress. I've drunk too much. I no longer have clear thought.'

'All too clear. You think we are both directionless.'

'It's possible. I think we both live in an ambience where we are allowed to be lazy, which suits us. I'm not really attacking you as much as my father, Roger Ingestre, Ben Oldfield, Peter Cameron. It's all so comfortable. Mendoza and Iris go out and scrap a bit. Then they come very quickly back. And we are all lazy, intellectually lazy. Except for Ferdinand and just possibly you.'

Isabel watched him, dispassionately, as his calm eyes travelled over her body. The challenge had been more or less deliberate and he was not going to rise to it. She was not distressed. Nor was Warrington.

'You are a cross young woman, aren't you?' he said.

'No. I'm not. But there is more to it all than playing games.'

Warrington shook his head in the thickening dusk.

'Not much,' he said. 'In a degenerate culture we all play private games, trying not to hurt ourselves first. And then whoever else is around.'

There was something real about an uneventful evening. Isabel and Evan Warrington walked back to the college with civilized composure. In spite of her own urges and something she could sense in him, it was reassuring. Compared to Warrington, with his books and his middle-aged headmistress, David Kelly was a joke: vacillating, directionless. The very word that Warrington had used, ironically, about Isabel and himself.

It was also an irony that, walking through the college lawns with him, there would be no gossip. What more civilized a couple than the Senior Tutor and the Master's daughter strolling decorously through a May evening. Warrington took her to the door of the lodgings, smiled warmly and turned away towards his own staircase.

Isabel went into the house, a little drunk and rather happy. She felt relaxed. Evan Warrington talked to her like a woman and treated her as an adult. He made no patronizing compromises in conversation. He did not rest a quasi-avuncular paw on her thigh, be it only for a moment. Not that she would have minded, rather envying the headmistress whom she hardly knew.

Always of a practical turn of mind, Isabel made herself a cheese and tomato sandwich, then found some cold ham. Since she had been drinking beer, she raided her father's store. She tried to read for a while but found it hard to concentrate, so she watched the television news which she found irritating.

'Why the hell don't you get out of this place?' Her answer had been glib and quick, but the question had thrown her. Was she so lacking in real confidence that, in spite of all the attributes in her favour, she dared not leave the security and charm of the world in which she had been brought up? People saw her as a woman, but Isabel was (in spite of her laughter) quite often frightened. For no reason. Unlike her sister, she relied on others to help her be herself. Perhaps this was all there was in what David Kelly called their 'sentimental friendship'. And Warrington who excited her? Isabel wished that she was her mother, Eve. Or, indeed, Iris Cameron.

*　　*　　*　　*　　*

'This is lovely,' said Francesca Oricellari. 'What a charming surprise.'

'I hope you like Indian cooking,' said Eve Darrow.

'I love it. I haven't been here before.'

'Nor have I. Some gourmet friend of Charles knew of it.'

'How is Charles?'

'Very well. He's at some dreary seminar about industry and education, so I telephoned on the off chance that you might be free for lunch.'

'I'm delighted. You are looking marvellous.'

'As far as you're concerned, that goes without saying. How's business?'

'Not so bad. I go to New York in two weeks to talk about an autumn show which will be quite big if it ever happens.'

'Sounds exciting.'

'It will be a lot of money. I don't like America.'

'I don't much. Not that I know a great deal about it. I was there for about six weeks once when Charles was giving a series of lectures. People were tremendously hospitable and kind, but a bit overwhelming.'

'Yes. And all those martinis and highballs.'

'At least you have a good head for heights. Do you still enjoy it all?'

'Not as much as I did. I like the business part. I get a kick out of arranging a good deal – particularly with some shrewd operator who thinks he or she has outsmarted me. The rest of it, parties and socializing, becomes a bore. I suppose it's because I'm getting old.'

'Don't! I look at my daughters, especially Isabel, and I feel a hundred. And looking at you, now, I think I've just turned seventy.'

'That's absurd. But, you know, a way of life that would suit Iris Cameron, I don't want any more. You understand?'

'I do. Her secret is that she never will. Shall we order?

'I have to be good and watch my figure. I need to lose some weight. It had better be the tikka kebabs.'

'That's a good idea. Or we could share a tandoori chicken. A half one.'

'Much better idea.'

'And papadums. I don't want to be a temptress, but the stuffed parata looks interesting.'

'What's it stuffed with?'

'Almonds.'

'My trouble is I have such a weak character.'

'We'll order one and go halves. Would you like another gin or shall we move onto wine?'

'No! Wine, please . . .'

'Good. I think a bottle of the Mâcon blanc. Thank you . . . Well, how are things in general? It seems ages since you came to see us.'

'I know. That was with Tom and Samantha Wilkins. It must have been in March and now it's almost June. Spring and Autumn seem to be the busiest times for us. Time passes.'

'At my age it bloody well rushes. I suppose it had to catch up with me some day, but I am finding it difficult being a mother.'

'I don't believe it.'

'It's true. For years Charles and I have rather smugly and tacitly congratulated each other that the girls were never any trouble. And Elaine isn't, except that she's a bit serious and might well be arrested climbing into some secret base. It's Isabel. She's almost twenty-five. Older than I was when I married Charles by several years. And yet she seems terribly young.'

'And vulnerable?'

'Not in the least. That's the trouble. And I can't really interfere in her life. Can I?'

'What's wrong?'

'I think she's having an affair . . .'

'Well, surely that's . . .'

'With someone already married who's a family friend.'

'With David Kelly.'

'You knew about it?'

'No. It's just I heard scraps of gossip over the last year perhaps. Anyway, does it matter that much?'

'In a curious way, yes . . . Here are the papadums and the wine. Thank you . . . In a strange way, it does. I've always assumed that someone her age and particularly someone who looks as she does would have a reasonably active sex life, even if my own was relatively modest. It's different, though, when you know both partners in a marriage fairly well. And David is quite a lot older.'

'What does Charles think?'

'Charles has a magnificent gift of not thinking about things which are not to do with the running of the college or academic gyrations of one sort or another. Oh, he'd be marvellous if there was any trouble or if anyone was hurt. My fear is that if anyone is likely to be hurt, it's not going to be Isabel. And not having Charles's temperament or his habit of seeing everything from a dozen different approaches, I find it difficult just to let things take their course.'

'But are you sure they are going to bed?'

'It seems to be commonly accepted. After all, you don't live in Oxford and you'd heard about it.'

'Here's our chicken. It looks marvellous. *And* the parata. I shall put on pounds.'

'We'd better have some raita as well, please . . . Sorry, I'd forgotten.'

'What we were talking about . . . ? Just consider, Eve. When you think about Isabel what comes into your mind – I don't mean you, her mother, but most people? First, she is beautiful; second, she is delightful; third, laughter. She is always teasing people. You don't think it is all a big joke.'

'Possibly. But I doubt if it is for Christina Kelly. And I can hardly believe that David would be stupid enough to be part of it.'

'I think you worry when there is no need to. I'll tell you. When I was seventeen, with Clodia, my sister, the serious, very intelligent, very elegant one, I was thought to be a very fickle and oversexed girl. Various people in my family had the idea suddenly I was sleeping with a protégé of my father who was about forty-two. He was very Venetian, proud. He disregarded magnificently all the nonsense. I laughed at it. At seventeen I was not having an affair with him. At nineteen I was. And no one suspected a thing. You have two daughters different in nature. The same is true of Clodia and me. I'd guess that she's been through many more emotional storms than I have.'

'So I should be more worried about Elaine?'

'No. But you shouldn't blame Isabel for being *l'allegra*.'

'Iris Cameron laughs a lot and plays games.'

'She doesn't laugh in the eyes.'

'I'm sorry, Francesca. I've turned into a fussy old hen. I didn't mean to bother you with all this.'

'Nothing. Relax like Charles. Hey, I've just noticed: I'm eating all the parata. It's delicious.'

'*Prego*. Odd isn't it that people who live happily together for twenty-seven years can relax in such completely different ways. Charles bothers about things I wouldn't blink about and I find myself in a controlled panic about what he would see as domestic trivia. I suppose it's because I was once an actress and miss the mildly paranoiac drama.'

'I've often meant to ask you. Do you regret you left the theatre?'

'Sometimes. Not much. I worked for a while until I had Isabel. Doesn't that sound antiquated? Anyway, it's what happened. And while she was still a toddler, there was Elaine. I went back for a while in rep. And I did a very little radio. But Charles was becoming more and more important, so that was it. I miss the company more than the job which was often quite tedious. One big night or two and then repetition. Actors are more amusing than dons, but Charles mattered more to me than actors.'

'You'd look marvellous on television.'

'Yes. And I can imagine in what kind of part. Smooth middle-aged barrister's wife falling for some criminal thug; clinically minded laboratory technician devoted in an entirely unerotic way to brusque and single-minded surgeon or pathologist; devastated wife of unfaithful minister casting her knickers to perdition in favour of some silky party hack with fashionably flat vowels, on the way up a lot more than me. No thanks. Once I'd like to have played a lot of parts. Now I'm just about right for Electra's mum in O'Neill or Antigone's nurse in Anouilh. I suppose I could *ju-ust* manage Hedda Gabler or one of Chekhov's older characters.'

'You sound – excuse me, Eve – you sound a little bitter.'

'I don't think so. I'll confess to you and to not many others that I sometimes wonder how much more exciting life might have been. But then there wouldn't have been Charles. Look at you and Clodia, for example. You've both . . .'

'Seen the world?'

'I suppose so.'

'And often with what boredom. I like making money. I admit it. My sister likes being a greyish eminence when the politicians are "negotiating". A lot of the time it is ashes in the mouth. The unending hangover that goes away after the first stiff drink, until the second and the third. Then it's all right until tomorrow. I come into your world and it is all different . . .'

'Civilized? Erudite? Tolerant? I've heard it all. You know as well as I do that it's not. It's as mean and as devious as any other. And *less* exciting. But I love Charles. I've never been unfaithful – although sometimes I might have been: quite of my own volition. Elaine can't escape and doesn't want to: but what the hell is Isabel wasting her time for?'

'Eve . . . aren't you a little envious of Isabel?'

'Why should I be?'

'Because she still has the choice.'

'I think we'd better have some more of the Mâcon. I keep having to apologize. Apart from Samantha, who seems entirely happy, there aren't many people I talk to. I suppose, in a way, I'm still acting: the Master's wife, Isabel's once glamorous mother, elegant hostess to all the Ben Oldfields . . .'

'There are worse guests.'

'Oh, of course. I meant nothing against Ben. I only wish that Isabel . . .'

'What?'

'Nothing. Just a wishful thought.'

'Good. Here's the wine. What have you been doing in London while you've been here?'

'A couple of theatres and exhibitions. Discreet shopping. I suppose that's it. And you're right. I envy Isabel because she doesn't miss it.'

*   *   *   *   *

ET OLDFIELD IN OGYGIA ERAT

Each one who enters imagines himself to be the first to enter whereas he is always the last term of a preceding series even if the first term of a succeeding one, each imagining himself to be first, last, only and alone, whereas he is neither first nor last nor only nor alone in a series originating in and repeated to infinity. Joyce of course. Bloom rationalizing Molly's suitors as I am rationalizing the lovers of Iris, from whom I have heard no more and for whom my longing sometimes returns.

In its way also applicable to an approach to myth. As I reel between Graves and Kirk and Eliade and Barthes, someone has more or less been there before.

Barthes! May the President of the Immortals save us from intellectuals – but especially from French intellectuals. I skipped through the stuff a few years ago, quite uncritically. Now I find myself sizzling with wrathful stricture.

(I suppose that Sartre and Camus can be excused because they wrote plays and novels. And I fear that there I give myself away. Oldfield will never be a philosopher.)

(Therefore with angels and archangels let us give thanks to the above named President that he made Oldfield even less a semiologist and least of all a structuralist.)

'The very end of myth is to bring the world to a standstill.'

'The purpose of myth is to empty reality.'

The French lap up this sort of thing all four paws in the air, which even the intellectuals are quite good at when it is feeding time. Barthes' bourgeois and proletariat don't go in for such displays. They tie their napkins appropriately and get stuck in. It is instructive to know that through drinking wine the intellectual discovers in himself a new virility and is reassured that he is more at one with the proletarian. Barthes should have cracked a bottle of Chambertin with Ingestre, or better still Blakemore! Or, for that matter, a carton of supermarket plonk. That kind of intellectual doesn't even drink *beer* to identify with proletarian virility. He drinks it because he is bloody thirsty.

Nevertheless, sticking to the point: myth is storytelling for comfort or reassurance or even amusement. As the generations rise and pass away there is a certain amount of palimpsestery. And each of us invests and betrays paradigms, as they betray us. Look what happened to Puig and Rita Hayworth one way and another. We cannot live without stories, even when we make them up for ourselves and they are what others call fantasies.

Myth is surely much more than some elaborate conspiracy of signs and symbols, linked to a linguistic theory that denies the normal function of language. (Didn't someone or other write a comic book *How to Talk Roland-Barthes?*) It is certainly more than an ingenious system which seeks to perpetuate bourgeois complacency and the attendant profit motive at the expense of the gormless proletarians sweating and shouting at wrestling matches, witnessing 'the euphoria of men elevated from the constitutive ambiguity of everyday situations to confront the panoramic view of Nature.'

(I wonder if Ferdinand knew that boxing, by contrast, was a Jansenist sport, determined by the manifestation of excellence. He is a bit old and fat to take it up now and I suspect too tired.)

Myths are a means of palliating fear of evil rather than of sustaining well-heeled comfort and maintaining a social and political *status quo*. We need stories – grand or absurd, even if these occur in adverts. No one is fooled for long. Listen to the news headlines at 1.35: earthquake; terrorist attack; threat and counter-threat; famine in Africa. And now it's time to find out what's happening in Ambridge. Things are fairly tense at Home Farm where Jennifer seems set upon a showdown.

Myths may be determined by history: but they are *not* history any more than all history or all biography is an aspect of fiction. Myths are certainly not a matter of disguising an abrasive detergent (which might cause dermatitis or exzema) in a cloud of fluffy bubbles. What happened to common sense? . . .

. . . I wonder what Iris would make of the ultimate triangle of the G-string, which 'by its pure, geometrical form, by its hard and shiny fabric, bars the way to the sexual part like a sword of purity and definitively drives the woman back into a mineral world.' Only Barthes could take the sex out of a woman taking her clothes off. I can imagine Iris's response – but the image would inflame me, so I won't.

It's odd that when I seek some touchstone of reality to steady my intellectual giddiness I think of Iris or Isabel. And, of course, Samantha Wilkins. That is something quite new and quite hopeless. The similarity is that all three are cheerfully unconcerned with all the matters of the mind that bother the rest of us. (Perhaps they bother me more than they do others!) Iris, alas (or perhaps alas), is in the past. Marvellously sensual and determinedly not destructive. Parting is not to be sweet or sorrowful. When we've talked at all, she seems clear-minded, uncomplicated, dispassionate – nothing like as subtle as her brother (whom I am still barely able to look in the eye – that bloody silk kimono draped over . . . yes, well). Isabel doesn't laugh as much as she once did. She is, nevertheless, refreshing. Ferdinand, like many others, is infatuated – but much too careful and perhaps kind to be embarrassing. He has been talking to her about Baudelaire (in whom he is unaccountably interested) and Madame Sabatier. Such is Ferdinand's idea of seduction, bless him. In consequence, Isabel has read some Baudelaire and, more significantly, Enid Starkie's biography of the sombre aesthete. She thinks he was a wimp, pestering his poor old ma when he should have been getting down to work, even if it meant polishing floors like Monsieur Oscar. Perhaps he might have for Isabel La Douce. I talked to her about the contrasting industry of Balzac. His immense output and the detail of his research, his appetite for work. Isabel replied that he had the time after all: for a start he didn't have to read Balzac. What can one do? I recall that Barthes talks about the Balzacian joy of creation in an essay about women writing novels while still contriving to give birth to children. I shall introduce Isabel to Barthes. I give Barthes two rounds and a submission.

Samantha Wilkins is something different. I've known her for a long time, I suppose. We've always liked each other and I have sometimes been asked to delight in her cooking: but she has always and evidently been 100 per cent Tom's wife. And so, although she is very attractive and (in her way) sassy, I have never thought about her lasciviously or sentimentally (even). We met quite by chance in the National Portrait Gallery. She was to meet Tom at Heathrow the same evening, after he returned from some colloquy in Canada. I took her to an Indonesian restaurant where I ordered the dishes that Francesca had ordered when she had taken me there. It appeared that Samantha was impressed. But then: she would have made it look like that. It was completely relaxed, unfussed, easy. Samantha couldn't give a stuff about Barthes, or Baudelaire, or Eliade, or Eliot, Stevens, Joyce and the rest. But she dismissed nothing and no one. Not wanting the evening to end, I suggested going to the airport with her – as company. Since she was meeting her husband there was no question of treachery. She agreed and said that she would then drive us all back to Oxford. Tom's flight was five hours late because of turbulence somewhere or other across the Atlantic. So Samantha and I got ourselves a bottle or two of wine and chatted. And, as is the Oldfield custom, I fell in love again.

She is of medium height, fair-haired, with a mobile, alert face, easily prompted to laughter. She has a full but well-shaped figure and strong firm legs with delicate ankles. She does not gossip. At no time during all the hours that we spent together did she say a word about (let alone against) any of our friends or acquaintances – even if I was tempted to. The conversation was of no consequence, but never boring. In the abstract I can think of few experiences more tedious than waiting in an international airport for an overdue flight. In fact I've seldom enjoyed an evening and half the next morning more. When Tom eventually arrived he was surprised to see me and roared with laughter. So I was clearly not a threat. Samantha drove us back quietly. Tom, not yet jet-lagged, was ebullient and very funny about his conference. They put me down at Carfax, where Samantha leaned out of the window and hugged me. She hugged me for 'looking after her' and said we must have tea or something. Her husband approved and recommended her chocolate cake. It won't happen because what intimacy we shared was accidental and could not again be contrived. I don't know if there was any sexual arousal for her, but I dare imagine there was a little. For me it became idyllic. Imagine a bloody idyll in the arrivals lounge at Heathrow! On a beautiful June night, I did not depart from Calypso. She drove away with her husband . . .

Good-bye Wendy! Send the fairies, pinewood elf and larch
tree gnome,
   Spingle-spangled stars are peeping
   At the lush Lagonda creeping
Down the winding ways of tarmac to the leaded lights of home.
   There among the silver birches,
   All the bells of all the churches
Sounded in the bath-waste running out into the frosty air.
   Wendy speeded my undressing,
   Wendy is the sheet's caressing
   Wendy bending gives me blessing
Holds me as I drift to dreamland, safe inside my slumber-wear.

208

I wonder what to make of the semiology of tights and stockings. What is the correlation here of signified, signifier, sign. If Samantha had said to me casually at Heathrow I am wearing stockings which I prefer to tights, that would surely be something signified. (Also involving the use of language.) In so doing she would have drawn attention to her sexual entity, even if I had not been aware of it – so playing the part of signifier. And the sign to which I might have responded would have been the secondary invitation. The sign to which I most certainly would have responded would have been the sight of the thighs, stockingtops and suspenders flashingly displayed.

Isabel has often joked about the male obsession with female underwear. Now if there is anything that Isabel cares less about than semiology, I imagine it is whether or not she wears tights. And, as it applies to her, I can be properly academic. I must though confess to a mild form of this relatively harmless preaccupation. I don't buy what Mendoza calls wank mangazines, but I have been known to speculate on the colour of Henrietta Ball's panties, or (indeed) whether Samantha Wilkins was wearing stockings or tights. Nothing sinister intended. With Iris Cameron there would be no doubt.

Perhaps I should ask her. She would answer freely. So would Francesca Oricellari. So would Isabel. I am wasting my time with Wallace Stevens when I could be investigating the semiology of stockings and tights, the linguistic spin-off, the mordant throwaway conclusion about bourgeois-induced decadence. And what fun the research would be.

Occasionally I think of Isabel as a woman and wonder that I do not and never have desired her. She is so beautiful. Ah! But is her face an idea (like Garbo's) or an event (like Audrey Hepburn's)?

Perhaps Barthes had not seen the photograph of Greta Garbo on the front cover of Alexander Walker's book about her. For proletarians like me that is, in itself, an event.

I'm going to give this up. I'll grow up sooner or later . . .

. . . A drink with Ferdinand in mildly doleful mood. The French aristocratic lady complained that *les paysans ont trop lu Proust*. Ferdinand had been reading too much Donne: although he is not a peasant and Donne is a darker philosopher than Proust. To lighten the tone of things, I put up the notion of Donne as the hypochondriac genius. Although it was not unfamiliar, it amused Ferdinand. I am sometimes hypochondriac. There the resemblance ends. As for Ferdinand, he is too clever for his own mental comfort. He examines unceasingly (as far as I can tell) the quality and sincerity of his own thoughts. And he longs for Isabel Darrow. This is not obvious, but the wistfulness across even a semi-crowded room is observable. Celibacy and chastity have become a habit. Perhaps it is just as well: the most he might expect would be kindness. I don't think he can reconcile the honesty of what he thinks he should think with unwelcome tumescence in unguarded moments. But how can I tell? And who am I to judge – with my regular playmate of the month.

Samantha *did* ask me to tea. Not at the Wilkins household which would have been suggestive and inconvenient. We met (for tea) at four o'clock in front of the Martyrs' Memorial. (I bet Barthes could have made something of that!) Samantha does not have red hair and her sulky lips aren't shaped for sin, because they are not remotely sulky. But she does have strong legs and for an hour or so I was wandering wantonly in the Licorice Fields of Pontefract. It was delightful and entirely friendly – apart from my wanton wandering, which she (I assume) knew nothing about. It must happen to everyone . . . So there we were in the teashop inglenook. She certainly not an ordinary little woman: funny, attractive, sexy without being provocative. And yet she must have been quite a girl, one of Betjeman's officers' mess syrens – the strong legs, round knees, the prominent breasts in a sensible jumper . . . or in uniform with those black stockings! I chased such thoughts away and we took tea as ceremoniously as Barthes tells us the British Royal Family do.

Then there was one of those events which, even if we never touch again, has set up a sort of intimacy between us that will not readily go away. As we walked along St Giles, I noticed Christina Kelly's car stopped near the Taylorian. I pointed it out to Samantha and was beginning to cross, when she laid her hand on my arm. Prudently. In the car Christina was kissing Peter Cameron. It was not a long orgiastic kiss, but it was no affectionate buss either. Cameron got out of the car. Samantha said, 'I don't think we saw that, do you?' I shook my head. 'Shall we have a pact? Keep it absolutely to ourselves?' I agreed. 'Good,' she said. 'You must come round to dinner with the lady of your choice soon and I'll see what I can do in the way of rococo cookery or frenzied baroque dishes.'

. . . The notion of parallax as applied to individuals which I have been playing with (after showing off to Francesca) is related to neutral perspectives. The pace of events is only properly judged or clearly estimated when we are some distance away; just as when I visit a city that I don't know, I find it difficult to remember detail a few days after my return, while a month or so later fragmentary images recur in memory until I build up a picture of the place. This naturally fades again with time until I make my next visit.

It would be overdramatic to suggest that coming upon Christina and Peter Cameron was anything like a shock, but I did experience that sort of frisson of alarm with which we hear other people's bad news. Although we are 97 per cent vexed and sympathetic, there is that small percentage of *Schadenfreude*.

Considering this event and Samantha's reaction, as well as my own, I do not think that my parallax theory is all that farfetched. And it is *not*, as Ferdinand insists, synaesthesia. For a moment Samantha and I were immediately involved as observers in a secret moment in the lives of two other people. I cannot speak for her – but I went away thinking of deceit, passion, the latent irony of the whole situation in view of past gossip about Isabel and David Kelly. (Part of me was mildly pleased at having, in my turn, caught Cameron with his kimono off.) Now it is not a very considerable event. If he and Christina are having the wildest affair, it will not rock the world and it is not of much importance. Yet my response and I suspect Samantha's was emotional: although hers was distinguished by control and good sense. As time passes, even if there are no further developments, we will see that moment in a different perspective. And eventually it will be just a fleeting incident forgotten for most of the time.

There are, however, in most lives moments of very great pain or happiness, triumph or failure, in which we are involved ourselves or which happen to people we care about in some way – not necessarily people we love. For a while we participate in such moments fully: then we rationalise whatever it was happened and it is not too much to say that we fictionalize it. We make a story of it. It becomes an entry in a commonplace book of personal myths.

At the most trivial level, I was quite worried when I thought that Isabel and Kelly were seriously entangled – partly on Isabel's account, partly because it might have meant that Christina herself would be involved in a difficult situation which might end in a wretched divorce. Never entirely reassured, I rationalized what might be or what was happening into a convenient story which might resolve itself in different ways, not reckoning on a twist in the plot.

Needless to say my own infatuations all assume highly comic even farcical dimensions in retrospect. Even the very positive and vivid business with Iris is now just an erotic novella which I try not to reopen too often. And soon Samantha will be something in my dithering past. Except for the confidence we share and have promised each other not to break.

Of course, what I remember as comic are the occasions when I have emerged with some dignity, or where I have been let down lightly!

Summer half over. The marathons have been run. The colour has been trooped. Reagan has been to Tipperary and Normandy where a lot of elderly people (not politicians) remembered the days when they were young, frightened and quite brave, forty years ago. Some very brave. The flower trees in north Oxford have lost their blossoms long ago, Eights Week is almost a year away, the Cherwell is flowing smoothly again, there is no cricket in the Parks. It has been one of those sunlit times, even when I was not aware of it: with light playing through waving branches and dancing off the water. And even in these days of jeans and track suits, some pretty girls in wafting light dresses with soft hair and that clear glitter of youth in their eyes before it is corrupted by whatever it is that corrupts: the artificial paradises of sex and drink and drugs, ambition, predatory vanities, viraginian ideologies. June is not yet over and I am already nostalgic for another summer, a time that I have always loved in this town and which has always brought some particular memory which is rueful or senti-mental or warming. The summer of '84 I shall remember,

I think, for an evening in a stuffy crowded lounge of what used to be called London Airport, drinking wine with a woman of gentle wit and surpassing charms on a hot night, before I went on my way and she was content to let me go. Why not?

So much for parallax? I wonder. 'So for us a last time is bright light made.' No. Overstating the case.

. . . I find myself sometimes in agreement with Barthes. Gide reading Bossuet going down the Congo. It reminds me of the specious colour supplement journalism: a room I can live in, rosy ruins where I have had a surreptitious piss. Fantasies of a not very good and thoroughly ineffectual academic . . . Except for one. Yes, except for one.

*　*　*　*　*

Partly curiosity, partly because I was bored and had a week or two with nothing much to do. Partly because I admit and without shame I wanted my contemporaries to see me as the tangible genial success I've become. 'Well, he-*llo* Malcolm! How is bloody old Bancroft after all these years? Not wearing badly at all. Given up pursuing the barmaids, no doubt.' Mean-spirited little sod he always was and now it shows. Wavy hair going grey but still plentiful. Same dark resentment in the eyes which were always suspicious. 'And Vernon Clift. My God! Dr Vernon Clift, well on his way to a top consultancy. Aha! Vernon, I have my spies everywhere.' All the promised pomposity has flourished and he has a paunch. Good rolling voice suitable for the bedside. Both married. Sourly or insipidly I expect. No, I do not share the joys of a family. Surprisingly rewarding. Yes. I *have* done well. 'Good heavens, no! Just luck. Being in the right place when it mattered. Well . . . a little ambition. But we all have that. Look at you two. What are you doing now, Malcolm?' I can hear them . . . Giles Mendoza. Pha! Knew him at Oxford. Always a bit full of Giles Mendoza. Lot of talent but basically what he is now. A performer. Lucky with women. I think he had quite a lot of money behind him . . . Bancroft is deputy headmaster of a large – he insists *large* – comprehensive. Needn't listen other than to put in the jovial 'C'mon!' or appreciative chuckle to

213

prove that the acid life of television has done nothing to pollute the old college spirit. Sheer vanity on my part to come at all. College Gaudy, be buggered, with Walter Harrington cruising around like some academic dreadnought out of the Snows of yesteryear and a lot of people I had no desire ever to see again. Still, apart from Philip Carey, already a junior minister, and Dick Dryden, star *Economist* columnist, I'm easily top of the bill. For my year. 'Get away with you, Vernon! Don't believe a word of it!' What a fucking waste of time.

Christina . . . Well, she didn't say yes etcetera and she did agree to have lunch next time we coincided in London. Fourth of July. Week before I go to America. Nice and leisurely, I said. She laughed. All the stops. White Tower or the Caprice. Somewhere she'll have heard of. And no rush, though that might be difficult, if she's wearing that white dress which is virtually transparent when she stands against the light. Lace bra, close-fitting pants. No tights or stockings if this weather holds. Perfect legs. She doesn't need them. *Festina lente* . . . Oh fuckeration, now I've done it. Even the flicker of a Latin tag across the fevered brain conjures up G. G. Julien, Vice-Principal and Tutor in Classics. Ye who have jokes to crack prepare to shatter them now. *A toute à l'heure*, Christina. 'G.G. How splendid to see you! How *are* you, sir?' Smirking as smugly as of yore, domed as though by Wren. Stiff little handshakes, stiff little twitches of the smirk, curt nods. Could have made a fortune as a television puppet. But remembers all the names. No doubt prides himself on it. Appropriate words: Bancroft – still fashioning the image of the future though I doubt with Quattrocento finger; Clift – modestly concealing his caduceus along with more sinister instruments in that elegant waistcoat pocket; Whitbread and Fenchurch don't merit an empyrean quip – it's enough that he remembers their names. And Mendoza! Here it comes. 'Well, it would be impossible to forget, Mendoza. He's seen to that. *Conticuere omnes intentique ora tenebant.*' Roughly I suppose: the intent gaze of all those gawping dumbly. Oh thanks G. G. Yes I'm doing quite well. 'Tell me, Mendoza, how does someone so essentially (in a non-Platonic sense) – perhaps I should say fundamentally (ohohohoho – what a wag, old G.G.) – genial become, as it were, professionally acerbic?' 'I'm not sure, G.G. Who was it said: "Anger makes a dull man witty but it keeps him poor"? I'm certainly not poor.' Freeze of smirk. Sharp military look, an abrupt turn to those unlikely to talk back to G.G. 'It was Bacon, Mendoza, whom you have quoted inaccurately. I'm sure all present wish you continued prosperity.' Gentlemen. Little bow. At least I got rid of the old fart . . .

At last the beaming shamble of Henry Sussex, black tie askew as his teeth. 'Seen you on the box, Giles. Don't like the show, but you're all right. Come and talk to Dick Dryden. Was he up with you?' Dryden – naturally alert and pleasant, the Frank Loesser of up-market journalism, not happy unless juggling with five or six topics simultaneously, tall, thin, balding, sharp of eye and mind, but kind. All the things I'd like to be. Joined by Philip Carey MP, darkly immense, a Conservative it seems by accident and mildly unhappy about being a digit of the present government. Gentle but curiously detached. Nothing much matters except the task in hand. Tall enough to look over the head of Henry Sussex who stoops a little these days, scanning some horizon where perhaps those biding their time (as he is) see some Conservative future and hope. Dryden is leftish. But this is no time for chit-chat. It is the Gaudy.

Even here, though, interest in the 'programme'. Dead-eye Dryden has heard that it's coming off, which raises Carey's massive eyebrows in concern and makes Henry Sussex shake loyally all over. Henry is easily moved to loyalty and affection. One could wish there were more of us like him, but I suppose it would be less amusing. The programme (as they call it) is safe. Such was the antagonism that Mabel and I were able to slide it through almost unnoticed except by Danby Austin (who was complaisant). And while we are sliding it through . . . who knows? Less frost and more gleam in the executive eyes. Nothing like a look across the committee room to let you know that she *is* quite interested. Not the point. Tell them about the trip to New York and Washington. Very crafty. Filming for new series and covering options from Rupert Bamberg, which they need not know about. Envious eyes in our direction. Mabel would be quite good for my career, so why am I still furious about Isabel and longing to get inside Christina's knickers. If only these tall grinning

215

suave gents, all safely married, all in their black ties, clutching their drinks, knew how difficult it was to be Mendoza. But here we are: Member of Parliament, Top Journalist, Television Personality with everyone's favourite don.

Dinner. Ivor Probert on one side, on leave from his regiment, keeping up the florid witticisms for which he was once famous when we were all so much younger. Hamilton Kinross on the other, drawling imperturbably, immaculate in all respects except sincerity. And who of us can say . . . ? Opposite Winrow, chap I hardly knew as a freshman. Red and raucous. In advertising. Shortly I should judge to be put down by first Probert (crossly), then Kinross (smoothly), then his neighbour Loughlan (drunkenly). Loughlan appears to be an estate agent. Not though by Mendoza, chuckling at the sallies. Quite easy taking the cue from the laughter of others notably Probert who was never slow at enjoying his own jokes. And thinking the while of a cool afternoon with Christina Kelly. Not so cool in this heat. But autumn will advance. Don't rise, Mendoza. *Ipse.* A public figure does not snap at trash bait. Just think of autumn as they talk. Christina in Knightsbridge knickers standing above me saying Darling I'm dying for it. Hahahaha. Bloody good, Ivor. Never heard that. Kinross snorting like a horse in some distress. That's the way he laughs.

Shan't do this again. Meanwhile somewhere in Oxford Kelly and Isabel Darrow . . . I'll do . . . I know not what I shall do . . .

★   ★   ★   ★   ★

Lady Margaret Hall
Oxford
11 July 1984

Dear Rachel,
Thank you for the invitation which I very much wanted to accept. The trouble is that Chiltern have come up with a very good offer, now that Dorf is asserting himself. Or so it would appear. I know perfectly well that I don't need the money, though it is a lot and will keep me in baked beans and beaujolais for many years. At the same time it gives me something to think about even if what

ultimately appears is less than profound. The theme is hegemonies throughout history. They will no doubt think up a much sexier title. I asked, 'Why me?' Dorf was candid. 'You have a good figure, long legs, dark red hair which looks splendid on television and an austere manner that turns on husbands without switching off wives.' It will involve much travelling and seems as good a way as any I have hitherto thought of of using my sabbatical. It will, naturally, bring me to America at least once, so I shall hope to see you and Oliver, however briefly. Everything is at the talking stage – an endless process in television, though Dorf looks determined and seems to have organized the necessary support.

So, with hegemony on the mind, it is interesting that it is now getting into space. Whatever its merits or demerits Reagan's laser umbrella has been instantaneously trivialized over here (and probably more so over there) as 'Star Wars'. There seems a determination on the part of so many to relate very serious things to utterly inconsequential fantasy, whether it be Star Wars or those frightful serials about rich Americans, where the men are crazed with power and the women with sex. Not that we do not have our own problems. Princess Margaret has appeared on 'The Archers', which no doubt lends that vapid diurnal chronicle the credibility that it needs. I'm not a secret listener. It's just that I'm often in the bath and can't get at the bloody wireless in the other room.

Much more serious. A theologian by the name of Jenkins is to be made Bishop of Durham. I'd never heard of the man, but he is apparently heterodox about things like the Virgin Birth, the Resurrection and (as far as I can make out) life after death. This has prompted much mirth among colleagues who are not on the one hand theologians, or on the other in holy orders. No sooner had the said Jenkins been appointed than lightning struck York Minster where some appropriate ceremony is due to take place. Well! Such testimony of God's wrath! Ingestre, not celebrated for his Christian devotion, thinks that the bishop elect or presumptive should be arraigned under the Trade Descriptions Act and threatens to write to the Advertising Standards

217

Authority and the Consumers' Council in an entirely Platonic way, having, of course, no personal axe to grind. I don't think that historians have ever fully grasped what Plato was on about, incidentally.

The miners' strike proceeds with endless repetitive rhetoric on both sides. And there seems no end in sight. There is quite a lot of violence which is more or less contained. In the existing circumstances, this is quite possible: because the protagonists (Scargill and MacGregor) are both so convincingly dislikable and it is a very limited confrontation which so many have chosen to ignore. The portents are nevertheless not attractive. I've been reading a book by Edward Crankshaw, *The Shadow of the Winter Palace*, which suggests to me that revolution against the tsars was unavoidable, in spite of Marx's prognostications. As you know I am not a historian (so Roger Ingestre could claim a draw so far), but I am less afraid of revolution, although I shouldn't welcome it, than anarchy. I was talking the other day to a visiting American, whom I may have mentioned, called Ivan Whitehart. Without presuming to comment on American life, I said I thought that we lived in a decadent society. Then, said Whitehart, you must be very right wing or very left wing. This is nonsense. It means I am a liberal who recognizes that it is impossible to be a *militant* liberal. For the first time I realized what people like you and Roger Ingestre have been agonizing about for years. At least the conversation settled one dilemma: however charming and physically attractive, I don't think I could surrender my body (so to speak) to someone as obtuse as Whitehart.

It made me think too about decadence in general. How could the Greeks of fifth-century Athens be the ancestors of the scruffy, shiftless people who stand so unmercifully upon their dignity today – most notably the men? How could the rot which set in when the hideous Commodus succeeded Marcus Aurelius run the gangrenous riot that it did? I am not hopeful about Western society generally, particularly the born-again right over on your side: but the anti-social belligerence that is to be seen all around here alarms me. The violence is directionless and mindless: it is, as the same time, exploitable. Clodius and Milo were perhaps better organized, but there is so much resentment and envy in our society that I fear it will only be contained by law enforcement (so called) of a savage nature which in our complacent way we have associated with 'less happy lands'.

Too much, too much! You will remember no doubt the lecherous eye and foxy sidelong speech of Professor G. S. Walton. Thank heaven he has abandoned making even putative passes at me: but he is as unrepentantly self-absorbed as ever. I don't think he's registered a word of anyone's replies for about fifteen years. Our latest conversation (after some unregenerate comments on how fetching I looked – in full academic dress) went: *Walton* – I suppose you're about to go on holiday, Philippa. *Me* – Henrietta. *Walton* – Always go to Greece, don't you. Marvellous. You'll have a splendid time. *Me* – I thought of going to France, as it happens. *Walton* – Yes! Nowhere like Greece. You've really taken to Greece, haven't you, Philippa. Jolly good. *Me* – I was thinking about the Pyrenees. Biarritz to Perpignan. Taking in the mountains. You know . . . *Walton* – Terrific mountains. Ouzo. Retsina. I imagine you've picked up a bit of Greek, haven't you? Jolly useful. *Me* – I suppose it depends on how many Greeks there are in southwest France. *Walton* – Goes a long way with them, you know, Margaretta. *Ne. Parakalo. Kalimera.* They like it. Feel very flattered. *Me* – I think I'll have to make do with *oui* and *s'il vous plait* and *bonjour. Walton* – I don't think you'll get very far with French, Antonia. Greeks are very bad at languages. A little English perhaps in the main tourist centres. But keep off German. They understand it. But they tend to spit at you. Happened to me in Rethymnon. Just because I have reddish hair. So have you. And very beautiful it is. Form atavism I suppose. Nice to see you, Philippa. Have a good holiday. Wish I was sharing a berth, as it were, with you . . .

I think I *shall* drive off to the Pyrenees as a matter of fact for a week or two to think about hegemonies and decadence among those amiable dogs who pant at one without threat apart from a wag and a lick.

Nothing much is happening. I try not be become involved in other people's lives. The David Kelly–Isabel Darrow relationship is almost an embarrassment. I met his wife, Christina, the other evening. Without any probing on my part she said that David claimed it was all an elaborate game to flabbergast the gossips. She hinted that it might also be an elaborate ruse to disguise a very real affair. It didn't seem to bother her. Perhaps I haven't changed with the times as much as I might have.

And so. I find myself contemplating a paperweight with all the solemnity of a neurotic existentialist, appalled by the thinginess of things which I am none the less not able to relate to *mauvaise foi* or bourgeois complacency. Yesterday's spaghetti, perhaps; or the dish in which I cooked lamb chops. But not a paperweight. It doesn't matter that it exists whether I am here or not and will exist when I don't. That is the road to feeling sorry for tablets of soap and old toothbrushes, one way or another. I'll opt for the nausea I understand.

How very uncheerful this all is. I would have loved to come over but if the Chiltern thing works, we shall start in August and there is planning beforehand. I shall probably write next from Babylon or Macedonia.

Love to you both,
Henrietta

★

Now is midsummer come and all fools slaughtered
And spring's infuriations over and a long way
To the first autumnal inhalations, young broods
Are in the grass, the roses are heavy with a weight
Of fragrance and the mind lays by its trouble . . .

Not entirely. Under the influence of some fairly benign summer virus, I have been even more lethargic than usual in that pleasant euphoric abstraction which a slight temperature induces. Not my fault, after all. Accordingly I was listening to some innocuous programme of light music – hardly listening, letting it drift around me. I was transported back to my childhood when I had scarlet fever, a dramatic complaint which I thoroughly enjoyed because it had such an exciting name and because I didn't feel at all ill. My mother had put some kind of portable radio at my bedside through which I heard Geraldo, Billy Cotton and so many others. Most pertinently, in this recollection of fevers past, Joe Loss and his band playing 'In the Mood'. It was this particular tune (played by Glen Miller's ensemble in the course of someone's nostalgic essay) which reminded me of the euphoric times when I did not think at all. There were only sensations. By association I was reminded of the flying bombs which used to frighten us in the Home Counties, because of a dramatic scene in a film where the same tune was played which moved my eighteen-year-old soul (as I then believed it was) beyond philosophy in the Ritz or the Super or the Electra. All came flowing comfortably back in a haze which was almost entirely pleasant. Of course it made no sense and it was very different from Donne's pestilent and infectious fumes. And I fear that much more trivial.

Recovering from this state of cachexy, I have reassumed the dismal habit of thought. It seems to me that my misfortune has been a substantial lack of Baudelaire's *guignon*. He lamented his terrible luck, whereas everything has gone rather well for me, in the material sense. What, after all, is a faith, an academic purpose, a philosophic substitute lost, when there are amiable friends, pleasant diversions, when there is good food and drink, ample means to pursue a comfortable life. And no Marie Daubrun. No Madame Sabatier. Not even a Jeanne Duval.

It is, when I call it to mind, painful. All men call *Misery*, *Misery*, but *Happinesse* changes the name by the taste of Man.

I do not believe Mendoza, who is activated by malice, that Isabel is promiscuous – although it may be true that she is in dangerous liaison with David Kelly. But her laughter exasperates me as Madame Sabatier's did Baudelaire . . .

âme toujours ravie
Bouche au rire enfantin . . .

221

And this is a comment upon my own failing of courage. I dare not be laughed at. Fat, elderly, amicable: incapable even of disguising my handwriting. And melancholy. At the same time I wish she would have a violent relationship with someone much younger, so that I need not be jealous! Ben Oldfield would be splendid. It is no longer within my prerogative to give blessing, but I should at least send them a large box of chocolates and a bottle of decent champagne. Dear old Ben doesn't seem to be aware of her, any more than he is of Francesca Oricellari, in whom I have discerned a mild affection for him. He needs to brood on someone at least ten if not twenty years older and I rather suspect is much too interested in corsetry, whether or not the woman in question needs it.

> But in our amours amorists discern
> Such fluctuations that their scrivening
> Is breathless to attend each quirky turn.
> When amorists grow bald, then amours shrink
> Into the compass and curriculum
> Of introspective exiles, lecturing . . .

Ben is balding a little. I am still sleek of head if not of mind. Try as I might, she still means to me life and movement because of the dance of her eyes and a wildness I guess (or perhaps merely wish) to be in her. No wildness will ever be aroused by the likes of Marcus Ferdinand. How, after all, does the girl think of herself. Perhaps I am wrong in dismissing Oldfield's notion of parallax. All things are done in *time* too; but if we consider *Tyme* to be but the *Measure of Motion*, and howsoever it may seem to have three *stations*, *past*, *present* and *future*, yet the *first* and *last* of these *are* not (one is not now and the other is not yet) and that which you call *present*, is not *now* the same that it was when you began to call it so in the *Line* . . .

It is all more immediate in Donne than in Eliot. When did she stop being a child and become a woman whom it was legitimate to desire and want to love. I shan't take refuge in the contradictory forms of grace. How, indeed, does she think of herself? For all her laughter, for all what others read as her folly.

222

Perhaps I am oppressed by the irreducible fact that my own existence is justified by this longing for a beautiful young woman. *Of course* it is absurd! But then the fact of my existence is in itself absurd. And there is absolutely no excuse for someone without faith, philosophic purpose, political drive to continue living – unless it is love. Not a generalized soapy love of humankind, but love focused on another person in spite of her irrepressible laughter who is more important than I am – at least to me.

Yet, although I am convinced of evil (nothing to do with sin) as a motivating force, I am not able to subscribe to an aesthetic of evil, which seems to me effete and self-indulgent. Nevertheless, Stevens's stoical acceptance of evil as an existential human fact which must be rejected seems to me to be admirable when considered alongside Baudelaire's God-ridden diagnostic self-contempt.

Compare Stevens: 'Men in general do not create in light and warmth alone. They create in darkness and coldness. They create when they are hopeless, in the midst of antogonisms, when they are wrong, when their powers are no longer subject to their control. They create as the ministers of evil . . .' with Baudelaire:

Dans ton île, O Venus je n'ai trouvé debout
Qu'un gibet symbolique où pendait mon image . . .
An Seigneur! donnez-moi la force et le courage
De contempler mon coeur et mon corps sans dégout

I am not sure that I understand what creating as a minister of evil means and I am more inclined to the view (as was Donne) that all moral suffering is a step towards wisdom and all physical suffering a step towards death – an advertisement for the vanity of life. But the courage of Stevens hurts my conscience more than the pitiless self-scrutiny of Baudelaire, which demands its own particular strength of mind.

I do not think of myself as a minister of evil in any sense: but I am not (and never have been even during my ministry) either a scourge. And I should have been: not as someone threatening hell fire and ascertaining that there was a certain level of misery in the lives of all around, but as one asking questions and refusing to be put off by the answers. There is a certain evil in being negative. Of this I am guilty. My kind betrays itself and in so doing betrays others. It's not a matter of sensual indolence. It is rather one of intellectual cowardice which disguises itself as laziness. Even those of us who take an active interest in politics, such as Ingestre and Warrington, are putting up some sort of front. Peter Cameron, Ben Oldfield, Charles Darrow, Robert Blakemore – all in our different ways frittering time and talent: so that Giles Mendoza makes better use of his time making meretricious television programmes and Francesca Oricellari designing pretty clothes; Iris and Isabel looking lovely and making love as they list (one assumes). It is no retreat. Even so, as the last Edwardians fluttered pretty wings above the late summer flowers before 1914, so are we all futile butterflies in the last brightly coloured dance before the end of civilization. And that is less a problem of nuclear devastation than of spiritual entropy. It is the consequence of intellectual, moral and spiritual treachery. I stand guilty in one of the lesser rows of the accusing tribunal. The charge against Marcus Ferdinand is culpable futility: where others arraigned thought that they were fulfilling some purpose, Ferdinand recognized at the age of forty that he had none but persisted in remaining alive. He perpetrated no evil: but he did no good. He contributed nothing.

. . . so when he awakes from *sleepe* and saies to himself, shall I be no otherwise when I am dead, than I was even now, when I was asleep, hee may bee ashamed of his waking *dreames*, and of his *Melancolique* fancying out a horrid and an affrightful figure of that *death* which is so like sleepe.

. . . why since I have lost my delight in all objects, cannot I discontinue the facultie of seeing them, by closing my eyes in sleepe.

Sacré nom. . . .

6

There were times when Isabel thought her quiet, academic sister was distinctly feline. She had a way of coiling her legs about her and of moving her long hair with a languorous turn of the head that was defiant as well as proud and perhaps predatory. Engaged in such reflection she had at first not registered what Elaine had said as she wound into position.

'*What* did you just say?'

'I asked you if you thought it would be a good idea for me to go to bed with Giles Mendoza.'

'This isn't a joke, is it?'

'Not a bit. He put the idea quite delicately to me. And I thought it might be fun.'

'I've no doubt you'll do whatever pleases you and I've no desire to play the Ugly Sister, but he's no fucking Prince Charming.'

'You must have been reading fashionable novels. You don't usually use such language. Anyway, who can tell? And as you are perfectly well aware no one can accuse you of being the *ugly* sister.'

'But he's such a creep . . . I mean . . .'

'Look at it dispassionately, Isabel. He's relatively attractive, quite funny, socially adept. And these things don't matter much any more, do they? I'm sure he's very experienced. And you know that I'm always eager to learn. Anything.'

'That is simply silly. How experienced are *you*?'

'Not quite in Iris Cameron's league. Or even yours, perhaps. But I'm not entirely innocent. I don't spread it around, of course.'

225

Isabel was not in the habit of playing the big sister. For the first time she found herself entirely thrown off guard by someone she had watched coolly deflecting ardour of one kind and another at home and abroad. Elaine was in command. It was evident that Mendoza was making as much mischief as possible and that the seduction of Elaine was some perverse way of getting at her. If he dared, he would try Eve as well. According to David Kelly, he was working on Christina.

'Christ, this is absurd!' Isabel said. 'Now tell me the truth: Mendoza has actually asked you to let him fuck you.'

'*You* put it indelicately . . .'

'I put it as it is. That's all it would be.'

'I know that. I told him I'd think it over.'

This coolness was evidently an act. From the age of fifteen Isabel had herself evaded propositions with skill and laughter. Elaine didn't laugh very much. And possibly it wasn't the involuntary shudder but her persistent laughter that had goaded bloody Mendoza. It would be stupid to suggest to Elaine that the bastard's interest in her was only a tactic of revenge – humiliating, vain and calculated to make her . . . let him fuck her. Surely not.

Elaine, coiled and snug in a pretty summer dress, was watching her.

'I just thought I'd ask your advice,' she said.

'But, love, Mendoza chases anyone.'

'I know he didn't make it with you, but that should hardly matter. Your friend Iris Cameron isn't what one might call selective. And for my part I don't think I'd fancy David Kelly much.'

Isabel was furious with herself. Whether it was true or not that Mendoza had tried his luck with her sister, Elaine was using the situation to attack her. She was clever, but not quick enough when it came to such things. Elaine had invented an imaginary moral fable to intrude into something that was not her concern. It was no one's concern and there was nothing. She had always been good at concealing temper.

'Well, I hope you enjoy it,' she said. 'I take it that you're on the pill.'

'I've no intention of bringing little Mendozas into the world before I've taken my degree. Or indeed my D.Phil. What about you?'

226

'I don't share your academic ambitions.'

Elaine uncoiled suddenly with a springy taut alertness. For a moment, Isabel felt, for the first time ever, submissive, as though offering her throat to the dominant claw. The sisters stared at each other for a mere few seconds. Then the amiable sounds of Daddy with Marcus Ferdinand rumbling away encroached on a moment of unprecedented hostility. If Elaine understood it, Isabel did not.

For a while, as her father poured sherry for everyone, the confusion remained. Even as children, Isabel and Elaine had seldom quarrelled. They had taken holidays together without the slightest acrimony when their interests conflicted and certainly no jealousy. She was upset. Elaine was apparently calm. Eve, if she had been there, might have noticed. Her father did not. Marcus was his usual comfortable self, his big friendly face beaming as he took generous sips from a beaker of sherry.

'I'll get some little biscuits,' Isabel said.

Daddy and Marcus were enchanted by the idea of little biscuits. Isabel was afraid that the ridiculous tears stinging her eyes were going to overflow. She went into the kitchen, trying to be rational, which was not her habit. Mendoza had probably made a pass at her sister, in which there was nothing very unusual, but Elaine had used it, quite deliberately, to try to hurt her. She had succeeded. While she was sure that Elaine had no interest in David Kelly, she sensed something that she had never before suspected – a resentment directed at her.

She returned with two dishes of little biscuits.

'Where's Elaine?'

'She's meeting someone for dinner,' her father said. 'It's about time she got about a bit.'

Why the resentment? She listened vaguely to her father and Marcus Ferdinand talking about the miners' strike, the forthcoming American election, born-again Christians, reactionary politics in America, the decline of liberal tolerance the world over. But her thoughts were fixed on that sudden moment when she and Elaine had faced each other with intense unspoken dislike. What they had said amounted to very little, but their mutual anger was no less real. If it had come as a surprise to Isabel, Elaine had planned it. Why? The whole nonsense of Mendoza need not have been mentioned between them. Surely there had always been an understanding. Isabel was prettier and not entirely dim; Elaine was cleverer and attractive in quite a different way. And when either of them brought young men home, they fell for Mummy. So Elaine did not. Isabel laughed – or had laughed – knowing that she had none of Mummy's class (yet) but had everything else in trumps. At last she was admitting something she had tried to forget about for years: the vanity of her own body and face and hair and eyes. What she would not forgive Elaine for was that reminder. What she had liked about David Kelly was that he had treated her as a woman who was neither an intellectual nor a sex object. Someone was talking to her. Daddy was dining at All Souls: Marcus Ferdinand was inviting her to an evening snack. She would have to concentrate, but it would be civilized.

'I'd love to,' she said. 'Sorry. I was miles away. Among your sectarian Californians. I don't think I know how to be a fanatic.'

Daddy and Marcus laughed.

'Darling,' her father said, 'in the privacy of the company of Marcus who has a confessional purity, will you remind Elaine that it is our wedding anniversary on the 23rd . . .'

'I hadn't forgotten . . .'

'I didn't imagine for a moment that *you* had. But it matters quite a lot to Eve.'

'Of course.'

Her father left them. Isabel poured Marcus another copious sherry and went off to make up properly. As far as she was concerned, if she was being taken out to McDonald's, it was only polite.

Marcus Ferdinand's idea of an evening snack was a full-blown dinner at the Cherwell Boathouse in Bardwell Street. While Isabel was prettifying herself, he had rung to book a table, on the roof. It was a fine, warm late-summer night.

She looked across the table at the warm large presence of Ferdinand, solicitous and funny, remembering her father's mild joke about confessional purity.

'I hope you won't mind this,' he said, 'but may I say just once that you are a remarkably beautiful woman.'

'Thank you . . .'

'No. It stops exactly there. Why were you distressed?'

'When?'

'When Charles and I came in. Your sister wasn't. You were.'

'Was it so obvious?'

'No. But to me you are rather more than a remarkably beautiful woman. I've known you, after all, for a very long time.'

'You've known Elaine as well. And . . .'

'And your mother and Henrietta and Iris Cameron. Of course. It's not quite the same.'

'All I can say is thank you, Marcus . . . I can't help the way I look and I've always tried to play it down.'

'By laughter and kindness. I've noticed.'

'Not always. I have hurt people.'

'Inevitably.'

'It would be so easy . . .'

'To be Iris?'

'If that's what I'm implying, it must sound horrible. I like Iris and she's much kinder than so many others. That doesn't include you. But I'm so bored with *me*. Eve wanted me, I think, to go into the theatre. I didn't. I would hate people looking at me in a way that she doesn't. And I'm not stupid, but I hated the idea of spending my life burrowing or ferreting after this or that little scrap of banana peel or rabbit fur. So I took the easy way out, without having the courage to go right away. I'm equipped to be a high-grade whore – physically and temperamentally . . .'

'Hush, my dear. There is something in the spirit which prevails. That is why I – and others – find you beautiful. Not because you are made the way you are. Although I confess it helps.'

Isabel laughed. It seemed several weeks since she had last smiled wanly. Marcus Ferdinand laughed too and almost, across the table, touched her. Then he withdrew his hand abruptly from her arm. It was fanciful, perhaps, but she thought there was beneath the jovial face some suggestion of pain.

He started talking about wine.

*   *   *   *   *

'I do not believe it,' said Francesca Oricellari. 'What is a brilliant young political scientist doing in the zoo?'

'I could ask the same question,' said Peter Cameron, 'of an elegant and successful couturier.'

'That is easy. I come for ideas. Colours, trimmings, finery, outlines.'

'And I come because I'm interested in animals. After all, I *am* a political scientist. The truth is I have a few hours with nothing much to do before an appointment, it's a pleasant day and I genuinely do like the place. There's quite a pleasant bar where one can sit under the trees. Can I offer you a drink?'

'That would be nice. My sketch pad is just about to run out.'

'It's this way. Past the gibbons and the parrots. What are you sketching for? A new collection?'

'No . . . Just trying out one or two things perhaps for next year.'

'Iris heard on the grapevine that you had an autumn show in New York lined up.'

'That is true. But all the work for that is done. How is your sister? I haven't seen her for months.'

'So I understand. She seems to be busy keeping her chorus line in order. She's bought a new car which she drives far too fast. Here's the bar. Just along there. What will you have?'

'Beer, I think. Lager.'

'Any special kind?'

'Australian. I'll come inside with you and choose.'

'Ah! It's empty. Will Foster's do?'

'Foster's will be fine. Only a half-pint. I am weight-watching.'

'I'm sure you don't need to. Pint and a half of Foster's, please. Well, this is an unexpected pleasure. We don't often have the chance of talking.'

'No. Strange that it should be here somewhere between the panda and the jaguar.'

'Thank you . . . How much? Thanks. Let's go outside.'

'It is nice here on a day like this. How are things at Oxford?'

'Somnolent. And with Parliament in recess I'm not much in demand as an instant unconsidered trifler.'

'What about the miners striking?'

'That's industrial not political. You must know how compartmentalized experts have become . . .'

'But isn't it political?'

'Oh God, yes. It is *very* political: but it is for politicians and others to sound off about. And I must say I'm quite glad about it. Things will liven up when the party conferences start, but I shall have to watch what I can on television, apart from the odd flying visit, because term will be on its way.'

'You know . . . I hope you don't mind this . . . I'm sometimes surprised you are teaching at Oxford at all. Sorry. I mean, Roger Ingestre is an old friend I've known since I was seventeen or eighteen. And I have got to know a lot of others. I mean from Robert Blakemore to Ben . . .'

'Oldfield?'

'Yes. Ben Oldfield. I don't know you so well, but you are different. They love the place and the life. You stand apart. You watch and smile. But you don't care like they do. Forgive me: I'm sure you work just as hard and consider your students, but . . . sorry . . . I'm speaking too much.'

'Not at all. Is your beer all right?'

'Lovely.'

'Good. You're quite right, of course. It's a matter of self-preservation. What else, after all, could I do. Imagine working full time for the *Guardian* or the BBC, looking over your shoulder for the shadow of Casca, illusory or not. I am no civil servant and I should hate to be a politician pretending to believe things which I know to be improvisations upon what is convenient. The university is reasonably polite, I rather enjoy challenging young minds – not in any aggressive way, and I am able, as you have astutely noticed, to keep my distance. Iris, who has no patience with academic niceties, and I share a very comfortable house and live our own lives – both separately and together.'

'That is very frank.'

'Perhaps not as frank as you may be imagining. We're not poor, obviously. Quite apart from what we already own, we both earn quite a lot of money. Our father died when Iris was twenty-three and I was twenty-one. We decided that the existing arrangement suited us both. What about you? I've met your enchanting sister. Without being any less enchanting, you are very different.'

'Because Clodia is calm and diplomatic and I am supposed to be volatile? I don't know. She is older than I am, so she remembers things I don't. She resembles in temperament our father. I don't. Perhaps you're right. But then you and Iris are close and different. And so are the Darrow daughters. Isabel is gay . . . that is not a permitted word now, is it? Isabel is happy, laughing; Elaine is serious.'

'You think I'm serious and my sister is not?'

'I don't have a professional relationship with you. But I think your sister when I meet her is *bloody* serious.'

'That's funny. I shall tell her.'

'Don't! She'll garotte me with a wire coathanger. No. It's just something that happens in any family. My father adored Clodia and he loved me. But she was intellectual . . . She isn't doing badly, but I'm rich. Except it doesn't matter to me. Do you understand? I do what I do because it gives me pleasure. If I didn't I'd stop tomorrow. You know . . . one month I think I only like making money, being clever. The next I'm here in the zoo playing with textures and colours and I'm almost a little girl again.'

'If I may say so, a long way from "almost". Do you not miss Venice? I mean apart from being so beautiful, I should have thought it was so much more alive.'

'It is when you're on holiday. Like everywhere else.'

'Including Oxford?'

'Oxford is different. It is for me peaceful. I couldn't work in Venice. Roma perhaps. Even then I don't know. My sister is a good European and travels out of duty. You know, even in Africa or the Middle East or the Pacific or South America, she is the perfect European. I've always wanted to be different.'

'From your sister?'

' . . . Yes . . . I suppose that is part of it. But more than that. Different from people I meet every day as I would at home.'

'So it is still "home"?'

'Of course. Not in any sentimental way. But if I wasn't a foreigner, I wouldn't be exotic, would I? And that would be bad for business. Why doesn't Iris go to Italy for a couple of years? She'd be a sensation.'

'I've no doubt. But I can't imagine the consequences.'

232

'They'd be interesting.'

'I'm rather surprised you think of yourself as a foreigner. Surely you've been admitted to most of the charmed circles that have any attraction for you? I should think you have a much more varied social life than I do.'

'From what I hear your own isn't exactly dull.'

'It depends who you've been listening to. I'll admit it's not dull. But it's anarchic. Partly because Iris is naturally impulsive and because I don't like charmed circles. Your judgement of me was astute. I like being an outsider. Of course, one is drawn into the obligatory seasonal festivals and has to take one's place in the tribal dances and what Ben Oldfield calls food rituals; but, I pretend to myself, merely as an observer.'

'So you submit to the anarchy?'

'As long as it's not destructive. Iris and I live happily together because we're unlikely to hurt one another, although we've obviously been very close always. Why do you dislike each other so much?'

'Now you *are* being frank. I don't know. Perhaps it's just the colour of our hair and eyes. As natural as that.'

★   ★   ★   ★   ★

HAZARDS AND DISTRACTIONS ON OLDFIELD'S VOYAGE

The myth of Ben Oldfield is slowly taking over from reality. It is ridiculous. In one of my rare dismal phases, I was able to see that all this scribbling is wayward waffle and that my serious work on Stevens will come to nothing unless I go to America, which will involve applying for some kind of grant and time off from the college. Michaelmas Term approaches and I have to teach. There are hints (only bloody hints) that I may be offered a full fellowship – something I could not possibly turn down. While all this is churning around, Henrietta Ball chooses to recommend me to someone in television as 'a literary critic who is at the same time entertaining and relaxed'. Would you believe it? A year ago she didn't know I was crossing Market Street in a sunburst of passion at the sight of her retreating left ankle. The downshot is that I passed the screen test, did the show, evidently relaxed and entertaining enough to be invited to do others. I have since

appeared, however briefly, on 'Kaleidoscope' and 'TV a.m.'
Henrietta's mentor, a large, suave, dangerous man called
Dorf, assures me I have a career in television. Now, as much
as it would delight me to enrage Mendoza by nonchalantly
breaking into his territory, there to set up my disreputable
gypsy caravan, I am not Mendoza. It would drive me mad.
On the one hand am I to be devoured by the Scylla of public
drivel or on the other swirled into the Charybdis of academic
insignificance?

Anyway, why should Ben Oldfield be significant? I will
cool my sweating soul with fabrications. What I need is the
love of a good woman.

However. . . .

Let us return to Eliot on Joyce: The use of myth 'is simply
a way of controlling, of ordering, of giving a shape and a
significance to the immense panorama of futility and anarchy
which is contemporary history.'

Reference, of course, to the application of ancient myth as
a disciplinary control upon modern experience. But I am
concerned with the folktale myth of everyday life – which
means the actual history of ourselves, the fictions we construct
about ourselves and the lies we tell one another and our
shaving mirrors or dressing tables.

Here, of course, categories are necessary. The admirable
G. S. Kirk explaining the nature of myth (rather than why
we need myths, stories, fictions, lies) makes the distinction:
'Folktales are not concerned with large problems like the
inevitability of death or . . . the justification of kingship.
Their social preoccupations are restricted to the family. Difficulties with stepmothers or jealous sisters are folktale topics,
worries over incest and the limits of permissible sexual
encounter are not.'

(With the utmost respect to the professor, I'm not so sure:
the relationship of Iris and Peter Cameron is something of a
local folktale and these days the 'limits of permissible sexual
encounter' are the substance of popular journalism rather than
myth.)

Kirk also points out the essentially aristocratic nature of
Greek myths, especially when they are heroic. This is coherent
with an aristocratic view of tragedy. If we seek to ennoble the

234

proceedings of our own monochrome lives, we have recourse to myth or to the catharsis offered by high tragedy.

It is difficult (for me at least) to apply the same word in the way that it is used on radio, television and in the press to the miseries and disasters, atrocities and individual sufferings which are regularly reported. The murder of some innocent child is profoundly shocking and distressful; the death in an accident of someone who is much loved (whether or not that person is of singular promise) is lamentable. Neither is tragic, because both are real, while tragedy is invariably contrived – artificial to a degree which works upon the imagination, the spirit, rather than the rational mind. The rational mind shows anger and pity when some act of deliberate cruelty or some misfortune is brought to its notice: but it is the imagination which surrenders itself to the cosmic misfortune focused upon hubris.

Professor Kirk describes the interplay of folktale and myth convincingly, but I wish to go further in introducing the interplay of myth and personal fiction. Ancient myth may have been aristocratic and may sustain us when we feel more than usually ignoble: the myths we concoct for ourselves are decidedly not aristocratic or noble. The grand myths are based on ritual or distant historical fact, folktales are based on paradigms which we can recognize even if they are not part of our own experience. Fiction is based on fantasy regarding the lives of others as they impinge directly or peripherally on ourselves. Lies, in this context, are strictly personal.

. . . I heard myself the other day, in a moment of distraction, saying aloud, 'I love you.' And I realized I had no idea who it was. Certainly there was some generalized female presence with all the attributes. But who? Eventually I realized it was a sterile plaint: Ben Oldfield wants to love someone, but can't find the bloody woman. After my fling with Iris (her word for it) I told myself for a while that I had come to love her. I did not dare confess as much, which is as well because it would have been a lie rather than a fiction. The fictions were Henrietta, Eve Darrow, Christina and most particularly Samantha. Iris was real: not a fantasy. She is also honest and would have laughed. If she makes fictions at all, I suspect they would all have lovely Francesca as some wicked man-eating enchantress who in the very last scene will turn into a frightful hag: but she would never lie to herself. Francesca wouldn't make up fictions; but she might, while not exactly lying, participate in self-deception.

And we have the real-life moving drama of Christina and Peter, Isabel and the odious Kelly. Samantha apart, if we could only combine the fictions made of the last two. God, I wish I was Henry James! (As must many others.) Except that Henry would not have been likely to involve himself in the sexual *enjambement*, as it were. I do not know, because I'm not myself involved. Isabel is more cautious and less laughing. No longer *dulce ridentem, dulce loquentem*. Mendoza says there is intense envy between the sisters. Certainly nothing to do with Mendoza! (I hope.) There is also the new soap opera of Oldfield and the latest sirens. Steve Kent, whom I knew, but not very well, in the mid-seventies has married a delightful woman, a little older, who was a contemporary of Mendoza. She is brilliant, but quiet. And very pretty.

Her name is Charley (a diminutive for Carlotta, which she rejected at the age of eight). Apart from being delightful, she has read more than I have (and then some!) with greater discernment. She is *happy* to talk about Eliot, Stevens, Joyce, Pound and all my chaps, but she also knows all the contemporary people whom I neglect, as well as the Latin Americans and Russians. Her eyes sparkle when she talks of *Notes Towards a Supreme Fiction*. Ferdinand has also taken to Stevens: but Ferdinand does not have sparkling eyes, slender hips and pretty legs. I dimly recall Kent going around with a beautiful red-haired girl whose name I have forgotten, with whom he was besotted. So what became of her? He is now an aspiring politician, locally adopted by the SDP. Although he is not putting up at Oxford, it will mean their frequent visits. I don't give a toss about Kent, but it will be good to see the lovely Charley over the next year or so. Sparkling conversation and there an end. She loves Kent very much and in his way he is devoted to her.

My other siren must be approaching sixty, still amazingly sexy. (Charley *isn't* consciously.) A friend of Ingestre and various others called Marie White. Much married, very worldly, gentle, temperate. Her figure is voluptuous, her eyes are round, guileless and surprisingly young, her smile is quick and she is generous. Without being predatory, I sense that she is still actively interested in sex. It would surely be more than cynical to essay the seduction of someone almost twice my age, however charming, because she happened to be there. She is probably much too wise to tangle with such ineffectual wing-flappers as your average Oldfield.

Back to what passes for thinking . . .

Apart from the fictions we make to amuse ourselves and to scandalize our fellow bourgeois, the more sinister aspect of present-day myth making seeks to influence a largely unsuspecting public through image making, story telling, covert ritual. It is most obvious in television presentation and advertising, but its exploitation is not new. Politicians must have, these days, an effective televisual presence. No doubt Old Orange Dye is going to grin Mondale into the ground in the forthcoming American campaign.

All quite legitimate in a democratic system. (Would Attlee have got the better of Churchill on the flickering living-room menace?) Are politicians to be judged by the figures invented for them? Does it matter?

Let us remind ourselves of the Cabinet of Dr Goebbels and its contents. The use of ceremony, ritual and the creation of quite underserving cult heroes (Horst Wessel) was not invented by the Nazis to legitimize the assumption of power. And it has not stopped with their demise. At the same time in those vast organized rallies there was a terrifying assurance in stage management which no American political convention could touch. Compared with either, the dear old shambles of our domestic party conferences, in spite of the block votes and traditional Tory discipline, is an eleventh-hour relief.

Nevertheless, the ghost picture on my television screen is Adolf Hitler with Josef Goebbels up in the gallery and Leni Riefenstahl calling the shots. Forget *Triumph of the Will* (a dangerous word if ever there was): think of the *Berlin Olympics 1936*. I suspect only with hindsight is it possible to see the ideological perversion of genius.

The early morning news has brought a report on the IRA attempt to blow up the Conservative Party during their conference. Many injured. The Prime Minister narrowly escaped. Reality has a way of banging Theory about the ears most painfully. No more dear old shambles . . .

. . . I was taking a holiday from theorizing while bedazzled

(I hope temporarily) by *The Auroras of Autumn*. Consequently in that helplessly undirected state of mind where having a pee is a spiritual effort and shaving requires intense moral purpose. At this point Iris rang up to suggest lunch. Would I be Tannhauser or Parsifal? I did not much care. My sombrero went once more over the windmill.

As it happened the gardens of Venus and Klingsor, with all their pleasures, were as firmly closed as Iris's thighs. The purpose of the meeting was to make sure that in spite of what happened and what might still happen again (always the tantalizing threat) we would remain friends.

Iris, in spite of her demure black-tighted (I hotly imagine) posture, did little for my sang-froid by insisting on a cool appreciation of our hectic weekend. If this is part of a calculated effort to keep my interest *up*, lest it be needed for some future blank date in her calendar, she succeeded. Then just as calmly she started chatting about foreign travel.

I am repeatedly astounded by the amount that women eat and the speed with which they consume it, without a suggestion of inelegance or gluttony, while managing to talk all the time. Isabel has the gold medal for sheer speed, Iris for quantity. Francesca and Charley Kent qualify for silvers. Yet each of them creates an impression of fastidious daintiness and they all have lovely figures. It is only when I see an empty plate opposite me and look down to see that my own is still two thirds full that I realize what sterling performers they are. I am incapable of eating and talking at once. If I were not engaged in my labyrinthine journey around myth (a myth is as good as a meal), I might essay a dissertation on the miseries of food rituals. For the sensitive person food can be dreadfully threatening. I wish that all the gastronomic scouts and good food guides understood what it is like to feel sated, especially in someone's house where everything has been prepared with concern. Or to feel sick in a smart restaurant alongside the one you love who will most certainly belong to somebody else. Worst of all, the splendid occasion when, even if you can flee from the elevated table, you can't find the gents. But the abovementioned sylphides flutter through course after course with bantering glissades, chassés and arabesques like shadows across a cloudless cyclorama.

It was all most enjoyable. Iris is quite explicit that any

relationship between us must be either civilized or sensual: it will not be allowed to become sentimental. This makes for a relaxed ambience.

'The Greek mouth that has never been twisted in prayer.' And yet I cannot think of you as a white goddess or a white Venus. You would not let me. Rather a priestess at some bawdy mystery to which I am now initiate. Beside all those women generated in dream factories, it is your cool reality that makes you radiant for me; the uncompromising sexuality that will hear no word of love outside the fury of some climactic embrace, or the long slow mutual relaxation of tension which comes in a gentle fire. No: I do not love you. But the memory of the arrogance of your naked body, your games with lace and silks and satin, your erotic joy inflames me still, for which I thank you. My dreams of fair women ramble everywhere. You were no dream. Revels you will permit: but you are not such stuff as dreams are made on.

I protest too much. For all that talk of reality, I am making a myth out of her. She would be scornful.

In response to her question, I told her that I did not see Isabel very often these days. Iris was thoughtful. She cannot understand why someone as high-spirited and as beautiful concerns herself only with flirtations. It occurred to me that she probably knew all about her brother and Christina Kelly. I dared not ask and she offered nothing. 'I think,' Iris said, 'that she wastes her time and talents in more ways than one. She'd be better employed working for me.' I wonder.

Isabel, Isabel, didn't worry,
Isabel didn't scream or scurry.
She showed no rage and she showed no rancour,
But she turned the witch into milk and drank her.

Hardly fair to either of them. Perhaps I, too, am becoming nastier as I grow older. Does it mean that I recognize a kind of ruthlessness in Isabel which isn't in Iris? Or is it just that I have been reading Ogden Nash? It would do no harm to take her out one evening to discover if she had recaptured the old laughter . . .

239

. . . Perhaps I'm in a fractious frame of mind. Dinner in college I found supremely irritating. There weren't many people there, but those that were had brought their malice with them: I can't count the number of times I have heard the well-planned trap, only to see the smirk of foxy malignancy congeal swiftly into a mask of pallid mortification as it is neatly, sometimes triumphantly, avoided. All the Aristophanic characters were on parade: the aloof visionary who insists that she is living in the real world, the buffoonish bubble-burster of no mean wit delighting in poking fun at quite serious hypotheses and arguments, the cunning devil who delights in his duplicity and who has let it take precedence over scholarship, critical judgement and any ideals he might once have had. In an Oxford donnery/There is so much connerie/Just a pack of pundits in clover/They're all there semestering/With dry footnotes festering/Teaching scruffy students moreover . . . Ah well! I'm not human tonight.

So where am I in all this? I am Snodgrass to Mendoza's Swozzler, the *eiron* who dissembles with consummate irony his worth to his *alazon* bragging about attributes that he does not have.

Not convincing: the comic catharsis described by Kenneth MacLeish is not for me 'the ironical satisfaction of seeing characters who have failed to reach manifestly impossible goals accept their alternatives.' Ben Oldfield, his story. But no catharsis.

Nevertheless, I have enjoyed Pretty Halcyon Days. I should not be grumbling.

Praise the spells and bless the charms,
I found April in my arms
April golden, April cloudy,
Gracious, cruel, tender, rowdy . . .

It's time I set my mind to serious work.

★   ★   ★   ★   ★

Here we all are again – our very exclusive dining club, founded soon after we left Oxford and characterized essentially by ambition, a sense of privilege, a determination to succeed. As the years go by, some of us become more pompous and wear our black ties with a difference. Not me, of course. But then Mendoza *is* already successful. The typical fruit salad I suppose: television men, journalists, literary agents, publishers, a doctor, some lawyers, a barrister, a dentist. Chaps to a man. I need not have come after all. Never any women, which is the pity of it. Several thoroughly round-upable wives could be mustered, as well as the occasional delicious playmate. From observation one or two of the roundest wives are very inclined to be upable: but a *chap* can hardly make the first move. I wonder if I'd have made it with Elaine. Not likely. The Darrow females are not easily impressed, witness two years of Mendoza's schemes for laying Isabel. Have the feeling though that Elaine might either for the hell of it or because her sister gets on her nerves prick-teasing in the most genteel way. Taking after her mother. Elaine is quieter but hardly prim. Witness our last meeting when there was a generous display accomplished with female Darrow discretion and she did not recoil from the second phase of Mendoza sincerity.

Conscience strikes at about 5.30 in the morning. My lust is indiscriminate, but this time I want to hurt Isabel. Sure I would like to fuck her sister but the motive is darker. It is a form of revenge. How could I be *sure* she would find out. The image of her with Kelly tortures me. And Christina thinks I'm joking. Or pretends to.

Nevertheless, in we go. Alistair! Good to see you. Who are you with *now?* The ways we have of demonstrating the ever-ready flicknife. Crooked teeth and shifting eyes. The misleading charm which leaks with the right crony out of the side of his mouth when he is unable to conceal the delight of his entirely vapid contempt as his eyes flicker over the topic of his venom. No such crony, me! Peregrine! How elegant you look. You must have put on weight. And how are things in literature? Any best sellers on the way? Of course, it's the autumn. Any decent agent will be looking towards the major prizes. Naturally. Oh I'm fine. New series in the New Year and one or two interesting one-offs plus a trip to Washington to bide my time. The bastard drives a Rolls. Six foot three of clumsy etiolated inherited money tripping over his own ankles as he remembers to think and sneer at the same time. Difficult for him. The thinking bit. Bertie! Great success! I read about it in *The Times*. But was he guilty? I suppose I shouldn't ask. My God, you *are* doing bloody well. You can't be all that much older than I am. The mouth grimaces downward, the eyes hood for a moment. Bertie Joiner prepares himself for a measured statement. It wouldn't matter whether it was about his latest civil law proceeding, Auchinleck at Alamein or Irish poetry: it would be measured and ponderous. At least I don't have to listen. He won't be interested in what *I'm* doing.

Here they all are after seven or eight years. Wilkinson born with a tomahawk face and a tabloid mentality both honed to kill, like so many others the spotless socialist working for a militant Tory paper; Burbank (with a cigar) small and birdlike with the important pomposity that small birds manage so much better than the ones which can soar and glide; Roland Barton, his crulle lockes receding with the width of his smile, eyes consciously watchful; Finch clumsily boyish and cricketing, fresh of face, glib, knocking things over. Odd to think that we must once all have liked one another. Or at least got on. The coincidence of starting careers at the same time in London and meeting friends of the others. The English craving to be exclusive. That sounds like Ben bloody Oldfield whom rumour has it was having an expensive lunch with Iris Cameron. I can't believe it. Surely not with Ben! I don't understand why he is so popular with women – including Isabel. Must be something in being wistfully harmless. But Iris? It's farther than thought can reach. A dining club seemed a good lark at the time. It was an idea of old Brookers and he's stayed the same: jovial, back-thumping. Binns is all right: modest, gently staring into carious mouths day by day. Allport – for someone who works in my business even if its only radio unusually good-humoured. Cf. Burbank and Barton. I suppose we were drawn together by ambition, all determined to get on. And here we are in our mid-thirties getting on. None more so than *ipse* Mendoza except in one respect, but I couldn't stomach the idea of marriage however much I enjoy looking up the skirts of the rounder wives and the occasional hastily conferred grope . . . No Giles, stop it! That's *enough*. Lovely though: perhaps we can think of something . . . And an uxorial hand howevering flutteringly over my balls. No I am a satyr. That's all there is to it. But even in the head I don't rape. They always have to want Mendoza, even flutteringly, for himself. I'll have to think it out again. Catherine at the office? Edna the PA? Helena the researcher? The trouble is the fury that seethes through me when I think of Isabel's shudder. It is stupid in someone in my position. And yet revenge becomes a passion. Christina . . . Elaine . . . How can I hurt her and Kelly?

Time to contribute . . . Thanks I was drinking whisky and soda . . . Well then, Ian, how are things at the Bailey? Must have been a bit tricky your last one . . . What I notice is that our coterie is narrow. There is the smattering of lawyers and one or two people who are something vague in business, but no politicians, no one who does anything of consequence in the City, no academics, no writers, no actors. And surely we all knew people who now do these things. It may be that such people are not clubbable or drift naturally to gatherings of their own kind. Not clubbable myself for that matter. This place oppresses me. Brookers is tremendously proud at being a member. Why we meet here over the last two, no three, years. Well, what is it to be? *Potage St Hubert, gigot d'agneau garni*, cheese and celery, chocolate mousse, fruit. Moulin à Vent 1978. Château de Malle 1979. Port. Madeira. Going to cost a bob or two. *That* doesn't matter, but I think I'll be busy next year. Not bad I suppose. Might as well enjoy it.

Dinner is served. Bonhomous shuffle, laughter, baritone rhubarb, sudden cries of recognition cleverly timed to avoid chat. An empty tradition. Ritual of those clinging to some arbitrary bond, something imaginary in the past. Yet I'm the only one who still has anything to do with Oxford. Only because of Aunt Dorothy's house and recently bloody Isabel. Most of them are now faintly contemptuous. Theirs is the real world. In a way it is. Ah we were all going to do such fine things ten or so years ago. Then came marriage, nappies, ambition, various degrees of success.

Soup isn't bad. This is the time for serious conversation where everyone shows how concerned they are. Pleasanteries are deferred. On my left acid rain and the environment: Bertie Joiner listening sagely to the fanfaronades of Terry Burbank like a tired statue being hopped on by a rather uppish robin.

On my right Peregrine Marston wants to lock up Arthur Scargill which excites the wrath of honest Walt Wilkinson who thinks the miners *must* win. Across the table terrorism – the bombs at the Conservative conference and the Libyan Embassy siege. Much wagging of heads, tapping of the table, intent forward leaning of those only waiting for a flicker of silence in which to break in. The sinking of the *Belgrano*. (*Still?*) Unemployment and the *mauvaise foi* of the government. The ineffectuality of the SDP. The Pope. Really heavy stuff flying all around the table gleaming and glittering. Quite a decent drop of wine . . . You're pretty silent, Giles. Thought you had views on everything . . . Only for the public, Alistair. What about you? . . . Yes. Nicely under the ribs that one.

And so I nod and smile, interject appropriately. After years in television I am expert at pretending to listen when not really expected to comment. When it all gets lighter, I'll turn on Mendoza's famous channel of humour and innuendo. Meanwhile over the gigot I shall think of that lingering glimpse of Elaine Darrow's thighs accompanied by a shake of her hair and a little pout of her lips. And if I get bored with that, there's always Christina to be imagined in a picture hat and fishnets. What did the man say about a perpetual feast? I don't think of Isabel any more . . . The fucking little bitch.

★   ★   ★   ★   ★

Hotel Bristol
Sorrento
18 October 1984

Dear Rachel,
It is all great fun, but a bit tiring. As soon as the talking stopped, we were in action almost at once. I hope you had my postcards from Greece and Crete in September, since this is the first moment I've had to sit down and write a proper letter. The visit to Iraq has been postponed because Chiltern are afraid that we might all become Babylonian captives and Egypt is deferred until December. It is all going to take a great deal of time and an unthinkable amount of money. Nevertheless, I am writing looking out at Vesuvius over the Gulf of Naples

so I have no cause for complaint. We are put up in very good hotels with every comfort. Within reason, of course!

The scheme appears to be that we shoot a great deal of footage – once I should have said take a vast number of pictures – some of them with me in pretty frocks or else looking businesslike in a shirt and very tight jeans telling the camera things that various learned people have told me and which I have put into my own words. Most of it will be done next year some time in voiceover or in straightforward narration. At the same time, I have to know what I'm talking about which involves immense reading. That's the tiring part. Eventually all this film will be woven around my studio exposition and interviews with the appropriate scholars.

If you wonder what we are doing at Sorrento, it is thought to be a convenient and pleasant place for working at Cumae and Paestum (outposts of Greek hegemony) as well as Pompeii and Herculaneum. Naples would obviously be a much more efficient base, but our executive producer was once hit on the head by some perceptive Neapolitan and is terrified of the place. I can't say I'm sorry, even if it does mean driving through the most undisciplined traffic I have ever encountered. Happily the driver of our minibus (the one I travel in, at least) is Italian, probably a nephew of someone in the Camorra, who behaves with all-comprehending ruthlessness even to pantechnicons on the *autostrada*. Living in such fear sets the adrenaline going for work on camera. In Cumae (sacred to Apollo) it poured with the most torrential rain I have ever seen. In my sleek white shirt and tailored slacks, I might as well have been naked. The camera crew were appreciative, but we have to do the very miserable journey and try to shoot it all again.

Next we move to southeast France to Nîmes, Arles and notably Orange, where they are looking for shots of the amphitheatre with the effigy of Augustus. I shall no doubt be found musing in Les Alyscamps at Arles or rapt in the Maison Carrée at Nîmes. There is talk of further Roman hegemonimous travel to Asia Minor (as we called it) or Spain. I hope not: and since the executive

245

producer hates both locations, I suspect the budget will not stand it. Who knows? If only the public knew how unglamorous it all is.

I had a week or two at Oxford in between excursions towards the end of September. Not being used to all this travel, it was a curious sensation. There was a possibly notional distance between me and others, as though I were seeing people from some milieu I didn't know. It was not markedly comforting. Your great friend Roger Ingestre is much the same as always, delighted by the presence of Clodia Oricellari for a few days and in the most convivial mood. You probably know her better than I do, but that willowy cosmopolitan charm is captivating, don't you think? The effervescent and curvaceous Francesca wasn't present, which was a pity. She stirs up the bubbles. As it was, we had a still, unruffled evening. Just six of us. I've written to you about David Kelly, his wife and Isabel Darrow some time ago, but I'm now afraid that the marriage is irreparably damaged. I'm also afraid that at last I must confess my own declared interest. Perhaps you, married to Oliver, have never experienced a hazy kind of jealousy directed towards someone whose mild sexual attention you used to take for granted. I'm afraid that this is what has happened to me in regard to David Kelly, which is why I suppose I am aware of the tension between him and Christina where others do not notice it. I may, of course, be imagining it because I want to. I don't think so. After all when I was tempted, I didn't trespass because of his marriage to someone whom I thought vulnerable. Now she seems to me less uncertain than indifferent. His manner has always been nonchalant. What was noticeable was that there was none of the casual intimate interplay that occurs between couples who are reasonably happily married: they did not talk or glance across the table, there were no joky asides, no tangential anecdotes. In fact, Roger and Clodia seemed much more intimate. Because of the Chiltern arrangement, it hasn't been difficult to keep out of the way of both David and Isabel, whom I found myself beginning to dislike. I think now that I was not so much annoyed, because I thought she was being silly and destructive, as jealous. It is depressing in a woman of my assumed maturity and pretentions. I had not known other than Clodia, whom I wanted to meet again, who Roger Ingestre's other guests were to be. No doubt, I'd still have gone. My own partner at the feast was Marcus Ferdinand whom you must have met. He is a pleasant man who claims to have renounced everything he once believed in these days. Far from becoming cynical and misanthropic, however, he can't help being decent and sociable. He laughs at himself for what he calls vacillation and intellectual vacuity, but in moments of repose I detect a certain sadness. I've known him, though not well, for a good many years. Alas, he has always been rather frightened of me, so we have not become the good friends we might have been.

In spite of all the hassle of travel and my current brand of displacement activity, I was quite pleased to leave Oxford again, because I found it unsettling. England itself, seen on a flying visit, is quite simply depressing. The coal strike drags on, though there appears to be less violence on picket lines, even if there are allegations of intimidation. While expressing responsible concern, the political bit of Roger Ingestre is very pleased that the strike and its supporters are doing harm to the Labour Party, which, under Kinnock, had been gaining support partly at the expense of Roger's SDP. Thatcher and her immediate Cabinet chums are highly unpopular, at least in the circles in which I move.

You will be up to the neck in the election campaign. In more ways than one, I've no doubt. From what I read Reagan looks as though he's going to walk away with it. And that doesn't fill me with primavernal lightness of heart. It's a pity because I've always thought that Mondale is a thoroughly decent politician, whereas some of the far right Republican forces sound dangerous. As you can imagine most of your friends and mine are solid for the Democrats. I look forward to reading your account of it all (along with Oliver's footnotes). If you do write, while I am still gallivanting, could you send the letters to the Hall. I return every so often, as I've described, so it's lovely to have them waiting for me.

For the next few days we are working at Pompeii. The weather is good and the light (so I am told) perfect. Also the executive producer has gone home. He does not hit it off with Dorf who is not averse to displaying the power of his elbow-wrestling. I'll write when I have a proper moment of leisure.

Incidentally, Ivan Whitehart who was at Oxford during the last academic year, is visiting Berkeley. Inadvertently I told him that Oliver and you were in California, so he may look you up. He 'certainly intends to'. He is very charming in his way, if not especially bright. You'll like him well enough, but Oliver will have to be patient.

I hope to see you in 1985. As yet I don't know when. Until then, my love to you both.

Ever,
Henrietta

*   *   *   *   *

Donne cites the statuary which was the ancient way of celebrating the *memorie* of such as deserved well of the *State* for their counsel, which was then called *Hermes: the head and shoulders of a man, standing upon a Cube*, but those *shoulders* without *armes* and *hands*. He goes on to explain this *Hieroglyphique* – the *Counsellor* should bee without *hands*, so farre as *not to reach out his hands to forraigne tentations of bribes, in matters of Counsell;* and that it was not necessary that the *head* should employ *his owne hand;* that *the same men* should serve in the *execution*, which assisted in the *Counsell;* but that there should not belong *hands* to every *head, action* to every *counsell*, was never intended, so much as in *figure*, and *representation*.

Ah me! As God must say to himself at the beginning of a liturgy. Donne's Hieroglyphique means something quite different to Marcus Ferdinand who has certainly done nothing to deserve well of the state or much else. A head without arms and hands, immobile and effectually impotent. Donne's stern words lash my conscience. It is not necessary to believe in the soul to have a conscience; guilt, in whatever form, is born in the intellect. I despair of my inactivity over so many years, even if I am not alone. Whether of the right or left, passive intellectuals are at fault. We have shirked responsibility, abandoned standards of thinking and judgement, ignored the deterioration of behaviour. Out of egalitarian mania or in the name of liberal generosity we have succumbed to every type of laxity and laziness. We have tolerated political cant to a degree where it threatens society and freedom. Freedom does not mean the maximum commercial exploitation of systems and people. Democracy is not the dishonest rant of the Trotskyist left. People are bored and have been encouraged to be idle. Television bears much of the blame, but the sychophancy of intellectuals has acquiesced in a steady deterioration of values. It started in the ghastly sixties and it is still with us. I know quite well that I have long been irrelevant, but with the exception of the doctors and biochemists and the necessary technologists, all those around me (including the pure scientists) are playing elaborate games in that we have helped to encourage a society in which ideas for their own sake do not matter. The smallness of our own lives and preoccupations is no more despicable than the smallness of most other lives: but so many of us cling to the desperate illusion that we, in some way, still matter.

> The war between classes is
> A preliminary provincial phase
> Of the war between individuals. In time,
> When earth has become a paradise, it will be
> A paradise full of assassins.

Thus Wallace Stevens in 'Life on a Battleship'. Written a long time ago but still apposite. Very apposite in the light of industrial and urban chaos. It would indeed be massive irony if this government (for all its glaring insensitivities and injustices) should lay the foundations of a kakistocracy. I suppose, in all fairness, that some would argue it had already achieved one. Against all this, there is Ingestre approaching fifty and there is Warrington past forty still struggling on at some liberal Verdun. To no avail. At least they will not be condemned for cowardice.

Thinking back a few weeks to Ingestre's highly polished

dinner party, I looked around the table to decide that Christina Kelly was probably the most useful person present. This may seem churlish to the charming Clodia Oricellari who is never indiscreet about her international diplomacy. But what, after all, is diplomacy? Consider Machiavelli. The rest of us were snow people. Even less substantial, we were the figures etched with a thumbnail upon frosted windows in a cold house such as the one I lived in as a child. Christina Kelly, by contrast, though no more exuberant, has gained in poise and confidence. From what little private conversation I had with her, I understand that she has now become head of public relations in her electronics firm which is about to be involved in a spectacular merger. This is obviously important to her, for which I am glad: especially if as I suspect Kelly has now mastered, or succumbed to, Isabel.

Symptoms of futility abound. I watched him throughout the evening. He is never obtrusive, but always polite. Once in the presence of Henrietta Ball, he would make efforts to be witty, even epigrammatic. Not any more. Clodia engaged him slightly: for the rest of the evening he was somewhere else. It is silly to resent him. But I do. I imagined him thinking of Isabel.

I met her briefly a few days ago and took her for a drink. She is sparkling again, laughing, careless, very beautiful. We talked of nothing very much. We never do. I was magniloquent but funny: she was pert and funnier. That is all there is. Looking at her, the perfect mouth tilted in a smile, black hair tumbling onto her shoulders, her eyes a darker blue than I remembered, her beautiful body in a relaxed curve of sensual, completely unprovocative ease, I was brushed by the wing of my own desperation.

> Oui! telle que vous serez, o la reine des grâces
> > Après les derniers sacrements,
> Quand vous irez, sous l'herbe et les floraisons grasses
> > Moisir parmi les ossements.

> Alors, o ma beauté! dites à la vermine
> > Qui vous mangera de baisers
> Que j'ai gardé la forme et l'essence divine
> > De mes amours décomposés!

250

It is an acutely morbid state of mind that can look at a lovely young woman and think of Baudelaire's 'Une Charogne'. *Sacré nom*. In my case it is not spleen but despair. Fortunately, Isabel knows nothing of that horrible flash of thought which frightens and disgusts me. My face remains broad and bland whatever terrors are passing through my sickening imagination.

In a roundabout way I mentioned David Kelly's name as though in passing. Isabel looked at me quickly, intelligent eyes twinkling, an irrepressible, entrancing pursing of the lips as for a chaste kiss. She said she understood he was working on a book quite busily as well as teaching: she saw him only on library business once or twice a week. She was being deliberately evasive and artful, even so there was an intentionally mischievous hint that she was dissembling – as though playing some kind of game.

Our conversation was, as always, inconsequential, but while it lasted delightful. As always, I struggled to think of some way of letting her know that I loved her for many years. It was too absurd. So I burbled and she chirruped until it was time for her to go. She did not say where. Isabel does not favour anoraks and jeans or modified dungarees. She dresses as carefully, though less idiosyncratically, as Iris Cameron. As it happens both women have the beautifully moulded *croupe* which would look fine in trousers and which so many others do not possess. I helped her into a close-fitting dark blue coat, so that it was one of those rare occasions when I have touched her. We left the pub. I watched her lilt away along the street for a moment, feeling in some way hollow.

                                        You
Become the soft-footed phantom, the irrational

Distortion, however fragrant, however dear.
That's it: the more than rational distortion,
A fiction that results from feeling. Yes, that.

Days later the hollowness is still there and the same feeling of absurdity. I know that I have distorted Stevens's meaning, but he seems to me to talk of the imagination and the supreme fiction which is a hedge against mortality as to a woman in

251

loving sometimes erotic tropes, so I claim licence to think of Isabel in such a way – as if it would help to pretend that she is a fiction which I (and perhaps others) have made of her and so does not really exist.

Distracted and idle, I turned on the radio some ten minutes ago to hear Mendoza, one of the leading *entrepreneurs du bonheur public*, being sharp on a quiz programme. It is *l'instant de boire*, so I reflect on what Aldous Huxley called 'the joylessness of contemporary pleasures'. The passivity and vicarious interests of those who are bored or lazy or cannot be bothered to make their own amusement. Possibly this is why youths go to football matches to fight rather than to watch football. The consequent violence is inevitable just as the consequence of the more extreme forms of sexual experiment is usually cruelty.

> The desert is not remote in southern tropics,
> The desert is not only around the corner,
> The desert is squeezed in the tube-train next to you,
> The desert is in the heart of your brother.

And in my own. Irrecoverably. I do not know how it became so. My childhood, adolescence and early manhood were far from unhappy. It was simply that I learned the habit of asking questions. And I have asked too many. Self-pity? Perhaps . . .

Who would not be affected to see a cleere and sweet *River* in the Morning, grow a *kennell* of muddy water by *noone*, and condemned to the saltnesse of the *Sea* by *night?*

*   *   *   *   *

21 October 1984
Not much more than a year has passed since our last holiday, but Christina and I are not the same people. For the first time that I recall she did not want to go away. The explanation was entirely feasible. She travels a great deal, she is now highly placed in her firm with responsibility for a smooth transition into the affairs of another. And I am working on my book on aesthetic theory after what she describes as months of just kicking around. She reminds me that I have often

complained about dozing or boozing by the sea when I might have been working. I don't remember it in quite the same way.

It doesn't matter. I'm happy that she is doing well, delighted by her work. In the past, she has been unfailingly pleasant to my colleagues (even the ones who made her wince); now I am, as the occasion demands, benign host to hers. Part of the 'give and take of marriage' after all. Occasionally we make love, though very much less frequently. Most of the time it works well enough, but it is technical rather than passionate. And those, sometimes contrived, are our only intimate moments: for the rest she is either preoccupied or indifferent.

I do not know how much I am to blame. I explained about the game with Isabel after Mendoza's initial calumnies and I thought she had accepted what I said. It's possible the game has gone on longer than it should have. Isabel is affectionate and cool when we are alone. If someone else appears who is likely to talk, I am given the occasional burning look or the intimate caressing glance, to which I suppose I respond. What is beginning to worry me is that the burning looks have started to strike kindling. It was all a thoroughly stupid idea which I should have called off months ago. Now I'm not sure that I want to. It's possible that Christina has a lover with whom she works at home or in Europe. As I was leaving her last evening, Isabel looked up at me with those violet eyes lingering and moonlit. We did not touch or kiss. We don't any more when alone. But, by God, it was a formidable example of the Will in action!

The attitudes of others are not exactly troubling but irritating. Eve Darrow, who must have studied *froideur* at RADA, gives me the full treatment. We are seldom invited to the hospitable table. Charles does his best to avoid me. Elaine almost perceptibly curls her lip. Mendoza grins knowingly, while trying his luck with Christina: she tells me about it, so I doubt that he has succeeded, unless I have completely misunderstood Christina whom I do not suspect to be devious. Even Ingestre and the pretty Francesca, Samantha and Tom Wilkins are less warm. In any event, what business is it of theirs? Ferdinand and Ben Oldfield (after an initial bout of puritan horrors on Ben's part) are the only ones who treat me

253

as I once was. Warrington would disdain any interest. Iris Cameron similarly. Her brother is as friendly as ever, but he never gives much away. It is all ridiculous. Late 1984. One of my former pupils who was a disastrous philosopher but has become quite a successful actor complained to me the other day, 'As soon as the curtain comes down, they seem to think that we're at it like knives. It just isn't true. Apart from anything else, we're too tired.'

This is nonsense. Christina and Isabel begin to obsess me. I shall take refuge in the temperate islands of aesthetics but without the statutory records and unlimited supply of pins and needles.

23 October

The kidnapping of the Polish priest, whom I suppose few of us knew about until now, is distressing. We live such circumscribed lives that I doubt whether we give a thought, other than during the morning or evening news, to what is happening in Poland or the Lebanon or to Sakharov or to hostages here there and everywhere. I don't mean cloistered academics only: I mean all of us who live busy, industrious, altruistic, thoroughly *comfortable* lives. Altruism stops at the end of the avenue or beyond the square where self-interest takes over. The threat to our own necessary equilibrium.

Today Mitterand comes on a state visit. A clever man adapting to the arrogance of power. He will meet someone whom it fits like a glove. I daresay other garments fit her as snugly but prefer not to think about it. I heard the First Lady of the Treasury a little while ago on early morning radio: 'Philosophy's all right,' said she, 'and I frequently indulge in it myself.' So now we know. Poor Mitterand. I wonder if he went to the Ecole Supérieure Normale.

I am bad-tempered because I have learned that two of my pupils (former pupils) have completely failed to find a job since going down. Neither was very good – one took a poor second and the other a third. At the same time they were good enough to be employed at something moderately demanding. Understandably, neither of them wanted to teach in a school of any description or to join the police or become minor administrators. There is no choice any more for philosophy students who haven't quite made it, other than the scrap heap. I daresay the politically inclined ones will be welcomed somewhere if they are convincingly 'politicized' in either direction, but my forlorn two had no clear idea what they wanted to do. They both did reasonably at Latin and Greek, but they should never have been allowed to read Greats. It may sound elitist but philosophy is only much use to people with first-rate minds, whatever Mrs Thatcher indulges in. I find myself guardedly guiding the undergraduates I am currently teaching in the direction of certain careers, trying not to hint that I do not expect them to do well in Schools. It has brought home to me for the first time the frustration of young people who have had much more limited or extremely limited education, to whom I regret to say I have seldom given much attention.

24 October

With Christina away for the weekend at some 'brainstorming' session (Ye elves and spirits!), I dined in college with Ferdinand as my guest. He appeared at first to be a little subdued. My tentative arguments about education reanimated him. Ferdinand believes that we have created a self-perpetuating elite which has betrayed standards. I pointed out that the Marxists I teach, some of whom are very intelligent, have no interest in the perpetuity of people like Ferdinand and myself and despise the standards which we observe. He believes Marxism to be destructive in that it is hostile to natural excellence, creating its own hieratic order. Any such order depends on rigid doctrine and all doctrine that is rigid is hostile to excellence. It must be said that he is just as contemptuous of *laissez faire* conservatism. With his capacious memory, he quoted (of all people) James Joyce: 'If we must accuse of madness every great genius who does not believe in the hurried materialism now in vogue with the happy fatuousness of a recent college graduate in the exact sciences little remains for art and universal philosophy.' (I don't suppose that Mrs Thatcher indulges much in Joyce. And I doubt that many of her colleagues have heard of him.)

It is not immediately perceivable that Ferdinand is deeply pessimistic. From time to time in exclusive, late conversation he has voiced some quite startlingly gloomy views of the human condition, while always refuting the idea of sin. For the most part this is concealed under his jovial fluency, his love of food and drink and good company, his appreciation (always discreet) of pretty women, his enjoyment of and contribution to laughter in any gathering.

Listening to his arguments – they were not so much arguments as postulates – about the elitist betrayal, I found myself thinking about Juvenal's fulminations against the Roman aristocracy upon whom he laid much of the blame for the decline of his society. Both attitudes seem to me conservative, if not reactionary. Resistance to change is not merely a matter of preserving the status quo, it is pining for a retreat into a world of values which have fallen into abeyance, where they have not been outrightly rejected. Without anything like the ferocity or bitterness of Juvenal, Ferdinand laments what he regards as the decline in excellence. From the time that he left the Church, I have little idea of what he thinks of as 'spiritual', although he sometimes uses the word. I am, however, sure that he refers to moral as well as intellectual qualities. An arch-Conservative such as Robert Blakemore accepts social change where he rejects political deviation in any form from benign paternalism. He is no reactionary. Others such as Ingestre and myself are cautious and may not welcome change for its own sake, but are prepared to resign ourselves to the inevitable. Politely I suggested to Ferdinand that his stance was reactionary. As urbane as ever, he referred to a Wallace Stevens poem: 'Rather than the revolutionary, I am, as you suggest, the reactionary stopping for orangeade. Except that I should ask for *orange pressé*.'

We were joined by Wilfred Noakes, another guest, chaplain of his college. To the best of my knowledge, Ferdinand is completely at ease with clerics, even when they fall upon him like the wasps of Assisi on spilt beer. They buzz and nag at him. My own speculation is that they are envious or resentful. Ferdinand lost his faith and had the courage to declare it publicly by resigning his ministry. There must be others who have not dared as much. Again there are those who cling to their Christian belief who are genuinely annoyed by an apostate and feel the need to attack him.

On this occasion, Noakes chose to go on at length about Ultimate Truth. Ferdinand and I were, for the most part, quiet. Then there came something of an outburst from Ferdinand, whom I have never known to lose his temper. It went something like: 'I've heard the arguments that Ultimate Truth, as you call it, is an accident of cosmic chemistry. And I refute them.' Noakes smiled confidently. 'The word "accident",' said Ferdinand, 'implies its opposite, which presupposes purpose. There is no purpose. There is no Ultimate Truth. There is only sub-atomic chaos.' Professionally, it was not difficult to see the flaws in what he said; personally, I was impressed by the intensity of feeling. Noakes might have been hit by an explosive blast. He sipped what was left of his coffee and withdrew.

Naturally, I walked with Ferdinand to the lodge. He thanked me for the evening and shook hands. Then, looking at me solemnly – Ferdinand is hardly ever solemn – he said, 'I hope you will be kind to Isabel.' The expression in his eyes had nothing of his usual geniality. Before I could say anything, he had gone.

26 October

One of the things I have most valued about my relationship with Isabel is that we are often quiet together. Apart from her physical attractions, what most people find irresistible is her effervescence. And so I have come to see as special the quiet times we spend in each other's company, sometimes not speaking at all for several minutes, both quite happy. Yesterday was different: her quietness was brooding rather than placid. Not morose, because she doesn't know the meaning of the word: rather, worried.

I waited for her to speak, but she didn't. So I asked her, at last, if there was anything troubling her. At first, she tried to shrug it off, making some unconvincing jokes. Eventually she said, 'I'm worried about Elaine. Mendoza is after her and I think he's going to make it.' I was incredulous. Elaine may have shown some distaste for me recently, but in the past I have always been impressed by her maturity and cool assurance. 'Indirectly,' Isabel said, 'it's because of us. I can't explain it. But I think I've been rather silly and made you play a game you didn't really want to. I'm sorry.' Typically, I fell back upon rationalization: Elaine was entitled to live her own life; she and Mendoza were both entirely free; Mendoza was lecherous but otherwise not a bad fellow (this Isabel

257

wouldn't countenance – he repels her, which is probably what is so upsetting for her); there was no reason to suppose he would not be thoughtful and considerate. I asked tactfully if Elaine was sexually experienced. She said she thought so, but apart from joking (which they no longer did) they did not talk about erotic things. It took some time to reassure her, during which I found that I had moved closer to her along the banquette until our bodies were touching from shoulder to thigh. It has happened before and we have remained comfortably in that way. It was the first time that I remember her moving away.

This morning I saw her on the corner of Turl Street and Broad Street talking to Evan Warrington. Nothing unusual in that. Senior Tutor at her father's college. Casual meeting. They were not touching, but she was looking at him in the way she looks at me when we have been playing her game. I had an instinct that she was not playing this time. Warrington was his usual impassive self. They parted company: Isabel laughing, Warrington smiling. I was savagely jealous, every nerve end seeming to tingle with pain.

7

'*I*'d love to,' said Isabel Darrow. 'How kind of you to ask me.'

'It's only a small private show at a hotel in Mayfair,' said Francesca Oricellari. 'But if you can spare the time, it's quite fun.'

'I'm sure I have the time. I'm owed yonks of Saturday mornings at the library. When is it?'

'Fifteenth November.'

'Great. I'll look forward to it.'

'Then we can have dinner, or a snack in my apartment. If you wish you can stay the night.'

'If it's midweek, I'll have to look up early trains. I'd like to. You know Evan Warrington, don't you?'

'We – at least I – have had the pleasure at one of the Master's Sunday gatherings,' said Evan Warrington.

'The pleasure was, I promise, mutual,' said Francesca.

'This isn't one of Daddy's Sundays,' said Isabel. 'It's my mother's birthday, so all the guests are hand-picked.'

'I'm honoured . . .'

'And I haven't brought a present. Oh Isabel– Why didn't you tell me?'

'I'd have been shot, Francesca. Not by Daddy, but by Eve. She says she doesn't have birthdays. It's all something to do with time passing.'

'Well, I'm sure you'd both agree that it has passed her by. As no doubt it will do both of you.'

'She thought it was another of his Sundays, so we plotted it between us with an entirely fake guest list.'

'Where's Elaine?'

259

'I . . . I imagine she'll be along later. Elaine has chosen to become wayward rather late in life.'

'At twenty?' said Warrington.

'I didn't say drop out. Far from it. After years of being the good sister, she's suddenly fractious.'

'I know all about it, Isabel. It is very difficult having a clever sister.'

'If neither of you ladies will think it a liberty, I might say it must be as difficult to have a beautiful sister.'

'Papageno!'

'Indeed?'

'Yes. You agree, Isabel? He charms the birds out of the trees . . .'

'But I don't trap them, Francesca, even if it were true.'

'No. I believe that.'

'Excuse me: I think I'm being summoned.'

'Yes. That's one of my mother's old theatre friends whom she obviously wants to impress.'

'Oh, Isabel: *now* who's doing the charming?'

'He's a nice man,' said Francesca. 'You like him?'

'I like him *very* much. And I *would* very happily. But there are difficulties. Do you find that a certain type of man is much more inhibited by age difference than women are?'

'A certain type, yes. A lot of others, no.'

'Apart from that Evan is Senior Tutor here and it would involve the most awful subterfuge. Most importantly, he already has a long-standing relationship which is casual and stable. And that's the best of all worlds. I suppose you've heard about me and David Kelly who was *not* invited. Daddy's veto.'

'So . . .'

'No: it's not true. But no one appears to believe it. I'm very fond of him and sometimes I find him physically tempting, though not in the way that Evan Warrington is. Do you know what I mean?'

'Oh yes! Very well. For a long time people thought that I was the mistress of Roger Ingestre. Not at all. I think Roger has always wanted my sister but is frightened of her. Most of all he is frightened of being hurt again. You know about his marriage?'

'Not very much. I know it ended in emotional carnage . . .

Ah here are Tom and Samantha, how lovely to see you. Thank you for keeping the secret, Tom.'

'I have a natural aptitude for secrets,' said Tom Wilkins. 'I think it goes with being a philosopher. We know pretty accurately what we understand and the rest we keep a mysterious secret.'

'I'm sure that's not true, Tom.'

'Very nice of you to say so, Francesca. You recognize a dissembler. How are you both? I don't think I know any two women who always look more blooming. And it's almost November!'

'Samantha doesn't look terrible. With me, it's just make-up. With Isabel the bloom is natural.'

'It's not bloom, it's just rosy bloody cheeks. Even when I'm ill no one believes it. I went to school with a girl who was so naturally pale that if she wanted time off or a day in bed she only had to wash her face. I *envied* her!'

'I'm glad I was not at school with Isabel for a lot of reasons. When I look at you, *cara*, I don't see a beautiful girl, I see my bathroom scales and a diet sheet.'

'Outrageous! Perfection assumes different forms.'

'How long have you been married, Tom?'

'Twenty-seven years.'

'Then, Isabel, I shall accept the compliment.'

'So shall I.'

'For a philosopher you don't look so bad yourself, Tom.'

'I'm very well fed, Francesca. And looked after in all other ways: so I'm not disposed to mope. In any case I'm an interpretive rather than a creative philosopher. Like Isabel's friend, David Kelly.'

'Oh . . .'

'I don't know much about it. But I would prefer to spend an evening with Voltaire than Hegel.'

'Yes, well . . .'

'Voltaire, Voltaire, lead me to the halter.'

'That's very *good*, Isabel.'

'Perhaps Voltaire wasn't a philosopher at all, I don't know.'

'Strictly speaking, I suppose not. Will you excuse me for a moment? Roger Ingestre is making signals that suggest I have just conceded four byes or that he wants a word aside with me. College politics, I suspect. Forgive me.'

'It didn't upset you, did it? What he said about David?'

'No. It made me cross. Coming from Tom. You know: tears of anger.'

'I know, *cara*. I know.'

'Do you think he noticed?'

'Tom? I doubt it. You covered well.'

'By making a silly joke.'

'Jokes can be useful.'

'It's just that I'm so fed up with all the insinuations now. I know it's my own fault for deciding to be bloody-minded, but it all went wrong.'

'Can I ask you something very personal?'

'Yes . . .'

'How do you feel about Ben Oldfield?'

'Ben?'

'You're very good friends, aren't you? I thought . . .'

'Ben! Good God! Yes, we're very dear friends. As we have been for years. But if you're talking about sex, Ben would be much more interested in my mother than in me. A few months ago he couldn't take his eyes off her. Eve knew it perfectly well, but she handles such situations effortlessly and kindly. Daddy's used to it and has perfect confidence in her. No: there's never been anything between Ben and me other than a hug or a kiss on the cheek.'

'Thank you.'

'What for?'

'Oh nothing. I just wonder about him.'

'Quite honestly I think he is a romantic *magna cum laude*. He becomes impassioned, but I'd guess he was amazingly chaste. I don't mean he's not heterosexual. Ben's a worshipper though, not a goat.'

'Interesting. I think we're being called in to lunch. We'll arrange the details for the 15th after. You can always trust me, you know.'

'Yes. I think I do. Thank you, Francesca.'

*   *   *   *   *

ITHACA AT LAST

I am resolved to be the man on the dump. Isabel said, with her customary laughter, that I am an incurable romantic. I am *not* a bloody romantic. I am there sitting among the mattresses of the dead, bottles, pots, shoes and grass . . . Yes, but I'm still liable to be murmuring *aptest Eve*, as I once did.

Stevens in *The Necessary Angel:* 'The imagination is one of the great human powers. The romantic belittles it. The imagination is the liberty of the mind. The romantic is a failure to make use of that liberty. It is a failure of the imagination precisely as sentimentality is a failure of feeling.'

So there! I am *not* a romantic. And from the ivory tower where I otherwise sit it is not possible *not* to have an exceptional view of the dump, even if I don't take a rotten newspaper. (Well, not *that* rotten, even if fings ain't what they uster be.)

The trouble with Isabel is that she thinks in clichés and is dim. She is a lovely girl and great fun, but I can't see why so many people lose their heads about her.

Forlornly, I realize I am one of the very few who could become so furious because a pretty woman accused me of being a romantic.

I was flattered to be asked to a pub lunch with Evan Warrington's old teacher, Jack Maddox and the lovely woman to whom he is perhaps married, called Jean. Warrington is always much the same, acerbic, slow to smile but warm in smiling. Watching Maddox I sensed his model: an emotional man who betrayed as little as possible of his feelings. Jean was quite different: smiling, gold-red hair as curling and tumbling as Isabel Darrow's, bright eyes and full lips, a quiet voice. She works for an insurance company!

Conversation was not slow. Maddox was attacking the kind of exhaustive scholarship that tracks down all allusions, arguing that it was the impact of someone's densely compounded cultural experience that mattered. Warrington disagreed. The scholar and the teacher should be friends . . . And of course they are. Nevertheless the argument was fervent. I recalled vaguely an epigrammatic (or so it seemed to me) paragraph in a book on Eliot by a very learned priest

263

Genesius Jones. I could only, out of memory, paraphrase: 'where is the wisdom we have lost in the knowledge . . . where is the knowledge we have lost in the information.' It was very well received. Jean had read less than the rest of us but was perceptive and quick in spotting inconsistent argument and quite impartial. Lovely woman indeed . . .

This morning there was the news of the assassination of Mrs Ghandi and the fearful violence which followed it. I was about to continue my notes on myth. With no special enthusiasm for the dead politician, who was pretty ruthless, we must all be sickened by such fanaticism. In the past I have thought that Ferdinand has exaggerated the evil wrought by religion. Now I am not so sure. Just as alarming, however, is the ruthlessness of the political terrorist, who shows complete disregard for the innocent, indeed often makes them a particular target. The bomb at the Brighton Conservative Party hotel has given many people (including me) some idea of what happens virtually every day in Beirut. What possible means of prevention are there? Urban terrorists planting bombs in crowded shops or shopping centres; hi-jackers of aeroplanes; those who set off devices by remote control aiming at some symbolic adversary but watching their other victims as they stroll by without any suspicion of danger and imminent death. The disintegration of civilization in the West portends an embattled society – repressive, increasingly vengeful in its own right, necessarily watchful and suspicious. Fanatics no longer stay at home: worse though, they are home-bred and of startling ferocity. Unlike my friend Marcus Ferdinand, who is a closet pessimist, I have always thought of myself as an optimist. Optimism is hardly justified when the alternative to intense policing and military reinforcement is the KGB and psychiatric prisons. If it is a matter of martial law, there is little reason to suppose that Western soldiers, given licence, would not behave with the same barbarous violence that we hear of in Africa and South America. Armies have reacted inhumanly to the defenceless for ever.

It might be argued, then, that there is nothing new in this turmoil, that apart from a hundred years or so in Britain and the United States and France and Scandinavia, there has always been a seething of social violence just below the civi-

lized crust. And those hundred or so years saw two cata-
strophic wars.

There is nothing novel in political assassination: consider
the last years of the Roman Republic and virtually the entire
era of the Roman Empire (apart from the rule of the Anton-
ines). When it happens it is no less grim, a reminder of the
ever-present threat to decency and compassion. It is the area
where history may be seen to be incontrovertibly different
from myth. It is fact. With the possible exception of
Agamemnon (and that would be arguable), there are few
assassinations in myth, even if there are countless murders
and deaths in battle. History is littered with the murders of
prominent men and women perpetrated in the name of some
ideology or faith. And it is these murders we describe as
assassinations.

I have no stomach for my scribbling today . . .

. . . An unlooked-for meeting with David Kelly outside
Balliol. I was surprised to be asked for a drink. I've always
disliked and distrusted Kelly and always thought he had very
little time for me. I have assumed him to be a covert woman-
izer (though Iris says he is not) and he has given every appearance of assuming me to be a numbskull. I expected the inevitable sherry in his rooms but instead we went to the White
Horse. Kelly was drinking large brandies. He is a contained,
very controlled man who does not usually betray his mood.
Now he seemed morose, miserable. It might be, I thought,
that he had found out about Peter Cameron and his wife,
though surely he must see it in the context of himself and
Isabel. There was a sparring of politeness: work, college
affairs, the undergraduates. I asked if Christina was well. He
said he assumed so: she was certainly busy and much involved
with her job. Unexpectedly, Kelly turned the conversation to
Isabel. It was all oblique, at first. Then he wanted to know
how well I knew her. I told him. Did she confide in me? In
all truth, I said that I doubted that Isabel hid much from
anyone. Kelly, almost thinking aloud but needing an audience, said that she was captivating but feckless; or did her
gaiety conceal a subtle and more devious purpose. I am not
very bright about these things and it took me some time to
realize that he was jealous. Not because of Christina, but
because of Isabel. He did not name the suspect. It would have

been supremely tactless to ask, since it would have probably embarrassed him. Kelly said he worried about her volatile temperament. 'It could,' he said, 'get her into trouble.' After all the nonsense between the two of them! I distrust him no less, without being able to help feeling sorry for his evident misery. What can she have done?

Returning to my own college I began thinking, because it has become a habit, of ancient mythic parallels. Kelly as Jason, Christina as Medea and Isabel as Glauce does not work. In the first place, from the diplomatic observations of Samantha and myself, Christina isn't likely to be smouldering with jealousy and is unlikely to try to set Isabel on fire. In the second, Isabel is adroit enough to avoid any suspect overtures. Dim but adroit. Thirdly, it is Kelly who is having bottle-green paroxysms, which never happened to thick-thewed old Jason. So that makes him that archetypal thickie, Theseus, who deserted Ariadne, who then had the dubious fortune of interesting Dionysus. It doesn't work. It is Isabel who is being wayward and there is no one I can think of in the class of Dionysus. I have to resort to fairytale: Oberon, Titania and Bottom. Oberon would despise Bottom utterly, but then it was he who brought about the enchantment and humiliation of Titania. (Suppose she was not humiliated and not disenchanted? Good plot.) Not good enough.

A little soberer and in less facetious mind, I wondered about how far myth and story and even soap opera are the means of alleviating the ecstasy (in which there is often fear) or the pain (in which there is sometimes hope) of loving someone.

And then everything changed. The lodge telephoned to say that there was a Miss Oricellari (well, he did his best) to see me. I went down delightedly. Francesca came up to my rooms but declined the inevitable sherry. I took away her coat. She accepted coffee. She was wearing a plain grey winter woollen dress in which she looked ravishing. She crossed her legs discreetly. While we drank the coffee, we chatted as we always have. She seemed very beautiful. Then she stood up in one sinuous movement and held out her hand. 'Dear Ben,' she said, 'take me at last to bed. I have to say it because you won't.' It was one of those glowing afternoons that sometimes happen in early November . . .

266

. . . I do not believe it. It was wonderful and I hope it was for her. (A guilty passing thought for Iris.) She called me a lot of names in Italian for being obtuse. Now I know what it is like to love someone.

So to hell with aphorisms. I'll try again to write poems or something out of my own head. I'll round up the Oxen of the Sun and put them in a pen. Or else I'll drown my book, thinking of

> . . . the logicians in their graves
> And of the worlds of logic in their tombs.

A poet looks at the world as a man looks at a woman. And what a woman!

*   *   *   *   *

What a week! Two salmon and the offer if not of the Exchequer a profitable and prestigious number . . . What has *ipse* Mendoza done to deserve all this lying here alongside Mabel Senior who is placidly smoking through a long cigarette holder half covered across the thighs so that the abundant bush peeps above the spotless (as it were) sheet. Blessedly quiet and it was amazingly good though not as good as Elaine might be if eventually . . . But that was a surprise. I don't think I should be thinking this. Surprise that she agreed to have dinner at all. The most chic place in Oxford. Surprised that she accepted a nightcap at Aunt Dorothy's. Then it was only a quarter past ten. All through the evening she had been stroking her own long fair hair. Preening gesture. Body language. An aspect of female display when the hair is long enough. Back at Aunt Dorothy's she sat on the sofa while I poured the Cognac. Frothy white blouse and black skirt quite short. Up till then talk about anthropology and television. Disguised that I was thoroughly pissed off that an amateur like Henrietta Ball had been swanning about all over the world because someone at Chiltern fancies her. The Beeb don't see me in that way, until perhaps now. But the fucking promise of her. Stroking her hair, unsmiling. Laughing sister never touches herself. I'd got them completely wrong. Hand on her knee I didn't know what – slap across the face or instant outrage. A little spurt of laughter and she opened her legs. Tights but very sheer. For such a girl an opulent crotch. Deep, deep kiss. Surge as I fondled the sacred mount. Drew away. That's it? 'Not going to fuck,' she said, cool as you please. 'Understand that. Where's the bathroom?' Came back still fully dressed but without tights. 'Lots of other things though,' she said and flung herself at me, reaching most elegantly for my cock. Elaine, for fuck's sake! Quiet, scholarly Elaine! She hadn't taken her panties off. 'More fun that way,' she said. We kissed more and I got inside the frothy blouse to lick her nipples. I came just after I had the panties off before I started going down on her. She was wild. Went on for some time. Then calm she said, 'Time I went home. I'll dress.' Held up her panties. 'What to do with these?' 'Put them under your pillow or send them to my sister,' she said. 'Think about it while you're walking me home.' Got me raging again. Just as well because Mabel's stirring. The sly hand. She wriggles her arse. Very nice it is too. 'Next time?' I said to Elaine. 'Who knows?' 'Will there be a next time?' 'Oh yes. Lots more next times, bastard.' Oooffh. And Mabel turns ready . . . Thrust? No: languorous this time. Groping. Haven't tried head yet, which should be quite exciting. Aah! That's it. I've got her. Not sure how but she doesn't want to wait. All right ma'am. Shriek. Hear myself grunting. Not poetic but it fucking worked. Blessed pause. Don't think of Elaine or of Mabel. Think of work and Mendoza's rosy-fingering future. We lie quietly . . . 'Fetch us a drink,' she says. 'Then we'll talk.' 'What do you want?' 'Whisky. You'll find ice in the kitchen. And bring some more cigarettes. They're in the sitting room.' So *this* is a working dinner!

Not even sure how it came about. Wolfe retired or got the push in a discreet way. Mabel became Danby Austin's Number Two whereupon Danby's arse collapsed (or something) and she finds herself in charge. Chagrin all round and needs her *pied-à-terre* while her husband cultivates the garden. Where are the bloody fags? She *is* quite something though. I'll stick to gin. Safer for me. Then she said have dinner with me I have plans for you. Such plans she had! Nice little Italian place around the corner. Back for a drink. (Oh Elaine . . .) Have to keep my head. Find the fucking ice.

There she is in a nightdress which covers very little

especially the burning bush and shimmering uplands. 'You took a long time,' she says, relaxing, fine legs (as they turned out to be) stretched out, wide-thighed, letting one tit escape through a slipping strap. What a week! I wouldn't have believed it. 'Thanks.' Takes the drink and fits a cigarette into the long holder. Of course Mabel knows it is too early for me to make a decision on the offer, but let's kick it around a bit more. Already explained she wants an upmarket chat show with *ipse* Mendoza up front. Not just the arts, but emphatically not showbizz. And then who knows? So much over the *costa di manzo alla pizzaiola*. Who knows what? Dabbing her quite pretty mouth with her napkin. 'I don't.' She explains over the *pallottole d'aranci* that she is forty-nine and has no intention of stopping. 'But I need someone I can create.' I thought I was created.

Bizarre sitting opposite a high-powered potential employer whose second tit is uncovered, eyes straying to that bewitching muff. Which she knows perfectly well shrugging her shapely arse from time to time in case attention is wandering. Seated as she is, it would be unlikely even without the shrugs. Amazing. After decorously pouring the drinks she sat down with *ipse* expecting tough examination and said, 'Do you enjoy looking at my legs at formal meetings?' From then it was a sort of gradation ending in two great fucks. So far but who knows. This is no time to have doubts, Mendoza. Very much not. Concentrate on the fur pie just in case she isn't tired. Doesn't look it. And I dare not let her down.

Of course we go ahead with the second series which we're already working on. Then we start thinking again. Mendoza is very good at agreeing at suitable moments. What are my ideas? Well Mabel . . . Never liked the name. 'When we're alone call me anything, but *not* at work.' Other people call her Fuzzy and I can guess why. Surely they all don't *know*. She doesn't either. I think I'll call you sugartwat, then there'll be no margin for error. Thighs twitch and close. She gets up. Crack. Haven't been hit as hard for years. What I expected from Elaine. 'Later,' she says. 'Now what are your ideas?' Nightdress abandoned in movement but legs now clamped. Difficult to think of ideas in the circumstance. Well we should go for something big on the lines of the Chiltern series that Henrietta Ball is working on. No she says that's not how we make *you* big. Henrietta Ball is one off and everyone including Dorf knows it. She had the time, they had the money and she didn't much care about it. You're professional and so am I. Forget about Henrietta Ball. Dorf's improving. No ideas? No. Then think of some when you've decided on the offer. 'Meanwhile pour us another drink.'

If I accept it will mean being based in London. No question of commuting. 'I want you within reach.' So be it. I can let Aunt Dorothy's house to passing Americans and visit so that everything is going well . . . Elaine . . . I was tempted to send your panties to Isabel but I think now I shan't. Mabel (what the hell *am* I to call her?) stands up imperious, fine legs tense. And parted. A man's got to do . . . And I adore it. Best interview I ever attended. Good dinner too. And now.

★

Hôtel Cheval Blanc
Nîmes
2 November 1984

Dear David,

It may surprise you to receive a letter from me, but you may remember that I like writing letters. I also miss our occasional conversations, even though they have been rare of late. On jaunts like this there is the company of the camera crew and the production team, which can be great fun. There are moments when I like to be alone, however. Reading is one way of passing the time: writing letters makes me feel that I'm talking to someone I want to say something to.

And I discover that what I want to say is commonplace. It is quite easy to be intellectual and clever in a casual way because it is expected. You will know as well as I do how pleasant it is to exchange banalities about the scenery, about passers-by, window shopping, sitting in a café, strolling through a market. Somehow this isn't expected of me. When I appear the chat becomes highfalutin. You must know how tedious that can be. One of the crew made a very half-hearted pass which I naturally dodged, but no one suggests we take a walk through the shops or go off and have a drink. Intellectuals are not trusted. The fault, dear Brutus . . . And possibly it is. Merriment is strictly for the bar.

This is a comfortable hotel in the Place des Arènes. I prefer, for no clear reason, the smaller circus at Arles. Who's complaining? I'm resolved to come back here for one of the operas they put on in the summer. The Camargue light is marvellous in a spell of good weather, so everyone is happy because everything is moving at great pace. Furthermore Dorf has sacked the executive producer without replacing him, which means that everything happens without pointless wrangling. I am personally relieved because this individual, whose name was (is) MacSomething, thought himself to be something of a thinker, so he used to corner me with interminable, turgid concepts about life, art and the higher reality when I just might have been having a jolly drink with the others at the opposite corner of the bar. Dorf will assign someone new to the project after our return from France. We go to Spain in early December: unfortunately ignoring all the Moorish relics, except perhaps for the desecration at Cordoba, in favour of Roman sites and the launching pads of the conquistadores.

I shall be sorry when we leave France. In spite of the long-standing *mésentente* between the French and everybody else, there is a civil surface, while the country itself and the way of life is enrapturing. The break from university routine is refreshing. I don't miss Oxford where I have spent too much of my adult life, but I do miss certain friends. How are things with you? I shall be back towards the end of next week, so perhaps we could meet. Since I am now very rich, I could take you and Christina out to dinner. Or else, if Christina is busy, just you. It would be nice to talk again.

All this wandering must eventually cure my restlessness. I know that people like Ingestre and Blakemore and even you are contented at Oxford, but don't you sometimes feel like standing on the high table and screaming? I've been at the university for more than twenty years, during which, as you well know, I have always believed in 'nothing in excess'. Too often, I now discover, that there was little question of excess.

Comparing myself (however seldom) with Iris Cameron, I wonder which of us is not so much evidently debonair, but happier. Without being vicious, Iris has denied herself very little – except her natural intelligence – and I suspect this is also true of the elder Darrow daughter, Isabel. I have indulged only my intellectual vanity. So that often I am now at odds with myself. I remember a phrase from Montaigne: 'We are double in ourselves, so that we believe what we disbelieve and cannot rid ourselves of what we condemn.' This is as applicable to too much conscious virtue as it is to too much hopheaded licence. And much else. Although able to grapple with difficult technical philosophy, we are both essentially moral philosophers – European rather than English. I don't know about you, but for me the isolation of the moral imperative became a habit to a point where, at times, it unsexed me. I exaggerate, of course. I could wish, though, that I had been less severe. This is where I was English rather than European. No matter.

Working on this series has been instructive. We've only done the Greek and Roman segments (Roman not yet finished), all of it to be collated and edited and presented God knows when. I've been reminded of something I read, without remembering where: 'Latin literature should be studied with a view to understanding Roman history, while Greek history should be studied in order to understand Greek literature.' It is very close to the mark.

As we have progressed in recent weeks, I have become more and more impressed by *romanitas*, the quality of identifying with Rome, which I suppose was characteristic of parts of the British Empire. Quite apart from all the Italians with their different tribal prejudices, they romanized most of Western Europe. It was efficiency rather than inspiration. But after the fifth century, the Greeks fell apart. It is as though there was a sequential decline. One of our scholars is inclined to explain the Greek incoherence by means of geography. Our resident Roman blames the inevitable collapse of society when simple values (*disciplina, clementia, frugalitas*) have been displaced by authoritarian government and permitted vice. You will immediately note a certain political conflict. I wonder about the numen of our own times. You know much more than I do about the will and its relation to action, so *are* we losing our sense of purpose? Is the West in inevitable decline? Tell me when we next meet.

After Spain there is a Christmas respite which I could well do without. I can usually do without Christmas. Subsequently we go to America: North, Central and South, no doubt with our new executive producer. I don't know the schedule yet, though I'm hoping to snatch a few days off to see my oldest and closest friend Rachel Bailey and the massive Oliver. Ivan Whitehart has also cordially invited me to stay with him and I shall accept.

I hope that all is well with you and Christina. Give her my love. It will be good to see you both, if you can make it. Anyway I hope to see *you*. Apart from our gossip, I very much miss someone to think with, however irreverently.

Much love,
Henrietta

★

The party is arranged for 4 November which I have said is my birthday. Most people have accepted. It will be lavish without vulgarity. I shall have paid my debts of hospitality and kindness after a fashion. Man hath no *centre* but *misery; there* and onely *there*, hee is *fixt*, and sure to finde himselfe. I have found myself. It will be as happy an occasion as I can make it.

I imagine them all. My beautiful, unattainable Isabel; her lovely elegant mother and my old friend Charles; Elaine, sulky but interesting. And Ingestre gingerly but wholeheartedly smiling with Francesca buxom in something blue, while Iris Cameron is dressed in black and white with waistcoat and trousers like a highway robber without the mask. Her brother never gives himself away. Mendoza dressed in his smile and a lady he wants to bring along from the BBC whom I cannot imagine. Though I suspect that it bodes something in favour of Mendoza. Samantha and Tom who are Samantha and Tom. Robert Blakemore and Cornelia (I was surprised that they accepted), both uncompromising but full of goodwill unless compromised. Dear old Ben Oldfield with a crumpled collar, poacher's pockets of enthusiasm and a brand new theory long discarded. Evan Warrington, inscrutable, who has promised to bring his delightful Maggie Eden. David Kelly and Christina. And everyone else. Ingestre is entertaining Marie White, who is very good at parties. Llewellyn Gray is visiting. All most welcome. Masters all.

So there it is at last.

C'est la Mort qui console hélas! et qui fait vivre;
C'est le but de la vie, et c'est le seul espoir
Qui comme un élixir nous monte et nous enivre,
Et nous donne le coeur de marcher jusqu'au soir.

I have taken a fine room. There will be good food and excellent drink. I shall be at my most convivial, no longer secretly yearning. The news is of murder whether of a politician or priest or by lethal injection of a woman who has been for six years on what is called 'death row'. Radio, television and newspapers seem to take an unwholesome interest in this last event. Execution, assassination, retributive political killing all amount to murder.

I look around me without conspicuous regret, more relieved than ever that I have no religion, no faith . . . I have taken a *farme* at this *hard rent* . . . no part of my *body*, if it were cut off, would *cure* another part . . . There is nothing in the same *man*, to helpe *man*, nothing in *mankind* to help *one another* but that hee who *ministers* that *helpe* is in as ill case as he that *receives* it would have beene, if he had not had it; for hee from whose *body* the *Physicke* comes is *dead*.

And so good night Doctor Donne. The emergent occasions are quieted. Lines I spoke with solemnity for so many years without meaning or understanding them: I heard a voice from heaven saying unto me, Write. From henceforth blessed are the dead which die in the Lord: even so saith the Spirit: for they rest from their labours. Hardly so. Whatever Spirit is, I am spiritually redundant.

274

Yet there was a man within me
Could have risen to the clouds,
Could have touched these winds,
Bent and broken them down,
Could have stood up sharply in the sky.

Was there? I wonder.

I was tempted to ask Isabel to have dinner with me, but it would have been too ceremonious and might, however fleetingly, afterwards have hurt her. I shall miss that *levitas*, that carefree tossing of the dark tumbling curls. Well, of course the point is that I shan't miss it. There will be nothing. If man knew the *gaine of death*, the *ease of death*, he would solicite, he would provoke *death* to assist him, by any hand, which he might use.

There is eventually the protean irony. It is not in the university, not even in the twists and turns of our own thoughts as separate individuals. It is something beyond our understanding:

Proteus is hard to approach and harder still to grasp, he can be forced to answer specific questions, but never volunteers a corollary; and he yields the truth only after having exhausted all appearances.

Being a reluctant prophet . . . Proteus comes ashore at high noon, the time of greatest light, not to prophesy but to sleep, surrounded by a protective herd of stinking seals: 'bitter is the scent they breathe of the deeps of the salt sea.'

And now I must be immaculate for the party. Ferdinand's Wake. *Sacré nom.*

*

6 *November 1984*
There is a kind of cruelty about fate which is impenetrable. I suppose I noticed that Ben Oldfield and Francesca Oricellari were more than usually affectionate at Marcus Ferdinand's party, but I thought he was playing up to Isabel. Within hours of the happy news that they had been married in London under special licence, I heard of Marcus's death. He

was knocked down and killed by a mail van. Charles Darrow and I went to the police to find out what we could. Witnesses agreed that the unfortunate driver could not have avoided the accident. He was travelling at speed when Marcus, it appears, looking in the other direction, walked straight into the van's path. There will be an inquest, but it seems that no one was to blame. Between us, Charles and I will take charge of the funeral and obsequies. So far as we can tell, Marcus had no relatives or anyone closer than his Oxford friends. I am glad (although it is hardly the right word) that Ben and Francesca are out of the country, so that they will not hear of it for a while. Both knew him, but Marcus was fond of Ben in an avuncular tutorial way. He teased him a great deal intellectually, but I think he learned from him. I don't know Oldfield, other than as a friend of Isabel's, at all well. I've noticed a headlong enthusiasm which many of us wouldn't tolerate for long. And yet Warrington and others say his Schools papers were wonderfully perceptive. Marcus, always composed, delighted in what he used to call 'passionate alarm or alarmed passion". This he found in Ben Oldfield. It is bitter that these events should be coincident.

For the first time Isabel came around to my house, very upset. Christina was away. We talked for a while. I gave her a drink and took her home. Almost without noticing, many of us liked Marcus Ferdinand very much. Indolent and indecisive as he was, there was no doubt that here was a fundamentally good man who wished no one harm.

I remembered his last words to me when we were alone: 'You will be kind to Isabel, won't you?' It is ridiculous to suppose anything beyond affection and concern in the light of pervading rumour, but there may have been love which he may have declared which may account for her distress. It is a sorry business. Not a tragedy. Good, jovial men and good, life-enhancing women die every day. Ferdinand, at least, did not waste in great pain.

At Marcus's party I had a rare conversation with Iris Cameron. We have always been cordial and I have obviously admired her physical attractions without desiring her. She has shown no interest in me. More to the point I like her. Her Messeliniac reputation is probably exaggerated. While she is certainly quite without inhibition, she is kind and well intentioned. It was not a long chat, for the most part as trivial as party exchanges are. Then, surprisingly, she referred to Isabel. She asked me if I knew how much Isabel depended upon me. I was taken aback. Watching Evan Warrington with the splendid woman who is said to be his mistress, I had already realized that my furious jealousy was unfounded and unbalanced. What Iris said made me wonder if I had hurt Isabel by coldness or assumed indifference. Then, it was hardly likely that Isabel would choose Iris as confidant. She said, 'It doesn't matter what people say. Beneath the laughter and life, there is an uncertain, rather lonely, very sensitive girl who happens to be a beautiful woman. I know. I was there once when I was a lot younger than she is now. *I* was also highly sexed and ever since I have let instinct take over. Whatever happens, I shan't complain. Look after her.'

I still do not fully understand what she was saying or why she said it.

*

Knowing that Christina was away for several days, Isabel hesitated when David suggested that instead of going to the pub she came to his house for a drink. It was early evening. The warmest November for years.

As they walked through the leaves now falling steadily, he talked about the absurd ritual of the state opening of Parliament and the Queen's speech. Unlike so many others, David was interested in politics only in that he chose to vote, so she was surprised that he was almost vehement about the iniquities of Conservative policy.

Then he turned to Reagan's landslide victory. 'You ain't seen nuthin' yet.'

'My own fear is that it will happen, but few of us will be here to see it,' David said. 'Did you hear someone on the early morning radio? What they call vox pop: "He's the leader of the free world and you'd better believe it." '

David went on about momentous days which were of no moment, smiling and easy. She realized he was keeping away from the death of Marcus Ferdinand who had loved Isabel without ever telling her. It would have been nonsense and perhaps eventually cruel, but she now wished that she had shown him some kind of affection in return. She tucked her hand into the crook of David's arm. He turned his head and smiled down at her.

At his house he made gins and tonic in the spotless wooden kitchen which was, like the rest of the place, scrupulously neat. They took the drinks through into the sitting room.

'I've often noticed that you have a lovely home,' Isabel said, immediately aware of her banality.

'Except that no one lives in it,' David said.

'I don't understand.'

'Well, look around you. If we were vapourized by aliens from outer space without damage to property, what would they make of this?'

'That's a new idea. Archaeologists from outer space.'

'You take the point. What would they be able to surmise about us? I mean Christina and me. If they fossicked around in my rooms at college, they might discern something. I daresay in your bedroom. Even so, how little they would know about the kind of people we were. Ben Oldfield is right in a way – about the nature of myth-making.'

'Ben's busy making his own myths with Francesca. I still don't believe it.'

'D'you know, I always thought that there was a sort of thing between you and Ben?'

'What! He never laid a finger on me. Not that I should have minded especially. It wasn't like that. We were friends. Ben thought that I was fairly stupid and always fancied older women . . . I'm not being catty about Francesca . . .'

'Of course not.'

'Did it matter to you?'

'In a word: yes.'

Isabel was pleased in spite of everything that she was telling herself. The conversation drifted around David's private work, her own future. David did not think she could stay where she was. It would be a waste. Then what was she to do? He had no answer.

David went back into the scrubbed pine kitchen to make more drinks. Isabel followed. There was a wooden bowl of pears and apples on the window ledge. She suddenly wanted to eat a pear.

'Oof. Blast!'

'What's the matter?'

'Bloody wasp in the fruit bowl. It must have been dormant.'

'Perhaps it was born again. Shall I kiss it better?'

Isabel thought for a moment.

'Oh David,' she said, 'after all that. It takes a goddam wasp.'

'I love you.'

'Yes. There isn't much else, is there?'

'There's you. And that's all.'

'Thank you. But I hope not . . .'